TEARS
OF THE
MOON

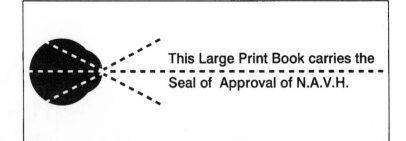

This Large Print Book carries the
Seal of Approval of N.A.V.H.

TEARS

OF THE

MOON

Nora Roberts

G.K. Hall & Co. • Thorndike, Maine

Copyright © 2000 by Nora Roberts.

Published in 2000 by arrangement with The Berkley Publishing Group, a member of Penguin Putnam Inc.

G.K. Hall Large Print Core Series.

The text of this Large Print edition is unabridged.
Other aspects of the book may vary from the original edition.

Set in 16 pt. Plantin by Elena Picard.

Printed in the United States on permanent paper.

Library of Congress Cataloging-in-Publication Data

Roberts, Nora.
    Tears of the moon / Nora Roberts.
        p. cm.
    ISBN 0-7838-8991-7 (lg. print : hc : alk. paper)
    ISBN 0-7838-8992-5 (lg. print : sc : alk. paper)
    1. Composers — Fiction. 2. Ireland — Fiction.
    3. Large type books. I. Title.
    PS3568.O243 T43 2000
    813'.54—dc21   00-039678

For Bruce,
my personal man of all work

Ah, kiss me, love, and miss me, love,
and dry your bitter tears.

— IRISH PUB SONG

One

Ireland is a land of poets and legends, of dreamers and rebels. All of these have music woven through and around them. Tunes for dancing or for weeping, for battle or for love. In ancient times, the harpists would travel from place to place, playing their tunes for a meal and a bed and the loose coins that might come with them.

The harpists and the *seanachais* — the storytellers — were welcome where they wandered, be it cottage or inn or campfire. Their gift was carried inside them, and was valued even in the faerie rafts beneath the green hills.

And so it is still.

Once, not so long ago, a storyteller came to a quiet village by the sea and was made welcome. There, she found her heart and her home.

A harpist lived among them, and had his home where he was content. But he had yet to find his heart.

There was music playing in his head. Sometimes it came to him soft and dreamy, like a lover's whisper. Other times it was with a shout and a laugh. An old friend calling you into the pub to stand you for a pint. It could be sweet or fierce or full of desperate tears. But it was music that ran through his mind. And it was his pleasure to hear it.

Shawn Gallagher was a man comfortable with his life. Now there were some who would say he was comfortable because he rarely came out of his dreaming to see what was happening in the world. He didn't mind agreeing with them.

His world was his music and his family, his home and the friends who counted. Why should he be bothered overmuch beyond that?

His family had lived in the village of Ardmore in the county of Waterford, in the country of Ireland for generations. And there the Gallaghers had run their pub, offering pints and glasses, a decent meal and a fine place for conversation as long as most cared to remember.

Since his parents had settled in Boston some time before, it was up to Shawn's older brother, Aidan, to head the business. That was more than fine with Shawn Gallagher, as he didn't quibble to admit he had no head for business whatsoever, or the desire to get one. He was happy enough to man the kitchen, for cooking relaxed him.

The music would play for him, out in the pub or inside his head, as he filled orders or tweaked the menu of the day.

Of course, there were times when his sister, Darcy — who had more than her share of the family energy and ambition — would come in where he was working up a stew or building some sandwiches and start a row.

But that only livened things up.

He had no problem lending a hand with the serving, especially if there was a bit of music or dancing going on. And he cleaned up without complaint after closing, for the Gallaghers ran a tidy place.

Life in Ardmore suited him — the slow pace of it, the sweep of sea and cliff, the roll of green hills that went shimmering toward shadowed mountains. The wanderlust that the Gallaghers were famed for had skipped over him, and Shawn was well rooted in Ardmore's sandy soil.

He had no desire to travel as his brother, Aidan, had done, or as Darcy spoke of doing. All that he needed was right at his fingertips. He saw no point in changing his view.

Though he supposed he had, in a way.

All of his life he'd looked out his bedroom window toward the sea. It had been there, just there, foaming against the sand, dotted with boats, rough or calm and every mood in between. The scent of it was the first thing he'd breathe in as he leaned out his window in the morning.

But when his brother had married the pretty Yank Jude Frances Murray the previous fall, it seemed right to make a few adjustments.

In the Gallagher way, the first to marry took over the family home. And so Jude and Aidan had moved into the rambling house at the edge of the village when they returned from honeymooning in Venice.

Given the choice between the rooms above the

pub and the little cottage that belonged to the Fitzgerald side of Jude's family, Darcy had decided in
favor of the rooms. She'd browbeaten Shawn, and
whoever else she could twist around her beautiful
finger, into painting and hauling until she'd turned
Aidan's once sparse rooms into her own little
palace.

That was fine with Shawn.

He preferred the little cottage on the faerie hill
with its view of the cliffs and the gardens, and its
blessed quiet.

Nor did he mind the ghost who walked there.

He'd yet to see her, but he knew she was there.
Lady Gwen, who wept for the faerie lover she had
cast away and waited for the spell to run its course
and free them both. Shawn knew the story of the
young maid who'd lived three hundred years before in that very same cottage on that very same
hill.

Carrick, prince of the faeries, had fallen in love
with her, but instead of giving her the words, offering his heart, he had shown her the grandeur of
the life he would give her. Three times he brought
her a silver bag of jewels, first diamonds cast from
the fire of the sun, then pearls formed from tears
dripped from the moon, and finally sapphires
wrung from the heart of the sea.

But doubting his heart, and her own destiny, she
refused him. And the jewels he poured at her feet,
so legend had it, became the very flowers that
thrived in the dooryard of the cottage.

Most of the flowers slept now, Shawn thought,

bedded down as winter blew over the coast. The cliffs where it was said the lady often walked were stark and barren under a brooding sky.

A storm was biding its time, waiting to happen.

The morning was a raw one, with the wind knocking at the windows and sneaking in to chill the cottage. He had a fire going in the kitchen hearth and his tea was hot, so he didn't mind the wind. He liked the arrogant music it made while he sat at the kitchen table, nibbling on biscuits and toying with the lyrics for a tune he'd written.

He didn't have to be at the pub for an hour yet. But to make sure he got there at all, he'd set the timer on the stove and, as a backup, the alarm clock in his bedroom. With no one there to shake him out of his dreams and tell him to get his ass moving, he tended to forget the time altogether.

Since it irritated Aidan when he was late, and gave Darcy an excuse to hammer at him, he did his best to stay on schedule. The trouble was, when he was deep enough in his music, the buzzing and beeping of the timers didn't register and he was late in any case.

He was swimming in it now, in a song of love that was young and sure of itself. The sort, to Shawn's thinking, that was as fickle as the wind but fun while it lasted. A dancing tune, he decided, that would require fast feet and flirting.

He would try it out at the pub sometime, once it was polished a bit, and if he could convince Darcy to sing it. Her voice was just right for the mood of it.

Too comfortable to bother going into the parlor where he'd jammed the old piano he bought when he moved in, he tapped his foot for rhythm and refined the lyrics.

He didn't hear the banging at the front door, the clomp of bootsteps down the hallway, or the muttered curse.

Typical, Brenna thought. Lost in some dream world again while life went on around him. She didn't know why she'd bothered to knock in the first place — he rarely heard it, and they'd been running tame in each other's houses since childhood.

Well, they weren't children anymore, and she'd as soon knock as walk in on something she shouldn't.

He could have had a woman in here, for all she knew. The man attracted them like sugar water attracted bees. Not that he was sweet, necessarily. Though he could be.

God, he was pretty. The errant thought popped into her head, and she immediately hated herself for it. But it was hard not to notice, after all.

All that fine black hair looking just a bit shabby, as he never remembered when it was time for a trim. Eyes of a quiet and dreamy blue — unless he was roused by something, and then, she recalled, they could fire hot and cold in equal measure. He had long, dark lashes that her four sisters would have sold their soul for and a full, firm mouth that was meant, she supposed, for long kisses and soft words.

12

Not that she knew of either firsthand. But she'd heard tell.

His nose was long and just slightly crooked from a line drive she'd hit herself, smartly, when they'd been playing American baseball more than ten years before.

All in all, he had the face of some fairy-tale prince come to life. Some gallant knight on a quest. Or a slightly tattered angel. Add that to a long, lanky body, wonderfully wide-palmed hands with the fingers of an artist, a voice like whiskey warmed by a turf fire, and he made quite the package.

Not that she was interested, particularly. It was just that she appreciated things that were made well.

And what a liar she was, even to herself.

She'd had a yen for him even before she'd beaned him with that baseball — and she'd been fourteen to his nineteen at the time. And a yen tended to grow into something hotter, something nervier, by the time a woman was twenty-four.

Not that he ever looked at her like she was a woman.

Just as well, she assured herself, and shifted her stance. She didn't have time to hang around mooning over the likes of Shawn Gallagher. Some people had work to do.

Fixing a thin sneer on her face, she deliberately lowered her toolbox and let it fall with a terrible clatter. That he jumped like a rabbit under the gun pleased her.

13

"Christ Jesus!" He scraped his chair around, thumped a hand to his heart as if to get it pumping again. "What's the matter?"

"Nothing." She continued to sneer. "Butterfingers," she said sweetly and picked up her dented toolbox again. "Give you a start, did I?"

"You damn near killed me."

"Well, I knocked, but you didn't bother to come to the door."

"I didn't hear you." He blew out a breath, scooped his hair back, and frowned at her. "Well, here's the O'Toole come to call. Is something broken, then?"

"You've a mind like a rusty bucket." She shrugged out of her jacket, tossed it over the back of a chair. "Your oven there hasn't worked for a week," she reminded him with a nod toward the stove. "The part I ordered for it just came in. Do you want me to fix it or not?"

He made a sound of assent and waved his hand toward it.

"Biscuits?" she said as she walked by the table. "What kind of breakfast is that for a man grown?"

"They were here." He smiled at her in a way that made her want to cuddle him. "It's a bother to cook just for myself most mornings, but if you're hungry I'll fix something up for the both of us."

"No, I've eaten." She set her toolbox down, opened it, started to rummage through. "You know Ma always fixes more than enough. She'd be happy to have you wander down any morning you like and have a decent meal."

"You could send up a flare when she makes her griddle cakes. Will you have some tea in any case? The pot's still warm."

"I wouldn't mind it." As she chose her tools, got out the new part, she watched his feet moving around the kitchen. "What were you doing? Writing music?"

"Fiddling with words for a tune," he said absently. His eye had caught the flight of a single bird, black and glossy against the dull pewter sky. "Looks bitter out today."

" 'Tis, and damp with it. Winter's barely started and I'm wishing it over."

"Warm your bones a bit." He crouched down with a thick mug of tea, fixed as he knew she liked it, strong and heavy on the sugar.

"Thanks." The heat from the mug seeped into her hands as she cupped them around it.

He stayed where he was, sipping his own tea. Their knees bumped companionably. "So, what will you do about this heap?"

"What do you care as long as it works again?"

He lifted a brow. "If I know what you did, I might fix it myself next time."

This made her laugh so hard she had to sit her butt down on the floor to keep from tipping over. "You? Shawn, you can't even fix your own broken fingernail."

"Sure I can." Grinning, he mimed just biting one off and made her laugh again.

"Don't you concern yourself with what I do with the innards of the thing, and I won't concern my-

15

self with the next cake you bake in it. We each have our strengths, after all."

"It's not as if I've never used a screwdriver," he said and plucked one out of her kit.

"And I've used a stirring spoon. But I know which fits my hand better."

She took the tool from him, then shifting her position, stuck her head in the oven to get to work.

She had little hands, Shawn thought. A man might think of them as delicate if he didn't know what they were capable of doing. He'd watched her swing a hammer, grip a drill, haul lumber, cinch pipes. More often than not, those little fairy hands of hers were nicked and scratched or bruised around the knuckles.

She was such a small woman for the work she'd chosen, or the work that had chosen her, he thought as he straightened. He knew how that was. Brenna's father was a man of all work, and his eldest daughter took straight after him. Just as it was said Shawn took after his mother's mother, who had often forgotten the wash or the dinner while she played her music.

As he started to step back, she moved, her butt wriggling as she loosened a bolt. His eyebrows lifted again, in what he considered merely the reflexive interest of a male in an attractive portion of the female form.

She did, after all, have a trim and tidy little body. The sort a man could scoop up one-handed if he had a mind to. And if a man tried, Shawn imagined Brenna O'Toole would lay him out flat.

The idea made him grin.

Still, he'd rather look at her face any day. It was such a study. Her eyes were lively and of a sharp, glass green under elegant brows just slightly darker than her bright red hair. Her mouth was mobile and quick to smile or sneer or scowl. She rarely painted it — or the rest of her face, come to that — though she was thick as thieves with Darcy, who wouldn't step a foot out of the house until she was polished to a gleam.

She had a sharp little nose, like a pixie's, that tended to wrinkle in disapproval or disdain. Most times she bundled her hair under a cap where she pinned the little fairy he'd given her years before for some occasion or other. But when she took the cap off, there seemed miles of hair, a rich, bright red that sprang out in little curls as it pleased.

It suited her that way.

Because he wanted to see her face again before he took himself off to the pub, Shawn leaned back casually on the counter, then tucked his tongue in his cheek.

"So you're walking out with Jack Brennan these days, I'm hearing."

When her head came up swiftly and connected with the top of the oven with a resounding crack, Shawn winced, and wisely swallowed the chuckle.

"I am not!" As he'd hoped, she popped out of the oven. There was a bit of soot on her nose, and as she rubbed her sore head, she knocked her cap askew. "Who said I am?"

"Oh." Innocent as three lambs, Shawn merely

17

shrugged and finished his tea. "I thought I heard it somewhere, 'round and about, as such things go."

"You've a head full of cider and never hear a bloody thing. I'm not walking out with anyone. I've no time for that nonsense." Annoyed, she stuck her head back in the oven.

"Well, then, I'm mistaken. Easy enough to be these days when the village is so full of romance. Engagements and weddings and babies on the way."

"That's the proper order, anyway."

He chuckled and came back to crouch beside her again. In a friendly way, he laid a hand on her bottom, but he didn't notice when she went very still. "Aidan and Jude are already picking out names, and she's barely two months along yet. They're lovely together, aren't they?"

"Aye." Her mouth had gone dry with that yen that was perilously close to need. "I like seeing them happy. Jude likes to think the cottage is magic. She fell in love with Aidan here, and started her new life, wrote her book, all the things she says she was afraid even to dream of once happened right here."

"That's lovely, too. There's something about this place," he said half to himself. "You feel it at odd moments. When you're drifting off to sleep, or just waking. It's a . . . a waiting."

With the new part in place, she eased out of the oven. His hand slid up her back lazily, then fell away. "Have you seen her? Lady Gwen?"

"No. Sometimes there's a kind of movement on the air, just at the edge of your vision, but then nothing." He pulled himself back, smiled carelessly, and got to his feet. "Maybe she's not for me."

"I'd think you the perfect candidate for a heartbroken ghost," Brenna said and turned away from his surprised glance. "She should work fine now," she added, giving the dial a turn. "We'll just see if she heats up."

"You'll see to that for me, won't you, darling?" The oven timer buzzed, startling them both. "I've got to be going," Shawn said, reaching over to shut it off.

"Is that your warning system, then?"

"One of them." He lifted a finger, and on cue there came the cheerful bell from the clock by his bed. "That's the second round, but it'll go off on its own in a minute as it's a windup. Otherwise, I found I'd be having to run in and slap it off every bloody time."

"Clever enough when it suits you, aren't you?"

"I have my moments. The cat's out," he continued as he took his own jacket from the hook. "Take no pity on him should he come scratching at the door. Bub knew what he was after when he insisted on moving out here with me."

"Did you remember to feed him?"

"I'm not a complete moron." Unoffended, he wrapped a scarf around his neck. "He has food enough, and if he didn't, he'd go begging at your kitchen door. He'd do that anyway, just to shame

19

me." He found his cap, dragged it on. "See you at the pub, then?"

"More than likely." She didn't sigh until she'd heard the front door close behind him.

Yearnings in the direction of Shawn Gallagher were foolishness, she told herself. For he would never have the same aimed her way. He thought of her as a sister — or worse, she realized, as a kind of honorary brother.

And that was her fault as well, she admitted, glancing down at her scruffy work pants and scarred boots. Shawn liked the girlie type, and she was anything but. She could flounce herself up, she supposed. Between Darcy and her own sisters, and Jude for that matter, she would have no limit of consultants on beautifying Brenna O'Toole.

But beyond the fact that she hated all that fuss and bother, what would be the point in it? If she polished and painted and cinched and laced to attract a man, he wouldn't be attracted to what she was in any case.

Besides, if she put on lipstick and baubles and some slinky little dress, Shawn would likely laugh his lungs out, then say something stupid that would leave her no choice but to punch him.

There was hardly a point in that.

She'd leave the fancy work to Darcy, who was the champion of being female. And to her sisters, Brenna thought, who enjoyed such things. As for herself — she'd stick with her tools.

She went back to the oven, running it at different temperatures and checking the broiler for good measure. When she was satisfied it was in good working order, she turned it off, then packed up her tools.

She meant to go straight out. There was no reason to linger, after all. But the cottage was so cozy. She'd always felt at home there. When Old Maude Fitzgerald had lived in Faerie Hill Cottage, for more years than Brenna could count, Brenna had often stopped in for a visit.

Then Maude had died, and Jude had come to stay for a while. They'd become friends, so it had been easy to fall back into the routine of stopping in now and then on her way home, or into the village.

She ignored the urge to stop in more often than not now that Shawn was living there. But it was hard to resist. She liked the quiet of the place, and all the pretty little things Maude had collected and left sitting about. Jude had left them there, and Shawn seemed content to do the same, so the little parlor was cheery with bits of glass and charming statues of faeries and wizards, homey with books and a faded old rug.

Of course, now that Shawn had stuffed the secondhand spinet piano into the dollhouse space, there was barely room to turn around. But Brenna thought it only added to the charm. And Old Maude had enjoyed music.

She'd be pleased, Brenna thought as she skimmed her finger over the scarred black wood, that someone was making music in her house again.

Idly, she scanned the sheet music that Shawn forever left scattered over the top of the piano. He was always writing a new tune, or taking out an old one to change something. She frowned in concentration as she studied the squiggles and dots. She wasn't particularly musical. Oh, she could sing out a rebel song without making the dog howl in response, but playing was a different kettle of fish altogether.

Since she was alone, she decided to satisfy her curiosity. She set her toolbox down again, chose one of the sheets, and sat down. Gnawing her lip, she found middle C on the keyboard and slowly, painstakingly, picked out the written notes, one finger at a time.

It was lovely, of course. Everything he wrote was lovely, and even her pitiful playing couldn't kill the beauty of it completely.

He'd added words to this one, as he often did. Brenna cleared her throat and attempted to match her voice to the proper note.

When I'm alone in the night, and the moon sheds its tears,
I know my world would come right if only you were here.
Without you, my heart is empty of all but the memories it keeps.
You, only you, stay inside me in the night while the moon weeps.

She stopped, sighed a little, as there was no one

to hear. It touched her, as his songs always did, but a little deeper this time. A little truer.

Moon tears, she thought. Pearls for Lady Gwen. A love that asked, but couldn't be answered.

"It's so sad, Shawn. What's inside you that makes such lonely music?"

As well as she knew him, she didn't know the answer to that. And she wanted to, had always wanted to know the key to him. But he wasn't a motor or machine that she could take apart to find the workings. Men were more complicated and frustrating puzzles.

It was his secret, and his talent, she supposed. All so internal and mysterious. While her skills were . . . She looked down at her small, capable hands. Hers were as simple as they came.

At least she put hers to good use and made a proper living from them. What did Shawn Gallagher do with his great gift but sit and dream? If he had a lick of ambition, or true pride in his work, he'd sell his tunes instead of just writing them and piling them up in boxes.

The man needed a good kick in the ass for wasting something God had given him.

But that, she thought, was an annoyance for another day. She had work of her own to do.

She started to get up, to reach for her toolbox again, when a movement caught the corner of her eye. She straightened like a spike, mortified at the thought of Shawn coming back — he was always forgetting something — and catching her playing with his music.

23

But it wasn't Shawn who stood in the doorway.

The woman had pale gold hair that tumbled around the shoulders of a plain gray dress that swept down to the floor. Her eyes were a soft green, her smile so sad it broke the heart at first glance.

Recognition, shock, and a giddy excitement raced through Brenna all at once. She opened her mouth, but whatever she intended to say came out in a wheeze as her pulse pounded.

She tried again, faintly embarrassed that her knees were shaking. "Lady Gwen," she managed. She thought it was admirable to be able to get out that much when faced with a three-hundred-year-old ghost.

As she watched, a single tear, shiny as silver, trailed down the lady's cheek. "His heart's in his song." Her voice was soft as rose petals and still had Brenna trembling. "Listen."

"What do you —" But before Brenna could get the question out, she was alone, with only the faintest scent of wild roses drifting in the air.

"Well, then. Well." She had to sit, there was no help for it, so she let herself drop back down to the piano bench. "Well," she said again and blew out several strong breaths until her heart stopped thundering against her rib cage.

When she thought her legs would hold her again, she decided it was best to tell the tale to someone wise and sensible and understanding. She knew no one who fit those requirements so well as her own mother.

She calmed considerably on the short drive home. The O'Toole house stood back off the road, a rambling jigsaw puzzle of a place she herself had helped make so. When her father got an idea for a room into his head, she was more than pleased to dive into the ripping out and nailing up. Some of her happiest memories were of working side by side with Michael O'Toole and listening to him whistle the chore away.

She pulled in behind her mother's ancient car. They really did need to paint the old heap, Brenna thought absently, as she always did. Smoke was pumping from the chimneys.

Inside was all welcome and warmth and the smells of the morning's baking. She found her mother, Mollie, in the kitchen, pulling fresh loaves of brown bread out of the oven.

"Ma."

"Oh, sweet Mary, girl, you gave me a start." With a laugh, Mollie put the pans on the stovetop and turned with a smile. She had a pretty face, still young and smooth, and the red hair she'd passed on to her daughter was bundled on top of her head for convenience.

"Sorry, you've got the music up again."

"It's company." But Mollie reached over to turn the radio down. Beneath the table, Betty, their yellow dog, rolled over and groaned. "What are you doing back here so soon? I thought you had work."

"I did. I do. I've got to go into the village yet to help Dad, but I stopped by Faerie Hill to fix the oven for Shawn."

"Mmm-hmm." Mollie turned back to pop the loaves out of the pan and set them on the rack to cool.

"He left before I was done, so I was there by myself for a bit." When Mollie made the same absent sound, Brenna shifted her feet. "Then, ah, when I was leaving . . . well, there was Lady Gwen."

"Mmm-hmm. What?" Finally tuning in, Mollie looked over her shoulder at Brenna.

"I saw her. I was just fiddling for a minute at the piano, and I looked up and there she was in the parlor doorway."

"Well, then, that must've given you a start."

Brenna's breath whooshed out. Sensible, that was Mollie O'Toole, bless her. "I all but swallowed me tongue then and there. She's lovely, just as Old Maude used to say. And sad. It just breaks your heart how sad."

"I always hoped to see her myself." A practical woman, Mollie poured two cups of tea and carried them to the table. "But I never did."

"I know Aidan's talked of seeing her for years. And then Jude, when she moved into the cottage." Relaxed again, Brenna settled at the table. "But I was just talking to Shawn of her, and he says he's not seen her — sensed her, but never seen. And then, there she was, for me. Why do you think that is?"

"I can't say, darling. What did you feel?"

"Other than a hard knock of surprise, sympathy, I guess. Then puzzlement because I don't know what she meant by what she said to me."

"She spoke to you?" Mollie's eyes widened. "Why, I've never heard of her speaking to anyone, not even Maude. She'd have told me. What did she say to you?"

"She said, 'His heart's in his song,' then she just told me to listen. And when I got back my wits enough to ask her what she meant, she was gone."

"Since it's Shawn who lives there now, and his piano you were playing with, I'd say the message was clear enough."

"But I listen to his music all the time. You can't be around him five minutes without it."

Mollie started to speak, then thought better of it and only covered her daughter's hand with her own. Her darling Mary Brenna, she thought, had such a hard time recognizing anything she couldn't pick apart and put together again. "I'd say when it's time for you to understand, you will."

"She makes you want to help her," Brenna murmured.

"You're a good lass, Mary Brenna. Perhaps before it's done, help her is just what you'll do."

Two

As the air was raw and the wind carried a sting, Shawn set out the makings for mulligan stew. The morning quiet of the pub's kitchen was one of his favorite things, so as he chopped his vegetables and browned hunks of lamb, he enjoyed his last bit of solitude before the pub doors opened.

Aidan would be in soon enough asking if this had been done or that had been seen to. Then Darcy would begin to move about upstairs, feet padding back and forth across the floor and the ghost echo of whatever music her mood called for that day drifting down the back stairs.

But for now Gallagher's was his.

He didn't want the responsibility of running it. That was for Aidan. Shawn was grateful he'd been born second. But the pub mattered to him, the tradition of it that had been passed down generation to generation from the first Shamus Gallagher, who with his wife beside him had built the public house by Ardmore Bay and opened its thick doors to offer hospitality, shelter, and a good glass of whiskey.

He'd been born the son of a publican and understood that the job was to provide comfort of all sorts to those who passed through. Over the years, Gallagher's had come to mean comfort, and it became known for its music — the *seisiun*, an informal pub gathering of traditional music — as well as the more structured sets provided by hired musicians from all over the country.

Shawn's love of music had come down to him through the pub, and so through the blood. It was as much a part of him as the blue of his eyes, or the shape of his smile.

There was little he liked better than working away in his kitchen and hearing a tune break out through the doors. It was true enough that he was often compelled to leave what he was doing and swing out to join in. But everyone got what they'd come for sooner or later, so where was the harm?

It was rare — not unheard of, but rare — for him to burn a pot or let a dish go cold, for he took a great measure of pride in his kitchen and what came out of it.

Now the steam began to rise and scent the air, and the broth thickened. He added bits of fresh basil and rosemary from plants he was babying. It was a new idea of his, these self-grown herbs, one he'd taken from Mollie O'Toole. He considered her the best cook in the parish.

He added marjoram as well, but that was from a jar. He intended to start his own plant of that, too, and get himself what Jude had told him was called a grow light. When the herbs were added to his satisfaction, he checked his other makings, then began to grate cabbage for the slaw he made by the gallons.

He heard the first footsteps overhead, then the music. British music today, Shawn thought, recognizing the clever and sophisticated tangle of notes. Pleased with Darcy's choice, he sang along with Annie Lennox until Aidan swung through the door.

Aidan wore a thick fisherman's sweater against the cold. He was broader of shoulder than his brother, tougher of build. His hair was the same dark, aged chestnut as their bar and showed hints of red in the sunlight. Though Shawn's face was leaner, his eyes a quieter blue, the Gallagher genes ran strong and true. No one taking a good look would doubt that they were brothers.

Aidan cocked a brow. "And what are you grinning at?"

"You," Shawn said easily. "You've the look of a contented and satisfied man."

"And why wouldn't I?"

"Why, indeed." Shawn poured a mug from the pot of tea he'd already made. "And how is our Jude this morning?"

"Still a bit queasy for the first little while, but she doesn't seem to mind it." Aidan sipped and sighed. "I'm not ashamed to say it makes my own stomach roll seeing how she pales the minute she gets out of bed. After an hour or so, she's back to herself. But it's a long hour for me."

Shawn settled back against the counter with his own mug. "You couldn't pay me to be a woman.

Do you want me to take her a bowl of stew later on? Or I've some chicken broth if she'd do better with something more bland."

"I think she'd handle the stew. She'd appreciate that, and so do I."

"It's not a problem. It's mulligan stew if you want to fix the daily, and I've a mind to make bread-and-butter pudding, so you can add that as well."

The phone began to ring out in the pub, and Aidan rolled his eyes. "That had best not be the distributor saying there's a problem again. We're lower on porter than I like to be."

And that, Shawn thought, as Aidan went out to answer, was just one of the many reasons he was glad to have the business end of things in his brother's keeping.

All that figuring and planning, Shawn mused, as he calculated how many pounds of fish he needed to get through the day. Then the dealing with people, the arguing and demanding and insisting. It wasn't all standing behind the bar pulling pints and listening to old Mr. Riley tell a story.

Then there were things like ledgers and overhead and maintenance and taxes. It was enough to give you a headache just thinking of it.

He checked his stew, gave the enormous pot of it a quick stir, then went to the bottom of the steps to shout up for Darcy to move her lazy ass. It was said out of habit rather than heat, and the curse she shouted back down at him was an answer in kind.

Satisfied altogether with the start of his day,

Shawn wandered out to the pub to help Aidan take the chairs off the tables in preparation for the first shift.

But Aidan was standing behind the bar, frowning off into space.

"A problem with the distributor, then?"

"No, not at all." Aidan shifted his frown to Shawn. "That was a call from New York City, a man named Magee."

"New York City? Why, it can't be five in the morning there as yet."

"I know it, but the man sounded awake and sober." Aidan scratched his head, then shook it and lifted his tea. "He has a mind to put a theater up in Ardmore."

"A theater." Shawn set the first chair down, then just leaned on it. "For films?"

"No, for music. Live music, and perhaps plays as well. He said he was calling me as he'd heard that Gallagher's was in the way of being the center of music here. He wanted my thoughts on the matter."

Considering, Shawn took down another chair. "And what were they?"

"Well, I didn't have any to speak of, being taken by surprise that way. I said if he wanted he could give me a day or two to think on it. He'll ring me back end of week."

"Now why would a man from New York City be thinking of building a musical theater here? Wouldn't you set your sights on Dublin, or out in Clare or Galway?"

"That was part of his point," Aidan answered. "He wasn't a fount of information, but he indicated he wanted this area in particular. So I said to him perhaps he wasn't aware we're a fishing village and little more. Sure, the tourists come for the beaches, and some to climb up to see Saint Declan's and take photographs and the like, but we're not what you'd call teeming with people."

With a shrug, Aidan came around to help Shawn set up. "He just laughed at that and said he knew that well enough, and he was thinking of something fairly small-scale and intimate."

"I can tell you what I think." When Aidan nodded, Shawn continued. "I think it's a grand notion. Whether it would work is a different matter, but it's a fine notion."

"I have to weigh the this and that of it first," Aidan murmured. "Likely as not, the man will reconsider and head for somewhere more lively in any case."

"And if he doesn't, I'd talk him 'round to building it back of the pub." As it was part of the routine, Shawn gathered up ashtrays and began to set them out on the tables. "We've that little bit of land there, and if his theater was in the way of being attached to Gallagher's, we'd be the ones to benefit most."

Aidan set down the last chair and smiled slowly. "That's a good notion altogether. You're a surprise to me, Shawn, working your mind around to the business of it."

"Oh, I've a thought in my head every once in a while."

Still, he didn't give it much of another thought once the doors were open and the customers rolling in. He had time for a quick and entertaining spat with Darcy, giving him the pleasure of seeing her flounce out of his kitchen vowing never to speak to him again until he was six years in his grave.

He doubted he'd have luck enough for that.

He scooped up stew, fried fish and chips, built sandwiches thick with grilled ham and cheese. The constant hum of voices through the door was company enough. And for the first hour of lunch shift, Darcy kept her word, glaring silently as she swung in and out for orders, and giving new ones by staring at the wall.

It amused him so much that when she came in to dump empties, he grabbed her and kissed her noisily on the mouth. "Speak to me, darling. You're breaking my heart."

She shoved at him, slapped his hands, then gave up and laughed. "I'll speak to you right enough, you bonehead. Turn me loose."

"Only after you promise not to brain me with something."

"Aidan'll take the breakage out of my pay, and I'm saving for a new dress." She tossed back her cloud of silky black hair and sniffed at him.

"Then I'm safe enough." He set her down and turned to flip over a hunk of sizzling whitefish.

"We've a couple of German tourists who want to try your stew, with brown bread and slaw. They're staying at the B and B," she went on as Shawn got thick bowls. "Heading toward Kerry tomorrow, then into Clare, so they say. If it were me, and I had holiday in January, I'd be spending it in sunny Spain or some tropical island where you didn't need anything but a bikini and a coating of sun oil."

She wandered the kitchen as she spoke, a woman with a stunning face, clear, creamy skin, and brilliant blue eyes. Her mouth was full, unapologetically sexual whether it was sulking or smiling. She'd painted it hot red that morning to keep herself cheerful on a chill and dreary day.

She had a figure that left no doubt she was female, and her love affair with fashion had her outfit it in bold colors and soft fabrics.

She had the Gallagher yen to travel, and the determination to do so in the style to which she longed to become accustomed. Lavish.

Since today wasn't the day for that, she picked up the order and started out just as Brenna came in. "What have you been into this time, then?" Darcy demanded. "You've black all over your face."

"Soot." Brenna sniffed and scrubbed the back of her hand over her nose. "Dad and I've been cleaning out a chimney, and a right mess it is. I got most of it off me."

"If you think so, you didn't look in a mirror." Giving her friend a wide berth, Darcy went out.

"She'd spend all her days looking in one if she had her choice," Shawn commented. "Are you wanting lunch, then?"

"Dad and I will have some of that stew. Smells fine." She moved over, intending to ladle it up herself, but Shawn stepped between her and his precious stove.

"I'd just as soon do that for you, as you didn't get off as much of that chimney as you might think."

"All right. We'll have some tea as well. And, ah, I need a word with you later."

He glanced over his shoulder. "What's wrong with now? We're both of us here."

"I'd rather do it when you're not so busy. I'll come back after the lunch shift if that suits you."

"You know where to find me, don't you?" He set the stew and the tea on a tray.

"I do, yes." She took the tray from him and carried it out to the back booth where her father waited.

"Here we are, Dad. Stew hot from the pot."

"And smelling like heaven."

Mick O'Toole was a bantam of a man, small and spare of build with a thick thatch of wiry hair the color of sand and lively eyes that drifted like the sea between green and blue.

He had a laugh like a braying donkey, hands like a surgeon's, and a soft spot for romantic tales.

He was the love of Brenna's life.

"It's good to be warm and snug now, isn't it, Mary Brenna?"

"That it is." She spooned up stew and blew on it

36

carefully, though the scent of it made her want to risk a scalded tongue.

"And now that we are, and about to have our bellies filled as well, why don't you tell me what's worrying your mind."

He saw everything, Brenna thought. That was sometimes a comfort, and other times a bit of a nuisance. "It's not a worry so much. Do you know how you told us what happened when you were a young man and your grandmother died?"

"I do, yes. I was right here in Gallagher's Pub. Of course, that was when Aidan's father manned the bar, before he and his wife took off for America. You weren't more than a wish in my heart and a smile in your mother's eye. There I was, back where young Shawn is right now, in the kitchen. I was fixing the sink in there, as it had a slow and steady leak that finally made Gallagher give me a whistle."

He paused to sample the stew, dabbing his mouth with his napkin, as his wife was fierce on table manners and had trained him accordingly.

"And as I was on the floor, I looked over and there was my grandma, wearing a flowered dress and a white apron. She smiled at me, but when I tried to speak to her, she shook her head. Then lifting a hand in a kind of farewell, she vanished. So I knew at that moment she'd passed over and that what I'd seen had been the spirit of her come to say good-bye. For I had been her favorite."

"I don't mean to make you sad," Brenna murmured.

"Well." Mick let out a breath. "She was a fine woman, and lived a good and long life. But it's left to us still living to miss those who aren't."

Brenna remembered the rest of the story. How her father had left his work and run down to the little house where his grandmother, two years a widow, lived. And he found her in her kitchen, sitting at the table in her flowered dress and white apron. She'd died quiet and peaceful.

"And sometimes," Brenna said carefully, "those who pass on miss others. This morning, in Faerie Hill Cottage, I saw Lady Gwen."

Mick nodded, and shifted closer to listen as Brenna told him.

"Poor lass," he said when she was finished. "It's a long time to wait for things to come 'round for you."

"Some of us do a lot of waiting." Brenna glanced over as Shawn came out with a tray piled with food. "I want to speak to Shawn about this when the pub quiets down a bit. Darcy says there's an outlet up in her rooms that isn't working proper. I think I'll go see to that after we've had our meal here, then take some time to talk to Shawn. Unless there's something else you have for me to do today."

"Today, tomorrow." Mick lifted his shoulders. "What we don't get to at one time, we'll get to another. I'll just take myself up to the cliff hotel and see if they've decided on which room they want renovated next." He winked at his daughter. "We could have ourselves a nice piece of work there for the whole of the winter. Where it's warm and it's dry."

"And where you can sneak down and check on Mary Kate in the offices where she's fiddling with a computer all day."

Mick grinned sheepishly. "I wouldn't call it checking so much. But I'm grateful she decided to take a job close to home since she's done with university. I expect she'll find work that suits her better in Dublin or Waterford City before much longer. My chicks are all flying the coop."

"I'm still roosting. And you'll have Alice Mae for years yet."

"Ah, but I miss the days when my five girls went tripping over me every time I turned around. Here's Maureen a married woman, and Patty going for a bride come spring. Don't know what I'll do, darling, when you hitch yourself to a man and leave me."

"You're well stuck with me, Dad." She crossed her booted feet as she finished off her stew. "Men don't lose their heads or their hearts over women like me."

"The right one will."

It took all her effort not to let her gaze wander toward the kitchen. "I won't be holding my breath. Besides, we're partners, aren't we, now?" She looked up and grinned at him. "So man or no man, it's always O'Toole and O'Toole."

Which, Brenna thought as she used Darcy's bathroom to wash away the rest of the soot, was just the way she wanted it. She had work that pleased her, and the freedom to come and go that no woman could manage with a man attached to her.

She had her room at home as long as she wanted it. The companionship of family and friends. She'd leave the fussing with keeping a house and pleasing a husband to her sisters Maureen and Patty. Just as she'd leave office work and marking her time by a clock to Mary Kate.

All she needed to get by were her tools and her lorry.

And her wanting Shawn Gallagher brought her little but frustration and annoyance. She imagined that one day, eventually, it would pass.

Knowing Darcy well, Brenna made certain she cleaned up every spot of dirt. She left the little white sink gleaming and used her own rags to dry her hands and face rather than the frilly fingertip towels Darcy had on the rod. Which, to Brenna's mind, were a complete waste of fabric, since no one who really needed to use them would dare.

Life would be simpler if everyone bought black towels. Then no one would shriek and curse when their fluffy white ones ended up grubby.

She spent a quiet few minutes replacing the broken outlet in the living area with the new box she'd brought along. She was just screwing on the cover when Darcy came in.

"I was hoping you'd get to that. It was irritating." Darcy dumped her tip money in what she called her wish jar. "Oh, Aidan said to tell you that he and Jude want to have some work done in what will be the baby's room. I'm going over to see Jude now, if you want to come along and see what she has in mind."

"I've something to do first, but you can tell her I'll come 'round in a bit."

"Damn it, Brenna! You've left dirty boot prints all over the floor here."

Brenna winced and hurried up with the screws. "Well, I'm sorry about that, Darcy, but I cleaned the sink."

"Well, now you can clean the floor as well. I'm not scrubbing up behind you. Why the devil didn't you use the loo in the pub? It's Shawn's week to clean up there."

"I didn't think of it. Stop bitching about it. I'll see to it before I go, and you're very welcome for the electrical work I've just done for you."

"Thanks for that." Darcy came back out, pulling on a leather jacket she'd splurged on as a Christmas gift for herself. "I'll see you at Jude's, then."

"I suppose," Brenna muttered, annoyed with the idea of washing the bathroom floor.

She muttered her way through the chore too, then cursed viciously when she noted she'd left little clumps of dirt and dried mud across the living room as well. Rather than risk Darcy's wrath, she dragged out the vacuum and sucked it all up.

As a result, the pub was quiet when she came

back down, and Shawn was nearly finished with the washing up.

"So, did Darcy hire you to clean her house as well?"

"I tracked mud in." At home, she poured herself a cup of tea. "I didn't mean to be so long. I don't mean to keep you if you've something to do before you're needed here again."

"I've nothing in particular. But I want a pint. You sticking with tea?" he asked with a nod of his head.

"For the moment."

"I'll just draw me one. There's a bit of pudding left if you want."

She didn't really, but having a weakness for such things, she dug out a few spoonfuls for a bowl. She was sitting and settled when he came back in with a pint of Harp.

"Tim Riley says the weather will be turning milder by tomorrow."

"He always seems to know."

"But we're in for wet before much longer," Shawn added and sat across from her. "So, what's on your mind, then?"

"Well, I'll tell you." She'd tried out a dozen different ways in her mind, and settled on the one that seemed best. "After you'd gone off this morning, I stopped off in your parlor to check your flue."

It was a lie, of course, and she was prepared to confess it to her priest. But she'd be damned if she'd tell him she'd been playing with his music.

Her pride was worth the penance.

"It's drawing well."

"Aye." She agreed and added a shrug. "But such things bear checking now and then. In any case, when I turned 'round, there she was, right in the parlor doorway."

"There who was?"

"Lady Gwen."

"You saw her?" Shawn set the pint down with a click of glass on wood.

"As clear as I'm seeing you now. She was standing there, sort of smiling at me in a sad way, and . . ." She didn't want to tell him what had been said, but felt obliged. It was one thing to tell a little lie and another to deceive.

"And what?"

The rare show of impatience from him had Brenna bristling. "I'm getting to it. And then she spoke to me."

"She spoke to you?" He pushed back from the table, paced around the kitchen, so uncharacteristically agitated that Brenna found herself gawking at him.

"What's crawled up your arse here, Shawn?"

"I'm the one who's living there, aren't I? Does she show herself to me? Speak to me? No, she doesn't. She waits until you come along to fix the oven and fiddle with the flue, then there she is."

"Well, it's sorry I am to have been the one preferred by your ghost, but I didn't ask for it, did I?" Brenna heaped her spoon with pudding and filled her mouth with it.

"All right, all right, don't get testy on me." Scowling, he dropped back into his chair. "What did she say to you?"

Keeping her face bland, Brenna stared through him while she ate her pudding. When Shawn rolled his eyes at her, she picked up her tea and took a dainty sip. "I'm sorry, were you speaking to me? Or is there someone else about that you've decided to snap at through no fault of her own?"

"I'm sorry." He flashed her a smile because it almost always worked. "Will you tell me what she said?"

"I will, since you've decided to ask politely. She said to me, 'His heart's in his song.' I thought perhaps she meant the faerie prince, but when I was telling Ma of it, she said it meant you."

"If she did, I don't know what she meant by it."

"I don't know any more than you, but I was wondering if you wouldn't mind me coming by now and then."

"You already do," he pointed out and made her squirm a little.

"If you don't want me there, you've only to say so."

"That's not what I said, or what I meant. I'm just saying you do come 'round."

"I thought I could come 'round when you weren't there as well. Like today. Just to see if she'd come back. I could do a few chores for you while I was there."

"You don't need to find work to come by. You're always welcome."

44

It softened her, not only that he said it, but that he meant it. "I know, but I like keeping busy. So I'll slip in from time to time since you don't mind."

"And you'll tell me if you see her again?"

"You'll be the first." She rose to carry her bowl and mug to the sink. "Do you think . . ." She trailed off, shook her head.

"What?"

"No, it's nothing. Foolish."

He came up behind her, gave her neck a quick squeeze with his clever fingers. She wanted to arch and purr like a cat, but knew better. "If you can't be foolish with a friend, who else is there?"

"Well, I was wondering if love really lasts like that, through death and time."

"It's the only thing that really lasts."

"Have you ever been in love?"

"Not so it took root, and if it doesn't, I suppose it's not love at all."

She let out a sigh that surprised them both. "If it takes root in one and not the other, it has to be the worst thing in the world."

He felt a quiver in his heart that he took for sympathy. "There, Brenna darling, have you gone and fallen in love on me?"

She jerked, whirled, gaped at him. He was watching her with such — such *bloody* affection, such patience and sympathy, she could have beaten him black and blue. Instead, she just shoved clear of him and snatched up her toolbox. "Shawn Gallagher, you are truly a great idiot of a man."

With her nose in the air and her tools clanking, she stalked out.

He only shook his head, then went back to his cleaning up. With that little quiver around his heart again, he wondered who it was that O'Toole had set her sights on.

Whoever, Shawn thought, slamming a cupboard door just a little too forcefully, the man had better be worthy of her.

Three

Brenna wasn't in the best of moods when she clomped into the Gallagher house. She didn't knock — didn't think to. She'd been breezing in and out of the old house, just as Darcy breezed in and out of the O'Tooles', for as long as either could remember.

The house had changed here and there over the years. Hadn't she and her father laid the new floor in the kitchen — as pretty a blue as a summer sky — not five winters back? And she herself had papered Darcy's room with that lovely pattern of baby rosebuds the June before last.

But though there'd been a bit of fussing here and fussing there, the heart of the house remained the same. It was a welcoming place, and the walls seemed to ring with music even when no one was playing.

Now that Aidan and Jude lived there, fresh flowers were always tucked into vases and bowls and bottles, as Jude had a fondness for them. And Brenna knew Jude had plans to do more planting in the spring and had talked of having Brenna build her an arbor.

Something old-fashioned was needed, to

Brenna's mind, to suit the look of the house with its old stone and sturdy wood and carelessly sprawling lines. She had something in her head she thought would suit, and would get to it by and by.

Even as she entered the house with a scowl, the sound of Darcy's laugh tripping down the steps had her lips twitching. Females, she thought as she headed upstairs, were so much more comfortable than men.

Most men, most of the time.

She found them in what had been Shawn's room, though there was little left of him there save the bed and his old dresser. He'd taken the shelves that he'd had crammed with music with him to Faerie Hill, and his fiddle and bodhran drum as well.

The rug was still there, a faded old maroon. She'd sat on it countless times, pretending to be bored while he'd played some tune.

The first time she'd fallen in love, it had been with Shawn Gallagher's music. So long ago, she thought now, she couldn't remember the song or the time. It was more an always sort of thing. Not that she'd ever let him know that. To her way of thinking you got a body moving quicker with pokes than with strokes. Though God knew, so far neither had inspired the man to move off his butt and do a blessed thing with his tunes.

She wanted it for him, the mule of a man. Wanted him to do what he'd been destined to do and take his music to the world.

But, she reminded herself, it wasn't her problem, and gnawing over it again in her mind wasn't why she'd come here today.

This, she thought, pursing her lips, was Jude's problem.

The walls were a mess, Brenna decided with a quick scan. Outlines where Shawn had hung pictures and whatnot stood out against the sun-faded paint. Dozens of nail holes pocked the walls as well, proving the man didn't have a way with a hammer.

But she could recall that whenever his mother had a whim to deal with his room, he'd just smiled and told her not to bother. He liked it just as it was.

Brenna leaned against the doorjamb, already visualizing how to turn the neglected male space into a cheery nursery. And thinking, she let her gaze rest on her friends, who stood by the window looking out.

Darcy with her gorgeous hair falling wild and free, Jude with her deep, rich brown hair bound neatly back. They were a contrast in styles, she supposed, with Darcy bright as the sun, and Jude subtle as a moonbeam. They were about the same height, about average for a woman, Brenna mused. Which put them both a good three inches over her. Their builds were similar as well, though Darcy had more in the curve department and didn't trouble to hide it.

They were both easily, unmistakably female.

It wasn't something Brenna envied — of course it wasn't. But she did wish, just now and again, that she didn't feel like such a fool whenever she put on a skirt and girl shoes.

Since it wasn't something she cared to dwell on, she stuck her hands in the pockets of her baggy pants and cocked her head.

"How are you going to figure out what you want done in here if you stare out the window all day?"

Jude turned, grinned so that her pretty, serious face lit up. "We're watching Aidan on the beach with Finn."

"The man ran out like a rabbit," Darcy put in as Brenna strolled over, "the minute we started talking paper and paint and fabrics. Said he had to exercise the dog."

"Well, now." Brenna peeked out the window herself, spotted Aidan and the young dog, Finn, sitting on the beach and watching the water. "That's a fine sight, anyway. A broad-shouldered man and a handsome dog on a winter's beach."

"He's thinking deep thoughts, I'll wager, on impending fatherhood." Darcy shot her brother a last look of affection, then turned, hands on hips. "And it's up to us to deal with the practicalities of the matter while he sits and philosophizes."

Brenna gave Jude's flat belly a friendly pat. "How's it all going, then?"

"Fine. The doctor says we're both healthy."

"I heard you're still queasy of a morning."

Jude rolled her sea-green eyes. "Aidan fusses. You'd think I was the first woman to conceive a child since Eve. It's just a little morning sickness. It'll pass."

"If it were me," Darcy announced and flopped onto her brother's old bed, "I'd play it up for all it

50

was worth. Pampering, Jude Frances, you should rake in all the fussing and pampering you can manage. For when the baby comes, you'll be too busy to remember your name. Remember when Betsy Duffy had her first, Brenna? She fell asleep every Sunday at Mass for two months running. With the second, she'd just sit there, wild-eyed and dazed, and by the time she had the third . . ."

"All right." Jude laughed and swatted at Darcy's feet. "I get the picture. Right now, I'm just dealing with preparing for one. Brenna . . ." She lifted her hands. "These walls."

"Aye, they're a sight, aren't they? We can fix them up for you. Clean them up, patch the holes . . ." She flicked a finger over one as big as a penny. "Paint them proper."

"I'd thought of papering, but I decided paint's better. Something sunny and simple. Then we can hang prints. Fairy-tale prints."

"You ought to hang your own drawings," Brenna told her.

"Oh, I don't draw that well."

"Well enough to sell a book with your stories and your drawings in it," Brenna reminded her. "I think your pictures are lovely, and it would mean more, wouldn't it, to the baby as it grew to have something its mother had done hanging here."

"Really?" Jude tapped a finger on her lips, the pleasure of the idea obvious in her eyes. "I suppose I could have some framed, see how they looked."

"Candy-colored frames," Brenna told her. "Babes like bright colors, or so Ma always says."

51

"All right." Jude took a deep breath. "Now these floors. I don't want to cover them, but they'll need to be sanded and revarnished."

"That's not a problem. Some of this trim needs to be replaced too. I can make some up to match the rest of it."

"Perfect. Now, here's this idea I've been mulling over. It's a large room, so I thought what if we made this corner here a kind of play area." Gesturing, Jude crossed the room. "Shelves up this wall for toys, a little table and chair that would fit right under the window."

"We can do that. But if you were to come 'round the corner with the shelves, you'd make better use of your space, and have it more like a separate spot, if you know what I mean. And I can make them adjustable so you can change the look of them as needs be."

"Around the corner . . ." Jude narrowed her eyes and tried to picture it. "Yes. I like that. What do you think, Darcy?"

"I think the two of you know just what's needed here, but it's up to me to get you into Dublin for some smart-looking maternity clothes."

Instinctively, Jude laid a hand on her stomach. "I'm not showing yet."

"Why wait? You'll need them long before the baby needs shelves, and you're already thinking of those, aren't you? We'll go Thursday next, when I've the day off." And the portion of her pay she allotted herself for fun in her pocket. "That suit you, Brenna?"

Brenna was already taking her measuring tape out of her toolbox. "Suits me for the pair of you. I've too much work just now to take a day being dragged around Dublin shops and waiting while you gasp over the next pair of shoes you can't live without."

"You could do with a new pair of boots yourself." Darcy skimmed her gaze down. "Those look like you wore them to march over to the west counties and back again."

"They do fine for me. Jude, tell Shawn to find a place for his junk here, and I'll start on this room first of next week."

" 'Tisn't junk," Shawn said from the doorway. "I spent many a happy night in that bed where Darcy's making herself at home just now."

"Well, junk's what it is now," Brenna shot back with a little sniff. "And in the way. And how many times, I'd like to know, do you have to hit a nail to put holes this size in a wall?"

"You put pictures over them, and it doesn't matter how big the holes are."

"Since that's your thinking on it, if you've a mind to put up anything in the cottage, call someone who knows one end of a hammer from the other. You'll want to make him swear to that, Jude," Brenna warned, "else the cottage'll be rubble by spring."

"I'll fix the damn holes meself if it'll shut you up." His tone was pleasant, dangerously so. And that was just enough to give Brenna's heart a little jerk and make her cover the reaction with sarcasm.

"Oh, to be sure, you'll fix them. Like you fixed the sink at the pub the last time it plugged up so I had to wade through an inch of water on the floor to repair the damage."

When Darcy snickered, Shawn sent her a cool and silent look. "I'll have what's left of mine out by tomorrow, Jude, if that's all right with you."

Recognizing scraped male pride, she started to step forward quickly. "There's no hurry, Shawn. We were just . . ." She trailed off as the room took a sick, slow spin.

Before she could stagger, Shawn darted across the room at a speed that had Brenna's mouth falling open and scooped his sister-in-law into his arms.

"It's nothing." Her head already clearing, Jude patted his shoulder. "I was just dizzy for a minute, that's all. It happens now and then."

"You're for bed," he said, already striding out. "Get Aidan." He tossed the order to Darcy over his shoulder.

"No, no, I'm fine. Shawn, don't —"

"Get Aidan," he repeated, but Darcy was already up and running.

Brenna stood where she was for a moment, her measuring tape in her hand. As the oldest of five, she'd seen her mother stretch right out on the floor during a dizzy spell while pregnant, so she wasn't particularly alarmed by Jude's behavior. What she was, was stunned by the fluid strength she'd just witnessed. Why the man had plucked Jude up as if she'd been weightless.

Where had that been hiding?

Shaking herself clear, she hurried into the master bedroom in time to see Shawn lay Jude gently on the bed and pull a throw over her.

"Shawn, this is ridiculous. I —"

"Lie down." He jabbed a finger at her in a way that made Jude obey and Brenna goggle. "I'm calling the doctor."

"She doesn't need the doctor." Brenna nearly flinched from the furious glare he aimed at her when he whirled around. But she also saw sheer male fear behind his eyes, and was touched by it. "It's just a part of carrying, that's all." She moved to the bed to sit and pat Jude's hand. "My mother used to lie right down on the kitchen floor when she had a spell, especially with Alice Mae."

"I feel fine."

"Of course you do. But a little rest doesn't hurt. Why don't you fetch our Jude some water, Shawn?"

"I think she should have the doctor."

"Aidan's likely to make her." Because Jude looked so unhappy at the thought, Brenna gave her a look of quiet sympathy. "Oh, don't take on now. Ma says that Dad did the same with her when she carried me. By the time the others came along, he was used to it. A man's got a right to panic, after all. He doesn't know what's going on inside you the way you do, does he? Shawn, let's have that water now."

"All right, I'll fetch it. But don't let her get up."

"I'm fine, really."

"Of course you are. Your color's back, your eyes

55

are clear." Brenna gave Jude's hand another squeeze. "Do you want me to go out and head Aidan off, try to calm him down?"

"If you think —" She broke off as she heard the front door slam like a gunshot, and then footsteps rushing up the stairs. "Too late."

Brenna got up and made it halfway across the room before Aidan came flying in. "She's fine. Just a little expectant-mother spell. She's —" Then she only sighed as Aidan dashed right past her.

"Are you all right? Did you faint? Did someone call the doctor?"

"We'll leave it to her to calm him down." Giving Darcy a little wave, Brenna nudged her out of the room and shut the door.

"Are you sure she's all right? She looked so pale for a minute."

"She's fine, I promise you. And Aidan'll likely keep her in bed the rest of the day no matter how she argues."

"Bad enough a woman has to get fat as a cow with a baby. But add to that the hanging over the toilet every morning and fainting without a moment's notice." Darcy blew out a breath and ordered herself to calm down. "It's a sorry state of affairs what a woman goes through. And you —" She stabbed a finger at Shawn as he walked down the hallway with a glass of water. "All the lot of you have to do is have your pleasure, whistle away nine months, then pass out smelly cigars."

"It just goes to proving God's a man," he said with a weak smile.

Darcy's lips quirked at that, but she shook her head. "I'm going to make Jude some tea and toast."

She sauntered away, leaving Shawn staring at the bedroom door.

"Let's give them a bit of privacy." Brenna took his arm and tugged him toward the stairs.

"Shouldn't I take her the water?"

"You drink it." Feeling kindly toward him, Brenna reached up and touched his cheek. "You're white as a sheet."

"Scared ten years off my life, she did."

"I can see that. But you acted fast and did just the right thing." She slipped into the next room, picked up her measuring tape again. "She's got all those changes going on inside her, and likely isn't resting as much as she might. She's all caught up in her plans," she added, taking a measurement, writing it down in her little book. "So much new in her life in so short a time."

"I guess it's easier for women to take such matters in stride."

"I suppose." Brenna continued to measure and take notes. "You must remember when your mother was carrying Darcy."

"Some." He sipped at the water, as his throat was still dry with nerves. Brenna was calm enough, he noted, moving gracefully around the room in those thick old boots, taking measurements, writing things down, making little pencil marks and noting numbers right on the wall.

Some of her hair was falling out of her cap. Just a

few long, spiraling red curls, loosened, he supposed, by her dash into the bedroom.

"What do you remember best?"

"Hmm?" He'd lost the thread somewhere, and now shifted his gaze from the red curl that teased her shoulder back to her face.

"About when your mother was pregnant with Darcy? What do you remember best?"

"Laying my head against her belly, feeling all those kicks and movements. It was like Darcy was fretting to get outside and get on with things."

"That's a nice one." Brenna put her tape and notebook away, lifted her toolbox. "I'm sorry I snapped and snarled at you before. I was in a bit of a mood today."

"You're in a bit of a mood most days." But he smiled and tapped the bill of her cap down over her eyes. "I'm too used to your nips to mind much."

The problem was, she wanted to take a real nip — right there, just along his jaw. To see how it tasted. And if she tried it, she imagined he'd be the one to faint. "I won't be able to get started in here until Monday or Tuesday, so there's no real rush getting your things out. But . . ."

She lifted a finger, tapped it against his chest. "I meant what I said about hanging pictures at the cottage."

He only laughed. "If I get the urge to pick up a hammer," he began, then threw her off balance by bending down to place a quick, friendly kiss on her cheek. "I'll be sure to call the O'Toole."

"Aye, do that." Irritated all over again, she

started to stride out. Aidan, looking frazzled, came to the doorway.

"She's fine. She says she's fine. I called the doctor, and *he* says she's fine. Just to rest a bit and keep her feet up."

"Darcy's making her some tea."

"That's good, that's fine, then. Jude's fretting some because she'd planned to take flowers to Old Maude this afternoon. I'd run them up myself, but —"

"I'll do it," Shawn told him. "You'll feel better if you can stay with her a bit longer. I can drive up, have a bit of a visit with Old Maude, then be back in time for the pub."

"I'd be grateful — am grateful," he corrected, his face clearing a little now. "She told me how you picked her up and carted her off to bed. Made her stay there."

"Just ask her not to go into a swoon around me again. My heart won't take it."

Shawn took flowers to Maude, the cheerful purple and yellow pansies that Jude had already gathered. He didn't often come to the old cemetery. He'd lost no one truly close to him who'd been laid to rest there. But he thought since the cottage was close, he could take over the task from Jude until she was more up to the climb.

The dead were buried near the Saint Declan's Well, where those who had made the pilgrimage to honor the ancient Irish saint had washed the travel from their hands and feet. Three stone crosses stood nearby, guarding the holy place, and perhaps, he thought, giving comfort to the living who came high on this hill to honor the dead.

The view was spectacular — Ardmore Bay stretched out like a gray swath under storm-ready skies. And the beat of the Celtic Sea, the heart that pulsed day and night, spread to the horizon. Between that drumming and the wind there was music, and birds, undaunted by winter, sang to it.

The sunlight was weak and white, the air damp and going raw. The wild grass that fought its way among the stones and cobbles was pale with winter. But he knew winter never had much of a march here, and soon enough fresh green shoots would brave their way among the old.

The cycle that such places stood for never ended. And that was another comfort.

He sat beside Maude Fitzgerald's grave, folding his legs companionably and laying the pansies under her stone where the words "Wise Woman" were carved.

His mother had been a Fitzgerald before her marriage, so Old Maude had been a cousin of sorts. Shawn remembered her well. A small, thin woman with gray hair and eyes of a misty, far-seeing green.

And he remembered the way she'd sometimes looked at him, deep and quiet, in a manner that hadn't made him uneasy so much as unsettled. Despite it, he'd always been drawn to her, and as a child had often sat at her feet when she'd come into the pub. He'd never tired of listening to her tell stories, and later, years later, had made songs out of some of them for himself.

"It's Jude who sends you the flowers," he began. "She's resting now, as she had a bit of a spell with the baby. She's fine, so there's nothing to worry about. But as we wanted her to lie down for a while, I said I'd bring her flowers to you. So I hope you don't mind."

He fell silent a moment, letting his gaze wander. "I'm living in your cottage now that Aidan and Jude have moved into the house. That's the Gallagher way, as I'm sure you know. And now with the baby coming, the cottage would be a wee bit small. Jude's granny, that would be your cousin Agnes Murray, signed the cottage over to her as a wedding gift."

He shifted to find more comfort on the ground, and his fingers began to tap on his knee in an unconscious match to the rhythm of the sea.

"I like living there, in the quiet. But I wonder that I haven't seen Lady Gwen. Do you know she showed herself to Brenna O'Toole? You'll remember Brenna, she's the oldest of the O'Toole girls who live down from your cottage. She's the redhead — well, most of the O'Toole girls are redheaded, but Brenna's got like . . . sunfire at the edges of it. You'd think it would burn your fingers to touch it, and instead it's just warm and soft."

He caught himself, frowned a little, cleared his throat. "In any case, I've been living there near to five months now, and she hasn't shown herself to me, not clearly. And there's Brenna come by to fix the stove, and the lady not only shows herself but speaks to her as well."

"Women are perverse creatures."

Shawn's heart gave one quick thud, as he hadn't expected anyone to speak back to him in such a place. He looked up and saw a man with long black hair, eyes of piercing blue, and a smile wicked at the corners.

"So I've often thought myself," Shawn said calmly enough, but his heart had decided one quick thud wasn't enough and began to gallop in his chest.

"But we can't seem to do without them, can we?" The man unfolded himself from the stone chair that crouched near the trio of crosses. His movements were graceful as he walked over grass and stone on soft leather boots, then sat on the opposite side of the grave.

The wind, the chilly snap of it, played through his hair, fluttered the short red cape tossed regally over his shoulders.

The light brightened, cleared so that everything — stones, grass, flowers — stood out in sharp relief. In the distance, entwined with the sound of sea and wind, came the dance of pipes and flutes.

"Not for any real length of time," Shawn answered, kept his gaze level and hoped his heart rate would soon do the same.

The man laid his hand on his knees. He wore hose and a doublet of silver, both shot through with threads of gold. And on one hand was a silver ring with a brilliant blue stone. "You know who I am, don't you, Shawn Gallagher?"

"I've seen pictures Jude's drawn of you for her book. She's clever with a sketch."

"And well and happy now, is she? Wedded and bedded?"

"Aye, she's all of that, Prince Carrick."

Carrick's eyes gleamed, both power and amusement alive in them. "Does it worry you to converse with the prince of the faeries, Gallagher?"

"Well, I've no desire to be taken off to a faerie raft for the next century or so, as I've things I prefer to do here."

With his hands still resting on his knees, Carrick threw back his head and laughed. It was a full, rich sound. Seductive, engaging. "Some of the ladies in court would enjoy you, I'm certain, for your looks and your musical gifts. But I've a use for you here, on your side. And here you'll stay, so don't trouble yourself."

He sobered abruptly, leaned forward. "You said Gwen spoke to Brenna O'Toole. What did she say to her?"

"Don't you know?"

He was on his feet without seeming to move at all. "I'm not permitted in the cottage, nor past the borders of its gardens, though my home is beneath it. What did she say?"

Sympathy stirred in Shawn's heart. The question had been more plea than command. " 'His heart is in his song.' That's what she said to Brenna."

"I never gave her music," Carrick said softly. He lifted an arm and with a flick of his wrist had the light blazing. "Jewels plucked from the fire of the sun. These I gave her, these I poured at her feet when I asked her to come with me. But she turned away from them, from me. From her own heart. Do you know what it is, Gallagher, to have the one you want, the only one you'll ever want, turn from you?"

"No. I've never wanted like that."

"There's a pity for you, for you're not alive until you do." He lifted his other hand, and darkness fell with silver beams and sparkles. Fog, thin and damp, crawled over the ground. "Even so, even when she took another at her father's bidding, I gathered the teardrops from the moon, and these I spilled into pearls at her feet. And still she wouldn't have me."

"And the jewels of the sun, the tears of the moon became flowers," Shawn continued. "And these she tended, year after year."

"What is time to me?" Impatience shimmering now, Carrick glared at Shawn. "A year, a century."

"A year is a century when you're waiting for love."

Emotion swam into Carrick's eyes before he closed them. "You're clever with words as well as tunes. And you're right."

Once more he snapped his wrist and the sun was back, winter pale. "Still, I waited, and too long I waited, to go to her that last time. And from the sea, through the deep blue depths of it, I took its heart. And from this, hundreds of sapphires I gath-

64

ered for her, and these, too, I poured at her feet. For my Gwen, all that I had and more for Gwen. But she told me she was old, and it was too late. For the first time, I saw her weep about it, weep as she told me if I'd once given her the words that were in my heart instead of jewels, instead of promises of eternities and riches, she might have been swayed to give up her world for mine, her duty for love. I didn't believe her."

"You were angry." Shawn had heard the story too many times to count. When he'd been a boy, he'd often dreamed of it. The dashing faerie prince astride a white winged horse, flying to the sun, to the moon, to the sea. "Because you had loved her, and didn't know how else to show it, how else to tell her."

"What more can a man do?" Carrick demanded, and this time Shawn smiled.

"That I can't tell you. But casting a spell that has you both waiting over the centuries was probably not the wisest action."

"I've my pride, don't I?" Carrick said, tossing his head. "And my temper. Three times I asked, and three times she refused. Now we wait until love meets love three times and accepts all. Flaws and virtues, sorrows and joys. You're clever with words, Gallagher," Carrick said, and the edgy smile was back. "I'll be displeased if you take so long to make use of them as your brother did."

"My brother?"

"Three times." Carrick was on his feet now, his eyes dark and brilliantly blue. "And one is met."

It was Shawn's turn to rise, and his fists were bunched. "Are you speaking of Aidan and Jude? Are you telling me, you bastard, that you put a spell on them?"

Carrick's eyes flashed, and thunder rumbled in answer. "You great fool of a man. Love spells are nothing but wives' tales. You can't play magic inside the heart, for it's more powerful than any spell. Lust you can order up with a wink, desire with a smile. But love is love, and there is nothing can touch it. What your brother has with his Jude Frances is as real as the sun and the moon and the sea. You've my word on it."

Slowly Shawn relaxed. "I'll beg your pardon, then."

"I'll take no offense at a brother standing for a brother. If I did," Carrick added with a thin sneer, "you'd be braying like a jackass. You've my word on that as well."

"I appreciate your restraint," Shawn began, then tensed up again. "Are you after thinking that I'll be the second stage in the breaking of your spell? For if you are, you're looking in the wrong direction."

"I know where I'm looking well enough, young Gallagher. It's you who doesn't. But you will, soon enough. You will." Carrick bowed gallantly. And vanished just as the skies opened and rain fell in a fury.

"Well, that's perfect, isn't it?" Shawn stood in the driving rain, angry and puzzled. And very late for work.

Four

He was a man who liked to take his time with things. To mull and consider, to weigh and to measure. So that's what he did, telling no one, for the moment, of his meeting with Carrick at the side of Old Maude's grave.

It concerned him a bit. Oh, not the meeting with a faerie prince so much. It was in his blood to accept the existence of magic, and in his heart to appreciate it. The manner of the discussion was what worried him, and the direction it had taken.

He'd be damned if he'd find himself picking out, or being picked out by, a woman, and stumbling into love just to fall in line with Carrick's plans and wishes.

He just wasn't the marrying and settling-in sort, as Aidan was. He liked women, that he did. The smell of them, the shape of them, the heat of them. And there were, well, so many of them out there. All fragrant and rounded and warm.

As much as he tended to write about love, in all its delightful and painful varieties, on the personal level he preferred to skirt around its edges.

Love, the sort that grabbed the heart with both hands and took it over, was such a bloody responsibility. And life was so pleasant just as it was. He had his music and the pub, his friends and his family, and now the little cottage on the hill that was all his.

Well, except for the ghost, who didn't appear to want his company in any case.

So he took his time, thinking it all through and going about his business. He had fish to fry and potatoes to slice and a great whopping shepherd's pie cooking in the oven. The sounds of Saturday night were beginning to heat up in the pub beyond his kitchen door. The musicians from Galway that Aidan had booked were slipping into a ballad, and the tenor was doing a fine job singing about Ballystrand.

Since Darcy had gotten in her shopping fix with Jude in Dublin, she was in a rare mood, all smiles and cooperation. Orders she called out to him like a song, then danced back out with them when he'd finished his part. Why, they hadn't had a hard word between them for the whole of the day.

He thought it might be a record.

When he heard the kitchen door swing open, letting in a flood of music, he slid a long slice of golden fish onto a plate. "I've all but got this last order done here, darling. And the pie needs only five minutes more."

"I'd love some of it when it's done."

He glanced over his shoulder and beamed. "Mary Kate! I thought you were Darcy. And how are you, then, sweetheart?"

"I'm fine and well." She let the door swing shut behind her. "And you?"

"The same." He drained chips and arranged the orders even as he studied her.

Brenna's younger sister had blossomed during her university years. He thought she'd be about one and twenty now, and pretty as a picture. Her hair was a sunnier, more golden red than Brenna's, and she wore it in soft waves that fell just past her chin. Her eyes had a touch of gray over the green, and she smudged them up prettily. She wasn't much taller than her oldest sister, but fuller at the bust and hip, and she wore a dark green Saturday-night dress to show off a very attractive figure.

"You look more than fine and well to me." He tucked the orders under the warmer, then leaned back on the counter so they could have a little chat. "When did you manage to grow up on me? You must be flaying the lads off with sticks on a daily basis."

She laughed, struggling to make the sound mature and female rather than the giggle that wanted to bubble out of her throat. The crush she'd developed on Shawn Gallagher was very recent, and very strong. "Oh, I've been too busy to do much flaying, what with working at the hotel and all."

"You like your work there."

"Very much. You should come 'round." She stepped closer, trying to keep her movements both casual and seductive. "Have yourself a busman's holiday and let me treat you to a meal there."

"That's a thought, isn't it?" He gave her a wink

that set her pulse skipping, then turned to open the oven and check his pie.

She moved closer. "That smells wonderful. You've such a hand with cooking. So many men are bumblers in the kitchen, it seems."

"When a man, or a woman for that matter, bumbles about in the kitchen it's usually because they know someone will come along and chase them out and deal with the matter to save the time and annoyance."

"That's wise." She all but whispered it, with reverence. "But though you're so good at it, I'll bet you'd like to have someone fix you a meal now and then instead of always fussing with it yourself."

"Sure and I can't say as I'd mind it."

When Brenna walked in the back door, the first and only thing she saw was Shawn Gallagher smiling into her sister's dazzled eyes.

"Mary Kate." Her voice was sharp as the tip of a whip, and at the sound of it her sister flushed and jerked back. "What are you doing?"

"I'm . . . just talking with Shawn."

"You've no business being back here in the kitchen wearing your good dress and getting in Shawn's way."

"She's not in the way." Used to being scolded by his elders, Shawn gave Mary Kate a comforting pat on the cheek. And being a man, he didn't see the dream clouds come into her eyes.

But Brenna saw them. Teeth gritted, she strode forward, took Mary Kate's arm in an iron grip, and pulled her toward the door.

The humiliation of it whisked away the mature sophistication Mary Kate had worked so hard to display. "Let go of me, you gnat-assed bully." Her voice spiked upward as she struggled. They very nearly plowed Darcy over when she came in while they were going out. "What's the matter with you? You've no right hauling me about. I'm telling Ma."

"Oh, fine, you go ahead." Without breaking stride, or loosening her grip, Brenna yanked her sister into the snug at the end of the bar, then shut the door of the little private room. "You go right ahead, you lamebrain, and I'll be sure to tell her how you were throwing yourself at Shawn Gallagher."

"I was not." Freed, Mary Kate sniffed, lifted her chin, and very meticulously smoothed down the sleeves of her best dress.

"You were all but biting his neck when I walked in. What's got into you? The man's nearly thirty, and you barely twenty. Do you know what you're asking for when you rub your breasts up against a man that way?"

Mary Kate merely lowered her gaze to her sister's baggy sweater. "At least I have breasts."

It was a sore point, a very tender area, as Brenna had resented the fact that every one of her sisters, including young Alice Mae, had more bosom than she did. "That being the case, you ought to have more respect for them than to go shoving them into a man's face."

"I was not. And I'm not a child who needs to be lectured by the likes of you, Mary Brenna

71

O'Toole." She stiffened her spine, rolled back her shoulders. "I'm a grown woman now. I've been to university. I have a career."

"Oh, that's fine, then. I suppose it's past time you jump the first man who catches your fancy and take a wild ride."

"He's not the first who's caught it." With a slow smile that made Brenna's eyes go cold and narrow, Mary Kate tossed her hair. "But caught it he has, and there's no reason not to let him know it. It's my business, Brenna. And not yours."

"Oh, you're my business, all right. Are you still a virgin?"

The utter shock in Mary Kate's eyes was enough to reassure Brenna that her sister hadn't been throwing herself naked around the corridors of the university in Dublin. But before she could so much as sigh, Mary Kate's temper lashed out. "Who the hell are you thinking you are? My romantic dealings are my business. You're not my mother or my priest, so mind your own."

"You are my own."

"Just stay out of it, Brenna. I've a right to talk to Shawn or go out with him or anything else I choose. And if you think you'll go running to Ma with tales on my behavior, well, we'll just see what she thinks about how I came on you and Darcy playing poker with your holy cards."

"That was years ago." But Brenna felt a little panic at the thought. Her mother wouldn't consider the years between. "Harmless girls' foolishness. What I came in on in the kitchen isn't harmless, Mary Kate, but it is foolish. I don't want to see you hurt."

"I can take care of myself." Mary Kate gave one last toss of her head. "If you want to be jealous because I know how to attract a man instead of going about trying to be one, that's your problem. Not mine."

The slice came so fast and true, Brenna stood frozen, hardly realizing that she bled until Mary Kate stormed out and slammed the door behind her. Tears stung at her eyes and made her want to slide into one of the old sugan chairs and just let them come.

She wasn't trying to be a man, she was just trying to be herself.

And she'd only wanted to protect her sister. To stop her before she did something that would hurt or embarrass her. Or worse.

It was all Shawn's fault, she decided. The little voice inside her head that whispered differently was ignored. It was Shawn's fault for luring her young and innocent sister into infatuation, and she was just going to deal with that right this minute.

She strode out, shaking her head as Aidan shifted to lay a hand on her arm and ask her what was the matter. When she stalked into the kitchen now, her eyes were bright. But not with tears. It was something closer to murder.

"Now, why did you go dragging Mary Kate out like that for, Brenna? We were just —"

He broke off because she'd marched up to him, the toes of her boots ramming hard against the toes of his, and her finger was drilling a hole in his chest. "You just keep your hands off my sister."

"What on God's green earth are you talking about?"

"You know damn well what I'm talking about, you bloody lecher. She's barely twenty, hardly more than a girl."

"What?" He shoved her hand away before she could stab straight into his heart. "What?"

"If you think I'm going to stand by idle while you add her to your string of ladies, then you'd best keep thinking."

"My . . . Mary Kate?" Sheer shock came first. Then he remembered how the young girl — no, no, young woman, he corrected — had looked when she'd smiled and fluttered her pretty lashes. "Mary Kate," he said, more thoughtfully, and with just a hint of a smile.

A hot red haze filled Brenna's head. "You get that gleam out of your eye, Shawn Gallagher, or I swear I'll blacken both of them."

Because her fists were raised, he took a cautious step back and lifted his hands palms out. They were well beyond the stage where he could, in all conscience, wrestle with her. "Brenna, calm yourself down. I never touched her, never thought to. Never thought of her in the way you're meaning until you mentioned it yourself. For Christ's sake, I've known her since she was in nappies."

"Well, she's not in nappies now."

"No, indeed, she's not," he said with perhaps an unwise hint of approval. So he supposed the fist that landed in his gut was his own fault. "Jesus, Brenna, a man can't be faulted for appreciating."

"You do that appreciating from a distance. If you make a move in that direction, I promise you I'll break both your legs."

It was rare for him to lose his temper, so he recognized that he was coming dangerously close. To solve the matter, he simply cupped his hands under her elbows and lifted her off her feet until their eyes were level. Both shock and fury fired in hers.

"Don't you threaten me. If I had thoughts of that nature regarding Mary Kate, then I'd act on them and that would be between the two of us, and not you. Do you understand that?"

"She's my sister," Brenna began, then subsided when he gave her one hard shake.

"And that gives you the right to embarrass her and take punches at me when we've done no more than stand in my kitchen and talk? Well, I'm standing here talking to you, too, and have countless times before. Have I ripped your clothes off and had my way with you?"

He dropped her down on her feet again and stung her beyond belief by merely turning his back. "You should be ashamed where you've let your mind run," he said quietly.

"I —" The tears were going to come after all. She struggled with them, swallowed viciously, then could only stare through them as Darcy came in. "I have to go," was the best she could manage. Then she fled through the back door.

"Shawn." Darcy dumped empties in the sink

and turned to glare at him. "What the devil did you do to make Brenna cry?"

Guilt, anger, and emotions he didn't care to explore waged an ugly war inside him. "Oh, just bugger it," he snapped. "I've had enough of females for one night."

She was mortified and full of misery. She'd upset, insulted, and embarrassed two people she cared about deeply. She'd butted in where it wasn't her business.

No, she didn't believe that. It *was* her business. Mary Kate had been flirting outrageously, and Shawn had been oblivious.

Typical.

But he wouldn't have stayed oblivious. Her sister was beautiful, she was sweet, she was smart. And she was most definitely a young woman in full bloom.

Protecting her hadn't been the mistake. But the method had been clumsy, and more than a little selfish. Because — and she had to face it — she'd also been a woman defending her territory.

Of which, Shawn was also oblivious.

All she could do now was mend her fences.

She'd taken a long walk on the beach. To cry it out, to think it through, to settle herself. And to ensure that when she did return home, her parents would most likely be tucked into their bed so that she could talk with Mary Kate alone.

There was a light on outside, shining over the porch, and another left burning in the front window.

She left them both on, as she doubted her sister Patty would be back yet from her Saturday date.

Another wedding, she thought as she took off her jacket. More fussing and planning and cranky tears over flowers and fabric swatches.

She couldn't for the life of her understand why a sensible person would want to go through all of that nonsense. Maureen had been a nervous wreck — and had set the entire family on its ear — before she'd finally walked down the aisle the previous autumn.

Not that she hadn't looked lovely, Brenna thought as she hung her cap on the closet hook. All glowing and fresh in her billowy white dress and the lace veil their own mother had worn on her wedding day. Happiness had been like sunbeams, all but shining from her fingertips, and seeing that wash of love over her sister had made Brenna stop, for a short while, feeling like ten times a fool in her own fussy blue maid of honor gown.

Now if she herself ever took the plunge — and since she wanted children, what else could she do but marry eventually — simplicity would be the order of the day.

A church wedding would be fine, as she imagined her mother's heart, and her father's as well, would be set on that for all their daughters. But she'd be damned if she would spend months looking at dresses and searching through catalogs and discussing the pros and cons of roses over tulips or some such.

She'd wear her mother's dress and veil, and

maybe carry yellow daisies, as she had a fondness for them. And she'd walk down the aisle on her father's arm to the sound of pipes rather than a fusty old organ. And after, they'd have a party right here at the house. A big, noisy *ceili* where everyone could loosen their ties and relax.

And what, she thought, shaking her head outside the door of the room that her youngest sisters, Mary Kate and Alice Mae, shared, was she doing dreaming of such things now?

She slipped into the room, stood in the candy-coated, female scent of it while her eyes adjusted, then picked her way over to the lump on the bed nearest the back window.

"Mary Kate, are you awake?"

"She is." Alice Mae's silhouette of a head and shoulders surrounded by a mass of wild curls popped up. "And I'm to tell you that she hates you like poison, always will until the day she departs this earth, and she's not speaking to you."

"Go back to sleep."

"How can I manage that, with herself there coming in and burning my ears off with abuse of you? Did you really shove her out the kitchen at Gallagher's, then curse at her?"

"I did not."

"She did," Mary Kate corrected in a stiff and formal voice. "And you'll kindly tell her, Alice Mae, to remove her skinny ass from my bedroom."

"She says you're to remove —"

"I heard her, for Christ's sake. And I'm not going."

78

"Well, then, if she's not going, I am." Mary Kate started to get up, but found herself pinned.

At the sound of muffled curses and struggle, Alice Mae eagerly switched on her bedside lamp to watch the show. "Ah, you'll never best her, Katie, for you fight like a girl. Did you never listen to anything she taught us?"

"Just hold still, you goose brain. How the hell can I apologize when you're trying to bite me hand off?"

"I don't want your flaming apology."

"Well, you're getting it, if I have to ram it down your throat." Annoyed and at her wits' end, Brenna did the simple thing. She sat on her sister.

"Brenna's been crying." Alice Mae, with the softest heart in Ireland, climbed out of bed to pad over to her sister. "There now." Gently, she kissed both Brenna's cheeks. "It can't be as bad as all that, darling."

"Little mother," Brenna murmured, and nearly started crying again. Her baby sister wasn't a baby any longer, but a slim and pretty girl on the verge of womanhood. And that, Brenna thought with a sigh, was a worry for another day. "Go back to bed, sweetheart. Your feet'll get cold."

"I'll sit here." She slid onto the bed, and plopped on Mary Kate's legs. "And help you hold her down. If it was enough to make you cry, she should at least have the courtesy to listen to you."

"Well, she made *me* cry," Mary Kate protested.

"Yours were temper tears," Alice Mae said primly, using one of their mother's expressions.

"Part of mine were, too, I suppose." With a sigh, Brenna snugged an arm around Alice Mae's shoulders. "She had a right to be angry with me. I behaved badly. I'm so sorry, Katie, for the way I acted, and the things I said."

"You are?"

"Truly." Tears swam up again, into her throat, into her eyes. "I just love you."

"I love you, too." Mary Kate sobbed it out. "I'm sorry, too. I said awful things to you. I didn't mean them."

"Doesn't matter." She shifted so that Mary Kate could scramble up to be held. "I can't help but worry about you," she murmured against her sister's hair. "I know you're grown up, but it's not easy to think of you that way. With Maureen and Patty it's not so hard. Maureen's barely ten months younger than me, and Patty came just a year after that. But with you two . . ." She opened her arms so Alice Mae could slip in as well. "I remember when each of you came along, so it's different somehow."

"But I wasn't doing anything wrong."

"I know." Brenna closed her eyes. "You're so pretty, Katie. And I suppose you have to test your skills. I just wish you'd test them on boys your own age."

"I have." With a watery laugh, Mary Kate lifted her head from Brenna's shoulder and grinned. "I'm thinking I'm ready to move up a level."

"Oh, Mother Mary." Brenna closed her eyes. "Just answer me this. Do you fancy yourself in love with Shawn?"

"I don't know." She moved her shoulders restlessly. "I might be. It's just that he's so handsome, like a knight on a white charger. And he's like a poet, so romantic and deep somehow. He looks at you, right in the eye. A lot of boys aim their eyes a bit lower, so you know they're not thinking about you, but about the possibility of getting you out of your blouse. Have you ever noticed his hands, Brenna?"

"His hands?" Long, narrow, clever. Gorgeous.

"They're an artist's hands, and you just know, looking at them, how they might feel if he touched you."

"Aye," she said on a long breath, then caught herself. "What I mean to say is I can understand how he'd stir certain, well, juices, being as he's pretty. I just want you to have a care, that's all."

"I will."

"There, now, you're all made up." Alice Mae got up, kissed both of them. "Now will you go away, Brenna, so we can all get some sleep?"

Brenna didn't sleep much, and when she did, there were dreams. Odd and jumbled dreams with moments of clarity that almost hurt the brain. A white-winged horse carrying a rider dressed in silver, with his long black hair flying away from a finely sculpted handsome face.

He flew through the night, with stars burning around him, higher and higher, toward the glowing white ball of a full moon. A moon that dripped light like tears, tears he gathered like pearls in his bag of shining silver. Pearls that he poured onto the ground at the feet of Lady Gwen as they stood outside the cottage on the faerie hill.

"These are the tears of the moon. They are my longing for you. Take them, and me."

But she shed her own tears as she turned away from him, denied him, refused him. And the pearls glowed in the grass and the glowing became moonflowers.

And it was Brenna who picked them, by night, when their delicate white petals were open. She laid them on the little stoop by the cottage door, leaving them there for Shawn because she lacked the courage to take them inside. And to offer.

The lack of sleep and surplus of dreams left her hollow-eyed and broody the next day. After Mass she piddled around, taking apart the engine of the old lawn mower, changing the points and plugs on her truck, tuning it though it didn't need tuning.

She was under her mother's old car, changing the oil, when she saw her father's boots.

"Your ma said I should come out here and see what's weighing on your brain before you take it into your head to strip the engine out of this old tank."

"I'm just seeing to some things need seeing to."

"I see that." He crouched down, then with a wheezy sigh, scooted under the car with her. "So you've nothing on your mind."

"Maybe I do." She worked a few moments in silence, knowing he would let her gather her thoughts. "Could I ask you something?"

"You know you can."

"What is it a man wants?"

Mick pursed his lips, pleased to see how quick and competent his daughter's hands were with a wrench. "Well, a good woman, steady work, a hot meal, and a pint at the end of day satisfies most."

"It's the first part I'm trying to figure here. What is it a man wants from a woman?"

"Oh. Well, now." Flustered, and not a little panicked, he started to scoot out again. "I'll get your mother."

"You're a man, she's not." Brenna caught his leg before he could escape. He was wiry, but she had a good grip. "I want, from a man's own mind, what it is he's looking for in a woman."

"Ah . . . well . . . common sense," he said a bit too cheerily. "That's a fine trait. And patience. A man needs patience from a woman, truth be known. Time was, he wanted her to make him a nice comfortable home, but in today's world — and as I have five daughters I have to live in today's world — that's more a give-and-take sort of arrangement. A helpmate." He grabbed the word like a rope tossed over the edge of a very high cliff with a very narrow ledge that was rapidly crumbling under his feet. "A man wants a helpmate, a life's companion."

Brenna gave herself a little push so she could sit out beside the car. She kept her hand on his ankle, for she sensed he'd bolt if she gave him the chance. "I think we both know I'm not talking about common sense and patience and companionship."

His face went pink, then white. "I'm not talking

to you about sex, Mary Brenna, so get that idea right out of your head. I'm not having a conversation with my daughter about such a matter."

"Why? I know you've had it, or I wouldn't be here, would I?"

"Be that as it may," he said and closed his lips.

"If I were a son instead of a daughter, we could discuss it?"

"You're not, so we aren't, and that's the end of it." Now he folded his arms as well.

Sitting as he was, he made Brenna think of an annoyed leprechaun, and she wondered if Jude had used him as a model for one of her sketches.

"And how am I to get my mind around something if it can't be discussed?"

Since Mick didn't give a hang about the logic of that at the moment, he simply scowled off into the distance. "If you must talk of such things, speak with your mother."

"All right, all right, never mind, then." She'd go at this from a different angle. Hadn't he been the very one to teach her there was always more than one way to approach a job of work? "Tell me something else."

"On another topic entirely?"

"You could say that." She smiled at him, patting his leg. "I'm wondering, if there was something you wanted, had wanted for some time, what would you do about it?"

"If I've wanted it, why don't I have it?"

"Because you haven't made any real effort to get it as yet."

84

"And why haven't I?" He arched his sandy brows. "Am I slow or just stupid?"

Brenna thought it over, decided he couldn't know he'd just insulted his firstborn. Then she nodded slowly. "Maybe a bit of both in this particular case."

Relieved to have the conversation turn to a safe area, he gave her a fierce grin. "Then I'd stop being slow and I'd stop being stupid and I'd take good aim at what I wanted and not dawdle about. Because when an O'Toole takes aim, by Jesus, he hits his mark."

That, she knew, was true enough. And was certainly expected. "But maybe you're a bit nervous and not quite sure of your skill in this area."

"Girl, if you don't go after what you want, you'll never have it. If you don't ask, the answer's always no. If you don't step forward, you're always in the same place."

"You're right." She took his shoulders, transferring a little grease from her hands to his shirt as she kissed him soundly. "You're always right, Dad, and that's just what I needed to hear."

"Well, that's what a father's for, after all."

"Would you mind finishing up this business here?" She jerked a thumb under the car. "I don't like to leave it half done, but there's something I have to see to."

"That's not a problem." He wiggled under the car and, delighted he'd put his daughter's mind at ease, whistled while he worked.

Five

Shawn steeped his tea until he could have danced the hornpipe on its surface, then unearthed the day-old scones left over from the pub. He had an hour before he had to be at work, and he intended to enjoy his little breakfast and read the paper that he'd picked up in the village after Mass.

The radio on the counter was playing traditional Gaelic tunes, and the kitchen hearth was crackling with a fine turf fire. For him, it was a small slice of heaven.

Before long he'd be cooking for the Sunday crowds, and Darcy would be in and out of the kitchen at Gallagher's, needling him about something or other. And this one or that would have something to say to him. He imagined Jude would slip in for an hour or two, and he'd make sure she had a good, healthy supper.

He didn't mind any of that, not a bit. But if he didn't grab a handful of alone time now and again, it felt as if his brain would explode. He could imagine himself living in the cottage for the rest of his life, with the bad-tempered black cat stretched out by the fire, wallowing in quiet morning after quiet morning.

His mind drifted along with the pipes and flutes flowing from the radio. His foot began to tap. And then the loud thud at his back door sent his heart shooting straight to his throat.

The big yellow hound grinned at him, her tongue hanging out and her massive paws pressed against the glass. Shawn shook his head, but he got up to go to the door. He never minded the O'Tooles' Betty. She was fine company, and after a bit of a scratch and stroke she would curl up and settle into her own dreams.

Bub arched his back and hissed, but that was routine rather than true annoyance. When the patient Betty didn't react, the cat merely turned his tail up and began to wash.

"Out and about, are you, now?" Shawn said as he let Betty in out of a brisk wind that hinted of rain. "Well, you're welcome to share a scone and the fire, no matter what that devil there says about it." But as he started to close the door again, he spotted Brenna.

His first reaction was a vague irritation, for here was someone who wouldn't settle for a scratch and a stroke but would demand conversation. He kept the door open and stood between the wind and the warmth as he watched her.

A few coils of hair had come loose from her cap and were flying around, red as rubies. Her mouth was set, making him wonder if he, or someone, had done something to annoy her. Which, now that he thought of it, was such a simple matter. Still, it was a fine mouth if you took the time to look at it.

For such a small woman, she had a long stride, he noted. And a purposeful one. She was moving as if she had something to do and wanted it over and dealt with quickly. Knowing the O'Toole as he did, he had no doubt she'd let him know just what that was in the shortest of orders.

She skirted around the little patch of herbs he was thinking of expanding into a full kitchen garden. The wind had whipped color into her face, so when she lifted her head and caught his eye, her cheeks were rosy.

"Good day to you, Mary Brenna. If you're out for a walk with your dog, it seems she's had enough of it. She's already sitting under my table here, and Bub's ignoring her as if she isn't worth his time."

"She's the one who wanted to walk with me."

"Sure, and if you walked now and then instead of marching as you do, she might stay along with you longer. Come in out of the wind." He started to move back as she stepped on the back stoop, then paused, sniffed. Smiled. "You smell of flowers and axle grease or some such thing."

"It's motor oil, and what's left of the perfume Alice Mae caught me with this morning."

"It's quite the combination." And very Brenna O'Toole, he thought as she strode past him. "Will you have some tea?"

"I will." She peeled off her jacket, tossed it on a peg, then belatedly remembered her cap and removed that as well.

It always gave him a little jerk in the belly to

watch all that hair spill out and down. Foolish, he thought as he moved to the pot. He knew it was up there, under that ugly cap. But each time she let it fall, it was a new surprise.

"I've scones."

"No, but thanks." She wanted to clear her throat, as it seemed coated with something thick and hot. Instead she sat at the table, casually kicked back. She'd decided as she'd walked over to ease her way into things, so to speak. "I wondered if you might want me to take a look at your car sometime this week. The last I heard it, it sounded sad."

"I wouldn't mind, if you've time." He watched as Bub sidled over to rub against Brenna's legs, then leap into her lap. The O'Toole was the only human person the cat had ever fancied. Shawn decided it was because they were both prickly creatures.

"Aren't you busy at the house, doing the baby's room for Jude?"

She stroked Bub's head so he purred like a freight train. "I've time enough."

He sat across from Brenna, and when Betty came begging, gave her half a scone. "How's it coming, then?" And decided it was comfortable after all, sitting with her in the warm kitchen, with the animals milling about.

"Oh, it's fine. It's mostly just fiddling Jude wants, prettying up and the like. But in the way of women, now she's thinking that when the one room's fixed and polished, the others will look shabby against it. She's thinking to spruce up the main bedroom now."

"What's wrong with it?"

Brenna lifted her shoulders. "Nothing I can see, but between Jude and Darcy they've come up with a dozen things. New paper for the walls, fresh paint for the trim, sanding the floors. Then I just mentioned how nice the view was from the front windows there, and Jude's saying that she longs for a window seat. I said if she wanted one, it was just a matter of this and a matter of that, and before you can blink, she's wanting me to do it."

Absently, Brenna took the second half of the scone and nibbled on it. "I wager Dad and I will be going from room to room in that house, and top to bottom. She's got the bit between her teeth now. Must be a nesting sort of thing."

"Well, if it pleases her and Aidan doesn't mind it . . ." Shawn trailed off, imagining how it would be to live in the midst of all that hammering and sawing. He'd rather be roasted over a slow fire.

"Mind it?" Brenna let out a quick snorting laugh. "He comes in during one of our discussions and just grins like a fool. The man's besotted with her. I believe she could say, well, let's just have Brenna turn this house around to face the other way and he'd never bat an eye." She sighed and sipped her tea. "It's lovely to see, really, the way they are together."

"She was what he was waiting for." At Brenna's puzzled look, Shawn shook his head. "Sure he was waiting. You'd only to study on him to see it. When she walked into the pub that first night, that was it. A life change from that instant, though neither of them knew it."

"But you did?"

"I can't say I knew precisely, just that I knew things would change."

Intrigued, she leaned forward. "And what are you waiting for?"

"Me?" His eyebrow quirked. "Oh, things are fine as they are for me."

"That's a problem with you, Shawn." She jabbed a finger at him. "You walk the same line until it becomes a rut, and never notice, for your head's in the clouds in any case."

"If it's a rut it's mine, and I'm comfortable in it."

"What you need to do is take charge." She remembered her father's words. "To move forward. If you don't move forward you're always in the same place."

Eyes mild and amused, he lifted his tea. "But I like this place."

"I'm ready for a change, for moving forward." Her eyes narrowed as she studied him. "And I don't mind being the one who takes charge if that's the way it has to be."

"And what do you have a mind to take charge of this time around?"

"You." She sat back, ignoring his smirk as he sipped tea. "I think we should have sex."

He choked, spilling hot tea over his hand and onto his paper as he coughed violently. She made a quick sound of annoyance and dislodged an irritated Bub to get up and thump Shawn briskly on the back. "It can't be that horrible a thought."

"Jesus!" was the best he could manage. "Sweet Jesus Christ!" When she plopped into her chair again, he simply goggled at her with eyes that continued to water. Finally he sucked in a breath and blew it out again. "What kind of thing is that to say?"

"It's plain speaking." Determined to hold back both nerves and temper, she hooked an arm over the back of her chair. "The fact is, I've a yen for you. I've had it for some time." This time his mouth fell open, and the shock on his face teased her temper closer to the surface. "What do you think? Only men can scratch an itch when they have one?"

He didn't, of course he didn't. But neither did he believe that one just plopped down in someone's kitchen and announced it. "What would your mother think, hearing you talk this way?"

Brenna inclined her head. "She's not here, is she?"

He pushed the chair back, abruptly enough to have Betty leap to her feet. Since none of the thoughts whirling around in his head would settle, he just marched to the door. "I need air."

For a moment Brenna sat where she was. She ordered herself to take long, slow breaths, to wait until she could be calm. To be reasonable and mature and clearheaded. Reason fought against temper for nearly ten seconds before it turned tail and deserted the field.

The nerve of the man! The bloody *nerve* of him. What was she, some kind of gargoyle a man couldn't think of cozying up to? Did she have to strut around in short skirts with her face painted before Shawn Gallagher took notice? The hell with that.

She was up and out the door and striding into the wind. "You're not interested, that's fine. You just say so."

She caught up with him, planted herself in front of him. He solved that problem by turning around and walking the other way.

And was a lucky man she didn't have a weapon in her hands.

"Don't you walk away from me, you yellow coward dog."

He shot a look over his shoulder, his eyes a ripe, glittering blue. "You ought to be ashamed of yourself." He looked away and kept walking.

He was mortified, right down to the bone. And God help him, he was . . . stirred as well. He refused to think of her that way. And always had. Well, if a time or two his thoughts had veered off in that direction, hadn't he cut them off, sharp and fast? And that's just what he was going to do now.

"Ashamed?" Her voice punched like a fist. "Who the hell are you to decide what should shame me?"

"I'm the man you just offered yourself to as easy as if you were offering me a pint and some crisps."

She'd caught up with him again, but his words struck her, drained the color from her face. "Is that what you think? That it's nothing more than that? Then it's you who should be ashamed."

He could see the hurt in her eyes, and it only added to the mass of confusion he found himself tangled in. "Brenna, you don't just go around saying let's have sex to a man. It's just not right."

"But it's fine for a man to go around saying it to a woman?"

"No. I don't think that either. It's a . . . it should . . . Mother of God, I can't have a conversation like this with you. You're all but family."

"Why is it the men I know can't speak of sex as a normal human function? And I'm *not* family."

It might have been cowardice, he thought, but it was also discretion. He stepped back from her. "Stay away from me."

"If you don't want to go to bed with me, you've only to say that I don't appeal to you in that fashion."

"I'm not thinking about you in that fashion." He took another step back, right through the little herb bed. "You're practically my sister."

She bared her teeth, a sure sign of temper about to snap. "But I'm *not* your bloody sister, am I?"

The wind caught her hair, sent it streaming so that he wanted to take it in his hands — something he might have done a hundred other times, when it would have been a harmless gesture.

Now he was afraid nothing between them would ever be harmless again.

"No, you're not. But I've thought of you — tried to think of you — that way most of my life. How do you expect me to just flip that about and . . . I can't do it," he said quickly when his blood began to stir again. "It's just not right."

"You don't want to have sex with me, that's your business." She nodded coolly. "Others do." With this she turned on her heel and started to march toward home.

"Wait a damn minute." He could move fast when he needed to, and he had her arm before she'd taken three full strides. He whirled her around and took as firm a hold on her other arm. "If you think I'm going to let you walk off with that in your head, you're badly mistaken. I'm not about to have you go off and throw yourself at some man because you're mad at me."

The flash in her eyes should have been a warning, but her voice was so calm, so cool, he missed it. "You think far too much of yourself, Shawn Gallagher. If I want to be with a man, with him I'll be. You've nothing to say about it. It may come as a shock to you, but I've had sex before, and I like it. I'll have it again when I please."

She might as well have plowed the business end of a sledgehammer into his gut. "You — who . . ."

"That's a matter of my concern," she interrupted with a smug look in her eye. "And none of yours. Now let go of me. I've nothing more to say to you."

"Well, I've plenty more to say to you." But he couldn't think of a thing, not with images of Brenna wrapped around some faceless man burning into his brain.

She tossed back her head, and her eyes burned once more into his. "Do you want to have sex with me or not?"

Truth or lie? He was suddenly certain that either answer would send him straight to hell. But he thought the lie safer. "No."

"Then that's the end of it." Humiliated, furious, she shoved away. Then — perhaps it was pride, or perhaps it was just need, but she acted before she thought.

In one easy leap, she was in his arms, her legs locked around his waist, her mouth fused to his. She thought she heard Betty bark — once, twice, three times in rapid succession, almost like a laugh. She clung like a bur when Shawn staggered, then bit, not so lightly, his bottom lip. Someone moaned, she didn't know or care who, and she poured everything she had into that fierce and hot mating of lips.

She'd caught him by surprise. That was why he didn't shake her loose. Of course it was. It was simply an instinctive reaction to grip that wonderfully tight bottom in his hands, then to let them slide up her back and get lost in her hair.

And that quick intake of breath had been shock. It wasn't his fault that the scent and flavor of her assaulted him and because of it, made his head spin.

He had to stop. For her sake, he had to stop this now . . . in just a moment. Sooner or later.

The wind spun around them in chilly ribbons. The sun buried itself behind clouds, shimmering out fragile light as a soft, soft rain began to fall. He all but felt the blood draining downward out of his head, leaving it empty but for the image of carrying her back inside and up the stairs so he could tumble her into bed and have more.

Then she was shoving him again, jumping down. Through the lust clouding his vision, he saw her sharp sneer. "I thought you should have a sample of what you've turned away."

While he stood there, aroused beyond speech, she brushed off the sleeve of her shirt. "I'll have a look at your car when I have a bit of time to spare. You'd best get down to the village. You're running late for work."

He didn't speak when she strolled away, and was still standing in the quiet rain when she and the yellow dog disappeared over the rise.

"You're late," Aidan said the minute Shawn came in the kitchen door of the pub.

"Then fire me or get out of my way."

At the unusually surly response Aidan lifted his eyebrows, watching as Shawn wrenched open the refrigerator and started pulling out eggs and milk and meat. "It's hard to fire a man who owns as much of the business as I do myself."

Shawn banged a pot onto the stove. "Then buy me out, why don't you?"

When Darcy pushed into the kitchen, Aidan held up a hand, shook his head, and motioned her back. She didn't look pleased about it, but she stepped back out again.

"What's the matter?"

"Nothing's the matter. I've things on my mind and work to do."

"I've never known you not to be able to work and run your mouth at the same time."

"I've nothing to say, and meat pies to make. What the hell's with women, anyway?" he demanded, spinning away from the stove to scowl at his brother. "First it's one thing, then it's another, and you never know which way they'll be coming at you next."

"Oh, well, then." Aidan's concern melted into amusement. He helped himself to tea and leaned back on the counter while Shawn muttered and worked. "We could talk all day and half the night and not come close to solving that particular puzzle. 'Tis a thorny one. But it's more pleasant to have a female causing you problems than to have no female at all, don't you think?"

"No, not at the moment."

Aidan only laughed. "Well, which one is it that's causing you grief?"

"It's no one. It's nothing. It's ridiculous."

"Hmm, not saying." Aidan sipped and considered. "Must be in the way of a serious matter, then."

"Easy for you to smile and look smug," Shawn tossed back with bitter annoyance. "All cozied up as you are with your Jude Frances."

"I reckon it is." Aidan nodded. "But it wasn't always, and you gave me good advice when I was at my own wits' end. Maybe you should take some time and give yourself some on this, if you don't want to hear from me."

"I don't want a woman in my life just at the moment," Shawn muttered. "And this particular one won't do at all. Just won't."

He tried not to think of that wild and wicked kiss, or the way Brenna's compact body had plastered itself to his.

"No, it won't," he said again, then adjusted the fire under the pot of meat filling with a sharp turn of his wrist.

"You'd know best what suits and what doesn't. I'll just say there comes a time when your head's telling you one thing, and the rest of you just won't listen. A man can be a child when it comes to a woman, wanting what he shouldn't have and taking more than he can handle. Knowing something's not good for you doesn't stop you from wanting it."

"I wouldn't be good for her." Calmer now, Shawn took out a bowl to make the pastry for the pies. "Even if there weren't other factors involved, I wouldn't be good for her. So that's the end of it."

With the flour and water mixed to a firm dough, he covered the bowl and stuck it into the refrigerator. "I'll be making poundies," he told Aidan while he creamed butter and suet for the next stage of the pastry. And I've some samphire that young Brian Duffy picked for me that I've pickled into jars, so we'll have that tonight as well, as it goes nicely with the salmon you bought this morning. You tell Jude to come over so I can fix her a plate."

"I will, thanks. Shawn —" He broke off as Darcy shoved through the door again, looking aggrieved.

"You ask me to come down early, then you push me back out the door. If the pair of you are going to stand in here and tell your little men's secrets, I'm going back upstairs and do my nails, since we don't open for nearly an hour as yet."

"Let me pour you a cup, darling, for I've abused you something terrible." Aidan gave her a little pat on the cheek, then pulled a chair out at the table with a flourish.

"Well, I'll have a cup, but I want some biscuits with it." She folded her hands on the table after she sat and gave her brother a challenging smile.

"Biscuits, then." Aidan got down a tin and set it in front of her. "I need to talk to both of you, as it concerns the pub."

"Then you'll have to talk while I work." Shawn retrieved the bowl from the refrigerator and began to roll out the pastry.

"Well, you were late, weren't you?" Aidan said easily. "The man from New York, the Magee? It seems he's interested in the idea of linking the theater he's planning with Gallagher's. It was my thought to lease him the land, long term, but he's holding out to buy it outright. If we do that, we forfeit the land, and some of the control we might have."

"How much will he pay?" Darcy asked and bit into a biscuit.

"We've only danced about the terms for the moment, but he'll meet the price we set, I'm thinking.

100

I'll need to call Ma and Dad on this, but as the pub is in our hands now, the three of us need to decide what we want to do."

"If he pays enough, I say sell it to him. We don't use it for anything."

"It's land," Shawn said, sending Darcy a glance as he covered the rectangle of rolled-out pastry with the mixture of suet and butter. "Our land. It's always been ours."

"And it'll be money. Our money."

"I've thought on both ends of that." Aidan pursed his lips while he turned his cup of tea around and around. "If we don't agree to sell, Magee could find himself another plot for his project. And the theater could be a benefit to the pub, if we keep some sort of handle on it. He strikes me as a sharp one, and one I'd rather deal with face-to-face than over the phone. But he says he can't come here now, as he's into some other business and can't leave it until it's done."

"So send me to New York." Darcy fluttered her inky lashes. "And I'll charm him into opening his wallet wide."

Aidan let out a quick hoot. "I don't think charm is what works with this one. It's a pounds-and-pence matter to him, to my thinking. I've a mind to ask Dad to take a trip into New York to meet with this Magee, as Dad's as sharp as any Yank wheeler-dealer. But before we do that, what do we, we three here, want from this?"

"Profit," Darcy said immediately and finished off a biscuit.

"That, yes, but what in the long term?"

"Reputation," Shawn said, and Aidan looked up at him. "We've been working around to making Gallagher's a center for music over the last few years. Have our name in the guidebooks, don't we, as a place for good food and drink, and for the music we have or bring in? Haven't you had bands calling you now, or the managers of them, inquiring about bookings?"

"Sure and we do well there," Aidan agreed.

"If this man Magee has a mind to expand the entertainment, the music in Ardmore, and bring in more tourists, more customers, it'll add to our reputation."

Shawn folded the pastry into three, then sealed the ends before putting it back in the refrigerator to chill. "But it has to be done the Gallagher way, doesn't it?"

Aidan leaned back in his chair as Shawn took potatoes from bin to sink and began to scrub them. "You're a constant surprise to me, Shawn. Aye, the Gallagher way or no way at all. Which means traditional, understated, and Irish. We'll have nothing flashy and foolish attached to our pub."

"Which means you have to convince him we need to work together," Shawn added. "As we know Ardmore and Old Parish and he doesn't."

"And for our input," Aidan decided. "We'll have a percentage of the theater. That was my thinking — and what I wanted to pass to Dad and have him work the Magee toward."

Darcy drummed her fingers on the table. "So,

we'll sell him the land at our price or lease it long term, on the condition that we have a part in the building, the planning, and the profits of the theater."

"Simply said." Aidan gave her a wink. She had a cool and sharp brain for business, did Darcy. "It's the Gallagher way." Aidan rose from the table. "We're agreed, then?"

"Agreed." Darcy chose another biscuit. "Let's see if this Magee can make us rich."

Shawn slipped potatoes into boiling water. "Agreed. Now the pair of you get out of my kitchen."

"Happy to." Darcy blew Shawn a saucy kiss and sailed out, already dreaming how she'd spend the Yank's money.

Because he considered that Aidan had it under control, Shawn didn't give another thought to land deals and building and profits from either. He prepared the dishes he'd planned and had the kitchen warm and full of scent by the time the pub doors opened.

He kept up with the orders, fell into the easy routine, but the music that usually filled his head kept stalling on him. He'd start to play with a tune while he worked, let the notes and the rhythm go their own way. Then he'd be back in the soft rain, with Brenna wrapped around him, and the only music he heard was the hum in his own blood. And that he didn't care for.

She was his friend, and a man had no business

thinking about a friend in that manner. Even if she'd started it herself. He'd grown up teasing her as he had his own sister. Whenever he'd kissed her, and of course he had, it had always been a brotherly peck.

How the hell was he supposed to go back to that when he knew what she tasted like now? When he knew just how her mouth fit to his, and how much . . . heat there was inside that small package? And just how was he supposed to get rid of this hard, hot ball of awareness in his gut, an awareness he'd never asked for?

She wasn't his type — no, not a bit. He liked soft women with female ways who liked to flirt and cuddle. And by God, women who let him make the moves. He was a man, wasn't he? A man was supposed to romance a woman toward bed, not be told to jump into one because she had a — what had she called it? A yen. An itch.

He'd be damned if he'd be anyone's itch.

He told himself he was going to steer well clear of Brenna O'Toole for the next bit of time. And that he wasn't going to be looking around to see that ugly cap of hers or to hear her voice every time he walked from the kitchen into the pub.

Still, his eyes scanned the crowd, and his ears were pricked. But she didn't come to Gallagher's that Sunday evening.

He did his work, and those who sampled it walked home at closing with full bellies and satisfaction. When he'd put his kitchen to rights and headed home himself, his own belly felt empty despite the meal he'd had, and satisfaction seemed a long way off.

He tried to lose himself in his music again, and spent nearly two hours at the piano. But the notes seemed sour somehow, and the tunes jarring.

Once, as he ran his fingers over the keys, shaking his head when the chords gave him no pleasure, he felt the change in the air. The faintest shimmer of movement and sound. But when he looked up, there was nothing but his little parlor and the empty doorway leading to the hall.

"I know you're here." He said it softly, waited. But nothing spoke to him. "What is it you want me to know?"

As the silence dragged on, he rose to bank the fire, to listen to the whisper of the wind. Though he was sure he was too edgy to sleep, he went upstairs and prepared for bed.

Almost as soon as his head settled on the pillow, he drifted into dreams of a lovely woman standing in the garden while the moonlight silvered her pale gold hair. The wings of the white horse beat the air, then settled as hooves touched ground. The man astride it had eyes only for the woman. As he dismounted, the silver bag he carried sparkled, shot light like little sparks of flame.

At her feet he poured pearls as white and pure as the moonlight. But she turned away from him, never looked at the beauty of the gems. Behind the sweep of her nightrobe, the pearls bloomed into flowers that glimmered like ghosts in the night.

And in the night, surrounded by those moon-washed flowers, Shawn reached for the woman. The pale hair had turned to fire and the soft eyes became sharp and green as emerald. It was Brenna he drew into his arms, Brenna he surrounded with them.

In sleep, where reason and logic have no place, it was Brenna he tasted.

Six

"Hand me my crooked stick, will you, darling?"

Brenna picked up her father's level — he had affectionate names for most of his tools — and walked across the paint-splattered drop cloth to pass it to him.

The nursery was taking shape, and already in Brenna's mind it was the baby's room rather than Shawn's old one. Some might not be able to see the potential of the finished project beyond the clutter of tools and sawhorses, the missing trim and the snowy shower of sawdust. The fact was, she loved the messy middle of a project every bit as much as she did the polished end of it.

She enjoyed the smells and the noises, the good, healthy sweat brought on by swinging a hammer or hefting lumber. Now as she stood back to watch her father snug the level onto the vertical length of the shelves they were building, she thought how much she liked the little pieces of work. Measuring, cutting, checking, rechecking until what you had built was the perfect mirror of what had been inside your head.

"Right on the money," Mick said cheerfully, then propped his level in the corner. Without realizing it, they stood as a pair: hands on hips, legs comfortably spread, feet planted.

"And as it's built by O'Toole, it's built to last."

"Aye, that's the way of it." He slapped her companionably on the shoulder. "Now there's a good morning's work here. How about we go down to the pub for a bit of lunch, then we'll finish the unit this afternoon?"

"Oh, I'm not feeling hungry." Avoiding his eyes, Brenna walked over to examine the trim they'd already made to frame the shelves. "You go ahead. I think I'll just go on and trim this out."

Mick scratched the back of his neck. "You've not been into Gallagher's all the week."

"Haven't I?" She knew damn well she'd not set foot in the door since Saturday last. And she calculated she'd need another day or two before her humiliation level bottomed out enough for her to stroll in and see Shawn.

"No, you haven't. Monday it was 'Well, I brought something from home,' and Tuesday it was 'I'll eat later.' Then yesterday it was how you wanted to finish something up and would come down when you had — which you didn't." He angled his head, reminding himself she was a woman, and women had their ways. "Have you and Darcy had a fight?"

"No." She was grateful he'd assumed that, and that she didn't have to lie about it. "I just saw her yesterday when she dropped over here. You'd gone on to see about the Clooneys' drainpipe."

Keeping her voice and movements casual, she

held up the trim. "I suppose I'm just anxious to see how this will all look when we're done. And I had a big breakfast. You go on and get your lunch, Dad. If I feel peckish after a while, I'll go downstairs and raid Jude's kitchen."

"As you like, then." His daughters, bless them all, were often a puzzle to him. But for the life of him he couldn't think of a thing that could be wrong with his Mary Brenna. So he winked at her as he pulled on his jacket. "We get this done, the least we can do is lift a pint at the end of the day."

"Sure, and I imagine I'll be thirsty." And she would find some excuse to head straight home.

When he was gone, she set the trim in place with the glue gun, then pulled nail and hammer from the tool belt slung around her waist. She wouldn't brood, that she'd promised herself. And by going about her daily business, she'd be over whatever these feelings were for Shawn soon enough.

There were plenty of things she wanted she couldn't have. A kind and generous heart like Alice Mae, a tidy nature like Maureen, the patience of their mother. Another bloody few inches in height, she added as she dragged the stepladder over so she could secure the top of the trim.

She lived without all that, didn't she, and managed very well. She could live without Shawn Gallagher. She could live without men altogether if it came to that.

And one day she'd build her own home with her own hands, and would live her own life her own way. She'd have a herd of nieces and nephews to spoil and no one cluttering up the place with demands and complaints.

A body couldn't ask for more than that, could she?

She wouldn't be lonely. Brenna fit the next piece of trim in place, precisely matching the edges. Why, she didn't think she'd been lonely a single day of her life, so why should she start now? She had her work and her friends and her family.

Damn it, she missed the bastard something fierce.

There'd been hardly a day in her twenty-four years when she hadn't seen him. In the pub, around the village, in his house or her own. She missed the conversations, the sniping, the look and the sound of him. Somehow she had to quash this wanting of him so they could go back to being friends.

It was her own fault, her own weakness. She could fix it. With a sigh, she rested her cheek on the smooth trim. She was good at fixing things.

The minute she heard footsteps in the hall, she jerked herself back and began to hammer busily again.

"Oh, Brenna!" Jude stepped into the doorway and glowed. "I can't believe how much you've gotten done in just a few days. It's wonderful!"

"Will be," Brenna agreed. She climbed down from the ladder to get the next piece of trim. "Dad's just gone off to have some lunch, but we'll have the shelves done today. I think it's coming along fine."

"So's the baby. I felt him move last night."

"Oh, well, now." Brenna turned away from her work. "That's lovely, isn't it?"

Jude's eyes misted over. "I can't describe it. I never thought I'd have all these feelings, or be so happy, have someone like Aidan love me."

"Why shouldn't you have all that and more?"

"I never felt good enough, or smart enough, or clever enough." Resting a hand on her belly, she wandered over to run a finger down the new trim. "Looking back now, I can't see why I felt so, well, inadequate. No one made me feel that way but myself. But you know, I think I was meant to be that way, feel that way, so that step by step my life would lead me right here."

"Now that's a fine and Irish way to look at things."

"Destiny," Jude said with a half laugh. "You know, sometimes I wake up at night, in the dark, in the quiet with Aidan sleeping beside me, and I think, here I am. Jude Frances Murray. Jude Frances Gallagher," she corrected with a smile that brought out the dimples in her cheeks. "Living in Ireland by the sea, a married woman with a life growing inside me. A writer, with a book about to be published and another being written. And I barely recognize the woman I was in Chicago. I'm so glad she's not me anymore."

"She's still part of you, or you wouldn't appreciate who you are now, and what you have."

Jude lifted her brows. "You're absolutely right. Maybe you should have been the psychologist."

111

"No, thanks all the same. I'd much sooner hammer at wood than at someone's head." Brenna set her teeth and whacked a nail. "With a few minor exceptions."

Ah, Jude thought, just the opening she'd been hoping for. "And would my brother-in-law be at the top of that list of exceptions?"

At the question Brenna's hand jerked, missing the mark and bashing her thumb with the hammer. "Bloody, buggering hell!"

"Oh, let me see. Is it bad?"

Brenna hissed air through her teeth as pain radiated and Jude fluttered around her. "No, it's nothing. Clumsy, flaming idiot. My own fault."

"You come down to the kitchen, put some ice on it."

"It's not much of a thing," Brenna insisted, shaking her hand.

"Down." Jude took her arm and pulled her toward the door. "It's my fault. I distracted you. The least I can do is nurse it a little."

"It's just a bump." But Brenna let herself be towed down the stairs and back to the kitchen.

"Sit down. I'll get some ice."

"Well, it won't hurt to sit a minute." She'd always been easy in the Gallagher kitchen. Little had changed in it since she'd been a girl, though Jude was adding her mark here and there.

The walls were cream-colored, and looked almost delicate against the dark wood that trimmed them. The windowsills were thick and wide, and Jude had set little pots of herbs along them to catch the sun. The old cabinet with its glass front and many drawers that ran along the side wall had always been white and comfortably shabby. Now Jude had painted it a pale, pale green so it looked fresh and pretty and somehow female.

The good dishes were displayed behind the glass — dishes the Gallaghers had used for holidays and special occasions. They were white with little violets edging the plates and cups.

The small hearth was of cobbled stone, and the carved fairy that Brenna had given Jude for her thirtieth birthday guarded the fire that simmered there.

It had always been a home, Brenna thought, and a fine, warm one. Now it was Jude's.

"This room suits you," Brenna said as Jude carefully wrapped an ice-filled cloth around Brenna's injured thumb.

"It does, yes." Jude beamed, not noticing that she was already picking up the rhythm of Irish speech. "I only wish I could cook."

"You do fine."

"It's never going to be one of my strengths. Thank God for Shawn." She walked to the refrigerator, hoping to keep it casual. "He sent some soup home with Aidan last night. Potato and lovage. Since you didn't go to the pub for lunch with your father, I'll heat some up for both of us."

She started to refuse, but her stomach was threatening to rumble, so she gave in. "Thanks for that."

"I made the bread." Jude poured soup into a pan

and set it on to warm. "So I won't guarantee it."

Brenna eyed the loaf with approval when Jude took it out of the bread drawer. "Brown soda bread, is it? I favor that. It looks lovely."

"I think I'm getting the hang of it."

"Why do you bother, when you've only to have Shawn send some over for you?"

"I like it. The process of it. Mixing and kneading and rising." Jude set the slices she'd cut on a plate. "It's good thinking time, too."

"My mother always says so. But for me, I'd rather take a nice lie-me-down to do my thinking. You go to all that trouble to cook something, and . . ." Brenna snatched a slice from the plate, bit in. "Gone," she said with a grin.

"Watching it go is one of the cook's pleasures." Jude went to the stove, gave her heating soup a stir. "You've had a fight with Shawn, and not one of your usual squabbles."

"I don't know that it was really a fight, but I can't say it was usual. It'll pass, Jude. Don't worry yourself over it."

"I love you. Both of you."

"I know you do. It's a bit of nothing, I promise."

Saying no more, Jude got out bowls and spoons. How much, she wondered, did one friend interfere in the business of another? Where was the line? Then sighing, she decided there simply wasn't one. "You have feelings for him."

Brenna's nerves jittered at the quiet tone. "Well, sure, and I have feelings for the man. We've been in and out of each other's pockets all our lives. Which is only one of the many reasons he irritates me so I want to bash him with a hammer more often than not."

She smiled when she said it, but Jude's face remained sober. "You have feelings for him," Jude repeated, "that have nothing to do with childhood or friendship and everything to do with being a woman attracted to a man."

"I . . ." Brenna felt the color rush hot to her cheeks — the curse of a redhead. "Well, that's not . . ." Lies trembled on her tongue and simply refused to fall. "Oh, hell." She rubbed her uninjured hand over her face, then stopped abruptly, fingers spread around eyes that went suddenly wide and appalled. "Jesus, Mary, and Joseph, it shows?"

Before Jude could answer, Brenna was up, pacing, knocking the heels of her hands against the sides of her head, moaning out curses. "I'll have to move away, leave my family. I can go to the west counties. I have some people, on my mother's side, in Galway. No, no, that's not far enough. I'll have to leave the country entirely. I'll go to Chicago and stay with your granny until I get on me feet. She'll take me in, won't she?"

She spun back, teeth gritted once again as Jude ladled soup into bowls and chuckled. "Oh, well, now, maybe you find this a laughing matter, Jude Frances, but to me it's dire business. I'm humiliated in front of everyone who knows me, and all because I've an itch for some pretty-faced, soft-brained man."

"You're not humiliated, and I'm sorry to laugh. But your face . . . well." Choking back another chuckle, Jude set the soup bowls on the table, then patted Brenna's shoulder. "Sit down, take a deep breath. You don't have to leave the country."

When Brenna stood her ground, Jude took the deep breath herself. "I don't think it shows, not obviously. But I'm used to watching people, analyzing, and on top of it I think, really, that when you're in love you're more tuned to emotions. Something . . . I don't know, ripples in the air when the two of you are in the same room. After a while I realized it wasn't the usual affectionate animosity that friends and family sometimes have, but something more, well, elemental."

Brenna waved a hand in dismissal. She'd hooked on to only one point. "It doesn't show?"

"No, not unless you look really close. Now sit down."

"All right, then." She blew out a breath now as she sat, but she didn't feel completely relieved. "If Darcy'd noticed, she'd have said something. She wouldn't be able to resist needling at me about it. So if it's just you and Shawn that know, I can manage that."

"You've told him?"

"It seemed time I did." Without much interest, Brenna spooned up soup. "I've been having these urges, so to speak, for a long time where he's concerned. Thinking on it just recently, it seemed to me that if we just went to bed together a time or two I'd get it out of my system."

116

Jude set down her own spoon with a clatter. "You asked him to go to bed with you?"

"I did, and you'd think I'd smashed him in the balls with my wrench. So that's the end of that."

Jude folded her hands, leaned forward. "I'm going to pry."

Brenna's lips twitched. "Oh, you haven't started that yet?"

"Not nearly. What exactly did you say to him?"

"I said, plain enough, that I thought we should have sex. And what's wrong with that?" she demanded, gesturing with her spoon. "You'd think a man would appreciate clear, honest speaking."

"Hmmm" was all Jude could think of. "I take it Shawn didn't appreciate it."

"Hah. I'm like a sister to him, he says. And how I should be ashamed. Ashamed," she repeated, firing up. "Then he tells me right out he doesn't want me in that way. So I jumped him."

"You . . ." Jude coughed and picked up her spoon again. She needed something to soothe the tickle in her throat. "You jumped him."

"Aye. Planted a kiss on him that he won't forget anytime soon. And the man didn't exactly fight me off like his life depended on it." She tore a slice of bread in two, shoved half in her mouth. "After I was done with that, I left him standing there, looking shell-shocked."

"I imagine. He kissed you back?"

"Sure he kissed me back." She tossed that off with a shrug. "Men are predictable that way. Even if a woman isn't to their taste, they're likely to take a sample, aren't they?"

"Um, yes, I suppose." Unsure of her ground, Jude went back to *hmmm*.

"Now I'm steering clear of him for a while," Brenna continued, "as I can't decide if I'm more angry or embarrassed about the matter."

"He's been very distracted the last few days."

"Has he now?"

"And short-tempered."

Brenna found her appetite coming back. "I'm delighted to hear it. I hope he suffers, the donkey's ass."

"If I wanted a man to suffer, I think I'd want to watch him while he did it." Jude swallowed more soup. "But that's just me."

"I suppose there's no harm in stopping by the pub after work today." Brenna sent Jude a quick and wicked grin. "Thanks."

"Oh, anytime."

Brenna went through the rest of her workday whistling, her mood bright and her hands nimble. She supposed it wasn't very charitable of her to take such pleasure in the idea of another's unhappiness. But she was human, after all.

When she walked into Gallagher's, she was more cheerful than she'd been in days. It was early enough to be quiet, with only a scattering of the tables occupied. Far from being worked off her feet, Darcy was standing at the bar talking to big Jack Brennan.

"You go on and sit with your friends," she told Mick when she spotted a couple of his cronies already planted by the fire with pints. "I'll just sit at the bar and catch up with Darcy."

"I'll do that, and you'll have her bring me a pint, won't you, darling?"

"I will." Brenna angled left and slid onto a stool beside Jack.

"Well, now, here's a stranger." Aidan automatically put a pint and a glass under the taps, as he knew the preferences of his regulars. "Where is it you've been hiding yourself, Mary Brenna?"

"In your own home. You have a look at your baby's room when you get there, and let me know what you think."

"That I'll do."

"We left your bride sighing and sniffling over the shelves we've just finished." Even as she spoke, Brenna had one eye on the kitchen door. "And how are you, Jack?"

"I'm fine and well, Brenna, and you?"

"The same. You're not falling in love with our Darcy here, now, are you?"

He blushed like a ripe beet. Jack had a face as big as the moon and shoulders wide as County Waterford, and he never failed to color like a schoolboy when teased about women.

"I've more sense than that. She'd squash my heart like a bug."

"Ah, but you'd die a happy man," Darcy told him.

"Don't listen to her, Jack." Aidan worked the

taps as he spoke, expertly building the Guinness. "For she's as fickle and flighty as they come."

"All true," Darcy agreed with a careless and beautiful laugh. "I'm holding out for a rich man, one who'll set me on a pedestal and strew jewels at my feet. But in the meantime . . ." She played her fingertips over Jack's flushed face. "I enjoy the attention of big and handsome men."

"Ah, go on and take my father his pint, before our Jack here loses all power of speech." Brenna cocked her boot on her knee and lifted the glass Aidan passed her. "You're safe with me, Jack darling."

"You're as pretty as she is."

"Don't be saying such things loud enough for herself to hear you, or she'll skin us both." Touched and amused, she kissed his cheek. And Shawn came through the door.

It would have been comical, she decided, and was a pity that no one noticed but herself the way he stopped dead in his tracks, stared, then jolted when the door swung back and slapped him in the ass.

Secretly delighted, she merely lifted her eyebrows and left her hand cozily on Jack's broad shoulder. "Good evening to you, Shawn."

"Brenna." So much was going on inside him he couldn't separate one sensation from the other. He knew one was irritation, another was discomfort. And, damn it, another altogether was straight lust that had no business being there. But the rest of it was just a mess.

She sipped her beer, watched him over the foam. "I had some of your soup at lunch today with Jude. It had a fine flavor."

"We've *ciste* on the menu tonight; Mrs. Laury butchered some pigs this week."

"Well, that'll stick to your ribs, won't it, Jack?"

"That it will. Are you staying to eat, then, Brenna?"

"No, I'm for home after my Guinness."

"If you change your mind, you can have a meal with me. I've a fondness for *ciste*, and Shawn makes it well."

"He's a hand in the kitchen, isn't he?" She smiled when she said it, but the expression in her eyes was sharp and derisive. "Do you cook at all, Jack?"

"Sausage and eggs I can manage. And I can boil a potato." Being Jack, he took her question seriously and furrowed his brow as he thought through his culinary repertoire. "I can make a sandwich well enough when I have the fixings about, though that's not the same as cooking when it comes to it."

"That'll get you by." She gave Jack's shoulder a friendly pat. "You and me, we'll leave the cooking for the likes of Shawn here. Aidan, will you be needing me at all this weekend for working the pub?"

"I could use your hands on Saturday night if you can fit it in. The band we've booked is a popular one, and your Mary Kate let us know there's a tour group coming into the cliff hotel for Saturday as well. I'm thinking some of them will wander into Gallagher's."

"I'll come at six, then." She drained her glass, slid off the stool. "Will you be stopping in the pub here on Saturday, Jack?"

"I will, yes. I like the band."

"I'll see you then." She glanced back, noted her father was deep into talk with his friends. An hour more, she calculated, then called to him, "I'm for home, Dad. I'll tell Ma you'll be along by and by. Darcy, you see that the man's up and out within the hour now, won't you?"

"I'll show him the door." Darcy carted a tray full of empties to the bar. "I've a date Tuesday next with a Dubliner who passed through here. He's taking me into Waterford City for dinner. Why don't you get yourself a man and come along?"

"I might do that."

"Better, I'll ask the Dubliner to bring a friend."

"All right." Brenna didn't have any interest in having dinner in Waterford with strangers, but it was so satisfying to plan it with Shawn listening. "I'll just stay with you after, as I expect we'll get in late."

"He's picking me up at six, prompt," Darcy called out as Brenna started to the door. "So be here on time and looking like a female."

Jack sighed into his beer when Brenna strode out. "She smells of sawdust," he said more to himself than otherwise. "It's very pleasant."

"What are you doing sniffing at her?" Shawn demanded. Jack just blinked at him.

"What?"

"I'll be back in a minute." He shoved up the pass-through on the bar, let it fall with a bang that had Aidan cursing him, then rushed through the door after Brenna.

"Wait a minute. Mary Brenna? Just a damn minute."

She paused by the door of her truck, and for one of the first times in her life felt the warm glow of pure female satisfaction stream through her. A fine feeling, she decided. A fine feeling altogether.

Schooling her face to show mild interest, she turned. "Is there a problem, then?"

"Yes, there's a problem. What are you doing flirting with Jack Brennan that way?"

She let her eyebrows rise up under the bill of her cap. "And what business might that be of yours, I'd like to know?"

"A matter of days ago you're asking me to make love with you, and I turn around and you're cozying up to Jack and making plans to have dinner with some Dubliner."

She waited one beat, then two. "And?"

"And?" Flustered and furious, he glared at her. "And it's not right."

She only lifted a shoulder in dismissal, then turned to open the truck door.

"It's not right," he repeated, grabbing her again and turning her to face him. "I'm not having it."

"So you said, in clear terms."

"I don't mean that."

"Oh, well, if you've decided you'd like to have sex with me after all, I've changed my mind."

"I haven't decided —" He broke off, staggered. "Changed your mind?"

"I have. Kissing you wasn't altogether what I thought it would be. So you were right and I was wrong." She gave him a deliberately insulting pat on the cheek. "And that's the end of it."

"The hell it is." He trapped her against the truck, quickly and firmly enough to have both excitement and annoyance rising inside her. "If I want you, I'll have you, and *that's* the end of it. Meanwhile, I want you to behave yourself."

She couldn't speak. She was certain that if she tried she would strangle on the words. So she did the only thing she could think of. She plowed her bunched fist into his gut.

It cost him some breath, and the color that temper had brought to his face drained completely. But he held his ground. The fact that he did, that he could, when she knew she had a solid punch, sent another trickle of excitement sliding through her.

"We'll talk about this, Brenna, in private."

"That's fine. I've plenty to say."

Satisfied that he'd made his point, he stepped back. "You can come by the cottage in the morning."

Seething, she climbed into the truck, slammed the door. "I could," she told him as she started the engine, "but I won't. I came to you once, and you spurned me. I won't be back."

He stepped back again, to save his toes from being run over. If she wouldn't come to him, he thought as she drove away, he'd find another way to get her alone so they could . . . come to terms, he supposed it was.

In private.

Seven

A body would think the woman had never jumped into his arms and kissed him senseless. A man could start believing himself delusional and that she'd never sat across from him at his own kitchen table and suggested they have a romp in bed.

But she had done both of those things. He knew it because every time he came within a foot of her the muscles in his belly knotted.

Shawn didn't care for it, not a bit. No more than he cared for how easy and bloody *normal* she was acting as they fell into the Saturday night routine at the pub. Every time he came out of the kitchen for one reason or another, she'd shoot him that look of hers that was caught somewhere between a sneer and a smile.

It made him wonder why he'd ever enjoyed seeing that selfsame expression on her face in the past.

Brenna worked the set of taps at one end of the long chestnut bar while Aidan manned those at the other end. She talked with the customers, laughed with old Mr. Riley, who was in the habit of asking every pretty young thing to be his bride. If the musicians played a tune she was fond of, she joined in the chorus.

She did everything, Shawn noted, that she'd done on a hundred other Saturday nights when the pub was crowded and the music was fine.

It should have been a relief — he told himself it was — that the two of them appeared to be back on even and familiar ground again.

It irritated the living hell out of him.

She wore jeans and a baggy sweater. He'd probably seen that same sweater on her twenty times or more. So why was it that it had never made him think of the trim little body under it until now? The kind of body that was quick and agile and strong, with breasts small and firm as peaches just before they ripen.

Distracted, he burned his fingers on the hot oil as he scooped out chips, and cursed himself for thinking, even for a minute, of sliding his hands up and over that body, those breasts.

That had been her plan, he decided. The devious witch. She'd planted the seed in his brain, stirred up his loins, as he was only a man, after all, and now she could torment him just by being in the same vicinity.

Well, two could play this game.

Rather than waiting for Darcy to pick up the orders, he carried them out himself. Just to show Brenna O'Toole that she didn't trouble him in the least.

The perverse creature didn't even glance his way as he swung into the pub and wound his way through the crowd to the tables. No, just to annoy him, he was sure, she pulled taps and continued a conversation with a couple of tourists as if they were all the best of mates and this was their Saturday night reunion.

She wore her hair down, tied back with a bit of black ribbon. In the muted light it burned like fire.

He wished he could keep his mind off her hair. He wished he had his hands in it.

"Hello, Shawn." Mary Kate caught up with him just as he was serving the Clooney family their basket of chips. She angled as close as she dared, hoping he would like the new scent she was trying out. "Busy tonight."

"The music's lively. I think we've the whole of your tour group here."

"They're having a wonderful time of it." She pitched her voice over the music, struggling to keep it sexy as the band kicked into a rousing rendition of "Maloney Wants a Drink." "But I'd rather hear you play."

He flashed her a grin as he tucked the empty tray under his arm. "You can hear that for free anytime you like. These Galway lads have a spark to them." He glanced toward the front booth, admired the way the fiddler handled his bow. "Are you here with your family, then?"

Mary Kate's ego took a nosedive. Why did he always think of her as one of the O'Toole girls? She was a grown woman now. "No, I'm not with anyone." It wasn't a lie, she assured herself. She may have come in with her parents and Alice Mae, but she wasn't *with* them.

"That's fine playing," he murmured, forgetting her in his pleasure with the music. "Quick and clever and bright. It's no wonder they've made a name for themselves. The tenor's the strongest voice, but he knows how to blend in without over-powering his bandmates."

He wondered what they would do with one of his own ballads and was brought back to the moment only when Mary Kate touched his arm. "You could make a name for yourself, too." Her eyes were full of dreams when they met his. "A bigger one. A brighter one."

He avoided answering, or thinking too deeply on the possibilities by giving her a light kiss on the cheek. "You're a darling girl, Mary Kate. I'd best be back to the kitchen."

He'd no more than let the door swing shut behind him when it burst open again and Brenna charged through. "I told you to stay away from my sister."

"What?"

She planted herself in the stance he knew very well signaled a fight. "Didn't I stand here a week ago and tell you what the situation was as regards my Mary Kate?"

She had, of course. And, Shawn admitted as he shoved a hand through his hair, he hadn't given it another thought. "I just had a conversation with her, Brenna, nothing more than that. It was as harmless as tickling a baby."

129

"She's not a baby, and you kissed her."

"Oh, Jesus Christ on the Cross, I'd kiss my own mother in the same fashion."

"The Germans are hungry," Darcy said brightly as she carted in a tray loaded with empty plates and bowls. "They're after three servings of your stew and two of the fish. You'd think the lot of them hadn't eaten since they left their homeland."

Dumping the dishes, she measured the weight in the pocket of her apron with a drum of her fingers. "But, bless them, they tip often and they tip well, and only once did one of them give my bum a pat."

When she started to deal with the dishes, Brenna took a steadying breath. "Darcy, would you mind seeing to those later? I need a word with Shawn, in private."

Darcy glanced around, lifted an eyebrow. She could see it now, the tension running in waves from one to the other. As far as she was concerned, the two of them weren't happy unless they were spatting. But this seemed . . . different. "Is something the matter?"

"The O'Toole thinks I've designs on Mary Kate and is warning me off." He wrenched open the refrigerator to take out the fish he needed. But not before he saw Brenna flinch.

"I don't." Because she spoke without heat, without her usual bite, Shawn looked back at her. "But she's designs on you."

"Well, she's a crush on him, to be sure," Darcy

confirmed. "Not that he'd ever notice."

"All I did was talk to her." Uncomfortable with two pairs of female eyes staring at him with both pity and disgust, Shawn turned on the fire to heat the oil. "Next time I'll just give her a shove out of my way and keep going. Will that do for you?"

Darcy sighed. "You're such a knucklehead, aren't you, Shawn?" She gave Brenna's arm a quick, supportive squeeze, then left them alone.

"I'm sorry I came barreling in and snapped at you." Apologies came rarely off Brenna's tongue, and had that much more impact because of it. "Everything's so new for Mary Kate just now, with university behind her and her just getting her feet wet in her career. She looks at Maureen, all flushed with being newly married, and our Patty so excited about her own wedding coming this spring. And she . . ."

Helpless, she fluttered her hands. She was so bad at words when they mattered most. "She thinks she's all grown up, you see, and ready for everything in her life to begin. Inside, her heart's still a girl's and romantic with it. And it's tender, Shawn. You could bruise it."

"I won't."

"You'd never mean to." She smiled now, but it didn't reach up into her eyes as it usually did. "You don't have it in you."

"I'd rather you were mad at me than sad. I don't like seeing you unhappy. Brenna . . ." But when he reached out to touch her hair, she shook her head and backed away.

"No, now you'll say something kind and sweet, and I'm too much in the mood for it. We've both work to do."

"I think about you in a way I didn't," he said, his voice soft and quiet as she turned to go. "And I think about you often."

She felt her heart shiver, and took a breath to steady herself. "Well, it's a fine time you pick to bring up the subject. But then, you've never had the gift of timing except for your music."

"I think about you often," he repeated. He walked toward her, pleased when her eyes went wary.

"What are you about?" She was flustered, and she was *never* flustered by a man. Certainly not by Shawn. She could handle him, of course. She always had, always would. But she couldn't seem to make her legs move.

Now wasn't this interesting? he mused as he closed in. She looked nervous, and color was rising in her cheeks. "I never used to think about doing this." He slid a long-fingered hand around to cup the back of her neck, eased her a step closer, all the while watching her eyes. "Now I'm thinking about it all the time."

He played his mouth over hers. A teasing, whispering, devastating slide of lips.

She should have known he would kiss like this if he set his mind to it. Slow, soft, sexy, so a woman could barely keep a thought in her head. The hand at her neck squeezed and released, squeezed and released, and sent pulses dancing. Warmth washed into her, filling her throat, her breasts, her belly, loosening her knees until she felt herself begin to sway into him, into the seductive rhythm of her own pulse that he set with no more than his mouth.

She trembled. He absorbed the first glorious sensation of having Brenna O'Toole tremble against him. Then immediately wanted to feel it again.

But he gave way when she braced a hand on his shoulder to stop him.

"You took me by surprise when you kissed me last week," he told her while her eyes gradually cleared. "I seem to have done the same to you now."

Pull yourself together, girl, she ordered herself. This wasn't the way to handle the man. "Then we're in the way of being even."

His eyes narrowed in speculation. "So is it a contest then, Brenna?"

More at ease with the faint irritation in his voice than she'd been with the smooth, seductive tone, she nodded. "I've always thought of it so. But, in the fortunate way of sexual matters, we can both win. I've customers to serve."

Her lips still tingled from his as she walked out of the kitchen.

"Maybe we'll both win," he murmured, "but I don't think I'll be playing this your way, Brenna, my darling."

Pleased with himself, he went back to his stove to make the German tourists happy.

The sun decided to shine on Sunday, and the sky was clear and blue. The smudge of gray far away to the east told him the storm hovering over England would likely put in an appearance by nightfall. But for now it was a fine, fresh day for walking the hills.

He thought if he happened to wander over to the O'Tooles' he'd get himself invited in for some tea and biscuits. And he'd enjoy seeing how Brenna would react to having him sitting in her kitchen after what had passed between them the night before.

He thought he understood what was in her head. She was a woman who liked to get things done — her way. Step by step and at a smart pace. For some reason she'd set her sights on him, and he was starting to like the idea. Quite a little bit, if it came to that.

But he had his own way of getting things done. One step might not follow the other in such a straight line, and he preferred a meandering pace. After all, marching head-on you missed the little things that happened all around you.

He was one for treasuring the little things. Like the clear call of the magpie, or the shine of the sun on a particular blade of grass. And there, the way the cliffs stood strong against the incessant beat of the sea.

He could wander for hours, and did when he

forgot himself. He was well aware that most people thought he got nothing done during his dreaming time, and they smiled indulgently. But in truth he got everything done. The thinking, the restoring, the watching.

And because he was watching, he didn't see Mary Kate until she hailed him and ran in his direction.

"It's a fine day for walking." To be on the safe side, he tucked his hands into his pockets.

"Warmer than it's been in days." She smoothed her hair in case her little dash had mussed it. "I was just thinking I might walk down to your cottage, then here you are."

"My cottage?" She'd changed out of her Sunday dress, he noted, but she wore what looked to be a new sweater, and she had on earrings, scent, fresh lipstick. All the little lures women use.

He was suddenly sure that Brenna had been right about the situation. And it terrified him.

"I was hoping to take you up on what you said last night."

"Last night?"

"About how I could listen to your music anytime. I love hearing you play your tunes."

"Ah . . . I was just coming over to your own house, to speak with Brenna about a matter."

"She's not home." Deciding he needed a little encouragement, Mary Kate slid her arm through his. "Something needed to be fixed at Maureen's, so off she went, and Ma and Patty with her."

"A word with your father, then —"

"He's not at home either. He took Alice Mae down to the beach to look for shells. But you're welcome to come."

Knowing it was bold, she let her hand run up and down his arm as they walked. The feel of muscle — a man's arm, not a boy's — had her pulse dancing. "I'll be happy to fix you some tea, and a bite to eat."

"That's kind of you." He was a dead man. He caught sight of the O'Toole house as they topped the hill. Though thin smoke plumed from the chimney, it had the general air of being empty.

Brenna's lorry wasn't parked in the street. The dog was nowhere to be seen. Apparently even Betty had deserted him in his hour of need.

The only choice left was a quick and cowardly retreat.

"What was I thinking?" He stopped short and clapped a hand to his forehead. "I'm supposed to be helping Aidan . . . at the house. Slipped my mind." As quickly as he could manage, he untangled his arm, gently nudging her hand away, as he might a puppy who was inclined to nip. *Down, girl.* "Things are always slipping my mind, so I don't suppose he'll be surprised that I'm late."

"Well, but if you're already late . . ." She leaned toward him, nearly into him, in a gesture that even a distracted coward such as himself recognized as an invitation.

"He'll be looking for me." This time he patted her on the head, as he might a child, and saw from the pout beginning to form that she'd taken it as

136

he'd meant it. "I'll stop in for tea sometime soon. Give my best to your family, now, won't you?"

He was twenty strides away before he let out a relieved breath. And what, he wondered, was this with the O'Toole girls all of a sudden? Now instead of a quiet walk, perhaps a cup of tea in a friendly kitchen, and a little time alone in the cottage working on his music, he was honor-bound to go into the village and find something to do at Aidan's.

"What are you doing here?" Aidan asked him.

"It's a long and complicated story." Shawn glanced around cautiously as he stepped inside. "Is Jude at home?"

"She's upstairs with Darcy. Our sister's having some trouble deciding what to wear to drive this Dubliner she's seeing crazy."

"That should be keeping them busy for a while. Good. I've had enough of women lately," he explained when Aidan looked at him questioningly. "Now there's the handsome dog." He bent down to give Finn's head a scratch. "Growing into his feet, this one is, and fast."

"He is that, and good-natured with it, aren't you, lad?"

Finn turned adoring eyes on Aidan, and his tail swished with such enthusiasm that it drummed from Shawn's knees to the table by the door. "He grows much more, he'll be knocking lamps off the table with that whip of his. Can you spare a beer?"

"I can spare two, one for each of us. Women,"

Aidan continued as they made their way into the kitchen, "as we were on the subject, are always going to be giving you grief of one sort or another. It's that pretty face of yours."

Amused, Shawn sat at the table while Aidan got two bottles of Harp and opened them. He laid a hand absentmindedly on Finn's head when the dog bumped under it. "You did fair in the lady department yourself, as I recall. And you're not nearly so pretty as I am."

"But I'm smarter." With a grin, Aidan passed his brother the bottle. "I held out for the best of them."

"I can't argue with that." After tapping his bottle to Aidan's, Shawn took a long, appreciative swallow. "Well, then, it wasn't to talk about women that I came by, but to get away from them for a time."

"If you've a mind to discuss business, I've some of that." He got down a tin of crisps, set it between them before he sat. "I had a call from Dad this morning. He and Ma send their love. He was going to ring you as well."

"I was out walking. I suppose I missed them."

"Well, the immediate news is he's off to New York next week to meet with the Magee." Since his dog was looking at him hopefully, and Jude wasn't around to disapprove, he tossed Finn a crisp. "He wants a feel for the man before we go any further on this deal."

"No one sizes a man up quicker and more true than Dad."

"Aye. And in the meantime, Magee is sending his man here, to do some sizing up of his own. His name is Finkle, and he'll be staying at the cliff hotel. Dad and I agree we won't discuss hard monetary terms with Finkle until we've got a better handle on this Magee."

"You and Dad would know best about such matters. But . . ."

"But?"

"It seems to me that one of the handles we're looking to grip would be what we'll make out of the deal. In pounds, yes, but also in how this project of Magee's will enhance the pub."

"That's a fact."

"So the trick would be," Shawn said after a contemplative sip of beer, "how to gain information without giving so much of it in return."

"Dad'll be working on that in New York."

"Which doesn't stop us from working on it here." As easy a mark as Aidan, Shawn fed Finn another crisp. "What we have in our happy little family, Aidan, is the businessman" — Shawn tipped his beer toward his brother —" that would be you."

"So it would."

"And," Shawn aimed a finger at the ceiling, "upstairs we have two lovely women. One, gracious and charming, has a shyness of manner that masks, to those who don't look close enough, a clever brain. The other, flirtatious and beautiful, has a habit of wrapping men around her finger before they realize she has a steel spine."

Aidan nodded slowly. "Go on."

"Then there's me, the brother who doesn't have a brain cell working in his head for business. The affable one, who pays no attention to money matters."

"Well, you're an affable enough sort, Shawn, but you've as good a head for business as I do."

"No, that I don't, but I've enough of one to get by. Enough of one to know it'll be you Finkle concentrates on." He gestured absently toward Aidan with his beer as he thought it through. "And while he's doing that, the rest of us can surround him and poke in, so to speak, in our own fashions. I think by the time the deed is done, we'll know what we need to know. Then you make your deal, Aidan. And Gallagher's will be the finest public house in the country, the place they speak of when they speak of Irish hospitality and music."

Aidan sat back, his eyes dark and sober. "Is that what you want, Shawn?"

"It's what you want."

"That's not what I'm asking you." Before Shawn could lift the bottle again, Aidan gripped his wrist, held it firm enough that Shawn cocked his head in question. "Is it what you want?"

"Gallagher's is ours," Shawn said simply. "It should be the best."

After a moment, Aidan released him, then restless, rose. "I never figured you for staying."

"Where would I go? Why would I?"

"I always thought there'd come a day when you'd figure out what you wanted from your music, then you'd go to get it."

"I have what I want from my music." As the crisps were no longer coming his way, Finn settled under the table at Shawn's feet. "It pleasures me."

"Why have you never tried to sell it? Why have you never taken yourself off to Dublin or London or New York to play in the pubs there so it can be heard?"

"It's not ready to sell." It was an excuse, but all he had. The rest, at least, could be plain truth. "And I've no yearning to go to Dublin or London or New York, Aidan, or anywhere to sing for supper. This is my place. It's where my heart is."

He settled back, absently rubbing Finn's side with his foot. "I've no wanderer's thirst inside me like you had, or like Darcy and Ma and Dad. I want to see what I know when I wake in the morning, and hear sounds I'm familiar with. It centers me, you see," he went on while Aidan studied him, "to know the names of the faces around me, and to be home no matter where I look."

"You're the best of us," Aidan said quietly and made Shawn laugh with both surprise and embarrassment.

"Well, now, there's a statement for the ages."

"You are. You've the heart that draws in the land here, and the sea and the air and holds it with respect and with love. I couldn't do that until I'd gone off to see all I could see. And when I left, Shawn, I'm telling you I didn't think I'd be back. Not to stay."

141

"But that's what you did, what you've done."

"Because I came to realize what you've always known. This is our place in the world. By rights, if we went by heart instead of birth order, you'd head the pub."

"And run it into the ground within a year. Thanks, but no."

"You wouldn't, though. I haven't always given you the credit you deserve."

Shawn turned the Harp over in his hand, eyed it thoughtfully, and sent the dog at his feet a wink. "Just how many of these bottles did the man drink down before I got here, Finn, my lad?"

"I haven't been drinking. I want you to understand my feelings and thoughts before things change on us again. And they will change if we make this deal."

"They'll change, but we'll be the ones guiding the direction of it."

"It'll take more of your time."

He'd thought of that, and what use he would make of the time it took. "I've time to spare."

"And Darcy's — she won't be pleased with that."

"No." Shawn let out a breath. "But she'll be pleased enough with the baubles and trinkets she can buy with the profits. And she'll stand for Gallagher's, Aidan." Shawn met his brother's eyes. "You can give her credit for that."

"At least till she bags that rich husband."

"After she does, and she deigns to visit with those of us who remain peasants, you could still ask her to put on an apron and pick up a tray."

"And have her bash me head in with it." But Aidan nodded, understanding. "Aye, she'd lend her hand if the need was there, I know it."

"Don't take this weight all on yourself — the deal and the worry and the work of it," Shawn told him. "There's three of us — well, four now that we've our Jude Frances. Gallagher's is family. We'll do well with this business, Aidan. I've a good feeling about it."

"It's good you came by. I'm clearer in my head than I was."

"Well, then, that should be worth one more beer before I —" Shawn broke off as he heard voices, light and female. "Oh, blessed Mary, there's the women. I'm off. I'll use the back door."

"Next time, I'll get you drunk and pry out what's got you so spooked over women."

"If I don't figure out what to do about it in the next little while, I'll tell you." With this, Shawn escaped out the back door.

Eight

The tune waltzing its way through Shawn's head put him in the best of moods. While the smoke from his pots and pans drifted up, and the oil he was heating began to sizzle, he let it play through, bar to bar, then a key change for a bit of drama. The words weren't clear to him yet, but they would come. It seemed to him a summer song, full of light. And the thinking of it, the listening to it inside his head, chased the winter gloom away.

The shared beer and conversation in Aidan's kitchen the day before had settled him down. Which was just where Shawn preferred to be.

At the moment he couldn't understand why he'd gotten so nervy about matters. Little Mary Kate was just going through one of those phases girls went through, and it would pass as quickly as it had reared up. He'd gone through phases himself, hadn't he? He could remember clearly mooning and sighing over pretty Colleen Brennan when he'd been about eighteen. Fortunately, he'd never worked up the courage to do anything but moon and sigh, as pretty Colleen Brennan had been two and twenty at the time and engaged to marry Tim Riley.

He'd gotten over it in a matter of weeks, then had sighed over another pretty face. That was the way of things, after all. Eventually, of course, he'd done more than sigh and had discovered the rare wonder of having a woman naked under him. And that was a fine thing.

Still, he took care whom he touched and how he touched, so that when the time was over each could walk away happy with the experience. He wasn't a man to take the act of love as a casual matter. Which he supposed, was why he hadn't participated in that rare wonder for some months now.

And that, he imagined, was most likely why the O'Toole had set his glands to stirring.

Not that he was at all certain, as yet, if he intended to do anything about it. No, Brenna was a puzzle, and one he thought it might be best to leave unsolved. A little time, he decided, a little care, and the two of them would be back on their old familiar ground, if they could just let things be.

His mind would be quiet again, and life would slide along the way it was meant to.

All he had to do was forget how stimulating it was to have his mouth on hers.

He checked on the crubeens he was boiling with cabbage and jacketed potatoes. He added a bit more marjoram to the broth to flavor it up, a trick he'd learned by experimentation.

He particularly liked to present the dish when there were Yanks in the pub. Their varying reactions to being served pigs' trotters was always an amusement to him. Jude was doing the waitressing tonight, and he didn't think she'd disappoint him.

Meanwhile, he had fish to fry for the two hikers from Wexford. He slid the haddock into the oil, then glanced up as the back door opened.

Instantly his spine stiffened, his eyes narrowed, and a prickly ball bounced around in his gut.

"Smells good," Brenna said easily and sniffed the air. "Would that be crubeens you're doing there? I doubt we'll have such fare in Waterford City."

She was wearing paint, and sparkly things at her ears. And for God's sake a dress — one that didn't leave the matter of curves to a man's imagination and showed a great deal of slim, well muscled leg.

"What are you doing, done up like that?"

"Having dinner with Darcy and her Dubliners." She'd rather, much rather pull up a chair at the table, snag a portion and tuck into the crubeens, but she'd given her word. And that was that.

"You're going out with a man you've never laid eyes on."

"Darcy has, and I'd best go up and drag her away from her mirror or she'll primp another hour and I'll never get my dinner."

"Just a damn minute."

His tone alone would have stopped her, it was very sharp and un-Shawnlike. But even before she could turn back, he had her arm. "Well, what's lit into you, then?"

"Perfume, too," he said in disgust, as he got a good, heady whiff of her scent. "I should've known it. Well, you can just turn straight around and go back home. I'm not having you go off dressed like this."

Temper would have snapped out, would have bitten him on the neck, but it couldn't get through the thick wall of shock. "You're not having it? Dressed like what?"

"I'm not, no. And you know very well dressed like what. It's surprised I am that your mother let you out of the house this way."

"I'm twenty-four, if you've forgotten. My mother stopped approving my choice of attire some years ago. And it's surely no business of yours what I'm wearing."

"I'm making it my business. Now go home and wash that stuff off your face."

"I'll do nothing of the sort." The fact was, she'd used the lipstick and so forth only because she knew Darcy would have slathered twice as much on her if she'd shown up without it. But there was no reason to mention that, especially since that temper was busily gnawing through the shock.

"Fine, then, I'll do for you here and now." He hauled her up under one arm, ignoring her shrieked curse and the fist that swiped at his temple, and carted her toward the sink. He had a vision through the black haze of his fury of dumping her in headfirst and turning the water on full and ice cold.

He had his hand on the tap when Jude rushed in. "Shawn!"

The stunned and somehow maternal tone stopped him, but barely.

"What in the world are you doing? Put Brenna down this minute!"

"I'm doing what needs to be done. Look how she's flaunted herself up, Jude, and all to go out with some strange man. 'Tisn't right."

Between curses, Brenna managed to turn her head and try for a good chomp out of his torso, but she only got a mouthful of flannel. She threatened to do something so particularly vile and vicious to his manhood that Shawn cautiously tightened his grip.

Well, well, Jude thought and struggled not to be amused. "Put her down," she said quietly. "You should be ashamed of yourself."

"*I* should? She might as well be naked as wearing this dress, and I should be ashamed?"

"Brenna looks lovely." Seeing no other choice, Jude walked up to him, carefully avoiding Brenna's kicking feet and snagged him by the ear. "Put her down."

"Ouch! Bloody hell." The last woman to pinch his ear in such a manner had been his own mother — and he'd been every bit as unable to defend himself. "I'm only looking out for her. All right, leave off," he said when Jude ruthlessly twisted.

He dumped Brenna back on her feet, then took the deep breath of the aggrieved. "You don't understand the situation," he began, then staggered when Brenna snatched up a pan and rapped it smartly over his head.

"Bastard. I'm not your dog in the manger, and don't you forget it."

He gripped the edge of the sink and watched triple Brennas march to the back stairs. "She coshed me."

"You deserved it." But Jude took him gently by the hand. "You should sit down. It's lucky for you she didn't grab the cast iron, or you'd be flat on your back."

"I don't want her going out with some Dubliner." Dizzy, he let Jude nudge him into a chair. "I don't want her going 'round looking that way."

"Why?"

"Because I don't."

Patient, and more sympathetic than she let him know, Jude ran her fingers delicately through his hair. "You don't always get what you want. It didn't break the skin, but you're going to have a bump, a good one." Jude tipped his face up to hers, and touched by the stubborn and miserable look in his eyes, kissed him lightly. "I never realized you had such a hard head. If you don't want Brenna going out with someone else, why haven't you asked her to go out with you?"

He shifted in his chair. "It's not that way."

This time she cupped his cheek. "Isn't it?" Leaving him stewing over that, she walked over to turn off the fish that was already burned beyond redemption.

"I don't want it to be that way."

Her mouth tipped up at the corners. Keeping her back to him for now, Jude got out fresh por-

149

tions of fish. "I'll have to repeat, you don't always get what you want."

"I do." He got to his feet, gave himself a moment for the room to settle. "I'm careful about what I want."

"So was I once. Wanting more's what got me here."

"Well, I'm already where I want to be, so I can afford to be careful."

Still holding the fish, she gave him a bland stare. "Hard head, indeed."

"And that's the way I like it as well. No, don't trouble yourself there, I'll do it." He shoved the entire pan aside, and got out another to heat fresh oil. "Ask Aidan to serve the hikers another pint on me, with apologies for the delay in the meal, would you, darling?"

"All right." She started out, then turned back. This family business was still so new. "Shawn, maybe you do like where you are, maybe it's the right spot for you. But there are times when you have to make certain. Take a step forward or take one back. You're not being fair to Brenna or to yourself by running in place."

"Is that the psychologist talking?" He glanced back in time to see her wince, then lower her eyes. "I didn't mean that in a hard way, Jude. And you're right. I just haven't figured which direction to take." Brooding over it, he coated the fish. "The fact is, she gave me a push. I don't care to be pushed. It makes me want to dig in my heels."

"I can understand that, just as I can understand

150

Brenna's the type who needs to move things along. One way or the other."

"Aye." Scowling, he touched fingers cautiously to the bump on his head. "One way or the other."

"If you can stand one more piece of advice, make yourself busy in the storeroom when you hear Brenna coming back down the steps."

"You're a wise woman."

"It's going well, isn't it?" Darcy powdered her nose in the ladies' room of the restaurant and slid her gaze to Brenna's in the mirror.

"The food's very good."

"Well, that, yes, but I mean the whole of it. It's so nice to be out with a man of some sophistication for a change. Matthew lived in Paris for an entire year," Darcy went on, speaking of her date. "He speaks the language like a native. I think I'll have him come up with the idea of taking me there for a weekend before much longer."

Despite herself, Brenna had to laugh. "Oh, you'll let him think he thought of it."

"Naturally. Men prefer it that way. And Daniel's very taken with you."

"He's pleasant enough." Knowing Darcy would be ages yet before she deemed herself freshened up enough to go back to the table, Brenna took out her lipstick. Well, Mary Kate's lipstick, copped from the bathroom, if the truth be known.

"He's marvelous-looking and wealthy as sin. Why don't we let them take us both to Paris?"

"I don't have the time to go off to France, nor

the inclination to pay for the journey in the way a man would expect."

"We've nothing but time." Darcy fluffed at her hair. "And a clever woman doesn't pay, in any form, unless she wants to. I'm not after sleeping with Matthew."

"I thought you liked him."

"I do, yes. He just doesn't give me a tug that way. But that could change," she added cheerfully.

Lips pursed, Brenna studied the lipstick as she wound the tube up and down. "Have you ever wanted to sleep with a man who didn't want to sleep with you?"

"I've never known a man who wouldn't pull down his zipper at the least provocation. It's the way they're made, so you can't blame them."

"But there would be some, under certain circumstances, who just wouldn't find a particular woman attractive in that way."

"I suppose there are exceptions to every rule. But you've not to worry." She gave Brenna a supportive pat on the shoulder. "Daniel finds you very attractive. I'm sure he'd be glad to sleep with you if you wanted."

Heaving a breath, Brenna dropped the lipstick back in her bag. "Well, then, what a relief."

She had a wonderful time. The best time she'd ever had in her life. A civilized meal in a civilized place with civilized people.

She'd been bored half to death but wasn't ready to admit it.

With that block in place, she'd given Daniel her number and promised herself she'd go out with him again should he ring her to ask. He'd been polite and amusing, she reminded herself as she drove home from the pub, where she'd been let off after the date. He'd pretended to be interested in her work and had actually made the effort to find something they had in common. Which had turned out to be old American films, the *noir* type.

He had an extensive collection of them on video and had made casual mention of her coming up to Dublin, where they could have their own little film festival.

It might be something she'd enjoy. Just as she'd enjoyed the good-night kiss. He hadn't been overly familiar with it, he hadn't let his hands roam where they shouldn't so early in an acquaintance.

A perfectly nice individual.

And damn Shawn Gallagher for ruining her palate for the taste of another man.

She slowed, then stopped as she came to his cottage, letting her lorry idle on the road while the fragile fog swam around it.

Oh, he was in there, all right, the snake in the grass. See there, the parlor light was on. He was likely playing at his music. If he'd had a window open, it would have drifted out into the night so she could hear it.

She wished she could.

Because knowing that made her feel soft, she deepened her scowl. She was tempted, sorely, to whip the truck into his street, march right in the door to give him a piece of her mind and the back of her hand.

But that would put too much importance on his earlier behavior. She'd rather shun him. The bastard.

What kind of man was it who could kiss you one night as if he'd happily spend eternity with his lips on yours, then behave like a furious father the next?

Wash her face indeed.

She sniffed, started to turn back in the seat to take the wheel when the movement in the upper window stopped her. For a moment she was terrified, mortified, that Shawn was there, looking out while she stared at his cottage.

But the embarrassed flush never had the chance to heat her cheeks as she saw the figure of a woman and the shine of pale hair in the delicate moonlight.

So now Brenna sighed, and rolling down her window, crossed her arms there and rested her chin on them.

How many nights, she wondered, had poor Lady Gwen stood there in that window, alone and lonely and heartbroken? All because of a man.

"Why do we bother with them, Gwen? Why do we let them get into our heads this way? When you push all the rest aside, they're so bloody irritating."

His heart's in his song. Brenna heard the words as if they were whispered directly into her ear. *And so are you. Listen.*

She squeezed her eyes tight, as something frightening was trying to swell and shift in her head. "No, no, I'm done with that, and with him. I'm not giving more of my thoughts and more of my time to Shawn. He's had enough of them, and for too long already."

Almost violently, she shoved the truck back into gear and drove home.

He knew she was working alone because he'd checked. Mick O'Toole was seeing to some business up at the cliff hotel, and Jude was running some errands.

He could hear her banging away at something as he climbed the steps. Which meant, he realized, the woman was armed. It was a risk he'd have to take.

He'd spent most of the night thinking the situation over — which was becoming too much of a habit and costing him a great deal of sleep. He'd come to the conclusion that Jude was right. It was time to move one way or the other. He imagined the conversation to come would determine which direction he headed.

The banging, he noted, was from inside the baby's closet. Following impulse, a rare thing for him, he closed the door, locked it, and pocketed the key. That, at least, would keep her from walking out on him until he'd finished.

Braced for the explosion he was sure he was inviting, he walked toward the closet.

"Jude? Back so soon? Well, have a look at these shelves here and see if they're to your liking." From the third step on her ladder, she looked over her shoulder and saw Shawn in the doorway.

He waited, but rather than blistering him with her tongue, she just looked through him, then turned back to work.

That, he thought, was a very dire sign indeed.

"I want to talk to you," he began.

"I'm working. I've no time for chatting."

"I need to talk to you." He stepped in, laid a hand on her hip. It took a great deal of courage not to spring back when she stared down on him and took a fresh grip on her hammer. "Would you put that down?"

"No."

He might have had courage, but he also had brains. In a quick move, he yanked the hammer out of her hand. "I've a knot the size of a fucking golf ball on my head. I'm not after a second one. I just want a few words with you, Brenna."

"I've nothing to say to you, Shawn, and as I value the friendship we've had all our lives, I'll ask you to leave me be for now."

Dire indeed, he thought as a tongue of panic licked the inside of his throat. "I want to apologize to you." She shifted on the ladder again, gave him her back and pulled out her measuring tape.

The woman brought out the worst in him, was all Shawn could think as he gripped her by the hips and lifted her down from the ladder. She came around swinging, and though he'd expected no less, he didn't dodge the blow. Not after he'd caught the sheen of tears in her eyes.

"I'm sorry." Panic was more than a sly lick now. It simply coated his throat. "Don't cry. I can't stand it."

"I'm not crying." She'd let the tears burn her eyes out of her head before she let a single one fall in his presence. "I asked you to leave me be. Since you won't, I'll leave you."

She strode to the door, wrenched at the knob, then simply gaped in shock. "You locked the door!" She whirled back. "Have you lost your mind?"

"I know you — so I knew you wouldn't listen. Now you have to."

He saw her slide a look toward her toolbox, imagined she was thinking of the nice weapon supply inside. However sincere his apology, he wasn't prepared to have holes hacked out of him, so he stepped over to put himself between Brenna and temptation.

"You say our friendship matters to you. It matters to me as well. It matters a great deal to me. You matter to me, Brenna."

"Is that why you treated me like some tramp last night?"

Her voice broke, alarming him, so he bore down. "I suppose it was, yes. It's not a regular thing, after all, for me to see you looking that way."

Frustration had her throwing up her hands. "*What* way?"

"Lovely." He saw her eyes go round in shock, and took advantage of the moment to step a little closer. "You looked so polished up and female."

"I am female, for God's sake."

"I know it, but you don't usually trouble to make it an issue."

"Why should it be?" she demanded. It was a sore point, and one she hated probing. "Just because I know how to hammer a nail or fix a pipe, I'm not allowed to be a woman as well? Wearing a dress and some lipstick makes me a tramp?"

"No, it makes me a fool for letting you think I meant that. Clumsy, foolish, and spiteful. And I'm sorry for it."

When she said nothing, he stuck his hands in his pockets, pulled them out again. Best, he told himself, to get it all out and over. "The truth of it is, I was thinking of you, thinking about things when you walked in, looking the way you did and about to go off with another man. I was jealous. I didn't realize it at the time, didn't want to admit it later after my mind had cleared a bit. I've never been jealous before. I can't say I cared for it."

She'd calmed down enough to begin to speculate. And consider. "I didn't like it much myself."

"I told myself you'd done it — put on that dress and left your hair all falling down and made your mouth slick and wet to stir me up."

Yes, she considered. And she nodded. "Sure I might've, if I'd thought of it. My mind just doesn't work in those clever ways."

"No, you're a straightforward woman. I know it." He stopped, angled his head. For every step he took she took one in evasion. "Why is it, Brenna, that when I come toward you now, you back away?

Aren't you the one who started it all?"

"Aye, I did, but I've had time to reconsider. Just keep your distance, will you, while I'm mulling it over," she demanded when she caught the dark male amusement in his eyes. Not an expression to settle a woman's nerves. "We've been friends a long time, and I don't want to lose that part of my life. If we'd acted when I first mentioned sex, if you'd just grinned and said, 'Well, Brenna, what a fine idea, let's go up to bed,' it would've been fine all around. We'd have enjoyed ourselves, kept it simple, and parted friends as always. But now it's stopped being an impulsive sort of thing and it's complicated."

He solved the problem of keeping her still by reaching out, planting his palm on the wall just above her head. Before she could shift, he planted the other and caged her in. "You've a habit of acting on impulse, and I'm one for pondering over things. You move fast and I move slow."

Her blood was beginning to hum. But pride kept her in place now, as sure as his arms. "Jesus, Shawn, a glacier moves with more speed than you."

"But I get where I'm going just the same, don't I? I'm thinking, Brenna, that weighing impulse and consideration, speed and caution, we can still meet somewhere in the middle of things."

"It's too . . . sticky now."

"Your heart's pounding," he murmured as he eased closer. "I can almost hear it." Watching her, he laid his hand between her breasts. Awareness snapped into her eyes, breath trembled between her lips, then drew in, soft and sharp when he let his fingers spread. "Now I can feel it. I've wanted to touch you."

Her knees wanted to buckle. "You'd never have thought of it if I hadn't mentioned it."

"Sure and I can't say I mind it being your idea, as I'm thinking of it now." He lowered his head to nip lightly at her bottom lip. "And I'm finding it hard to think of much else. When I came up here today . . ." He shifted his head so his lips skimmed up along her jaw. "I thought I'd apologize, make things as right as I could between us. Then I was nearly sure, very nearly sure that I'd take a step back and leave it that way. But now I want to touch you." He toyed delicately with the nipple that strained against her shirt. "I want to taste you."

And finally, finally covered her mouth with his.

She gripped his hips, fingers digging in as she let her tongue dance with his, let her lips heat with his. She wanted faster, hotter, harder. She thought she might die from the gentle and glorious warmth.

"Wait." Something was breaking loose inside her. A vital something that needed to stay firmly in place. "Wait. You think I need all the fancy work." She turned her head, but that only meant his teeth found her ear.

Oh, Jesus, the man had the most magical of mouths.

"I don't need it." Her breath was coming hard

and fast and making her dizzy. "Or seductions."

"I do." He tilted his head so he could nibble down her throat.

"If you've decided — and it appears to me you have — that we should have sex after all, we'll take an hour now and go to your cottage."

His chuckle was muffled against her skin, skin that was soft as sun-warmed silk. "Somewhere in the middle, Brenna. I want you." He felt her shiver as his mouth found hers again. "But I've a mind to drive us both a bit crazy before I have you naked and under me."

"Why?"

"Because it's more enjoyable that way. Do you like it when I do this?" She drew in her breath in three short gasps when he feathered his fingers just under her shirt so the backs of them rubbed the curve of her breast. "I see you do. Your eyes are blurry."

"I'm half blind. The hell with the cottage, we'll just finish this right here."

But when she locked her arms around his neck, he laughed and swung her in a circle. "Oh, no, we won't. I won't short myself or you of the pleasure."

"It doesn't seem like middle ground from where I'm standing. It's leaning heavily toward your way of things."

"Maybe, but you'll thank me for it when we're done."

"So like a man," she said when he set her on her feet. "Always thinking you know what's best and how it all should be done."

His teeth flashed. "Brenna, darling, if I wasn't a man we wouldn't be having this conversation."

She blew out a breath, settled her cap more firmly on her head. "Well, you're right about that, aren't you?"

"You told me you had an itch, well, I'll scratch it for you, in my own time and my own way. That's fair."

She looked at him, nodded. "Frustrating, but fair."

"And wherever we stand now or after, we walk away friends at the end of it. As much as I want you, I won't touch you if we don't take a vow here to walk away friends."

How could she help but care for him, Brenna wondered, when he was the kind of man who would think of that? And would mean it. "Friends now, during, and after." She offered her hand on it. "I'll promise that to you."

"And I to you." He took her hand, held it. Then, just to see her reaction, brought it to his lips to nuzzle.

Her mouth fell open, delighting him into a rolling laugh.

"Mary Brenna, I believe you're in for a few surprises along the way."

"Maybe." She tugged her hand free, put it behind her back, where it continued to tingle. "But I'm not without a few tricks of my own."

"I'll count on that." Plucking the key from his pocket, he turned toward the door. "Why don't you come down tonight and I'll fix you supper, and

I can show you some . . . surprises in the store-room."

"In the storeroom?" Before she could laugh, a thought took root. "Just how many women, might I ask, have you surprised in the storeroom?"

"Mauverneen." He winked at her before he strolled out. "I'm not a man who counts."

Nine

"Magee's man Finkle's here." Darcy hissed it as she scurried into the kitchen.

Shawn glanced up from the trio of bookmaker's sandwiches he was making. "Is he now?"

"Big as life." Out of habit, she checked her face and hair in the little mirror she'd hung beside the door. "Aidan's pulling him a pint of lager and chatting him up at the bar, though the Finkle looks to be all business."

Knowing his sister's skills, Shawn gestured with his knife. "Give me him in a hundred words or less."

Darcy narrowed her eyes, tapped a finger to her lips. "Middle fifties and balding. Sensitive about it, as he does a comb-over. A prosperous belly that tells me he likes his food. Married, but not above casting an eye. An indoor man. A company man used to taking orders and giving them on down the line. Frugal, as Mary Kate tells me he bargained fierce on the room rate even though it's on his expense account. Urban through and through and a bit of a dandy. I could pluck my eyebrows in the shine off his shoes."

"Well done." Shawn's eyes glittered with anticipation. "You won't have any trouble charming him, will you?"

With the smuggest of smiles, Darcy examined her nails. "Shooting fish in a barrel."

"I'm not talking about leading him into temptation, Darcy, just making him stumble around the far edges of it."

"Give me some credit. I said he was married. I'm not a homewrecker."

"Sorry. It was the look in your eye. It's a terror you are to mankind."

She took a tube out of her tip pocket and freshened her lipstick, with her eye on Shawn's in the mirror. "Mankind loves terrors like me."

"I can't argue with you there, as I've seen too many of the fallen. I'll help you serve the sandwiches here, so the Finkle can get a look at the harmless brother."

In harmony with him, Darcy helped Shawn load the tray. "He's impatient, I'd say, to get a look at things, eye the land, talk his deal."

"He's in Ireland now," Shawn said easily. "Rushing isn't the Gallagher way."

He put the orders together and got some bowls of crisps for the bar. "I wasn't daydreaming," he said to Darcy's back, lifting his voice slightly as they passed through the kitchen door into the pub. "I was thinking."

Following his lead, Darcy sighed. "You can't put orders together in good time if your head's in the clouds. Try staying on the ground with the rest of us now and again."

Adopting a sulky expression, Shawn began to set bowls out on the bar.

"Shawn, come meet Mr. Finkle from New York City." Shawn let his face clear and moved down the bar in Aidan's direction, leaned on it to offer a friendly smile at the man with thinning hair and vaguely irritated black eyes.

"It's nice to meet you, Mr. Finkle. We've cousins in New York City, and friends as well. They say it's a fast and busy place, with something doing every minute of every day. Aidan, you've been to New York City. Is that how you remember it as well?"

Because he had to swallow a chuckle, Aidan merely nodded. Shawn had thickened his accent, just enough to add atmosphere and a touch of country bumpkin.

"Aidan's one for traveling. Sure, and it runs in the family, it does. But as for me, I'm one for staying where he's planted."

"Yes, well," Finkle began, obviously prepared to dismiss Shawn and get back to important matters.

"So, have you come on holiday to Ardmore, Mr. Finkle? Sure, and it's a fine spot for it. Quiet now, so you're lucky," Shawn went on. "By end of May, they'll come swarming to the beaches since we've such fine ones, and then they pack into the pub so I can barely keep up with the orders. A body can get a bit of a rest in the winter at least."

"I'm here on business." Finkle spoke precisely, and the hard edge to his consonants Shawn recognized as native New Yorker. "For Magee Enterprise."

166

At Shawn's convincingly blank look, Aidan shook his head. "Shawn, I told you about the possibility of doing a deal with Mr. Magee. His theater?"

"Well, now, I never thought you were serious." Shawn scratched his head. "A cinema in Ardmore?"

"Not a movie theater," Finkle said with obvious impatience. "One for live entertainment."

"I think it's a wonderful idea." Darcy sidled up to the bar, beamed approval at Finkle. "Just brilliant. You must come to the pub tonight, Mr. Finkle, so you can have a sample of the kind of local talent we could offer your theater."

"What about the man from London?" Shawn sent baffled looks to Darcy, then Aidan. "The restaurant man?"

"We'll talk about that later." Aidan gave Shawn a small and very obvious nudge. "That's not important."

Finkle's shoulders straightened, his eyebrows lowered. "Are you speaking with another investor, Mr. Gallagher?"

"It's not a serious matter. Not at all. Why don't I show you the land we'll be discussing? Sure, you'll want a look at it, won't you? You're not after buying a pig in a poke. Shawn, you man the bar here, there's a lad." Hastily, Aidan flipped up the pass-through. "We'll have a walk about the place, Mr. Finkle, and see what's what."

"Please do come back, won't you?" Darcy called out and had the satisfaction of seeing Finkle flush a little as he glanced back her way. "I'd love to sing for you."

She waited until they were safely out and away. "The man from London," she said, snickering. "That was inspired."

"Just came to me. And I'll wager a pound to a pence that the minute he gets back to a phone he's ringing Magee in New York to tell him we're playing two lines."

"It could backfire, you know, Shawn, and have this Magee looking elsewhere."

"Or it could pay off." He reached over to tug her hair, surprised at how much fun he'd had playing the game. "Life's a gamble, isn't it?"

He looked up as Brenna and her father came in for their lunch hour. "And that's half the fun of living. A good day to you, Mr. O'Toole," he said when Mick strolled to the bar. "Mary Brenna. And what can we do for you?"

"I've a thirst, Shawn." Mick sent Darcy a wink.

"We can help you there." Knowing his man's preferences, Shawn slid a pint glass under the tap and began the process of building a Guinness. "And for you, Brenna?"

"I'm more interested in that soup I see on your menu." She nodded toward the daily board. "But there's no hurry."

"None at all," Mick confirmed as he slid onto a stool. "We're all but finished at your brother's house this morning. My Brenna here will tidy it up by day's end, then we'll be back to renovating rooms at the hotel. Sure, and I'll miss coming in here for your cooking, Shawn. Not that the hotel doesn't serve a good meal, but no one has your touch."

"Will you have some soup today, and a sandwich as well, Mr. O'Toole?" Darcy slipped behind the bar to pour the tea she assumed Brenna wanted. "A man works as hard as you, he needs his fuel."

"Well, I will at that, Darcy darling. You'll make some fortunate man the best of wives one day, as you'll know how to tend to him."

With a quick and wicked laugh, Darcy slid the tea across to Brenna. "I'm looking for one who'll tend to me — and lavishly. Speaking of it, has Daniel rung you up, Brenna?"

"Daniel?" She caught Shawn's raised brow and fought not to squirm. "He did, yes."

"That's fine, that. Matthew said he would. That's a fine-looking and well-set-up young man has his eye on your daughter, Mr. O'Toole."

"And why shouldn't he? She's a pretty thing."

"All right, Dad."

"Well, you are, and what's wrong with saying so?" The slap on the shoulder he gave her was one most men would have given a son. "A man'd be fortunate indeed to snap up a lass like my Brenna, as she's fair of face and a good worker too. A bit of a temper, maybe, but that only adds the spice. A man doesn't go looking for a bland sort of woman, does he, Shawn?"

Shawn laid the next level of Guinness in the glass. "That would depend on the man."

"Well, a smart one doesn't, for he'd be bored

brainless within a year. Not that I'm in a rush to see my Brenna here off and married. My chicks are leaving the nest quick enough now, with Maureen already wed and Patty looking to be a bride in a few months." He sighed. "I don't know what I'll do without my Brenna when the time comes."

"You won't have to do without me, time or not. We're partners. I'll just go back and get the soup, since you're shorthanded here."

It was as good an excuse as any to get out of the spotlight and away from uncomfortable topics. She was behind the bar and through the kitchen door as quickly as she could manage without letting on she was in a hurry. When the door was behind her, she rolled her eyes heavenward and blew out a breath.

Her father was getting powerfully sentimental lately, and while she found it touching most times, this wasn't one of them. She got down bowls and tried not to wince when she heard the door open again. She didn't have to turn to know it was Shawn.

"I can get this. You're busy."

"And Darcy can man the bar as well as me — or anyone. Besides, your father wants a sandwich. You don't build as well with bread and meat as you do with wood and nails."

Because he wanted to, and because he knew it would fluster her, he came up behind, took her hips in his hands and bent down to nip at the back of her neck.

Heat flashed straight down to her toes. "What

are you about? You're to be working."

"You're work enough." He turned her, then slid his hands up her sides.

"I've only time to get a bite to eat. I have to get back to the house and finish up."

"I'll feed you soon enough." With his hands hooked under her arms, he boosted her onto the counter. "You feed me first. I've an appetite for you."

She started to protest, though her heart wouldn't have been in it, but then his mouth was nibbling on hers. "Someone could come in," she managed, but her hands were already in his hair.

"And why would that bother you? Just put your mind to this for a minute." He framed her face, tilted his head. And took her under.

He'd promised to drive her crazy, and she was forced to admit he was a man of his word. For days he'd kept her on a shaky sexual edge that was both frustrating and wonderful. It was never more than a kiss, long and slow and deep or fast and hard and hot. The bare, teasing brush of hand or fingertips. The quiet look that could send her pulse scrambling without a word spoken.

An appetite for her, he'd said. It must have been true, as he was sampling and savoring and consuming her in lazy, lingering bites. When she began to tremble he only made a sound of satisfied approval.

"Shawn." The man made her light in the head and wild in the belly. "I can't go on like this much longer."

171

"I can." He was dreaming in her. "I could go on like this for years."

"That's what I'm afraid of."

He chuckled, then drew back, pleased by the clouds of desire in her eyes. "What did you say to this Daniel?"

"Daniel who?"

His grin flashed, and her mind cleared. Swearing, she gave him a shove and jumped off the counter. "Damn you, Shawn, that's what this was about. Just softening me up and fogging up my brain so I'd boost your ego a notch."

"That was just a side benefit." He got out the makings for a sandwich. "But the fact is, Brenna, I've an interest in knowing if you're going out with the Dubliner again just now."

"I ought to, just to slap at you." She jammed her hands in her pockets. "That's what Darcy would do."

"Ah, but you're not Darcy, are you, darling?"

"No, I'm not, and I haven't the talent or the energy to juggle men like apples. I told the Dubliner I was seeing someone."

Shawn glanced over, met her eyes. "Thanks for that."

"What I'd like to know is when I'm going to be sleeping with someone."

He added the spiced mustard he knew Mick O'Toole favored, and kept his brows lifted. "In all the years I've known you, never did I realize you had such an obsession with sex."

"I wouldn't be obsessed with sex if I was *having* sex."

"Well, now, how can you be sure of that, as you've never had it with me?"

She wanted to pull her hair, decided to laugh instead. "Christ Jesus, Shawn, you're enough to drive a woman to drink."

"Go out and have Darcy pull you a pint on me," he began, then his head came up again as he heard the sound of voices through the back door. "No, wait. Follow along here."

"Follow what?"

"Ladle the soup." He gave a wag of his hand toward the bowls. "And just follow along."

The back door opened, and Aidan stepped back to let Finkle go through. "The kitchen's Shawn's territory, as you can see. We've added this and that as he's felt a need for it. Oh, hello, Brenna. This is our friend and occasional employee, Brenna O'Toole. Brenna, Mr. Finkle from New York."

"Pleased to meet you." Clueless, Brenna put on a company smile and ladled the soup.

"Mr. Finkle's here about adding a restaurant to the pub," Shawn began.

"A theater," Aidan said in a tone so sharp that Brenna nearly bobbled the bowl in surprise. "The theater, Shawn. You're confused again."

"Oh, aye, the theater. Sure and I can't keep business dealings straight in my mind for five minutes at a run."

"But you make a lovely soup." Brenna gave him an encouraging look, one she might have sent to a slightly slow twelve-year-old. And hoped that was what he'd had in mind. "Would you care for a bowl

173

of it now, Mr. Finkle, or have you eaten already?"

"No, I haven't." The kitchen smelled like someone's devoted grandmother's kitchen, and it had his mouth watering. "It's very aromatic."

"And tastes better, I can promise you. What kind of theater are you thinking of?"

"A small, tasteful entertainment arena. My employer wants something traditional."

"People like to eat and lift a glass or two before or after the theater, don't they?" Shawn dressed the sandwich with a bit of parsley and radish.

"As a rule." Finkle scanned the room, the shining pots, the scrubbed counters, the tidy workstation. The stove was enormous and looked older than Zeus, but it appeared to be in good working order.

It might do, he thought. He would make a note of it in his report.

"Well, then, they couldn't do better than Gallagher's for that," Brenna assured him. "Would you like to sit here in the kitchen, sir, or would you prefer a table?"

"A table, if you don't mind," he told Brenna. The better to observe the business flow.

"I'll get you settled." Smoothly Aidan gestured toward the door. "You just tell our Darcy what you'd enjoy for your lunch. On the house, of course."

Aidan shot one triumphant look over his shoulder as he led Finkle out.

"What's this about a theater? And why were you acting as though you'd misplaced a few brain cells since you woke up this morning?"

"Well, I'll tell you. Go on and get your father his lunch, then come back and have your soup here, and I'll give you the full story."

When he had, Brenna sat back, gnawing her bottom lip as she did when thinking hard business. "I know this Magee."

"Do you?"

"Well, not personal like, but I know of him. Them, actually. Father and son, they are, but the son is more in the way of doing the running of things now."

"A family business," Shawn mused. "Well, that's something I can appreciate."

"A well-established one at that. He builds beautiful things, does Magee. Mostly theaters and arenas and such. He's very big in America, and in England too, I'm thinking. My mother's cousin's nephew Brian Cagney went to work for one of his construction teams in New York. He wrote me a year or two ago and said if I were to come over, I'd have a job in a wink, as Magee doesn't look at how a carpenter's skin is stretched when he hires on."

"Are you thinking of going to New York?" It was such a shock, even the possibility of it, that he had to work to keep his tone level and casual.

"No." Her mind already elsewhere, Brenna answered absently. "I work with Dad, and we work here. But Brian writes me now and again. He says Magee treats his people well, pays top of the scale, and has been known to swing a hammer himself when the mood strikes. But doesn't suffer fools, and if you fuck up, you're out and gone. I'll write to Brian, see what he knows of this or can find out."

Then her eyes sharpened, latched on to Shawn's. "Is he bringing in his own crews or hiring local for this?"

"I wouldn't know about it."

"Well, he should hire local. That's how it should be. You want to build in Ireland, then you use Irish hands. You build in Ardmore, you hire from the village and Old Parish. Dad and I could use a piece of this."

"Where are you going?" Shawn demanded when she got up.

"To talk to Mr. Finkle."

"Wait, wait. God, woman, you never let a fly land on your nose, do you? Now's not the time."

"Why isn't it if I want to get in on the ground floor of it?"

"Let Aidan set the deal first." He caught her hand. "It's still in delicate stages. Once we have it as we want it, then you can move on into who should have the building of it."

She hated to wait, hated that she saw the sense of what Shawn was saying. "I need to know the minute the deal's done, then."

"That I can promise."

"I'll show you how it should be." She pulled a pencil out of her pocket and would have sketched right on the wall if he hadn't grabbed her and shoved a pad of paper under her nose. "This is your north wall. You open that up, an oversized doorway." She drew quickly, all lines and angles. "And you put a breezeway sort of thing here, for people to move from the pub to the theater and back again. You keep it as much the same as the pub as you can, the same wood, the same flooring, so you have a — what is it — a symmetry that leads to the lobby part. Better if the breezeway fans out, spreads as it goes so that the lobby becomes part of the pub, as on the other way, the pub would become part of the lobby."

She nodded, glanced up. And narrowed her eyes. "And what might you be grinning at?"

"It's just such an education watching you work."

"If I have my way, you'll be watching me work for months down the line, and Dad can slip into the pub daily for his lunch and pint. I've got to get on."

"Can you take an hour later?" He caught her hand before she could turn to go.

"I suppose I could. It shouldn't take longer than that for me to get your clothes off and finish with you."

"I had something else in mind. As for the other, I don't want timetables and deadlines." He brought her hand to his lips, rubbed them over her knuckles. "Have a walk with me on the beach."

It was so like him, she thought. An hour on a winter's beach with the sea and the wind. "Come and fetch me at Jude's. If you manage the time, so will I."

"Then come on and kiss me good-bye."

Willing to oblige, she rose to her toes, leaned in, and had just touched her lips to his when the door swung open.

"The Finkle believes he can fit in a bit of that soup and some —" Darcy stopped short, gaping at the sight of her dearest friend kissing her brother. "Well, for the sake of Jesus, what's all this?"

"It was just what it appeared to be before you interrupted. You haven't finished," Shawn said to Brenna, and started to pull her back from the full foot she'd jumped in retreat.

"Yes, I have. I've work to do." Considering it the best line of escape, she dashed out the back door.

"Soup, you say?" Casually, Shawn pivoted to the stove.

"Shawn, you were kissing Brenna."

"So I was, though I had hardly gotten a taste before you came barging in and scared her off."

"What are you thinking of, kissing Brenna?"

He glanced back, his face bland. "I was sure our mother explained such matters to you, but if you're needing a refresher course on the subject, I'll do what I can to educate you."

"Don't smart your mouth off at me." But she was too baffled to work up the kind of temper that entertained them both. "She's the next thing to a sister to me, and I won't have you teasing her that way."

He ladled soup into a thick, generous bowl. "Maybe you should have a word with her before you flay into me."

"Don't think I won't." She snatched up the

178

bowl. "I know how you are with women, Shawn Gallagher."

He inclined his head. "Do you now?"

"That I do." She said it in her darkest, most forbidding tone, added a toss of her head, and stalked out.

The minute she'd served Finkle his bowl and fussed over him enough to bring a rise of color to his cheeks, Darcy informed Aidan she was taking a fifteen-minute break. And was out the door before he could tell her different.

In her hurry she forgot to take off her apron or grab her jacket, so her tip money jingled cheerfully in her pocket as she raced down to her family home.

As a result, she was out of breath and pink of cheek when she dashed through the door. She headed straight upstairs to the door of the nursery, where Brenna was rolling varnish onto the freshly sanded floor.

"I want to know what's going on."

"Well, I'm putting on this first coat of sealer. It takes a day or two to dry good and hard. Then I'll put on another, and that will be that."

"With you and Shawn. Damn it, Brenna, you can't go around letting him kiss you that way. People'll get the wrong impression."

Brenna kept rolling. She hadn't worked up the nerve to look at her friend. "Actually, I imagine they'd get the right one. I should've told you, Darcy, I just didn't know how."

Darcy braced herself with a hand on the doorjamb as the blood drained out of her face. "There's — there's something to tell me?"

"Well, not so much, really. But not for lack of trying on my part." Time to face the music, Brenna told herself, and she turned around. "I want to sleep with him. That's all."

"You want to —" Because her throat had snapped shut, Darcy broke off and rubbed a hand over it. "You want to *sleep* with Shawn? Well, why?"

"The usual reasons."

Darcy started to speak, then raised a hand to hold Brenna off while she gathered her own thoughts. "All right, I'm thinking. You've been in somewhat of a sexual drought just recently, so I can see you'd . . . No, no, I'm not quite seeing. It's Shawn we're speaking of here. Shawn who's been a thorn in both our sides since we were babies."

"Sure and it's an oddity, I admit. But the thing here is, Darcy, I've had a bit of a . . . of a yen for him for . . . well, forever. I just thought it was time to act on it or I'd always have one, and where would that get me?"

"I'm sitting down." She did so, right in the doorway. "You acted on it."

"I did, and he was as surprised as you are by the idea, at least initially. And he wasn't very flattering about it, either. But he's in the way of interested now. It's just that I've discovered this is yet one more thing you can't rush Shawn over. And it's fair to killing me."

Meticulously, she coated her roller with varnish

and spread it thin and smooth. "I'm sorry you're upset about it. I'd hoped that we could just get it done, so to speak, with no one the wiser."

"Don't you have any feelings for him, then?"

"Of course I do." Brenna's head came up again. "Of course I do, Darcy. We're all like family. This is just . . . it's just different."

"It's different, that's the truth." Struggling to adjust, Darcy sighed out a breath. "I was going to protect you from him — knowing that he has a way with women that can make them softheaded over him, and him barely noticing half the time. But now that I've heard what you've said, Brenna, I have to turn that coin over."

Genuinely surprised, Brenna set her roller on the end of the pan. "You think he needs protecting from me? Darcy, I'm not exactly your femme fatale sort of woman." She spread her arms, knowing very well how she looked in her grubby work clothes and battered boots. "I think Shawn's safe from the likes of me."

"Then you don't understand him, not in his heart. There's romance in him, the kind of dreaminess that builds castles in the air. He has a delicacy of feeling. He'd cut off his arm before he'd cause hurt to another. Cut them both off because he caused a moment's pain to someone he cared for. And he cares for you. It's not so far a step from caring for to loving. What will you do if he falls in love with you?"

"He won't." She nearly took a step back, from the question and the idea. "Of course he won't."

"Don't hurt him." Darcy got to her feet. "Please don't hurt him."

"I —" But as Darcy had already turned away, Brenna had to hurry after her. "Darcy, you mustn't worry so." Brenna gripped the banister when Darcy turned, halfway down the stairs. "We both know what we're about, I promise you. We've already taken a vow to stay friends through it."

"Make sure it's a vow you don't break. You both mean a great deal to me." She worked up a smile because her friend seemed to need it. "Sleeping with Shawn," Darcy said with her usual bite. "What is the world coming to?"

Ten

After closing, when the village was so quiet that only the heartbeat of the sea could be heard, the Gallaghers gathered around the kitchen table of their family home with tea and with whiskey.

"Here's where we stand."

Aidan laid a hand over Jude's as he spoke, and hers turned under his so their fingers linked. He had a sudden, vivid picture of his parents joining hands in exactly the same manner when they'd sat at table's head for a family meeting.

The Gallagher way, he thought. One link leading to another in a chain of tradition.

"Well, where do we stand?" Darcy demanded.

"Sorry." Aidan shook his head. "My mind went wandering. So, at the start. Finkle may be a Yank, but he's no green one when it comes to horse trading. I wouldn't believe as successful a man of business as Magee is reputed to be would send any but a sharp individual to look after his interests."

"Be that as it may," Shawn considered, "he fell for the man from London."

Aidan grinned in appreciation and nodded. "Well, now, we're not green either, come to that. And the Irish were horse traders before those looking for America ever found her. But that's neither here nor there."

He started to toss the patiently waiting Finn a biscuit, then remembered the presence of his wife and cleared his throat. "Finkle, he liked the look of the land, the setup, the location, and so forth. I'm sure of that, though he made little noises and grunts and pulled on his lip rather than commit. He said again how the Magee is set on buying, and I said again how that was easy to understand, and a man likes his own and so on and so forth. But how we're set on leasing."

"We'd have more money sooner, and could put it to work for us making more if we just sold," Darcy piped up.

"That's true enough." Aidan nodded toward her.

"And we'd have more control," Shawn put in, "part of the profit, and a hand in what's done with what's ours if we hold the lease. Look ahead, Darcy, to ten years down the road. And twenty, and the legacy to your children."

"Who says I'm having any?" She shrugged her shoulders. "But I see your point. It's a hard thing for me to resist grabbing the money held out at the moment."

"A hundred years' lease is our offer."

"A hundred?" Darcy's eyes popped wide, and Aidan merely looked at his wife.

"A hundred's the number of magic."

"This is business, not fairy spells."

"You use the fairies where you find them."

Shawn added a drop of whiskey to his tea. It seemed to go with these dealings. "If Magee is forward-thinking, a lease of a hundred years will appeal to him. Brenna knows something of his company." He caught Darcy's jerk to attention out of the corner of his eye at his mention of Brenna. "From what she told me, he's a fair man, but far from green himself. So I'm thinking he'll look even beyond the century."

"As should we. A pound a year for a hundred years."

"A pound?" Darcy threw up her hands. "Why not just give him the bloody land, then?"

"For that price we ask for fifty percent of his theater."

Darcy settled again, her eyes sharpening. "And settle for?"

"Twenty. And at the end of the term the land, and the theater, are owned, equal shares. Gallagher and Magee."

"It's a sweet deal if the theater takes hold." Darcy agreed. "And leaning heavily in our direction."

"It'll take hold," Aidan said with a gleam in his eye. "With Gallagher luck and Magee money."

"I'm willing to trust that. Now, why should he agree to those terms?"

"I —" Jude started to speak, then closed her mouth.

"No, have your say." Aidan gave her hand a squeeze. "You're part of this."

"Well, I think he will agree. After some negotiations and posturing and perhaps a few more adjustments. You may have to give a bit more, but in the end you'll have fairly close to what you're after — because in the end, all parties want the same thing."

"Magee wants his theater," Darcy put in.

"More than that." In an automatic gesture, Jude slapped Shawn's hand before he could sneak Finn a biscuit. "He has a reason for choosing this place, and the kind of man who helms that successful a business can indulge himself from time to time. His people came from here," she went on. "His great-uncle was engaged to my great-aunt."

"Of course." Shawn tapped a finger against the whiskey bottle as it came to him. "John Magee who was lost in the first great war. His youngest brother — Dennis, was it — went off to America to make his fortune. I didn't put it together before now."

"I don't know how much sentiment is in the motive for this Magee selecting Ardmore," Jude went on, "but it's bound to be part of the motivation. If this Magee had anything like my background, he grew up on stories of Ireland, and of this area in particular. Now he wants a more tangible tie with the place his family came from. I understand that."

"That Yank sentiment over ancestors." Amused, Darcy helped herself to the whiskey. "I'll never understand it. Ancestors . . . sure and they've been dead for long years, haven't they? But if sentiment helps glue the deal, that's fine with me."

"That'll be part of it, but — sorry, it's the psychologist in me again — he'll also have his eye on profit. If he didn't, he wouldn't have one of the largest companies in the States. And for the same reasons, he'll have his eye on his reputation."

"And ours will be on our own." Shawn lifted his glass.

"You've quite the reputation, don't you?" Darcy sent Shawn a sour smile.

"Not as well rounded as yours, darling."

"At least I don't go around seducing childhood friends."

Slowly, and with a dangerous gleam in his eye, he set his glass down again. Before feathers could fly, Aidan stretched an arm between them. "Now what? What's all this?"

"Ah, she's got her nose out of joint because I kissed Brenna."

"Well, there's nothing to squabble about . . ." Aidan's hand dropped onto the table. "Brenna O'Toole?"

"Of course Brenna O'Toole."

"What were you doing kissing our Brenna?"

"Aidan." Jude tugged on his sleeve. "This is Shawn's business."

"It's ours as it's Brenna."

"Mother of God. It's not as if I grabbed her by the hair and dragged her to the kitchen floor to force myself on her in a carnal fashion while she tried to fight me off."

"You were on the kitchen floor?"

"We were not." At his wits' end, Shawn pressed his fingers to his eyes. "A man can't have a simple life in this family. I kissed Brenna, and not for the first time. Neither do I plan on it being the last. And I fail to see why that's such a puzzlement to everyone who knows us. And an outrage as well."

Darcy folded her hands. She'd learned something she'd hoped to by the poking at him. He hadn't mentioned that it was Brenna who'd initiated the shift in relationship. With another man she'd chalk it up to ego. But with Shawn she knew it was instinctive protection of the woman involved.

The fact both pleased and worried her.

"It's just . . . surprising," Aidan said.

"I'm not outraged." Darcy sent Shawn a sweet, sisterly look. "But puzzled I am. After all, Brenna's seen you naked already — some years ago, to be sure, but still such things linger in the mind. And having had a good look at your equipment, I can't think why she'd be the least bit interested."

"That's a question you'll have to put to her." He wanted to leave it at that, dignified, dismissive, but it rankled. "I wasn't more than fifteen, and the water was cold. A man's not at his best just out of frigid water, you know."

"That's your story, son, and you stick with it."

"And you shouldn't have been looking in that direction. But you always were a perverted sort."

"Why shouldn't I have looked? Everyone else was. He lost his trunks in the sea," she explained to Jude, "and didn't realize it till he was standing clear of the surf, jay naked. I've always regretted the lack of a camera."

188

Jude glanced at Shawn with sympathy. "I used to regret being an only child. But there are some circumstances when — oh!"

"What is it?" Aidan was on his feet like a shot, prepared to haul his wife into his arms, when she pressed her finger to her belly. "There, you've upset her with your bickering."

"No, no. The baby's moving." Thrilled, she grabbed Aidan's hand and laid it over her middle. "Do you feel it? It's like a rippling inside me."

Panic shifted to awe, filling his eyes, his heart. "He's lively."

"It's a family meeting, after all. Why shouldn't he be part of it?" Shawn raised his glass again. *"Slainte."*

He went to visit Maude. Since he'd been used to seeing her once or twice a week most of his life, Shawn saw no reason that should change after death. And her resting place was a good spot for thinking.

It had nothing much to do with the fact that he would stroll near the cliff hotel on his way. It wasn't likely he'd see Brenna, but, well, if he didn't walk in that direction, there was no chance at all of seeing her.

As he recalled, Maude Fitzgerald had been the romantic sort, and he thought she'd appreciate the logic of it.

The hotel sat dramatically on the cliffs, with the sea spread before it. And though the air was brisk with morning, a scattering of guests were out and about enjoying the view. Shawn gave himself the pleasure of it as well, and as he watched the boats bob and sail over the water, he thanked his ancestors for going into the business of a public house rather than fishing.

There was Tim Riley and his crew hauling in nets while the waves kicked and danced. There was a rhythm to it that had Shawn tapping his foot and set pipe against cello in a musical duel in his head.

Shawn imagined the tourists thought the boats looked picturesque. They probably viewed the idea of making a living from the sea as a kind of romantic venture steeped in history and tradition. But as he stood, wind flowing through his dark hair and doing its best to sneak under his sweater, he could only think it a cold and lonely and capricious life.

He'd take a warm pub and a busy kitchen any day of the week.

But it was romance that whirled through Mary Kate's mind when she rushed out after spotting him. She had to press a hand to her heart, as it filled with images.

She looked at Shawn, standing on the cliffs, legs spread, eyes on the horizon, and she saw Heathcliff, Rhett Butler, Lancelot, and every other heroic fantasy that might fill an infatuated young woman's dreams.

She was glad she'd borrowed her sister Patty's new blue blouse that morning, though Patty wasn't going to be pleased about it. Making a valiant attempt to smooth her hair, Mary Kate hurried forward.

"Shawn."

When he turned and saw her coming toward him, Shawn cursed himself. He hadn't thought of the possibility of running into Brenna's sister, not when he'd been so busy thinking of Brenna.

Mind your step, Gallagher, he warned himself. "Good morning, Mary Kate. I was forgetting the hotel is full of O'Tooles just now."

She had to untangle her tongue. His eyes were so clear in this light. If she looked into them deeply enough, she could see herself reflected back. It was so alluring.

"You should come in out of the wind. I've a break now, I'll buy you some tea."

"That's a kind offer, but I'm on my way to see Old Maude. I was just watching Tim Riley pull in his nets, and they looked heavy with fish. I'll have to go about bargaining with him later for some of his catch."

"Why don't you stop by on your way back?" She tilted her head, running a hand through her hair and looking up at him under her lashes in a look she'd practiced endlessly. "I can take my lunch most anytime."

"Ah . . ." She had more skill in flirtation than he'd given her credit for. It was just a little frightening. "I'm due at the pub before long."

"I'd love to be able to sit and talk with you." She laid a hand on his arm. "When there's not so much going on."

"Well, that's a thought, isn't it? I've got to be going. You should go inside. You shouldn't be standing out here in that thin blouse. You'll catch a chill. My best to your family."

As he made his escape, Mary Kate sighed. He'd noticed the blouse.

He'd handled that well, Shawn congratulated himself. Friendly, a sort of older brother to younger sister kind of thing. He was sure the little crisis had passed. And it was really rather sweet that she'd thought of him the way she had. A man had to be flattered, especially since he'd slipped through those sticky loops with no harm done.

But deciding a bit of backup wouldn't be out of order, he dipped into Saint Declan's Well and sprinkled the water on the ground.

"Superstitious? A modern-thinking man?"

Shawn's head came up, and his eyes met the clever blue ones of Carrick, prince of the faeries. "A modern-thinking man knows there's a reason for superstitions, especially when he stands and finds himself having a conversation with the likes of you."

Since he'd come for a purpose, Shawn walked away from the well and over to Maude's grave. "So, tell me, are you always here and about? I've come to this spot all my life, and it's only recently I've seen you."

"There was no particular reason for you to see me before recently. I've a question for you, Shawn Gallagher, and I'm hoping you'll be answering it."

"Well, you have to ask it first."

"So I will." Carrick sat by the grave across from Shawn so their eyes were level. "What the bleeding, blistering hell are you waiting for?"

Shawn raised his eyebrows, rested his hands on his knees. "All manner of things."

"Oh, that's typical of you." Disgust edged Carrick's voice. "I'm speaking of Mary Brenna O'Toole, and why you haven't taken her to your bed."

"That would be between Brenna and myself," Shawn said evenly, "and no concern of yours."

"Of course it's a concern of mine." Carrick was on his feet now, the movement too fast for the human eye to catch. The ring on his finger glowed a deep, deep blue, and the silver pouch hanging from his belt glittered. "I judged you to have the kind of nature that would understand, but you're more boneheaded than even your brother."

"Sure and you aren't the first to say so."

"It's in place, Gallagher the younger."

Because Carrick was now standing beside Shawn rather than across from him, Shawn got to his feet. "And what would that be?"

"Your part, your destiny. Your choices. How is it you can look into your heart for making your music, and not for living your life?"

"My life is as I like it."

"Boneheaded," Carrick said again. "Finn protect me from the foolishness of mortals." He threw up his hands, and thunder rumbled across the clear bowl of the sky.

"If you think to impress me with parlor tricks,

you won't succeed at it. That's just your temper talking, and I've one of my own."

"Would you dare match it to mine?" As a demonstration, Carrick waved a finger, and a bolt of blinding white light lanced into the ground in front of Shawn's feet.

"Bully tactics." Though Shawn had to fight the instinct to leap back. "And unworthy of you."

Fury turned Carrick's eyes nearly black, trembled from his fingertips in little licks of red flame. Then subsided as he threw back his head and laughed. "Well, now, you've more courage than I gave you credit for. Or it's just stupid you are."

"Wise enough to know you can cause mischief if you like, but no real harm. You don't worry me, Carrick."

"I could have you on your knees croaking like a bullfrog."

"Which would hurt my pride but little else." Not, Shawn thought, that he wanted to put the matter to the test. "What's the point of this? Threats don't endear you to me."

"I've waited six of your lifetimes for something you could have in an instant, just by holding out your hand." But this time he sighed. "Tears from the moon I gathered for her the second time." As he spoke he took the pouch from his belt. "And at her feet I poured the pearls they formed. And all she saw was the pearls."

Turning the pouch over, he poured a white waterfall of glowing white gems onto Maude's grave. "They glowed in the grass, in the moonlight then,

194

white and smooth as Gwen's skin. But she didn't see that it wasn't pearls I'd poured at her feet, but my heart — the longing in it, and aye, the purity of that love as well. I didn't know she needed to be told, or that it was already too late, as I hadn't given her the part of me she wanted."

Carrick's voice was full of despair now, and so ripe with unhappiness that Shawn touched his arm. "What did she want?"

"Love. Just the word. A single word. But I gave her diamonds — jewels plucked from the sun, and these pearls, then the final time the stones you call sapphires that I harvested from the heart of the sea."

"I know your story well."

"Aye, you would. And your new sister, Jude, has put it in her book of tales and legends. The ending is still an unhappy one as I cast the spell over my Gwen, in anger and in pain — rashly, Gallagher. Three times love would find love, heart accept heart with all the failings and the foibles. And then, my Gwen and I will be free to be together. A hundred years times three I've waited, and my patience is sore tested. You're a man who has words."

Considering, Carrick circled Shawn and the grave. "You use them well with your music — music others should hear, but that's another matter. A man who has such a gift of words is one who understands what's inside a person, sometimes before that person knows. It's a gift you have. I'm only asking you to use it."

In a long flourish, he waved his hand over the

grave, and the pearls blossomed into flowers. "The jewels I gave Gwen grew into flowers. Your Jude will tell you it was the flowers she kept. Some women want the simple things, Gallagher, so I've come to understand."

He lifted his finger. Resting on the tip was a single perfect pearl. With a thin smile, he flicked it toward Shawn, then nodded, pleased, when Shawn snatched it from the air. "Take it, keep it, until you realize who it is you're to give it to. When you do, give the words. They're more of magic than what you have in hand."

The air trembled, wavered, and Carrick disappeared into it.

"The man wears you out," Shawn murmured, then sat beside Maude's grave again. "It's very unusual companions you have."

Then, because he needed it, Shawn let himself fall into the quiet. He watched the moonflowers, blooms open despite the steam of sunlight, dance across the grave. He studied the pearl, rubbing it through his fingers. He put it in his pocket before reaching down to pick a single blossom.

"I don't think you'll mind, as it's for Jude," he said to Maude. He sat and kept her company another twenty minutes before going back home.

He didn't knock. It had been his home too long for him to think of it. But Shawn did think, the minute he'd closed the door behind him, that he was very likely interrupting Jude's work.

When she came to the top of the steps before he

could decide if he should go back out again, he glanced up in apology. "You'll be working. I'll come back 'round later."

"No, that's all right. I don't mind a break. Would you like some tea?" she asked as she started down.

"I would, yes, but I'll fix it for both of us."

"I won't argue with that." She smiled uncertainly when he held out the moonflower. "Thanks. Isn't it the wrong time for this to be blooming?"

"In most places. It's one of the things I'd like to speak with you about." He started back toward the kitchen with her. "How are you feeling today?"

"Good. Really good, actually. I think the morning sickness is passing, and I'm not sorry to see it go."

"And your work's going well?"

It would be Shawn's way, she thought, to wind his way around to the genuine purpose of the visit in his own time. So she found a little bottle for the blossom while he put on the kettle. "Yes, it is. I still have moments when I can't believe I'm doing it. This time last year I was still teaching, and hating my work. Now I have a book on its way to being published, and another one coming to life every day. I'm a little nervous because this one's a story out of my head instead of a compilation of others I've been told, but I really love the process of it."

"Being a little nervous you'll probably write a better story, don't you think?" At home, he got out the biscuit tin and filled a plate. "Meaning, you'll have more care with it."

"I hope you're right. Are you nervous when you're writing your music?"

"Not the tunes," he said after a moment's thought. "The words sometimes. Trying to find the right way of saying what the music's telling me. It can be frustrating."

"How do you handle it?"

"Oh, I bang my head against it for a while." After the pot was warmed he measured out the tea. "Then if all I get from that is a headache, I'll take a walk to clear it, or think of something else entirely. Most times, after I do, the words are just there, as if they'd been waiting for me to pluck them."

"I'm afraid to walk away when it's not working. I always think if I do I won't be able to write at all when I come back. Your way's healthier."

"Ah, but you're the published author, then, aren't you?" While the tea steeped, he got out cups.

"Do you want your music published, Shawn?"

"Maybe, one day. There's no rush about it." Which, he knew, he'd been saying for years already. "I write it to please myself, and that's enough for now."

"My agent might know someone in the music business. I'd be happy to ask."

His stomach jumped like a rabbit under the gun. "Oh, there's no need for that. Actually, Jude, I've come by to speak with you about another matter altogether."

She waited, letting him bring the pot to the table, pour the tea. When he'd settled, and the fragrant steam rose between them, he still didn't speak.

"Shawn, tell me what's on your mind."

"Well, I'm trying to figure out exactly how to say it. I'll just start this way." He reached in his pocket, and after drawing out the pearl, set it beside her cup.

"A pearl?" Puzzled, she started to reach for it, then her gaze whipped up to his, and her fingers stopped a whisper away from the round white gem. "Oh. Carrick."

"He speaks fondly of you."

"How odd. It's so . . . odd." Now she did pick up the pearl and cupped it in her palm. "And the moonflower. The rest of the pearls turned to moonflowers."

"On Maude's grave. What do you think of it all?"

"What does a modern, educated, fairly intelligent woman think of the existence of faeries?" She let the pearl roll in her palm, then shook her head. "I think it's marvelous. Literally. This one's arrogant and impatient, and a bit of a showoff, but coming into contact with him is one of the things that changed my life."

"I think he's of a mind to change mine. Or he wouldn't have given me that."

"Yes, I'm sure you're right." Jude gave the pearl back to Shawn. "And how do you feel about that?"

"That he's got a long wait in store, as I like my life just as it is."

"Are you . . ." Trailing off, Jude picked up her

199

tea. "I never had siblings, so I don't know what's out of line. But I wonder if you're thinking of Brenna."

"I've given the O'Toole considerable thought. And I've given more than a passing one to the notion that Carrick sees my linking with her as the next step for him."

"And?"

"Well, now." Shawn picked up a biscuit, bit into it. "I'd say again, he has a long wait in store." His lips twitched as Jude looked down into her tea. "Was that a bit of a matchmaker's gleam I caught there in your pretty eyes, Jude Frances?"

She sniffed. "I don't know what you're talking about."

"I'm talking about a happily married woman taking a look at her bachelor brother-in-law and thinking to herself, 'Well, now, wouldn't it be fine if our darling Shawn found himself the right woman and settled down — and what might it be that I can do to help that along.'"

"I wouldn't presume to interfere." However prim her tone, the laugh showed in her eyes. "Hardly at all."

"I appreciate it." He slipped the pearl back into his pocket. "And just so you're aware of my thoughts and feelings on this, I'll tell you that if there comes to be anything between me and the O'Toole it'll be because it's something we both decide upon, not because some bullying member of the gentry's decided for us. Or even because my new sister, whom I love dearly, wishes it so."

"I only wish you to be happy."

"I've plans to stay that way. And as I do, I'd best get into the pub so Aidan's not duty-bound to break my head for being late."

Eleven

Brenna didn't consider it spying. And she'd have challenged the one who accused her. It just so happened that she had a bit of work to do in Finkle's room. He'd complained the shower was slow to drain, and since she was there in any case, the hotel had asked that she deal with it.

Was it her fault he was on the phone with his employer when she came 'round? Certainly not. And could the blame be laid on her that he wasn't the sort of man who paid any mind to service people?

Unless, she imagined, they looked like Darcy, and then a man would have to be deaf and blind, and likely dead a year or so not to give her a long second look. But that was beside the point altogether.

He'd let her in himself, with a fussy and impatient wave of his hand. Then had simply gestured toward the bath and gone back to the phone. Such treatment didn't hurt her feelings. She was there to do some plumbing, after all.

But she had ears, and was there any reason not to use them?

"I apologize for the interruption, Mr. Magee, the young man's here to fix the plumbing."

Young man? Brenna bit her tongue and rolled her eyes.

"I'll fax the report as soon as I've put it all in a cohesive form. That may be after business hours in New York, sir, so I'll send copies to your private line as well."

In the bath, Brenna rattled her tools. From her angle she could see only Finkle's polished shoes and a thin strip of dove-gray sock.

"No, I haven't been able to get the name of the London firm that's interested in the property. The elder brother, Aidan, brushes it off, claims the other one is confused. I'd have to say it's more than possible for the younger to confuse things. He's amiable enough, but doesn't appear terribly bright."

Brenna snorted, then began the business of snaking the drain. As quietly as manageable.

"However, judging from the reaction, the body language, and the speed with which this lapse was covered, I'd have to say there has been some negotiation in that corner."

Finkle was silent for a moment. Brenna strained her ears and heard the light *tap-tap* of his fingers on wood. "Yes, it is a lovely place. Picturesque, unspoiled. 'Simple' would be my word. It's also remote. Having seen it, and having spent this short time here, I would have to go back to my original opinion, sir. I hardly see this theater project being a financial success. Dublin would be a more logical choice. Or failing that —"

Silence again, then the faintest of sighs. "Yes, of

course. I understand you have your reasons. I can assure you that the land the Gallaghers have is the best location in Ardmore. The pub appears to be just what you expected. It's off-season, of course, but it does a steady business, and it's well run under the elder Gallagher's hand. The food is first-rate, which I admit surprised me. Not at all your average pub grub. The sister? Yes, she's . . . she's . . ."

The bumbling had Brenna biting the inside of her cheek to hold back a bark of laughter. Men were so predictable.

"She appears to be efficient. Actually, I went back for a short time last evening, at their request. Darcy, the sister, Miss Gallagher, has an exceptional singing voice. All three of them, for that matter, are quite musical, and that could be an advantage. If you're determined to place this theater here, in Ardmore, connecting it with Gallagher's Pub is, in my opinion, the most logical decision."

Still on her hands and knees, Brenna wiggled her butt, since her hands were full and she couldn't punch a fist in the air.

"Oh, you can trust me to negotiate them down from the percentage they're asking. I know you'd prefer to buy the land outright, but this sentiment of theirs has thus far proven unassailable. In actual terms, the lease they offer is a less risky venture for you and would in the long term give you a tighter connection to the established business. I feel it's to your advantage to use Gallagher's, and the reputation it's earned, to launch your theater."

The finger tapping sounded again, and the shoes uncrossed, then recrossed at the ankle. "Yes, that's understood. No higher than twenty-five percent. You can trust me there. I hope to have the deal settled within twenty-four hours. I'm sure I can convince the elder Gallagher that he'd get no better offer from a London firm, or any other."

As she sensed the conversation was winding down, Brenna scrambled up and turned the taps on full and loud. She hummed to herself as she watched the water run. After she'd turned it off again, she did a bit more rattling, then hefted her toolbox and strolled into the adjoining room.

"Draining like a champ now, it is. Sorry for your inconvenience."

He never so much as glanced up, but waved her away as he'd waved her in and hunched over the laptop on the little desk.

"And a good day to you, sir," she called cheerfully and heard the keyboard clatter as she slipped out.

Once she was clear, she sprinted. Finkle wasn't the only one who knew how to do a report.

"Well, now, the London bit seems to have been inspired." Aidan gave his brother a slap on the shoulder and shot Brenna a look of approval. "It's got them shagging their asses, doesn't it?"

"Some people can't resist the competition." Since they were in the kitchen, Shawn turned to get four bottles of beer from the refrigerator. "I think we should drink to the O'Toole here, and her busy ears."

"I just happened to be where I was when I was." But she took the offered bottle.

"You're a fine field soldier, Sergeant O'Toole." Aidan clicked his bottle to hers, then to Shawn's and Darcy's in turn. "Twenty-five percent and no more. Pity for him he didn't know we'd have settled for twenty without a whimper."

"The man — the Magee," Brenna explained. "He's determined to have what he wants here, though Finkle doesn't approve. But approve he does of Shawn's cooking, Darcy's face, and your managing hand, Aidan. Oh, and he thinks you're none too bright, Shawn, but an amiable sort. And when he speaks of Darcy, he stutters."

Delighted, Darcy laughed. "Give me another day or so, and when he speaks of me, he'll babble. And we can get thirty percent."

Aidan slung an arm around Darcy's shoulders. "We'll take the twenty-five and wrap the deal. I'll let Finkle think he's turned the thumbscrews to get it, for why shouldn't he feel accomplished after all? I can tell you Dad likes what he's seen of Magee so far. He called only this morning to tell me that, and that he'll leave the details of the matter to us."

"Then we'll let Finkle wrangle over the terms." Shawn raised his bottle. "Until he gives us what we're after."

"That's exactly so. Well, it's back to work for now. Brenna, my darling, do you think you could make yourself scarce 'round the pub until we've got it hammered?"

"I can, of course. But I'm invisible to the likes of him. He doesn't see past my toolbox. Fact is, he thought I was a man."

"Then he needs glasses." Aidan tipped up her chin and kissed her. "I'm grateful to you."

"I tell you I could get us thirty without much more effort," Darcy claimed, but she followed Aidan out into the pub.

"She likely could," Brenna commented.

"No need to be greedy. I'm grateful to you as well."

She cocked her head, and the faintest of sneers twisted her lips. It was one of Shawn's favorite expressions. "Are you going to kiss me, then, as Aidan did?"

"I'm thinking about it."

"Sure and you think a long time about things."

"No longer than it takes." So he cupped her face in his hands, still enjoying the sneer, then tilting her head to please himself, laid his mouth on hers.

Slow, comfortably lazy, like a warm breeze on a summer morning. She relaxed against him, her lips just starting to curve at the easy sweetness. Then deeper, so gradually, so skillfully, he took her deeper, she was over her head before she realized she'd been going under.

She made a sound, caught somewhere between a sigh and a moan. As her heart battered against her ribs, she slid her hands up his back to grip his shoulders. Even as her body went on alert, braced for more, he was easing away.

"I can only be so grateful, at the moment."

The man had made her dizzy, damn it. And had left her system screaming. "You did that on purpose."

"Of course I did."

"Bastard. I'm going back to work." She reached down for her toolbox and, still off balance, rapped hard into the table when she turned for the door. Her head whipped around quickly, and her narrowed eyes warned him. But he was wise enough to keep his expression bland.

She sniffed, then strode around to wrench open the back door. There she paused, shot him one last look. "You know, when you stop thinking, you do a fine job of the rest of it."

He didn't grin until she was gone. "That's a fortunate thing, as I've about finished thinking altogether."

Shawn stayed out of the way when Finkle came in that evening. But he fixed the man a king's meal of baked plaice done with an herbed butter, served with cally potatoes to which he'd added a dash or so of thyme, and some curly kale.

Since word from Darcy when she popped in was that the man would have licked his plate if there'd been no one about to notice, Shawn felt he'd done his part.

So it was mischief, as much as business sense, that had him going out to take Finkle a portion of lemon cheesecake.

Relaxed from the meal, and Darcy's attentions, Finkle offered Shawn what might have passed for a smile. "I don't know when I've had better fish. You run a creative kitchen, Mr. Gallagher."

"That's kind of you to say, sir. I hope you'll enjoy this. 'Tis me own recipe, fiddled about somewhat from that of my dear old granny. I don't believe you'll find better when you return to London."

Finkle, just about to take the first bite, paused with his fork in the air. "New York," he said, very precisely.

Shawn let himself blink. "New York? Oh, sure, and it's New York I meant. The man from London was thin as a skate and wore little round glasses. You'd think I'd be able to keep it all straight, wouldn't you, now?"

Keeping his expression pleasant, Finkle casually took a sample of the cake. "So . . . you've spoken to someone from London about a restaurant, was it?"

"Oh, Aidan, he does the talking. I've no head for business at all. Is the cake to your liking?"

"It's excellent." The man had a slow brain, Finkle mused, but no one could fault his cooking skills. "The man from London," he pressed. "Would you happen to know his name? I have a number of acquaintances there."

Shawn stared up at the ceiling, rubbed his chin. "Was it Finkle? Oh, no, that would be you." With a sweet and harmless expression covering his face, he lifted empty hands. "I've a bad habit of forgetting names. But he was a very pleasant individual, as you are yourself, sir. If you find you've room for another portion of cake, just let Darcy know."

He strolled back to the kitchen, catching Aidan's eye with a wink.

Ten minutes later Darcy poked her head into the kitchen and hissed, "Finkle asked for a moment of Aidan's time. They've gone into the snug."

"That's fine, then. Let me know if you need help at the bar."

"Consider I've let you know. Frank Malloy's come in with his brothers."

"He had words with his wife again?"

"That's the face he's wearing. I'll not be able to keep up with them, and the rest of the customers."

"I'm coming, then."

He was pulling the second pint for the Malloys — all of whom were burly-built men with straw-colored hair who made their living from the sea — when Aidan and Finkle stepped out of the snug.

He nodded good night to Aidan, then to Shawn. And for a moment as he glanced toward Darcy, his stern face fell into lines as soft as a hopeful puppy's.

"Are you turning in for the evening so early, then, Mr. Finkle?" Darcy set her tray on the bar, then sent the poor man a smile that could have melted slab chocolate at twenty paces.

"I —" He had no choice but to tug at the meticulously knotted tie, as his throat was suddenly thick. "I'm afraid I must. I have a plane to catch in the morning."

"Oh, you're leaving us altogether?" She held out a hand for his. "I'm sorry you can't stay longer, and hope you'll come back again when you're able."

"I'm quite sure I'll be back." Unable to help himself, Finkle did something he'd never so much as considered doing before in his life, even with his wife. He kissed Darcy's hand. "It's been a great pleasure."

A faint flush of pink riding on his cheeks, he left the pub.

"Well?" Darcy demanded, spinning around to Aidan.

"Let's give this a minute, just to be sure Finkle doesn't turn about, rush back in, and throw himself to his knees to beg you to run off with him to Tahiti."

Darcy chuckled and shook her head. "No, the man loves his wife. Now he might allow himself a misty dream about what the two of us might do in such a place, but that's as far as it goes."

"Then I'll tell you." He laid a hand on hers on the bar, placed the other on Shawn's shoulder. "We've done the deal, as the three of us and Jude discussed, and we've shaken hands on it. He's going back to New York, and the papers will be drawn up as soon as lawyers can manage it."

"Twenty-five percent?" Shawn asked.

"Twenty-five, and a say in approving the design for the theater. There are details yet, but between us, Magee, and the lawyers, we'll iron them out."

"So we've done it?" Shawn laid down the cloth he'd been using to wipe the bar.

"It appears we have, as I've given my word."

211

"Well, then." Shawn put his hand over the one Aidan held over Darcy's. "I'll tend the bar. Go on and tell Jude."

"It'll keep. We're busy."

"Good news is more fun when it's fresh. I'll handle it here, and close up as well. And as a return, you can give me the evening off tomorrow. If Kathy Duffy will take the kitchen. I haven't had a free evening in some time."

"Fair enough. I'll call Dad as well," he added as he flipped up the pass-through. "Unless you'd both rather I wait until morning when we can all speak to him."

"Go on and call." Darcy waved him out. "He'll want to know straight off. He was distracted," she said to Shawn when the door closed. "I'm not. Do you have something with Brenna in mind for tomorrow?"

Shawn merely took the empty glasses off her tray, set them in the bar sink. "You've customers, darling, and so have I." And he leaned over a bit. "You've your business. And so have I."

Miffed, Darcy jerked a shoulder. "It's not your business I care a damn about. But Brenna. She's a friend. You're nothing but a brother, and an irritant at that."

And knowing her irritant, she let it alone. She'd get nothing out of Shawn Gallagher, if he'd decided otherwise, with dynamite.

He had a plan. He was good at planning. That didn't mean it always worked, but he was good at the figuring out of how it should work.

There was cooking involved, and so he was in his element. He wanted something simple, a dish he could put together, then leave to itself until it was needed. So he made a tomato sauce with a bit of bite and left it to simmer.

It required a setting of the stage. That was something he preferred and something he believed would give him an advantage. He thought a man could use every advantage when it came to Brenna O'Toole.

It required a phone call, which he made from the pub at the end of the lunch shift when he was certain Brenna would be up to her neck in whatever job she was doing.

Just as he knew that, being Brenna, she'd come by after her workday to take a look at the broken washing machine he'd reported.

So when he got home, the sauce he'd left warming added an appetizing scent to the air. He picked some of the petunias and pansies that were happy to winter over in the garden and put these in the bedroom along with the candles he'd bought at the market.

He'd already changed the sheets for fresh, which had given him the idea about the washing machine.

Next there was music. It was too much a part of his life not to include it in any venture. He selected the CDs he liked best, slipped them into the canny little player he'd bought himself months before, then left them going while he went down to the kitchen to see to the rest.

He put out the cat, who it seemed sensed something important was going on and so put himself in the way at every opportunity.

He didn't expect to see her till near to six, which gave him enough time to put together a platter of finger food. He hunted up wineglasses, polished them out, then opened the bottle of red he'd taken from the pub, setting it on the counter to breathe.

After giving his sauce a last taste and stir, he glanced around and nodded in satisfaction. It was all fine and done. The clock showed ten minutes before six when he heard her lorry pull into his street.

"She's a timely sort," he murmured, and was taken by surprise when nerves set to dancing in his belly. "It's only Brenna, for Christ's sake," he told himself. "You've known her all your life."

Not in the way he was about to, he thought. Nor she him. He had a sudden wild urge to dash into the little mudroom and rip something off the washing machine and forget the rest.

And since when had a Gallagher been a coward? Especially with a woman? With this lecture playing in his head, he started toward the front door.

She was already coming in, carrying her toolbox. Her jeans had a fresh rip in them, just below the right knee. There was a faint smear of dirt across her cheek.

She closed the front door, took two steps, then saw him. And nearly jumped out of her work boots. "Jesus, Shawn, why not just cosh me over the head as scare the life out of me? What are you doing here this time of day?"

"I've the evening off. You parked behind my car, didn't you?"

"I did, yes, but I figured you'd walked down or gotten a lift." While she waited for her heart rate to return to normal, she sniffed the air. "Doesn't smell as though you've taken advantage of a free evening. What are you cooking?"

"A sauce for spaghetti. I thought I'd try it out before we gave it a go at the pub. Have you eaten?" he asked, though he already knew.

"I haven't, no. Ma's expecting me shortly."

She wasn't, as Shawn had called down to tell Mollie he'd give Brenna a meal while she was there. "Have your dinner here instead." He took her hand, leading her back to the kitchen. "You can judge the sauce for me."

"I might do that, but let's have a look at your machine first to see what the matter is."

"There's nothing the matter with it." He took her toolbox, set it out of the way on the floor.

"What do you mean, there's nothing the matter? Didn't you call up the hotel and say it wouldn't run for you at all?"

"I lied. Try this." He plucked up a stuffed olive and popped it into her mouth.

"Lied?"

"I did, yes. And I'm counting on the sin being worth the penance."

"But why would you . . ." Realization dawned slowly, and left her feeling awkward and edgy. "I

215

see. So this is the time and the place that suits you."

"Aye. I told your mother you'd be staying awhile, so you've no need to worry about that."

"Hmm." She looked around the kitchen, paying more attention. Fragrant sauce simmering, a pretty plate of fancy appetizers, a bottle of wine. "You might have given me a bit of notice. A little time to settle in to the notion."

"You've time now." He poured wine into the glasses. "I know wine tends to give you a head the next morning, but a glass or two shouldn't hurt."

She'd risk the hangover, if the wine managed to cool her throat. "You know you didn't have to bother with all this fuss for me. I told you from the start I didn't need it."

"Well, I do, and you'll just have to tolerate it." He was more at ease again, because she wasn't. He took a step toward her. "Take off your —" He nearly laughed when her eyes widened. "Your hat," he finished, then did so himself, setting it and his wine aside so he could run his hands through her hair until it tumbled in a way that most pleased him. "Have a seat."

He nudged her into a chair, sat across from her. "Why don't you take off your boots?"

She leaned down, tugged on the laces, then sat up again. "Do you have to watch me? You make me feel foolish."

"If you feel foolish with me watching you take off your boots, you're going to feel like a real horse's ass before much longer. Take off your boots, Brenna," he said in a quiet voice that sent a ripple running up her spine. "Unless you've changed your mind about the matter."

"I haven't." Annoyed, she bent down again to work on the boots. "I started this, and I finish what I start."

But it wasn't at all the way she'd imagined it. She'd simply pictured the two of them already naked, in bed, getting on with business. She hadn't given a great deal of thought to the mechanics of arriving there.

She kicked her boots under the table and made herself look back at him, steadily back at him.

"Are you hungry?"

"No." She couldn't conceive of eating under the circumstances. "Dad and I had a late lunch."

"All the better. We'll eat later. Let's take the wine upstairs."

Upstairs. All right, they'd go upstairs. It had been her idea, after all. But when he took her hand this time, she had to force herself not to bolt. "This isn't a fair way, Shawn. I've just come from working all day, and haven't had a chance to clean up."

"Would you like a shower, then?" As they walked up the back stairs, he rubbed the smudge from her cheek. "I'm happy to wash your back."

"I'm just saying, that's all." She couldn't shower with him, for God's sake. Not just like that. The music drifted toward her, a whisper of harpsong. Her nerves were screaming.

She stepped into the bedroom, saw the flowers,

the candles, the bed. And gulped her wine like water.

"Easy now." He nipped the glass from her hand. "I don't want you drunk."

"I can handle my drink," she began, then rubbed her damp palms on her thighs as he wandered around lighting candles. "There's no need for that. It's not full dark yet."

"It will be. I've seen you in candlelight before," he said easily as he touched the flame of the match to the candles he'd set on the narrow mantel over the fire he'd already set to glowing. "But I didn't take time to appreciate it. I will tonight."

"I don't see why you have to make the situation romantic instead of what it is."

"Not afraid of a little romance, are you, Mary Brenna?"

"No, but . . ." He turned, and the subtle and shifting lights of flame danced over his face, behind him, around him. He might have stepped out of one of the pictures Jude drew. Of faerie princes and valiant knights and poetic harpists.

"There's something about the way you look," she managed, "that makes my mouth water half the time. I don't much care for it, to be honest with you, and I'd prefer getting it out of my system."

"Well, now." His voice was as smooth as hers was annoyed. "Why don't we see what we can do about that?"

Keeping his eyes on hers, he crossed to her.

Twelve

However odd the situation, Brenna thought, it was still Shawn, a man she'd known and cared for all her life. However ridiculous it all seemed, she still wanted him.

Nerves were as out of place as the harpsong and the candlelight.

So when he laid his hands on her shoulders, when he ran them lightly down her arms to link with her hands, she tipped her head up. "If I laugh," she told him, "it's nothing personal. It's just the whole business of this that strikes me funny."

"All right."

Since he only stood watching her, seemed to be waiting, she rose to her toes and took his mouth with hers. She didn't mean to rush it, as she'd already concluded he wouldn't allow that in any case. But at that first taste she wanted more, she wanted it all. And quickly. Her hands flexed in his as she chewed on his bottom lip.

"I've got this powerful urge for you. I can't help it."

"Who's asking you to?" He wouldn't rush, no, but it was tempting to pick up the pace. That fascinating little body of hers was already vibrating against his, and her mouth was like a fever. But he thought it would be much more satisfying all around to let her drive him crazy for a while yet.

"Come up here." He let go of her hands to take her hips, to hitch her up so that her legs wrapped his waist as they'd done once before. "And kiss me again. I like it."

Now she did laugh, and the nerves that had worried her flitted away. "Do you, now? Well, as I recall, the first time I did it . . ." She brought her mouth to within a breath of his, then drew back — once, twice. "You looked as though I'd coshed you over the head with my hammer."

"That's because I wasn't expecting it, and you turned my brain upside down." He gave her bottom an intimate, and friendly, squeeze. "Bet you can't do it again."

"Oh, so it's a wager, is it?" Eyes glinting with the challenge, with the fun, she fisted her hands in his hair. "You're about to lose."

She put herself into her work, he had to give her that. He could all but feel his eyes roll back in his head as her mouth attacked his. There were times when surrender wasn't a humbling experience at all. There was a hint of wine still on her tongue, warm and rich. Mixed with her own flavor, it spun into him, a lovely and intoxicating combination.

Harpsong and candlelight, a hot-blooded woman twined around him. He let both the passion and the romance pump into his system. Alluring. Arousing. Pleasure took on a fine, sharp edge.

She felt his fingers dig into her hips, heard his breath quicken like a man who'd done a fast sprint up a long hill. When he shifted, turning toward the bed, triumph flashed through her.

She would have him now. Her way. Fast and furious and done. Then this terrible pressure in her chest, her belly, her head, would find release. Her breath caught in a laughing gasp when he spilled her onto the bed, then covered her, pressed her into the mattress, tight body to tight body.

"I'll have to give you that one." There was a gleam in her eye that only sharpened when he pulled her hands over her head and cuffed her wrists. "But now it's my turn. As I recall, the first time I kissed you, your eyes went blurry and blind." He closed his teeth gently over her jaw. "And you trembled."

Deliberately she arched her hips, pressed against him. "I'll bet you can't do it again."

A man that aroused, that ready, wouldn't dawdle. She was sure of it. Still, she braced herself. And still she trembled when his lips skimmed tenderly, tormentingly over hers. Her arms went limp, her mind blank as glass. The pressure that had built to crisis point slid into a glorious aching.

The first hint of the rising moon slipped into the room to shimmer silver against the gold of candle flames.

He cupped her breasts, his fingers tracing the shape of her against her work shirt, before moving to the buttons. She wore a man's white T-shirt beneath. After he tugged the denim aside, Shawn found himself fascinated at just how sexy her small breasts looked, felt, under that simple white cotton.

"I've always liked your hands." She had her eyes closed now, the better to absorb the little shocks of sensation. "I like them even better now." But when he lowered again, when his mouth closed over her through the cotton, her eyes flew open. "Oh, sweet Jesus."

He might have chuckled, if he could have found the breath for it. But his lungs were clogged, and his head already starting to reel. Where had this been all his life? This taste, this texture, this shape? How much more had he missed?

She was tugging off his sweater as he dragged her up. Breath ragged, they stared at each other. Whatever shock there was on both sides, she nodded as he did. "Too late," was all he said and pulled the shirt over her head.

"Thanks be to God."

They dived at each other.

His hands might have been faster now, and just a bit rough here and there. His mouth might have been hotter, more impatient than it had. But it didn't stop him from being thorough. He wanted every bit of her, and would remember always, the taste of her flesh, that tender spot just under her breast, the way that angle went to curve from her rib cage to her hip, and the silken feel of it all under his palm and fingertips.

The strength of her was no small matter, and outrageously erotic as they rolled together, as he felt her muscles bunch. Erotic still when he made that strength waver toward weakness, feeling her shudder against him when he found some new spot that pleased her.

The music was flutes now, lilting and faerie-like, a rise of pipes beneath it. The moonlight strengthened, a pearl gleam on the air that was fragrant with candle wax and turf smoke.

She buried her face against his throat, fighting to catch her breath. "Shawn, for God's sake. Now."

"Not yet, not yet, not yet." He said it like a chant. He wanted those small strong hands of hers never to stop running over him. He wanted to find more and still more of her with his own. Didn't those lovely legs deserve his attention now that he'd tugged the ripped denim away? And the back of her shoulder was such a marvelous place to linger.

"For a little thing, there's so much of you."

Desperate, she sank her teeth into him. "I'll die in a minute."

"Here, now. Here." And his mouth took hers again as he slid his hand between her legs, slipped his fingers into the heat.

She came in a flood, fast and full with her body bucking against him. He swallowed her cry of shock and release, absorbed it, savored it even as his blood burned for more.

Then she was pliant, soft as the wax that pooled at the base of his candles, and he was free to feast on her mouth, on her throat, on her breasts.

"Just let me have you for a while."

The pressure built again, layer by layer, slick and slippery until she slid off the edge a second time. How could he bear it? she wondered. His flesh was damp as hers, his heart leaping as high and fast, his body as tensed and ready.

Once again she arched against him, once again she wrapped her legs tight around his waist. And their eyes met in the shifting light.

"Now." He murmured it as he slipped into her, silky and smooth, as if they'd mated a thousand times before.

Her breath trembled in, then out. His hands covered hers, and she laced her fingers with his. They watched each other as they began to move.

Easy and lovely, like a dance remembered. Rising and falling, pleasure met with pleasure. Then, as if the music demanded it, a subtle quickening of pace. His eyes were darker now, that dreamy blue going opaque as he lost himself. When she tightened around him, when her eyelids fluttered closed and the moan rippled her throat, he held on, held on.

Then he buried his face in her hair and let himself go.

She was going to need a minute. Perhaps an hour. A day or two might be best. After that, she imagined she could move again, or at the very least think about moving. But for now it seemed like the finest of ideas to just stay as she was, sprawled over

Shawn's bed with him plastering her into the mattress.

Her body was absolutely golden. She imagined that if she had the energy to open her eyes and look, she'd see it glow in the dark.

It was just as she'd said before. Once the man stopped thinking, he did a fine job of things.

"You aren't cold, are you?" His voice was muffled and sleepy.

"I doubt I'd be cold if we were lying naked on an ice floe heading for Greenland."

"Good." He shifted, settled in. "Let's just be here for a little while yet."

"Just don't fall asleep on top of me."

He made some sound, and nuzzled. "I like the way your hair smells."

"Sawdust?"

"There's some of that. It's nice enough. And there's a hint of lemon with it."

"It's probably the shampoo I stole from Patty." Her body was waking up again, and she began to take more notice to the way he fit against her, the way their legs were tangled. Even as interest began to stir, she also noticed the sheer weight of him.

"You're heavier than you look."

"Sorry." He tucked an arm under her and rolled. "Better?"

"It wasn't so bad before." But, now that he mentioned it, it was better to be able to cross her arms over his chest and look down at his face. It was so damn pretty, that face, that she didn't even mind, for now, the smug way his lips were curved. "I have to say, Shawn, you're better at the entire business than I figured on."

He opened his eyes. The blue of them was dreamy again. "Well, I'll admit to having some practice over the years."

"I won't complain about that, but there's a problem just the same."

"Is there?" He picked up a lock of her hair, twined the curl of it around his finger. "And what would it be?"

"Well, my idea, originally, was that we'd have sex."

"I recall you mentioning it." He let the curl unwind, then fall, then chose another. "And I have to admit, a fine idea it was."

"That was the first part. I mentioned as well that I was looking to do that in order to get this urge I had for you out of my system."

"I recall that as well. An itch, you said." He ran his nails lightly down her back. "I've done my best to scratch it for you."

"You did, and I'd never deny it. But that's the problem part." Watching him, she trailed a finger along his collarbone, up the side of his neck. And watched his lashes flutter until his eyes were a slit of blue behind them.

"Well, what's your problem, then, O'Toole?"

"You see, it hasn't appeared to work, as yet. It seems I've still got this itch. So we'll just have to have sex again."

"If we must, we must." He sat up, taking her with him. "Let's have a shower and a meal first, then we'll see what can be done."

Chuckling, she laid her hands on his cheeks. "We're still friends, too, aren't we?"

"We're still friends." He cuddled her closer, and intended for the kiss to be light and affectionate. But he sank into her.

Her mind was going fuzzy when he turned to lay her back on the bed. Her arms were reaching up for him as she said, "What about the shower and the meal?"

"Later."

It was later, and a great deal later, and they both ate like starving wolves. Here it was easy to fall back into friendship, to be two people who'd shared meals hundreds of times before.

Did you know Betsy Clooney's whole brood's down with the chicken pox?

Have you noticed Jack Brennan's eyeing Theresa Fitzgerald now that she and Colin Riley have broken things off?

Between bites she told him of her sister Patty's latest flood of tears over whether to have pink or yellow roses in her bridal bouquet. And they lifted a glass to toast the closure of the deal with Magee.

"Are you thinking he'll send a man out to get the lay of the land and design the theater?" Brenna got up to let Bub in when he came scratching at the door.

"If that's his plan, it hasn't come down to me as yet." He watched the cat slink over to Brenna to rub against her leg.

"Sure, it's the only way it can be done correctly." She considered another serving, then decided if she gave in to greed on that, she'd suffer. With a little regret, she pushed her plate away. "He can't be sitting up in his lofty office in New York City and design what should be here in Ardmore."

"And how do you know he has a lofty office?"

"The rich are fond of lofty." Grinning, she kicked back in her chair. "Ask Darcy if lofty isn't an aim when she finds the rich man she's hunting for. In any case, they have to see what we are and what we have before they set in their minds what we'll be."

"I'll agree with that." He rose to clear the table. "I liked your design. Maybe you could draw it up a little more formally. We could give Aidan a look at it. If he likes it as I do, there's nothing stopping us from passing it onto the Magee for his consideration."

For a moment she simply sat. "You'd do that?"

He glanced over his shoulder as he ran hot water and soap into the sink. "Why wouldn't I?"

"It would mean a great deal. Even if Magee laughs it off and tosses it aside, it would matter to me. I'm not an architect or engineer or anything that . . . lofty," she decided as she got to her feet. "But I've always had a yen to have a hand in the designing and the building of something, from the ground up."

"You get a picture in your head," he said. "An empty field or lot and what you'd put on it right down to the fancy work."

"That's right, yes. How did you know?"

"It's not so different from building a song."

Thinking of it, she frowned at his back. Never once had she considered that they had anything in common in that area. "I suppose you're right. I'll draw it up for you as best I can. Whether the Magee takes a look at it or not, I'm grateful to you for thinking of it."

She helped him clean up, then as it was nearing midnight, said she had to go.

He walked her out, and they'd made it nearly to the front door before he changed his mind. He settled it by simply plucking her up, hauling her over his shoulder and carting her up to bed once again.

As a result it was half-one when she crept into her house. Creeping was about all she had the energy for. Who would have thought the man could near to wear her out?

She switched off the light her mother had left on for her. Even in the dark she knew which boards, which part of the steps, would creak underfoot. She made it upstairs and into her room without a sound.

And since she wasn't a mother, she was comfortably unaware that her own had heard her despite the precautions.

Once she slipped into bed, she let out a long sigh, shut her eyes, and fell instantly asleep.

And in sleep dreamed of a silver palace beneath a green hill. Around it grew flowers and grand trees that stood out like paintings in the gilded light. A ribbon of river ran through them, with little diamonds sparkling on its surface in a flash here and there that shocked the eye.

A bridge arched over it, its stones marble-white. As she crossed it, she heard the click of her own boots, the bubble of the water below, and the quick skip of her own heart that wasn't fear but excitement.

The trees, she saw, were heavy with golden apples, silver pears. For an instant she was tempted to pluck one, to bite into that rich flesh and taste. But even in dreams, she knew that if you visited a fearie raft, you could eat nothing, and drink only water, or you were bound there for a hundred years.

So she only watched the jeweled fruit glint.

And the path leading under them, from the white bridge to the great silver door of the palace, was red as rubies.

As she approached the door, it opened, and out of it spilled the music of pipes and flutes.

She stepped inside, into the music and into perfumed air where torches as tall as men lined the walls with flames that shot as high and true as arrows.

The hall was wide and filled with flowers. There were chairs, with curvy arms and deep cushions, all the color of precious gems. But she saw no one.

Following the music, she climbed the stairs, trailing her hand along a banister that was smooth as silk and glinted like a long, slender sapphire.

Still there was no sound but the music, no movement but her own.

At the top of the stairs there was another long

corridor, as wide as the space two grown men would make were they laid head to foot. To her left as she traveled along the corridor was a door of topaz, and to the right, one of emerald. Straight ahead was a third that glowed white as pearls.

And it was from there that the music came.

She opened the white door and stepped inside.

Flowers twined and tangled up the walls. Tables the size of lakes groaned under the weight of platters filled with food. The scents were sensuous.

The floor was a mosaic, a symphony of jewels placed in random patterns.

There were chairs and cushions and plush sofas, but all were empty. All but the throne at the room's head. There, lounging in the grandeur, was a man in a silver doublet.

"You never hesitated," he said. "There's courage in that. Not once did you think of turning around. You just walked straight into what's unknown to you."

He offered her a smile, and with a wave of his hand, the gold apple that appeared in it. "You may have a taste for this."

"I may, but I haven't a century to spare you."

He laughed, and flicking his fingers, vanished the apple. "I wouldn't have let you, as I've more use for you above than here."

Curious, she turned in a circle. "Are you alone, then?"

"Not alone, no. Even faeries like to sleep. The light was to guide you. It's night here, as it is in

your world. I wanted to speak with you, and preferred to do so alone."

"Well, then." She lifted her arms, let them fall.
"I'm here."

"I've a question for you, Mary Brenna O'Toole."

"I'll try to answer it, Carrick, Prince of Faeries."

His lips twitched again with amused approval,
but his eyes were intense and sober as he leaned toward her. "Would you take a pearl from a lover?"

An odd question indeed, she thought. But after
all, it was a dream, and she'd had stranger ones. "I
would, if it was given freely."

With a sigh, he tapped his hand on the wide arm
of his throne. The ring he wore flashed silver and
blue. "Why is it there are always strings attached to
answers when dealing with mortals?"

"Why is it faeries are never satisfied with an
honest answer?"

Humor brightened his eyes. "You're a bold one,
aren't you? It's a fortunate thing I've a fondness for
mortals."

"I know you have." She walked closer now. "I've
seen your lady. She pines for you. I don't know if
that heavies your heart or lightens it, but it's what I
know."

Resting his chin on his feet, he brooded. "I know
her heart, now that it's too late for me to do much
more than wait. Must there be pain in love before
there's fulfillment?"

"I haven't the answer."

"You've part of it," he muttered, and straightened again. "You are part of the answer. Tell me

232

now, what's in your heart for Shawn Gallagher."
Before she could speak, he lifted a hand in
warning. He'd seen the temper flash over her face.
"Before you speak, mind this. You're in my world
here, and it's the simplest of matters for me to
make you speak truth. Only truth. We both prefer
you answer of your own will."

"I don't know what's in my heart. You'll have to
take that as your truth, for I've nothing more."

"Then it's time you looked, and time you knew,
isn't it?" He sighed again, not troubling to hide his
disgust. "But you won't till you're ready. Go on to
sleep, then."

With a sweep of his arm, he was alone with his
thoughts in the jeweled light. And Brenna slept,
dreamlessly now, in her bed.

She got no more than four hours' sleep, but went
through the day fueled with energy. Most often a
late night followed by an early morning left her out
of sorts and cross most of the day. But in this case,
she was so cheerful that her father commented on
her bright mood more than once.

She didn't feel she could tell him what she told
herself. It was good, healthy sex that had her
whistling through her work. As close as they were,
and as much as she loved him, she doubted her father would want to know how she'd spent her evening.

She remembered the dream, remembered it so
clearly, so precisely, that she wondered if she was
filling in some blanks without meaning to. But it

wasn't anything she was going to muddle over for long.

"That's about all for the day, wouldn't you say, Brenna darling?" Mick straightened up, stretched his back, then glanced over to where his daughter was squatted down painting the floor molding. His lips pursed when he noted she was painting the same six inches over and over with lazy swipes of the brush.

"Brenna?"

"Hmm?"

"Don't you think you might have just about enough paint on that space of wood by this time?"

"What? Oh." She dipped the brush again, then made sure to hit the fresh wood. "My mind must've wandered."

"It's time to call it a day."

"Already?"

With a shake of his head, he gathered up brushes, rollers, and pans. "What was it your mother put in your oatmeal this morning to give you such pep? And why didn't I have any?"

"The day went by fast, that's all." She got to her feet, looked around. With some surprise she noted just how much had been done. She'd gone through the day on automatic pilot, she supposed. "We've nearly finished in here."

"By tomorrow, it'll be on to the next. We deserve big portions of that roast your mother promised for tonight."

"You're tired, Dad. I'll clean this up." That, at least, would soften some of the guilt she was going to feel. "And you know, I was thinking I'd go on into the pub and see Darcy. Would you tell Ma I'll be grabbing a sandwich there?"

He looked pained when she took the brushes from him. "You're after deserting me, when you know sure as you're born your mother and Patty will be into the wedding plans and buzzing around me ears."

Brenna shot him a grin. She'd forgotten about that and the more genuine excuse not to go straight home. "Want to come to the pub with me?"

"You know I would, but then your mother'd have my head on her best china platter. At least give me your word that when your time comes 'round you won't ask me if I like the lace or the silk best, then burst into tears when I pick the wrong one."

"A solemn promise." She kissed his cheek to seal it.

"I'm holding you to it, girl." He shrugged his jacket on. "And if things get over sticky at home, you may see me down at Gallagher's after all."

"I'll buy you a pint."

When he was gone, Brenna put more time and effort into the cleaning than she had to. It made her feel a little less guilty, though truth to tell, she would be seeing Darcy when she went to the village. If she saw Shawn as well, how could she help it. He worked there, didn't he?

Despite the rationalization, Brenna made a point of seeking Darcy out the minute she walked into the pub. Since she was down at the end of the bar letting old Mr. Riley flirt with her, Brenna took the next stool, then leaned over to kiss the man's papery cheek.

"And here I find you making eyes at another woman, when time and time again, you've said you had them for none but me."

"Oh, now, darling, a man's got to look in the direction his head's pointed. But I've been waiting for you to come along and sit on my knee."

The man was so thin, and she suspected, his bones so brittle, that an attempt to sit on his knee would shatter it. "Oh, we O'Toole women are jealous creatures, dear Mr. Riley. Now I'm after taking Darcy here aside and giving her a stern piece of my mind for trying to beat my time with you."

When he cackled, she wandered to a table, gesturing for Darcy to follow. "I'm dying for a pint and a hot meal. What's Shawn got for us tonight?"

Darcy narrowed bright-blue eyes, cocked a dark brow, then fisted a hand on her hip. "Well, then, you've gone and slept with him, haven't you?"

"What are you talking about?" Though Darcy's voice had been quiet, Brenna's head swiveled in panicked embarrassment until she was assured no one was close enough to hear.

"You think I can't look at a woman I've known since I was born and not see she's had a tumble the night before? With Shawn, you can't be sure, as he's half the time got that dreaming look in his eyes. But you, that's a different kettle."

"So what if I did?" Brenna hissed it as she sat

down. "I said I was going to. And no," she said as soon as she caught the glint. "I won't be telling you about it."

"Who said I'd want to know?" But of course she did. She sat herself, leaned close. "One thing."

"No, not even one."

"One thing — we've had one thing no matter who or what our whole lives."

"Damn it." It was true, and to break tradition now would be breaking a bond. "Four times last night."

"Four?" Eyes widened, Darcy looked toward the kitchen as if she could peer right through the door and pin her brother to the opposite wall. "Well, I have to give him a raise in my estimation. And it's hardly a wonder you're looking relaxed."

"I feel wonderful. Does it really show?"

"You have to look for it. I've customers." Reluctantly, Darcy rose. "I'll get you a pint — and I'd try the poached chicken tonight. People have been pleased with it."

"I will then, but I think I'll see if I can't have it back in the kitchen."

"Fine. Get your own pint on your way. Do you want to stay up with me tonight? I'll bet I can get a bit more out of you."

"You probably could, as you're a sneaky, nagging sort, but I need to go home early. I didn't get much sleep last night."

"Braggart," Darcy said with a laugh and flounced off to take an order.

"And how are you, Brenna?" Aidan asked when

she came behind the bar.

"Why? How do I look?"

He glanced over, as her response had been so sharp. "Well, you look fine to me."

"I am fine." Cursing herself under her breath, she drew a pint of Harp from the tap. "I'm a bit tired, I suppose. I thought I'd have this and a plate back in the kitchen, if it's all right with you, before I head home."

"You're welcome, as always."

"Ah, will you need an extra hand at all this week, Aidan?"

"I could use yours both Friday and Saturday nights, if you have them free."

"They are. I'll come 'round." Casually, she hoped, she moved past and pushed open the kitchen door. "Can you spare a hungry woman a hot meal?"

He turned from the sink where he had the water running hot and full. His eyes warmed as she lifted her glass to his own lips. "I think I might have something you'll like. I wondered if you'd wander my way tonight."

"I wanted to see Darcy." She laughed and sat down with her beer. "And maybe I don't mind so much seeing you as well."

He turned the water off, pulled at the cloth tucked into his waistband, and dried his hands. "And how would your system be?"

"Oh, my system's doing well, thank you. Though there does seem to be a little bit of a hitch in it still."

"Would you be wanting some help with that?"

"I wouldn't mind it."

He walked to her chair, and leaning over the back of it, sent the system under discussion churning with his teeth on her ear. "Come home with me tonight."

She shivered, couldn't help it. There was something unspeakably erotic about the voice, the suggestion, when she couldn't see his face. "I can't. You know I can't. It'd be too hard to explain to my family."

"I don't know when I can get another night off."

Her vision wavered, doubled as he did something clever with his tongue behind her ear. "How about mornings?"

"It so happens all my mornings, for the foreseeable future, are free."

"I'll come by, the first chance I get."

He straightened, then plucking off her cap, ran a hand down her hair in a way that made her want to stretch like a cat. And purr. "The door's always open."

Thirteen

The morning was soft. Gentle rain pattered over flowers coming awake for spring. Fog, very thin and nearly white, skimmed along the ground and would be burned away at the first ray of sun to beam through the clouds.

Faerie Hill Cottage was quiet when Brenna stepped inside. Even faeries like to sleep, she remembered. Perhaps ghosts did as well, and chose gray and rainy dawns for their dreaming times.

For herself, she was full of energy, and she knew exactly how she planned to use it.

She sat at the base of the stairs to take off her boots, then decided it was as good a place as any to dispense with her jacket and cap as well. When she hung the cap on the newel post, she tapped a finger lightly to the little faerie pin she kept hooked there. It had outlasted a number of caps.

She wondered if anyone but Shawn would have thought to give it to her, as he had years before. Most, when they gave her gifts, chose something practical. A tool or a book, warm socks or a sturdy work shirt.

That was how most saw her, after all. How she saw herself if it came to it. A practical person with little time for the foolish or the pretty.

But from Shawn it had been a little silver faerie with slanted eyes and pointed wings.

And she wondered if someone else had given it to her, would she have worn it nearly every day since, without really thinking about it.

She didn't know the answer to either, nor the meaning of either. So she shrugged, thinking that was just the way it was between them.

However it was, her pulse quickened as she climbed the stairs.

He was sleeping, all but buried under sheets and blankets, and dead center of the bed, like a man who was used to having the place to himself. The cat made a black circle on the foot of the covers, but opened his eyes, a cool, steady gleam, when Brenna stepped in.

"Guarding him, are you? Well, he'll never hear it from me. Now then, unless you're after being embarrassed, or envious, in very short order I'd take myself off somewhere else."

Bub arched his back, then, as if it was an afterthought, leaped down to wind his way through Brenna's legs. She reached to give him one long stroke. "Sorry, darling, but I've a mind to pet someone else this morning."

The man surely made use of every inch of bed. Well, he was about to share it, she thought, and unbuttoned her shirt.

If he'd bothered to build a fire the night before, it had died to ash. Kindling one now to chase the chill away might wake him. She had plans to do that by other methods altogether.

He was a quiet sleeper, she noted as she stripped down to the skin. One who appeared to nestle into dreams without a lot of rolling about. As she recalled, he slept deep as well — hadn't she heard Mrs. Gallagher shout him awake dozens of times when she'd spent the night with Darcy down the hall?

So they would soon see how much time and trouble it took to wake him by other means.

It was exciting to watch him when he didn't know, when he was defenseless, when he had no idea of what she had in mind for him. His face held both strength and beauty, and, she supposed, a kind of innocence now. But then, she'd always considered Shawn a great deal more innocent than herself.

He believed in things. Believed they would just happen along at the right time without a body having to take a hand in it, put their back into it. That's what bothered her the most about him when it came to his music. What did the man think, that someone would just wander into the cottage and buy up the tunes he had scribbled on papers?

It wasn't enough to write them. Why didn't he see that? Bone-lazy, she supposed, then shook her head. If she kept thinking of that, she'd work herself right out of the mood. And that would be a terrible waste of a morning.

Naked, she walked to the bed, slipped under the covers, and straddled him. Her mouth fit over his.

She intended to start the process with a reverse on the waking of Sleeping Beauty. But she didn't intend to stop with a kiss.

He was steeped in dreams, all a blur of color and shape. A pleasant place to be. Sensation slowly weaved its way through. The warm flavor of woman that stirred the blood and roused the mind. Then the scent of her — subtle, familiar, so that the next indrawn breath thickened the pulse. And the shape of her, the feel of flesh sliding along flesh.

He lifted a hand, lost it in that wonderfully wild tangle of hair. Even as he murmured her name, she was shifting over him, surrounding him, taking him in. The first burst of lust exploded inside him while he was still half sleeping.

He thrust up into her, helpless, trapped in a web of need woven while he'd been dreaming. For the first time in memory he could do nothing to finesse control over his own body. Nothing but let himself be taken.

When he opened his eyes, she rose over him in the soft gray light, her hair bright as fire, her eyes sharp and green. Then she bowed back, fisting her hands in her own hair as she rode them both to finish.

"Mother of God," was all he could manage, and nothing could have pleased her more.

"Good morning to you." She felt golden and bright. "And that's all the time I have for you. I've got to be going."

"What? Why?" He grabbed for her hand, but she

slipped nimbly out of reach.

"Well, I'm finished with you, boyo, and I've work to do."

"Come back." He thought about sitting up, but only rolled to his side. "I'll do better by you now that I'm waking up."

"I did well enough by both of us." She tugged her T-shirt on, then shrugged the flannel one over it. "And I'm expected at the hotel. As it is, I've got to take at least a quick look at your car, since I told Dad that was why I was coming by here first."

"Tonight, then." He only grunted when the cat leaped up on his ass and nipped it with his claws. "Find a way and stay here tonight."

"Stay" was the word that made her uneasy, but she snuck a glance at him while she pulled on her work pants. His eyes were half closed. "I'm working at the pub tomorrow night. I can say I'm sleeping over with Darcy."

"Why do you have to lie?"

"You know how people would talk if anyone knew we were seeing each other this way."

"And that matters?"

"Of course it does." This time when she looked over at him, she was surprised to note his eyes weren't sleepy, but focused and alert.

"Is this something that shames you, then, Brenna?"

"No. But it's private. I'll have a look at your car now, and the fact is I'll give it a good going-over first chance I have." She leaned over to kiss him, then shoved back her hair. "I'll be back 'round soon as I can."

He rolled over onto his back, annoying Bub enough to set the cat to stalking off again. Alone, he stared at the ceiling until he heard her shut the front door behind her.

When, he wondered, had he started wanting more? Why should she be the one he wanted more from? What was this need that was growing inside him? Had it always been there?

Questions, he thought in disgust. Well, he seemed to have plenty of them, without the first answer.

He rolled out of bed and might have sulked off into the shower, but the sound of his own car starting up drew him to the window.

Brenna was just rounding to the bonnet, and as he watched she yanked it open, stuck her head under. He imagined she was already muttering curses because he'd neglected this or allowed that to get dirty. It never did him a bit of good to tell her that as far as he was concerned everything in there was dirty and mysterious and not of any particular interest to him. As long as the engine started when he turned the key, he didn't give a rat's ass what made the whole business possible.

She would, of course. A born tinkerer was Brenna. She was never happier than when she had something taken apart and all the pieces of it spread out for her examination. It made him think he should ask her to have a go at his toaster, as it was burning one side of everything he put in it.

245

Then she pulled her head out, slammed the bonnet smartly. She shot a look up at the window where he was standing, and her eyes, full of righteous annoyance, flashed to his. He sent her what he knew was a cheeky grin in return before she stomped off to her lorry. The way her mouth was moving, he assumed she was assigning him to the devil.

Rain sprinkled down on her as she hitched herself into her lorry. He watched as she, with her usual energy and carelessness, bulleted in reverse into the road, then zipped away over bumps.

But he was no longer smiling. Amusement had fallen away into sheer shock. He had one of the answers now, and he didn't care for it one bit.

He was in love with her.

"Bloody, stinking hell. What in the wide world am I supposed to do with that?" He started to jam his hands into his pockets, but got no satisfaction, as he was naked. He turned, intending to drown himself in the shower in the hopes the feeling would pass.

Lady Gwen stood just inside the doorway, her hands folded neatly, watching him.

"Sweet Jesus." However foolish it was, he snatched the blanket from the bed and wrapped it around him. "A man's entitled to his privacy in his own home."

Flustered and fumbling, he stared back at her. She looked as real as he felt, and as lovely as all the legends professed. Now her eyes were full of quiet sympathy, and an understanding that had his gut churning uneasily.

She was there, no question that she was there, and the cat had come back to ribbon around her skirts and purr ferociously.

"So, is this what you were waiting for before you showed yourself to me? For me to realize something that hurts? Well, it's said misery loves company, but I prefer to nurse my own wounds alone."

She walked to him, graceful, dignified, those soft eyes swimming with emotion. He saw her lift a hand, and though he felt no pressure, no slide of skin to skin, he felt the touch of it against his cheek as gentle comfort.

Then she was gone.

He did what he usually did when he came up against something he didn't want to deal with. He tucked it into a corner of his mind, trusting he'd work out some solution eventually, and dived into his music.

It balanced him, fed his heart. As close as he was to his family, he'd never been able to explain what it meant to him to be able to hear music in his head, to feel it inside him, then to be able to make it sound in the air.

It was the one thing he'd always had — and having, needed — and needing, feared losing.

Until Brenna.

He'd always had her as well, and needed her without realizing how deep that need was rooted.

247

And now knowing, he feared losing her, and what he'd just discovered.

Thoughtfully, he opened the little box he'd put on the piano. Inside he'd placed the pearl he'd been given at Maude's grave. He understood now what Carrick wanted him to do with it. But he was far from ready to offer that pearl, and himself, to Brenna.

Whatever others had planned for him, he would move in his own time, and in his own way. He'd promised Brenna friendship. He wouldn't go back on his word, but he was beginning to understand just what keeping it would cost him if he couldn't win the whole of her heart.

The woman who'd come to his bed that morning wasn't looking for romance and the promise of a future. She was looking only at the moment and the pleasures it could bring.

He hadn't been so different himself, at other times, with other women. It didn't sit comfortably to be the one pining. Since comfort was important to him, he didn't intend to pine for long.

It was just a matter of figuring which steps to take, in what order and in which direction. And as it was Brenna, he knew that he would get to his objective faster, and smoother, if he found a way to make her believe it was all her idea in the first place.

So . . . he ran his hands lightly over the keys. He just had to work it out so that he was in the position of being courted by Brenna O'Toole.

He was amused enough by the notion that his

fingers began to move faster, to make the tune live-lier. Even as he stopped to scribble down the notes, words began to jump into his head.

Come back 'round so you can catch me. I'll give you a dance as long as you please. But circle back soon, my red-haired lovely, for it's only you I'm wanting to tease. Now kiss me quick and say that you'll love me from now till ever birds sing in the trees. I'm waiting right here so you can convince me the time's come to get down on my knees.

It made him see the humor of it all, and smoothed out the knot of tension from the back of his neck. After all, how could anyone who knew the pair of them not see the absurdity of it?

She the planner, he the dreamer. Why, they rammed up against each other's basic personalities at least as often as they meshed. Well, what did the heart know about the logic of things? And, he was wise enough to know that if he'd fallen for someone more like himself, they'd while their lives away without getting the first thing accomplished.

And though he couldn't think of a man like Brenna, he imagined if she'd come across one, the two of them would hammer each other's brains out within a week.

So, in the big scheme of things, by falling in love with her, and arranging for her to decide they should make what was between them a permanent thing, he was only saving her from a brief, and certainly violent, life.

Though he thought it might be best all 'round if he kept that opinion strictly to himself.

Satisfied, he closed the pearl back in its box, left his music scattered about, and went off to start his day of work.

He baked apple tarts with Brenna's appetite in mind. If he was going to approach the business from a kind of role-reversal angle, baking one of her favorite weaknesses seemed rather canny.

He toyed with the idea of trying to talk himself out of being in love with her, as he imagined people did when the fit wasn't as comfortable as they might prefer. He even imagined he could do a fair job of it, starting with listing all the reasons why it wasn't a wise idea. The head of that would be the simple fact that he hadn't planned on falling in love, not seriously, for years yet.

And when he imagined the woman on the receiving end, it was always a soft, feminine, gentle-natured sort. A *comfortable* woman, he thought as he trimmed his pastry. There was nothing comfortable about the O'Toole, for all she was a blessing in bed. After all, much as it appealed, a man couldn't spend his life in bed with a hot-blooded, naked woman.

Which made him think about the morning, and the way she'd ridden him to a blind, sweaty finish before his brain had even waked up. Which made him a great deal less comfortable altogether. So, being Shawn, he put that thought away. For the time being.

It hadn't been the sex he'd fallen in love with. That had simply been the key that opened him up so he'd see what had been waiting inside him for her. She'd never be an easy woman. God knew she'd poke and she'd prod at him until he was ready to throttle her. She would pick fights and would always find the way to put his own temper on the boil.

But Jesus, she could make him laugh. And she knew half of what was in his mind before he'd gotten the words out. There was treasure in that. She knew his every flaw, and didn't hold any of them against him overmuch.

She didn't think much of his music, and that stung more than a little. But he chose to think it just a lack of understanding. Just as he had no interest or knowledge of what mysteries were under the bonnet of his car.

Whatever the weight of the scale, for or against, didn't matter. His heart was already hers. All he had to do was make her realize she wanted to keep it.

He fancied up the pastries, adding bits of dough in little designs, the way he'd seen in a picture somewhere. After brushing the lot of them with egg wash, he popped them into the oven.

When Darcy came in he was whistling over the Gallagher's Irish stew he had simmering in his big pot.

"My larder's bare as the top of Rory O'Hara's head. I need a sandwich before shift starts."

"I'll make it." Shawn cut her off before she could grab from the refrigerator. "You'll just leave a mess for me to clean up otherwise."

"I'll have some of that roast beef if there's any left."

"There's enough."

"Well, then, don't be stingy." She sat, propping her legs on the chair beside her, as much to admire her new shoes as to rest her feet before the long shift ahead. When she noted the bowls he'd yet to wash, she sniffed the air. "Is that apple tarts you have in the oven?"

"It might be. And I might see there's one left for you, if you don't badger me."

Experimentally, she ran a finger around the inside of the bowl that had held the filling and licked. "I seem to recall that Brenna favors apple tarts particularly."

Shawn sliced the sandwich neatly in two, knowing Darcy would complain otherwise. "I recall that as well." His expression bland, he slid the sandwich in front of her.

"Are you —" Darcy cut herself off, picked up the first half of her lunch. "No, I don't want to know. My best friend and my brother," she said over the first bite. "I never thought to have to work to keep that image out of my head."

"Well, keep working at it." Curious, he sat across from her. "You're friends with Jude, and it never seemed to bother you that she and Aidan —"

"I was *new* friends with Jude." Darcy stared at him over her sandwich with eyes that were blue and sulky. "It's a different matter entirely. It has to be your face," she decided. "Because she knows you through and through, so it's certainly not your riveting personality. She's just dazzled by the look of you, as there's no denying you've a strong and handsome face."

"You're only saying that because we look so much alike."

Her teeth flashed before she bit in again. "That's true enough. But we can't help being beautiful, can we, darling?"

"We can only do our best to bear the terrible weight of it. Then offer it up." He said it ponderously and made her snicker.

"Well, it's a burden I enjoy carrying. And if a man doesn't want to look any further than my face, I've nothing to complain over. It's enough that I know I've a mind behind it."

"Is the Dubliner you've been seeing treating you like a pet, then?"

She moved a shoulder, annoyed with herself for being dissatisfied with a relationship that held so much potential. "He enjoys my company and takes me nice places in fine style." And because it was Shawn, she could hiss out a breath. "Where he spends half the time bragging about himself and his work and expecting me to be impressed beyond speech. And the thing of it is, he's not nearly as smart as he thinks he is, and owes most of his accomplishments, such as they are, to family connections rather than his own hard work or skill."

"You're tired of him."

She opened her mouth, closed it again, then shrugged. "I am, yes. What's wrong with me?"

"If I tell you, you'll be after throwing that plate at me."

"I won't." As a sign of truce, she pushed it aside. "This time."

"All right, then, I'll tell you what's the matter. You underestimate yourself, Darcy, then you get annoyed when others do the same. You don't have any respect for the men who fall at your feet, promising to give you the world on a platter. You've filled your own platter all your life and carried it with your own hands. And you know you can keep doing it."

"I want more." She said it fiercely, finding herself inexplicably on the verge of tears. "What's wrong with wanting more?"

"Nothing. Nothing at all." He reached out to close his hand over hers.

"I want to go places, see things. *Have* things." She shoved away from the table, prowling the kitchen as if it were a cage. "I can't help wanting it. Everything would be easier if I could be a little bit in love with him. Just a little would be enough. But I'm not, and I can't talk myself into it. So I woke up this morning knowing I'd be breaking it off, and tossing away a lovely trip to Paris."

"That's the right thing to do."

"I'm not doing it because it's the right thing to do." Frustrated, she threw up her hands. "I'm doing it because I'm not having my first trip to Paris spoiled by sharing it with a man who'd bore my brains out. Shawn." She came back to the table, sat again, and leaning forward, spoke seriously. "I'm not a nice person."

He took her hand again, patted it. "I love you anyway."

It took her a minute, then her eyes lit with appreciation. "I should have known better than to expect you to list my virtues. But I feel better in any case." Because she did, she dipped her finger in the bowl again, scooped out another smear of filling. "I wish I could find someone to have a bit of fun and frolic with, like you and Brenna."

She might not have caught it, the quick change in the eyes before he rose to clear the table. But she knew him as well as, often better than, she knew herself. "Damn it all. I was afraid of this. You've gone and fallen for her, haven't you?"

"It's not for you to worry about."

"It is, of course it is, when I love both of you. You great blockhead. Couldn't you just enjoy yourself, like any other man?"

He thought of that morning, and licked a bit of apple filling himself. "I am enjoying myself."

"And how long will that last now that you've fallen in love with her?"

Interested, he glanced back at her as he began to work. "Does the fun go out of such matters when love walks in?"

"It does when it only walks through one of the doors and the other stays shut."

"You don't have much confidence in me, for finding a way of opening a closed door if I put my mind to it."

"Shawn, I don't want to hurt you, and neither

would Brenna, but she told me straight out that she only wanted to sleep with you."

"She was clear enough about what she wanted." This time he smiled. "I want more. What's wrong with wanting more?"

"This isn't the time to throw my own words back at my head. I'm worried for you."

"Don't be." He washed the largest of the bowls by hand rather than crowd the dishwasher. "I know what I'm about. I can't help my feelings. And before you say it," he continued, "I know she can't help hers either. But what's wrong with doing what I can to change her feelings?"

"The minute she thinks you're courting her —"

"But I won't be. She'll be courting me."

Darcy's first response was a snort, but then she stopped, considered. "Aren't you the clever one?" she murmured.

"Clever enough to know Brenna will prefer to do the persuading rather than be the persuaded." He checked his tarts, adjusted the heat. "I expect what we've said here to stay here, between the two of us."

"As if I'd go running off to tell Brenna what falls out of your mouth." Insulted, she grabbed a tray. His stare from under raised brows made her relent. "All right, in the general way of things that's what I do, but this is a different matter. You can trust me."

He knew he could. She might try to fracture his skull with a flying plate, but Darcy would bite off her tongue before betraying a confidence. "I suppose that means you won't be carrying back to me whatever she might have to say, about . . . certain things."

"It does, indeed. Look for your spies elsewhere, my lad." Nose in the air, she started to flounce out. Then there came a hiss of breath from her and she stopped. "She doesn't think she's built in a particularly attractive way."

Since it was the last thing he'd expected to hear, Shawn merely stared until Darcy cursed under her breath.

"I'm only telling you because she never said it outright to me in just those words. But she thinks of her body as a practical thing, and not as female as it could be. She doesn't think men find her particularly attractive — female-like. And that's why the sex is just sex in her thinking. She doesn't believe a man might look at her in a romantic or tender sort of way."

She paused a moment, tried not to wonder if Brenna would forgive her if her friend knew she'd said such things. "A woman likes to be told . . . well, if you've any brain in your head, you should know what a woman likes to be told. And it's not a matter of just grabbing hold of what's different from yours, but *telling*. Now, close your mouth because you look half-witted."

She let the door swing shut behind her.

Fourteen

"And you'll remember Dennis Magee who went off to America — well, neither of us remembers it precisely, as it's been fifty years if it's a day and we weren't yet born, or barely so in my own case, at the time he left Old Parish. But you'll remember hearing of it and how he made his fortune with land and building and such over in New York City."

Kathy Duffy sat cozily in the O'Tooles' kitchen, sipping tea and nibbling on iced cakes — though if truth be known the batter could have used just a splash more vanilla — while she shared news and gossip.

As she was used to having ten words to say for anyone else's one, she didn't notice her friend's distraction, but kept chattering away with the hottest bulletin in Old Parish.

"Always a clever one, was Dennis. So everyone who knew him said. And he married Deborah Casey, who was a cousin of my mother's and was reputed to have a good head on her shoulders as well. Off they went, across the foam with their first-born still in short pants. They did well for themselves in America, built up a fine business. You know Old Maude was betrothed to the John Magee who was lost in the war, and he was brother to Dennis. In all these years," Kathy went on as she licked a bit of icing from her finger, "it seems Dennis never did look back to Ireland, or the place where he was born. But he had himself a son, and the son a son. And that one, he's looking right enough."

She waited a beat, and Mollie roused herself to raise her eyebrows. "Is he?"

"He is, yes. And he's got his sights set on Ardmore. Planning to build a theater here."

"Oh, yes." Mollie stirred the tea she'd yet to taste. "I heard Brenna talking about it." Distracted she was, but not so deeply that she didn't notice Kathy's crestfallen expression. "I don't have the details of it," she said, to smooth her friend's feathers.

"Well, then." Delighted, Kathy edged forward. "There's a deal being done between the Magees in New York City and the Gallaghers. The word 'round is they'll be building the theater onto the pub. A kind of music hall if I'm hearing correctly. Imagine that, Mollie, a music hall right in Ardmore, and with the Gallaghers having their fingers in it."

"If it's to be, I'd be happier knowing one of our own had some say in the matter. Do you know if Dennis Magee, the younger, will be coming back to Ardmore?"

"I don't see how the matter can be done otherwise." Kathy sat back, patted her hair. Her niece had given her a home perm the week before, and she was well pleased with it. Each curl was like a soldier tucked up in his bedroll.

"Dennis and I had a bit of a flirt when we were both young and foolish and he came to visit one summer back some years." Kathy's eyes went dreamy as she looked back. "On his grand tour, was he, and wanted to see the place where his parents had been born and reared and where he himself spent the first years of his life. He was a fine-looking man, Dennis Magee, as I recall him."

"The way I remember things, you had a bit of a flirt with every fine-looking man before you plucked the one you were after."

Kathy's eyes went bright with humor. "What's the point of being young and foolish if you do otherwise?"

Because it was one of the things worrying her, Mollie managed a wan smile and let her old friend settle back into chattering.

Mollie was certain that her oldest daughter was having a great deal more than a flirtation with Shawn Gallagher. That wasn't such a shock, not really, but the fact that Brenna wasn't talking of it with her was both a shock and a concern. She'd raised her girls to know there was nothing they couldn't share with their mother.

She'd known the night her Maureen had fallen in love, as the girl had come in flushed and laughing and full of the wonder of it. And when Kevin had asked her Patty to marry, she'd known the minute her girl had come into the house and thrown herself weeping into her mother's arms. That was the way with them, Maureen laughing over joys and Patty weeping over them.

But Brenna, the most practical of her children, had done neither, nor had she, as Mollie had expected, sat down and spoken of what had changed with Shawn.

Hadn't she left that very morning saying that she would be staying over with Darcy that night and not quite looking her mother in the eye when she lied? It hurt, knowing your child had the need to lie to you.

"Where have you gone off to?"

"Hmm?" Mollie focused on Kathy's face again, shook her head. "I'm sorry. I can't seem to keep my mind on things these days."

"It's no wonder. You've one daughter married only months ago, and another planning her wedding. Is it making you blue?"

"A little, I suppose." Because she'd let her tea go cold and Kathy's cup was empty, Mollie rose to pour hers down the sink and refill both cups with fresh. "I'm proud of them, happy for them, but . . ."

"They grow up so much faster than ever you think."

"They do. One minute I'm scrubbing faces, and the next I'm buying wedding gowns." To her surprise, helpless tears rushed to her eyes. "Oh, Kathy."

"There, now, darling." She took both of Mollie's hands and squeezed. "I felt the same way when

261

mine left the nest."

"It's Patty's doing." Sniffling, Mollie dug a handkerchief out of her pocket. "I never cried with Maureen except at the wedding. Thought I'd go mad from time to time as my Maureen wouldn't settle for less than perfection, and her idea of it changed daily. But Patty, she gets weepy if we talk about what flowers she'll have. I swear to you, Kathy, I live in fear that the child will bawl her way down the aisle to poor Kevin. People would think we've a gun to her head, forcing her to take her vows."

"Oh, now, nothing of the sort. Patty's your sentimental one. She'll make a lovely bride, tears and all."

"Of course she will." But Mollie indulged herself with a few tears of her own. "Then there's Mary Kate. She's taken to mooning about — over some boy, I'm sure — and brooding and closing herself off to write in her diary. Half the time she won't let Alice Mae in the room."

"Sure, there's probably a lad at the hotel she fancies herself in love with. Is it worrying you?"

"Not overmuch, I suppose. Mary Kate's a great brooder, and she's of an age where having her younger sister in her pocket becomes a trial."

"Just growing pains. You've done a fine job of mothering your girls, Mollie. They're a credit to you, each and every one. Not that that stops a woman from worrying over her chicks. Well, at least Brenna's not giving you any grief at the moment."

Carefully, Mollie lifted her cup and sipped. "Brenna's steady as a rock," she said. There were some things you couldn't share, even with a friend.

With the pub closed for an hour between shifts, Aidan stuck his head in the kitchen. "Can you leave that for a few minutes?"

Shawn cast a look around the general disorder caused by a busy afternoon crowd. "Without a second's hesitation. Why?"

"There's something to talk about, and I want a walk."

Shawn tossed his dishcloth aside. "Where?"

"The beach'll do." Aidan came through the kitchen and started out the back door. He paused there a moment, studying the slight rise of land, the tidiness of it before it gave way to a smattering of trees the wind had bent seaward.

"Second thoughts?" Shawn asked him.

"No, not about this." But he continued to look and measure. The shops and cottages that ran along the sides of his pub, the back gardens, the ancient dog who lay claim to a shady spot for a nap, the corner at the far end of their land where he'd kissed his first girl.

"It'll change more than a little," Aidan mused.

"It will. It changed when Shamus Gallagher put up the walls of the pub. And every one of us since has changed it in one way or the other. This is your change."

"Ours." Aidan said it quickly, as it was very

much on his mind. "That's one of the things we'll talk about. I didn't catch Darcy. The girl was out of the place like a ball from a cannon. Do you remember playing out here?"

"I do." Absently, Shawn rubbed his nose. "Aye, that I do."

With a quick laugh, Aidan walked around the side. "I'd forgotten that. We had a ball game going out back from time to time, and that's where Brenna rapped one right in your face. Christ, you bled like a pig."

"The bat was as near as big as she was."

"True enough, but the lass has always had an arm on her. I remember you lying there, cursing and bleeding, and when she saw it was no more than your nose that was broken, she told you to stop shouting and offer it up. We had some fine games back of the pub."

"Impending fatherhood's making you sentimental."

"Maybe it is." They crossed the street, quiet this time of day, this time of year. "Spring's coming," Aidan added as they worked their way down to the curve of beach. "And the tourists and holidayers come with it. Winter's short in Ardmore."

Shawn dipped his hands in his pocket. There was still a bit of bite to the wind. "You won't hear me complaining over that."

Sand crunched softly under boots as they walked west. Where it met the horizon, the water was a dreamy blue. Here, where it rolled to land, it fumed, white against green, driven by small, choppy waves. Their tips sparkled in the generous stream of sun.

They walked in silence, away from the boats already docked for the day, and the nets hung for drying, and toward the cliffs that layered their way up toward the sky.

"I spoke with Dad this morning."

"He's well? And Ma, too?"

"They're well and fine. He's expecting to meet with the lawyers early next week. Papers, at least some of them, should be ready to sign. He's decided, while he's about that, to have more drawn up. Papers that would put the pub in my name, in a legal way."

"It's time for that, as we've known they've found their spot in Boston."

"I told him my thoughts, and I'll tell you. I feel it would be better, and more fair, if the pub was titled between the three of us."

When a shell caught his eye, Shawn bent, picked it up, examined it. "That's not our way."

Which had been precisely what his father had said. Aidan hissed out a breath, paced off, then back. "Christ, you're more like him than any of us."

"Sure, that doesn't sound like a compliment to either our father or myself just at the moment." Tickled, Shawn stood where he was while Aidan paced a bit more.

"It wasn't meant as one. You've both heads like bricks about certain things. Wasn't it you who just spoke of change as a good thing? If we can change the pub, why the devil can't we change the way it's passed down?"

Absently, Shawn tucked the shell in his pocket. "Because some things you change, and some you don't."

"Who decides, I'd like to know?"

Shawn cocked his head. "We do. You're out-numbered on this, Aidan, so let it go. Gallagher's is yours, and you'll pass it down to the child Jude's already carrying. It doesn't make it less ours, Darcy's and mine, not the heart of it."

"I'm talking about a legal matter."

"Exactly. It's going to be a fine, fresh evening," Shawn said, considering the matter closed. "Business should be good."

"What about your children when you have them?" Aidan asked. "Don't you want them to have some legal standing in all of it?"

"So why does it have to get legal all of a sudden?"

"Because it's changing, Shawn." Exasperation sparked from him as he threw up his hands. "The theater changes Ardmore, changes Gallagher's. Changes us."

"It doesn't, not the way you're worrying right now. More people will come, for different reasons," Shawn mused, trying to see it in his mind. "Another B and B might pop up along the way, and someone might be inclined to open another shop along the water. But Gallagher's will still be serving food and drink, and offering music as it always has. One of us will man the bar. And while we're about it, the boats will go out, nets'll be cast. Life goes on as it means to, whatever you do about it."

"Or whatever you don't?" Aidan asked.

"Well, now, some might disagree with that. It's the business of it that's weighing on you, Aidan. And better you than me. I mean it sincerely. Carrying the Gallagher name is standing enough, legal or otherwise, for my needs."

Shawn turned back so he could look at the pub, the dark wood, the cobbled stone, the etched glass that caught winks of sunlight. "It's done well enough till now, hasn't it? When the time comes, your children, and mine and Darcy's, will work it out for themselves."

"You might marry a woman with other ideas."

Shawn thought of Brenna, shook his head. "If a woman didn't believe in me and my family enough to trust in this, I'd have no business marrying her."

"You don't know what it is to be in love beyond reason. I'd have walked away from here, from this, from everyone, if she'd asked it of me or wanted it so."

"She didn't ask it of you, or want it so. You might have desired a woman who would have, Aidan, but you'd never have lost your heart to her."

Aidan started to speak, then huffed out a breath first. "An answer for everything. And it's not a little vexing that each one seems a right one."

"I've given the matter some thought over time. Now you give me one, as I've a question. When you love a woman, beyond reason, does it hurt, or give you pleasure?"

"Both, very often at the same time."

Shawn nodded as they started back. "I thought that might be the case, but it's interesting to hear it confirmed."

It was a fair and fresh evening, and business was brisk as the wind that tripped in over the sea. Music drew customers, some to listen while they sipped their pints, others to join in on the chorus, and more than a few who found the music pulled them to their feet to dance.

Despite the fast pace, Shawn found time to pop out now and then. And once, watching Brenna circling the tables in a pretty waltz with old Mr. Riley, he pondered an idea.

"I've a notion here, Aidan." Shawn served two orders of fish and chips at the bar himself. He took a glass to pull himself a Harp and cut his thirst. "You see Brenna dancing there?"

"I do." Aidan topped off the last layer of two Guinnesses. "But I don't believe she's running off with him to Sligo, no matter how often she promises."

"Women are born to deceive a man." Taking his moment, Shawn sipped, enjoying the way Brenna moved in the old man's bony arms. "But I'm watching them, and the others who'll get up now and then, and I wonder wouldn't it be interesting if when we shuffle things about with the theater, we found someplace for dancing."

"That's what the stage is for now, isn't it?"

"Not professional dancing, but this sort. You know, how they do in a beer garden, but I'm thinking more intimate."

"Well, you're thinking that's for certain." But Aidan paused long enough to watch, scan the faces, consider. "It's something we might slide around with Magee when we get to the design of it all."

"Ah, Brenna, she had a kind of design she sketched up. I have it in the kitchen still. Maybe you'd like to take a look, and if you like what you see, you might be interested in the more formal drawing I asked her to do."

Intrigued, Aidan looked away from the dancing and into his brother's eyes. "You asked her, did you?"

"I did, because I think she knows what we want and what Magee should build. Is that a problem for you?"

"Not a problem, no problem at all. It's making me think, Shawn, that you had it right about the legalities of things not changing the heart. I'd like to see what our Brenna has in her mind."

"That's fine, then. And if you like what you see, you could send it off to Magee for his thoughts."

"I could, but I'd think the man would have his own designers."

"Then we'll have to find a way to bring him 'round to it, if it's what we want. Couldn't hurt," Shawn murmured, still watching Brenna, "to have our fingers in it early on."

"It couldn't," Aidan agreed.

However prettily Brenna could dance, Aidan needed her back behind the bar shortly. He caught her eye, sent her a quick signal. But even as she acknowledged it, he saw her gaze slip past him to Shawn. Even though he was a bystander, Aidan felt the heat of it.

"I'll thank you not to distract my bartender when we're three-deep around here."

"I'm just standing, drinking my beer."

"Well, stand and drink in the kitchen, unless you're after having half the customers raising their eyebrows over the pair of you."

"It wouldn't bother me." He held the look another moment, a kind of test. "But it does her." Because it would annoy him if he dwelt on it, Shawn slipped back into the kitchen.

It wasn't a problem to keep himself busy until closing, and he calculated another hour at least to clean up before he could call it a night.

He was scouring pots when one of the musicians strolled in. She was a pretty blonde named Eileen, with sharp features and hair chopped short to show them off. She had a fine, clear voice and a warm disposition. Shawn had admired the first and taken advantage of the second, in a friendly sort of way, when her band had been booked at Gallagher's before.

"We did well by each other tonight."

"That we did." He rinsed off the pot, and angling his body toward her, started on the next. "I liked the arrangement you've put together for 'Foggy Dew.'"

270

"It's the first time we've tried it outside of rehearsal." She walked to him, turning to lean back against the sink while he worked. "I've been working on a couple of other numbers. I wouldn't mind running them by you." She ran her fingertip down his arm. "I don't have to be back tonight. Would you care to put me up as you did last time?"

Last time, they'd enjoyed music and each other for half the night. The woman, Shawn recalled, wasn't the least shy about her talents. The memory made him grin even as he contemplated the most polite way to turn her down.

The only thing Brenna saw — besides red — when she carted in the last tray of empties, was the way Shawn had his head tipped down and the way the blonde had her hand on him. She stalked over, slammed the tray down on the counter by the sink with enough force to make the glasses dance.

"Is there something you're after in here?"

Eileen was quick enough to read the threat in the eyes that were burning over her face, and the meaning behind them. "Not anymore." In a cheerful gesture, she patted Shawn's arm. "I guess I'm heading back after all. Some other time, Shawn."

"Ah . . . hmm." He had a split second to make up his mind, and going with instinct, fixed a guilty, sheepish expression on his face. "Well."

"Always a pleasure, coming to Gallagher's," Eileen added as she strolled to the door. She kept the snicker inside and wondered how the pint-size redhead was going to make Shawn suffer.

"Is this the last of it, then?" Shawn began scrubbing the pot again, as if he'd dedicated his life to that single purpose.

"It is. And what was that about, I'd like to know?"

"What?"

"You and the singer with the big breasts and boy's hair?"

"Oh, Eileen." Deliberately, he cleared his throat as he set the pot aside to deal with the glasses. "She was just saying good night."

"Hah." She skewered a finger into his side and made him jump. "If she'd been any closer, she'd have been inside your skin."

"Well, now, she's just a friendly sort."

"Just keep this in mind, while you and I are rolling on the sheets, you keep your distance from the friendly sorts."

Even while delight rippled through him, he straightened slowly. "Are you accusing me of something, Brenna?" It pleased him that he managed the right mix of hurt and insult. "Of making moves toward another woman while I'm with you? I didn't realize how little you thought of me."

"I saw what I saw."

He studied her a moment, then began to wipe off counters with a moody and injured air. It would be interesting, he thought, to see how much she worked to bring him around.

"She had her hand on you."

"I didn't have mine on her, did I?"

"That's not the —" Damn it. Brenna folded her

272

arms, unfolded them and jammed her hands in her pockets. She'd wanted to shred the skin off the blonde's face. Still did, she admitted, if it came to that. It wasn't in character at all. Not that she'd back down from a fight, but she wasn't one to start a brawl. And surely not over a man.

"You were smiling at her."

"I'll be sure not to smile at anyone unless you approve it first."

"It looked overly cozy." Her hand was still balled in her pocket. If she hadn't felt so foolish, she might have given in to the urge to pop him with it. "I'll apologize if I misunderstood."

"Fine." Leaving it at that, he walked over to push open the door and call out his good nights. When he turned back, she looked so frustrated and unhappy he nearly relented. But a man had to finish what he started. He spoke coolly, with just enough bite to let her know she had more making up to do. "Would you prefer staying over with Darcy?"

"No. No, I wouldn't."

"All right, then." He crossed to the back door, opened it, waited. She got her cap and jacket from the hook by the door, then bundled them under her arm and stepped out into the chill.

They didn't speak as they got into opposite sides of his car. She brooded out the window while he drove out of the village and up the road toward the cottage.

She told herself she'd had a perfectly normal reaction. And shifting in her seat, she told him the same. When he didn't answer, she had to struggle not to squirm. "Can we agree this is new territory for both of us?"

Ah, he thought, just the direction he'd hoped for. He sent her one quiet look, then nodded.

"And we never, I suppose you could say, discussed the boundaries of it."

"You wanted sex. You're getting it." Out of the corner of his eye, he saw her flinch. Perfect.

"That's true. That's true," she repeated in a mutter when he pulled up to his cottage. She was starting to feel a little sick to her stomach. "But I . . . it's only that I —" She cursed and had to scramble out of the car to keep up with him. "Damn it, you can at least hear me out."

"I'm listening to you. Do you want tea?" he asked, viciously polite as he walked inside.

"No, I don't want tea. And take that stick out of your arse for one bloody minute. If you don't have the sense to see that woman wanted to jump you, you're blind as six bats and twice as dim."

"More to the point would be what I wanted — and intended." He started up the steps.

"She's beautiful."

"So are you. What does that have to do with it?"

As her mouth was hanging open, it took a minute to get her feet moving. In all the years she'd known the man, he'd never told her she was beautiful. It threw her off her stride. She could feel her mind trip as she tried to keep it on track.

"You don't think of me that way, and that's all right. It's not what I'm trying to get to, anyway."

He'd make sure they came back to it, but for

now, he emptied the contents of his pockets onto his dresser. "What are you trying to get to, Brenna?"

"I know when we started this — when I started this — I never said what I expected." Wishing she had his clever way with words, she dragged a hand through her hair. "What I mean is, that while we're together this way, until one of us or both of us decide this has run its course, I wouldn't consider being with another man."

He sat on the trunk at the foot of the bed to take off his boots. "You're meaning that this area of our relationship should be an exclusive one? That neither of us sees anyone else? Is that the way of it?"

"Aye, that's my feeling on it."

They would be exclusive to each other, and it was her idea — even demand. A strong first step, he thought, to where he wanted her to lead him. He took his time, letting her believe he was considering. "That fits in with my feeling on it as well. But . . ."

"But?"

"How do we know, and who decides when that changes, Brenna?"

"I don't have an answer to that. I never expected this to be complicated. I didn't know it was until I saw that singer hanging all over you. I didn't like it."

"While I'm touching you, I'm touching no one else. You'll have to trust me."

"I can trust you, Shawn." Easier now, she

stepped toward him. "It's the big-breasted blondes I have trouble with."

"Recently, my taste is running strong for well-packed redheads."

Because she was relieved that the chill had gone out of his eyes, she laughed. "Well-packed, my ass. Have we made up, then?"

"It's a beginning." He patted the space beside him. "Let's have your boots off and we'll make up some more."

Happy to oblige, she sat, tugged on the laces. "I hurt your feelings. I'm sorry for that."

"I don't mind spatting with you, Mary Brenna." He stroked a hand over her hair. "But I don't like you thinking that I'd think of another woman in that way when I'm with you."

"Then I won't think it." After toeing off her boots, she straightened, but her eyes went wary at the way he was staring at her. "What is it?"

"I like looking at you."

"Nothing new to see here."

"Maybe that's part of it." He framed her face, then combed his fingers through her hair, drawing it back and away. "I know this face," he said quietly, "as well as I know my own. I can conjure it up in my mind, the way it runs from cheek to jaw." He skimmed his lips along the sweep. "The shape and color of the eyes, and the moods of them."

Just now, he noted, the mood was surprised, and not a little uneasy. "The mouth," he continued, brushing it lightly, retreating just as hers softened. "The curves and dips of it. Such a lovely face. I don't mind looking at it, even when you're not around."

"That's an odd thing to . . ." She trailed off as he brought his mouth back to hers, lingered there.

"Then there's the rest of you." He skimmed his hands down, a light play of fingers. Then captured her hands before she could tug the sweater off. "No, let me." He drew her to her feet, lifting the sweater, inch by inch. "It gives me pleasure to uncover you, to work my way through the layers to that amazing body of yours. It drives me mad the way you cover it up."

She might have gaped if she hadn't been so busy just trying to breathe. "It does?"

"I keep thinking, I know what's under all that." He loosened the hook of her trousers. "I've had that under me." He let the trousers drop, pool at her feet. "Step out of those, darling," he murmured, and toyed with the hem of her undershirt.

"I'm built like a twelve-year-old boy."

"As one who's been a twelve-year-old boy . . ." He slipped the undershirt over her head, then let his gaze run down her. "I can promise you that's not the case. Milkmaid's skin and strong shoulders." He dipped his head, touching his lips to one, then the other. "And here." Slowly, he trailed his hands from her waist to cup her breasts. Her breath caught, released, shuddered. "Soft and firm and sensitive."

She started to drift along, to cruise on the wonderful slide of his hands. Then gasped, half in shock, half in amusement, when he lifted her, stood her on the little chest.

But the humor that sparked in her eyes went dark when he closed his mouth over her breast, caught her nipple delicately between his teeth. "Oh, God."

"I want you to come." He traced a finger along the edge of cotton that still covered her, and his mouth worked down. "I want you to call out my name when you do." And slipped his finger under the cotton, inside her where she was already hot, already wet.

She rocked against him, a jerk of movement while her fingers dug into his shoulders. Pleasure rushed into her so fast it was almost a panic, built so high, so huge, she wondered her body could survive it.

And it was his name she called out.

Was she falling or flying? She felt her legs give way, like a melting of bone, tried to center herself again when she felt him lift her, carry her to the side of the bed.

"The light."

He laid her on the bed, knelt over her. "We'll see each other clearly this way. This time." Watching her, he took off his shirt. "Do you know how arousing it is to know I can take you up, again and again? That you have that much inside you for me?"

She reached for him, drew him to her. "I want you inside me."

"And I want you weak first." His mouth began

to taste, his hands to roam. "And sobbing my name."

"You bastard." The fact that she said it on a moan delighted him. "Just try to make me."

He thought it a lovely challenge, and set about meeting it.

His hands were light as faerie wings one moment, hard as iron the next. And each touch was a separate thrill. He had a way about him that she'd never imagined when she'd fantasized about having him for a lover. The men she'd known before him hadn't given her this, or lured her into giving so much back. There was a freedom here, with him. That odd mix of wicked surprise with easy recognition.

And trust. Absolute trust.

She opened herself to him willingly. Perhaps with his skill she'd have been helpless to do otherwise, but she was willing to take all he offered, and to match it.

Even as shocks of sensation lanced through her, she yielded. It was a surrender she'd given to no other.

As if he sensed it, he took her up again, slowly this time, almost torturously, so that her body was a raw, aching mass of nerves.

Her skin was damp and slick. The heat of her all but stopped his heart with need. She moved against him, under him, with a smooth and sinuous female rhythm that made him ache for joining. In the lamplight his eyes were narrowed, focused on her face as he strained against his own need and kept her shuddering on the edge.

Quaking, she sobbed out his name.

He drove himself into her, more violently than he meant to. But she arched up to meet him, accept him, matching the desperate pace that slapped flesh against flesh and had heart thundering against heart. Glorying in it, he lifted her hips, going deeper, pushing them both toward delirium.

"No one but you, Brenna." The throbbing in his blood was a drumbeat, primitive, constant. "Say it back to me. Say it back."

"No one but you." As she said it, her world exploded.

Swamped with love, he emptied himself into her.

Fifteen

It was her habit to wake early and get on with the business of the day. On the rare occasions when Brenna slept late, it was usually because she'd had more than her fair share to drink the evening past.

So as she'd had nothing but fizzy water the night before, it was a surprise to see the sun was well up when she opened her eyes. The second surprise came on the heels of the first when she noted the only thing keeping her from rolling off the bed was the arm that Shawn had banded around her.

He'd sprawled himself in the middle of the mattress, shoving her to the outer edge. But, she thought, at least he was considerate enough to see that she stayed there and didn't fall on her face.

She tried to shift around, gave him a shove so that she could get free and climb out. But he tightened his grip and pulled her back until she was curved against him in the cozy spoon position.

"You might be the lazy sort who lies in bed half the morning, but I'm not." She started to wiggle free, and wiggling, discovered the interesting fact that not all of him was asleep. "Wake up ready, do you?" She said it with a chuckle and pushed at his arms. "Well, I don't. I want a shower and some coffee."

His answer was a grunt, but his hand snuck up to cover her breast.

"And just keep your hands to yourself. I don't want any of this fooling around until I've had my coffee."

He simply parted her legs and proved her a liar. "Well." His voice was thick with sleep, but the arm that slid under her was strong enough to hold her in place. "You can just lie there, then, while I use you."

Later, when she staggered into the shower, she thought it wouldn't be such a sacrifice to be used in such a way of a morning every now and again.

She turned the water on, keeping it on the cool side, as her skin was still hot and flushed. After stepping into the old claw-foot tub, she tugged the curtain around, then ducked her head under the stingy spray to wet her hair.

It wasn't an easy business with so little water and so much hair, but she had nearly accomplished it when the curtain jingled back. She opened one eye and fixed it on Shawn.

"I don't suppose you can give me much trouble in here so soon after that."

"Care to wager on it?" he asked as he stepped in with her.

She'd have lost.

Her legs weren't quite steady when she snapped down a towel. "Keep your distance now," she warned, wrapping it around her while her hair dripped everywhere. "I've no more time for you. I've got to get home."

"I suppose you don't have time for any griddle cakes, then."

She shoved wet hair out of her eyes. "You'd be making griddle cakes?"

"I had a mind to, but if you're in such a rush, I'll just scramble an egg for myself."

He was already dried off and was brushing his teeth, an easy act of intimacy that barely registered. "I suppose I'm not in such a terrible rush. Have you a spare toothbrush around here?"

"I don't, but I think under the circumstances you can use mine."

She kept one at Darcy's, along with a few other essentials, but she'd been too distracted to remember to gather them up the night before. "Would you mind if I left a few things here, for convenience sake?"

He leaned over the sink to rinse so she didn't see the gleam of triumph in his eyes. Another step, he thought. "There's room." He handed her the toothbrush. "Use whatever you need for now. I'll go down and put on some coffee."

"Thanks."

Leaving her to it, he stepped out to pull on jeans and a sweater. If he hadn't been obliged to be at the pub, he would've found a way to talk her into spending the day with him. As it was, they only had an hour or so.

But he saw, clearly saw, how it could be with them. Mornings like this, begun with love and slipping into the easy routine of a meal before they went off on their ways. Brenna sitting in the pub kitchen for a while in the evening while he worked. Knowing she'd be waiting when he got home.

As he headed downstairs, he reminded himself there were a few steps left to take before they got there. But he couldn't believe, wouldn't believe, he could be so in love with someone and not find the way to spend his life with her.

They'd need their own house, one that belonged to them. A big kitchen, and bedrooms enough for the family they'd make. He had enough put by to see about acquiring some land. He put on water for coffee, and got out the makings for tea as well, as he preferred starting his day that way.

He assembled eggs, flour, buttermilk. Then nearly dropped the carton at the knock on the back door.

"I'm sorry." With a laugh in her voice, Mary Kate opened the door. "I didn't mean to give a start." Her cheeks were pink from her walk to the cottage, her eyes bright and cheerful. "I was just out, it being my day off, and I thought I'd stop by for a moment."

His mind raced for the way to get her out again, fast and smooth, with no harm done. Before he'd come up with anything other than yelling *fire!* it was too late.

"Why aren't I smelling coffee?" Brenna demanded. "You wear a body out before ten in the morning, then can't even . . ." Her voice simply died away as she walked in and saw her sister.

284

All the happy color in Mary Kate's cheeks died, and her eyes went wide and dark with hurt. For a moment no one moved. Actors in a bad play waiting for the curtain, knowing that when it lifted disaster would follow.

Shawn reached out, laid a hand on Mary Kate's arm. "Mary Kate." He said it gently, and the sympathy in the tone snapped her out of her shock. She smacked his hand aside, turned for the door.

"Mary Kate, wait!" Brenna rushed forward, skidded to a halt when her sister turned. There was color in her face again, the wild, deep color that came from shame and fury.

"You're sleeping with him. You're a liar and a hypocrite." She swung out, and as Brenna neither braced for nor tried to avoid the blow, the slap sent her sprawling. "And a whore as well."

"That's enough." Grimly, Shawn grabbed Mary Kate's arm. "You've no right to strike her or speak to her that way."

"It doesn't matter." Brenna got to her knees. That was as far as the horrible weight on her chest would allow.

"It matters a great deal. Be as mad as you want at me," he said to Mary Kate. "And I'm more sorry than I can say if I hurt you in any way. But what's here is between me and Brenna and has nothing to do with you."

She wanted to weep. She wanted to scream and was afraid she'd do both at once. Fighting viciously for one scrap of dignity, Mary Kate lifted her head, stepped back from him. "You didn't have to make a fool of me. You knew I had feelings. I still do, only now I hate you. I hate both of you."

She shoved the door open and fled.

"Jesus." Shawn bent to help Brenna to her feet, laid a hand over the cheek that flamed an angry red. "I'm sorry, so sorry. She didn't mean what she said."

"She does. Right now she means it all from the bottom of her heart. I know how it is. I have to go after her."

"I'll go with you."

"No." A part of her heart ripped as she backed away from him. "I have to do it myself. It would only hurt more to see us together. What was I thinking?" She shut her eyes, pressed her fingers to them. "What was I thinking?"

"You were thinking of me. We were thinking of each other. We've a right to that."

She dropped her hands, opened her eyes. "She thinks she loves you. I should have thought of that as well. I have to go do what I can."

"While I stay here, doing nothing?"

"She's my sister," Brenna said simply, and left.

She ran, but Mary Kate had a good head start and longer legs. By the time Brenna caught sight of her, she was already heading down the slope to the backyard of their house, the big yellow dog hurrying behind like a rear guard.

"Mary Kate, wait!" Brenna kicked into a sprint and caught up at the edge of the yard. "Wait now. You have to let me explain."

"Explain what? That you've been fucking

Shawn Gallagher. That was clear enough by the way you waltzed into his kitchen with your hair still wet."

"It's not like that." But wasn't that exactly how it had started? Brenna thought. Hadn't it been just like that at the beginning?

"The two of you must've had a fine laugh or two at my expense."

"No, not ever. I never thought —"

"Never thought of me?" Mary Kate rounded on her, shouting so now that the dog slunk off to hide. "That's fine, then, that makes it just fine. You go off playing whore with a man you know I have feelings for, but you didn't give me a thought."

The flash came into Brenna's eyes. A warning. "You called me that before, and I took it. You knocked me on my ass, and I took that as well. You've had your say. Now I'll have mine."

"You can go to hell." She gave Brenna one hard shove, spun on her heel, and marched toward the door.

Then let out a whoosh of air when Brenna tackled her from behind. "You want to settle this with slaps and shoves, that suits me." She grabbed a fistful of Mary Kate's hair and had just given one good, satisfying yank when their mother threw open the door and rushed out.

"What in sweet hell is this? Get off your sister this instant, Mary Brenna."

"The minute she apologizes for calling me a whore twice in one morning."

"Whore!" Tears of pain and rage blurred Mary

287

Kate's eyes, but she managed to shout it. "That makes three."

They rolled into a vicious tangle of arms and legs, and without a minute's hesitation, Mollie waded in, grabbed each by whatever she could snare, and hauled them apart. And since it was like separating spitting cats, she added a cuff on the side of the head to each to keep them there.

"It's shamed I am, *shamed* of the pair of you. Now in the house, and one word before you have my leave, it's the back of my hand for you."

Mary Kate got to her feet, brushed herself off, lowered her head. And when she caught Brenna's eye mouthed "whore." She had the dark satisfaction of watching Brenna start a swing and get another cuff for the trouble.

"A grown woman," Mollie muttered, herding her daughters toward the house, where Mick stood struggling to look disapproving, Alice Mae watched owlishly, and Patty stood peering over her father's shoulder with her best I'm-above-it-all look on her face.

"Sit!" She jabbed a finger at the table, then shot a steely look at her other daughters. "Patty, Alice Mae, I believe you have other things to do. If not, I can find plenty to occupy your time."

"She landed you a good one there, Brenna." Alice Mae clucked her tongue as she studied Brenna's cheek.

"She won't a second time."

"Quiet." At patience's end, Mollie snapped, "Out." She pointed to the door.

"Come on, Alice." Patty laid a hand on Alice Mae's shoulder. "There's no point in staring at the heathens." And the minute they'd rounded the corner, both of them hunkered down to hear what they could.

But when Mick started to slither out the door, Mollie pinned him with a hard stare. "Oh, no, you don't, Michael O'Toole, this baggage is as much yours as mine. Now." She planted her hands on her hips. "What started this? Brenna?"

"It's a personal problem between myself and Mary Kate." Her eyes clicked to her mother, then to her father when he moved to the pot to pour himself more tea.

"When it's a problem that has one sister calling another filthy names and the both of you tearing at each other like alley cats, it's no longer personal. You may be near twenty-five years of age, Mary Brenna Catherine O'Toole, but you live under this roof, and I won't tolerate such behavior."

"I'm sorry for it." Brenna set her hands on the table, folded them, and prepared to hold her ground.

"Mary Kate? What have you to say for yourself?"

"That if she lives under this roof I no longer care to."

"That would be your choice," Mollie said coldly now. "As all of my children are welcome here as long as they like."

"Even whores?"

"Mind your tongue, girl." Mick stepped forward. "You want to slap and wrestle, that's one

289

thing. But you'll speak with respect to your mother, and you won't use language like that about your sister."

"Let her deny it."

"Mary Kate." Brenna's voice was little more than a whisper, and more plea than warning.

Though Mary Kate's lips trembled, she couldn't fight off the rage. "Let her deny she spent the night in Shawn Gallagher's bed."

The teacup cracked as Mick fumbled and knocked it on the edge of the counter. All Brenna could do was close her eyes as shame and sorrow washed through her.

"I won't deny it. I won't deny I've been there before, and that every time I have, I went freely. I'm sorry that it hurt you." She got shakily to her feet. "But it doesn't make me a whore to care for him. And you know if you make me choose between you, I'll let him go."

It took all the courage she had left to turn and face her parents. The understanding in her mother's eyes might have been a balm if not for the shock in her father's. "I'm sorry for this, all of this. I'm sorry I haven't been honest with you. I can't talk about it anymore now. I just can't."

She hurried out, would have rushed right past her sisters, but Patty reached out. "It's all right, darling." She murmured it, giving Brenna a hard hug.

That broke her, set free the tears that were burning in her throat and the back of her eyes. Blinded by them, she rushed upstairs.

In the kitchen, Mollie kept her eyes on her younger daughter. Her heart was aching for both her girls, but comfort and discipline would have to be meted out separately.

The only sound now was Mary Kate's ragged breathing. Holding the silence a moment longer, Mollie slipped into the chair Brenna had deserted.

No one noticed when Mick walked out the back door.

"I know what it is to have feelings for someone," Mollie began quietly. "To see them as the brightest light, as the one who'll answer all the questions and fill all the holes, whether you're twenty or forty. I'm not doubting what you have in your heart, Katie."

"I love him." Defiance, still her only shield, edged her voice, but a single tear spilled over and slid down her cheek. "She knew."

"It's a hard thing to have those feelings for someone who doesn't have them for you."

"He might have, but she threw herself at him."

"Katie, darling."

There were many things she could have said. The man's too old for you, this was infatuation and would pass, you'll fall in love half a dozen times before it matters and takes a firm hold inside you. Instead, she took Mary Kate's hand.

"Shawn looked at Brenna," she said gently. "And has looked for a long time. And she at him. Neither of them is the careless sort who looks to hurt another. You know that."

"They didn't care about me."

"They had their eyes on each other, and for a

time they didn't see you."

It was worse, a hundred times worse, to be looked at with sympathy and still be made to feel like a fool. "You make it sound like it's all right, them having at each other that way."

Oh, a fine and shaky line, Mollie thought. "I'm not speaking of that, as that's between Brenna and her conscience and her heart. It's not for you to judge her, Mary Kate, nor for me. We cast no stones in this house."

Tears came faster now, and with them resentment. "You're taking her side in this, then."

"You're wrong, as I have two daughters hurt now and I love each in equal measure. If there's sides to be taken, Brenna's just taken yours. You've no way of knowing what her feelings are for Shawn or how deep they run, but she'll turn away from him for you. Is that what you want, Mary Kate? Would that soothe your heart and your pride?"

The turmoil inside her swallowed her up. Laying her head on the table, she wept like a child.

There was no choice for a man, for a father, but to deal with such matters. Mick would have preferred having his fingers broken one at a time rather than using them to knock on the door of Faerie Hill Cottage.

But there was nothing else to be done.

His daughter had given herself to a man, been taken by one, and that had shattered his comfortable illusions about his firstborn. He wasn't a stupid man. He knew that women, young ones and old ones and those in between, had certain needs. But when it was a matter of his pride and joy, he didn't care to have those needs shoved in his face.

And he knew, as well as any, about the needs of a man. He might have had a deep affection for Shawn Gallagher, but that didn't negate the fact that the bastard had put his hand on Michael O'Toole's baby.

So he knocked, and he was prepared to handle the matter in a straightforward and civilized way.

When the door opened, Mick rammed his fist into Shawn's face.

Shawn's head snapped back, and he took two steps for balance, but he stayed on his feet. Tougher than he looks, Mick decided, lifting his balled fists again, for that had been a fine punch if he said so himself.

"Come on, then, defend yourself. Ya son of a bitch. I've come to wipe the floor with you."

"No, sir." Shawn's head was ringing, and he wanted badly to swivel his jaw to make sure it wasn't broken, but he merely stood there, arms at his sides. The man was half his size and nearly twice his age. "You can plant another on me if you must, but I won't fight you."

"So, you're a coward, then." Mick danced inside, a boxer prepping for the next round. He gave Shawn a quick rap in the chest, faked another toward his face. Reluctant admiration bloomed. The boy didn't so much as flinch.

"You're standing up for your daughter. I can't fight what I'd do myself if I were you." But a sudden horrible thought flew into his head, and now his hands did fist. "Did you raise your hand to her over this?"

Insult mixed with frustration. "Bloody hell, boy, never have I raised a hand to one of my girls. I leave that to their mother if they've a need for it."

"She all right, then? Would you just tell me that she's all right?"

"No, we took a bat to her and bashed her brains to Sunday." With a windy sigh, Mick lowered his fists. He didn't have the heart to use them again. But he was far from done. "You've some answering to do, young Gallagher."

Shawn nodded. "Aye. Do you want me to do it here, in the doorway, or in the kitchen over whiskey?"

Thoughtfully, Mick rubbed his chin, measured his man. "I'll take the whiskey."

Temper was still bubbling under his skin, but he followed Shawn to the back, waited while the bottle was taken from the cupboard and good Jameson's poured into short glasses.

"Will you sit, Mr. O'Toole?"

"Well, you've manners, don't you, at such a time." Scowling, Mick sat, picked up his glass, and eyed Shawn over the top of it. "You've had your hands on my daughter."

"I have."

Mick set his teeth. His hand fisted again, braced and ready. "And what are your intentions toward my Mary Brenna?"

"I love her, and I want to marry her."

Mick's breath hissed out. He dragged one hand through his hair as he gulped down the whiskey, then held out the glass for more. "Well, why the devil didn't you say so?"

"Ah . . ." Gingerly, Shawn cupped his bruised jaw, moved it gently side to side. Not broken, he decided. Just battered. "It's a bit of a dilemma."

"And why would that be?"

"I haven't brought the matter up to Brenna herself as yet. If I do, you see, she'll determine to go the opposite way. I've been working at bringing the matter 'round so it seems her idea. That way, she'll make my life hell till I agree to it."

Mick stared, then shaking his head, set his whiskey down. "Well, Jesus, you do know her, don't you?"

"I do. And I love her with all my heart. I want to spend my life with her. There's nothing I want more. So . . ." Finished, and exhausted from it, Shawn knocked back his whiskey. "There you have it."

"You know how to take the wind out of a man's sails." Mick drank again. "I love my girls, Shawn. Each one of them's a jewel to me. When I walked my Maureen down the aisle and gave her away, I was proud, and my heart was breaking. You'll know how that is one day. I've to do the same with Patty soon. Both of them chose men I'm pleased to call son."

He held out his glass, waited while Shawn filled it again. "My Brenna has as good taste and sense as her sisters, if not better."

"Thank you for that." Relieved, Shawn took a second glass himself. "I'm wishing she'd come 'round to that sooner rather than later, but she's a bit of work, if you don't mind me saying."

"I don't. I'm proud of it." Mick settled in, frowned a little. "This business that's going on between you, I don't approve of it." He noted Shawn was man enough to meet his eye and wise enough to keep his thoughts to himself. By God, who'd have thought Brenna would meet her match in this one? "But she's more than of age," Mick continued, "and so are you. My approving or not isn't going to stop you from . . . well, I don't want to say any more on that particular thing."

They drank in cautious silence.

"Mr. O'Toole."

"I think, as things are coming 'round, you should call me Mick."

"Mick, I'm sorry about Mary Kate. I swear to you, I never —"

Mick waved a hand before Shawn could finish. "I can't blame you on that score. Our Katie has fancies, and a young and tender heart. I don't like knowing it's bruised, but there's no blame."

"Brenna'll blame herself, and she'll step back from me. If I didn't love her, I could let her."

"Time." Mick polished off the next whiskey and thought it was a fine morning to get a bit of a drunk on. "When you get older, you come to trust in time. Not that I'm meaning you sit idle and let it pass."

"I'm looking for land," Shawn said abruptly. The whiskey was starting to work in his head, and he didn't mind a bit.

"What's that?"

"For land, to buy. For Brenna. She'll want to build her house, don't you think?"

Tears of sentiment gathered in Mick's eyes. "It's been a dream of hers to do that."

"I know she's a dream to have a hand in building something from the ground up, and I'm hoping she'll have her chance with the theater."

"Aye, I've been giving her a hand in the drawing of that."

"Would you see that I get it, so I can pass it on? She may not feel as easy about giving it to me now."

"You'll have it tomorrow."

"That's fine, then. And the theater's an important thing, for Brenna, for us, for Ardmore. But a home — that's more important than a place of business."

"It is, and would be to her as well as to you."

"If you hear of something you think might suit, would you pass it on to me?"

Mick took out his handkerchief, blew his nose. And was pleased to see Shawn fill his glass without waiting to be asked. "That I'll do." Eyes narrowed and a bit bright from drink, Mick peered at Shawn's jaw. "How's the face, then?"

"Aches like a bitch in heat."

Mick laughed heartily, tapped his glass to Shawn's. "Well, that's something, then."

While Mick and Shawn bonded over Jameson's, Mollie had her hands full. It took nearly an hour of strokes and pats and sympathy before she could tuck Mary Kate in for a nap. Her own head was feeling achy, but she pressed her fingers to her eyes to relieve some of the pressure before crossing to Brenna's room.

She reminded herself she had wanted children, and a number of them besides. She'd been blessed. She was grateful.

And Blessed Mary, she was tired.

Brenna was curled on the bed, eyes shut. Sitting cross-legged beside her, Alice Mae stroked Brenna's hair. At the foot of the bed, Patty sat dabbing at her eyes.

It was a sweet sight, all in all. Patty was a romantic and would automatically throw her heart to Brenna on this. Alice Mae, bless her, couldn't bear to see anything or anyone in pain.

Mollie had only to gesture for Patty and Alice Mae to get up and take their leave. "I'll speak to Brenna alone." She shooed them out before questions could be asked and shut the door.

As Mollie crossed to the bed, she saw Brenna tense. "I'm sorry." Brenna kept her eyes closed, and her voice was rough and strained. "I don't know what else to say but I'm sorry. Don't hate me."

"Oh, what nonsense." Using a brisker tone than she had with Mary Kate, Mollie sat, gave Brenna's shoulder a little shake. "Why should I? Are you thinking I'm so old that I don't understand what feelings churn around in a woman?"

"No, no." Miserable, Brenna curled herself tighter, shifting so she could rest her head on her mother's lap. "Oh, Ma, it's all my fault. I started it. I wanted Shawn, so I went right up to him and said so. I kept at him until . . . well, he's a man, after all."

"Is that all there is between you, Brenna? Just the need and the act?"

"Yes. No." She pressed her face into the comforting give of her mother. "I don't know. It doesn't matter now."

"Nothing matters more."

"I can't be with him. I won't see him that way anymore. If you knew how she looked at us, at me. All the hurt on her face before the anger came into it. I never thought of her." She rolled onto her back now, stared at the ceiling. "I only thought of me and what went on inside me when I was with him. Because of it I lied to you and to Dad. How can you trust me again after this?"

"I'm not saying the lie was right, but I knew it was a lie when you told me." She nearly smiled when Brenna's gaze cut to hers. "Do you think I told my own mother that I was sneaking out of the house on a warm summer night to meet Michael O'Toole so he could make my head swim with kisses?" Her eyes warmed with humor and memory. "Twenty-six years we've been married, and five children we brought into the world, and to this day my mother believes I lay chaste in my bed every night before my wedding."

With a long sigh, Brenna sat up, and wrapping her arms around Mollie, laid her head on her shoulder. "I have a need for him, Ma, and it's so big. I thought after a bit it would quiet down, fade back and away, then we'd both get back to how things were before. But it isn't quieting down at all. And I've ruined it because I didn't say to Katie, 'This one's mine, so find another.' Or whatever I could have said or done. Now I can't go back to him."

"Answer me this, as honest as you can." Mollie drew her back, studied her face. "Would Shawn have looked in Mary Kate's direction if you hadn't been standing between?"

"But that's not the —"

"Just answer, Brenna."

"No." She let out a painful breath. "But he'd never have hurt her if not for me."

"Mistakes were made, there's no denying it. But Mary Kate's as responsible for her heart and its bruising as anyone. Martyring yourself won't change what was or what is. Have a rest," she said, pressing her lips to Brenna's forehead. "You'll think clearer when you're head's not aching. Shall I bring you some tea and toast?"

"No, but thanks. I love you so much."

"There, now, don't start crying again. Any more tears today and I'll need an oar. Let's have off your boots and tuck you in."

As she had with Mary Kate, Mollie fussed and stroked and settled Brenna under the covers. She sat a little while, and when Brenna was quiet, she rose to let sleep do a bit of healing.

As she passed the window, she stopped, stepped back, stared down at the sight of her husband weaving and stumbling his way home.

"Saints in heaven, the man's drunk and it's not yet noon." She pushed at her hair. "What a family this is."

Sixteen

Getting ready to go to work was quite an undertaking. He was dressed already, which was a fortunate thing. Shaving was out of the question. Even if he'd wanted to deal with scraping a razor over his tender jaw, he was just sober enough to fear cutting his face to ribbons in the process.

So he left it as it was, and stumbling over his shoes, he thought it might be a fine idea to put them on.

Bub, being the perverse creature that he was, took the opportunity to crawl all over him, then laid stinging furrows over the back of Shawn's hand when he tried to push him aside.

"Vicious bastard." He and the cat eyed each other with mutual dislike and from a respectful distance. "I might have to take a swipe from Mick O'Toole, but I don't have to take one from you, you black-hearted spawn of Satan." He lunged, missed as the cat streaked away, and ended up rapping his already sore jaw on the floor. "Fuck me, that's about enough."

With his ears ringing, he managed to get to his hands and knees. The fiend of a cat was in for dire consequences. Later. He'd let the fiend believe he'd won the war, then seek revenge at an unexpected moment.

Still sulking over it, Shawn nursed his hand as he headed out of the house. As a matter of habit, he turned toward his car, then paused, balancing himself on the garden gate.

He was certain he could drive. He was a man who could hold his drink, wasn't he? For Christ's sake, his name was Gallagher. But the way things were going, he'd likely run off the road and smash his teeth out on the steering wheel.

Much better to walk, he decided. Clear his head, settle his thoughts. He started down the road, mindful of the ruts and bumps, singing to entertain himself on the journey.

He stumbled a time or two, but fell only the one time. Of course, the one time was enough to have his knee find the single sharp rock in the bloody road. He was picking himself up from that, not far from the village proper, when Betsy Clooney, with her car full of her children, stopped beside him.

"Shawn, what's happened? You've had an accident?"

He smiled at her. She had a pretty brood of children, all of them fair of hair and blue of eye. The two in the back were squabbling, but the youngest, secured in her car seat, watched Shawn like a little owl as she sucked on a red lollipop.

"Well, hello, Betsy. How's it all going, then?"

"Did you have a car crash?" She pushed open her door to hurry around to him, grinning as he was at her baby and weaving like a man who'd gone a hard round with the champ.

"I didn't, no. I've been walking."

"Your hand's bleeding, and you're bruised on the face. Your trousers are ripped at the knee."

"Are they?" He glanced down, saw the mud and the tear. "Shit, look at that, will you? Begging pardon," he said quickly, remembering the children.

But she was close enough now to see, and to smell, just what the matter was. "Shawn Gallagher, you're drunk."

"I am, I suppose, a little." They'd gone to school together, so he patted her shoulder in a friendly manner. "You've darling children, Betsy, but your oldest girl there is trying to throttle her brother, and doing a damn fine job of it."

Betsy merely glanced back and barked out one sharp warning. The children broke apart.

"My mother could do the same." Sheer admiration shone on Shawn's face. "Half the time it only took a look to curdle the blood in your veins. Well, I must be going."

"Get in the back of the car, for heaven's sake, and I'll take you home."

"Thanks, but I'm for work."

She rolled her eyes, jerked open the car door. "Get in all the same, and I'll drive you the rest of the way." And let the Gallaghers deal with their own, she thought.

"That's kind of you. Thanks, Betsy."

The children were so entertained by drunk Mr. Gallagher that they behaved themselves until their mother dropped him off behind the pub.

He waved cheerfully, then opened the door, tripped over the threshold, and as his balance was already impaired, nearly went facedown on the floor for the second time that day. He caught himself, hung on to the side of the counter, and waited for the pub kitchen to stop revolving.

With the careful steps of the drunk, he walked over to the cupboard to get out a pan for frying, a pot for boiling.

He was weaving in front of the refrigerator, wondering what the hell he was supposed to do with what was inside it, when Darcy marched in. Fire in her eyes.

"You're near to an hour late, and while you're lazing in bed, we've got two bloody buses coming in full of tourists and nothing to put in their bellies but beer nuts and crisps."

"Sure I'll be dealing with that directly."

"And what, I'd like to know, are we to put on the daily while you —" She broke off, took a good look at him. His eyes, she noted, were all but wheeling around in his head. "Look at the sight of you. Dirty and torn up and bleeding. You've been drinking."

"I have." He turned, gave her the sweet, harmless smile of the very drunk. "Considerably."

"Well, you knothead, sit down before you fall down."

"I can stand. I'm going to make fish cakes, I'm thinking."

"I'll bet you are." Amused, she pulled him to the table and shoved him into a chair. She took a look at his hand, decided she'd seen worse. "Stay where you're put," she ordered and went out to get Aidan.

"What d'you mean, drunk?" Aidan said after Darcy hissed in his ear.

"I think you're familiar with the term, but if you need refreshing on it, you've only to go into the kitchen and have a look at our brother."

"Christ, I don't have time for this." The pub had only a scatter of customers, as the doors had barely opened, but within thirty minutes, there would be sixty piling in, hungry from the bus trip down from Waterford City.

"Mind the bar, then," he told her.

"Oh, no, not for a million pounds would I miss this." So saying, she followed him into the kitchen.

Shawn was singing in his break-your-heart voice, about the cold nature of Peggy Gordon. And with one eye closed, his body swaying gently, he dripped lemon juice into a bowl.

"Oh, fuck me, Shawn, you *are* half pissed."

"More of three-quarters if the truth be known." He lost track of the juice and added a bit more to be safe. "And how are you today, Aidan, darling?"

"Get away from there before you poison someone."

Insulted, Shawn swiveled around and had to brace a hand on the counter to stay upright. "I'm drunk, not a murderer. I can make a goddamn fish cake in me sleep. This is my kitchen, I'll thank you to remember, and I give the orders here."

He poked himself in the chest with his thumb on

the claim and nearly knocked himself on his ass.

Gathering dignity, he lifted his chin. "So go on with you while I go about my work."

"What have you done to yourself?"

"The devil cat caught me hand." Forgetting his work, Shawn lifted a hand to scowl at the red gashes. "Oh, but I've plans for him, you can be sure of that."

"At the moment, I'd lay odds on the cat. Do you know anything about putting fish cakes together?" Aidan asked Darcy.

"Not a bloody thing," she said cheerfully.

"Then go and call Kathy Duffy, would you, and ask if she can spare us an hour or so, as we have an emergency."

"An emergency?" Shawn looked glassily around. "Where?"

"Come with me, boy-o."

"Where?" Shawn asked again, and Aidan hooked an arm around his waist.

"To pay the piper."

"If you're taking him upstairs," Darcy called out as she reached for the phone, "I'll thank you to clean up whatever mess is made during the sobering."

"Just call Kathy Duffy and mind the bar." Aidan took Shawn's weight and dragged him upstairs.

"I can cook, drunk or sober," Shawn insisted. "I don't know what you're in such a taking over. It's just fucking fish cakes." And he pressed a noisy kiss to Aidan's cheek.

"You always were a cheerful drunk."

"And why not?" Shawn hooked an arm around Aidan's shoulder, stumbled. "My life's in the toilet, and it looks better through the whiskey."

Making sympathetic noises, Aidan half carried him into Darcy's tidy little bathroom. "You had words with Brenna, did you?"

"No, but with everyone else in God's creation. I spent the night making love to the woman I want to marry. I tell you, Aidan, it's a different matter altogether being inside a woman when you love her. Who knew?"

Aidan considered the trouble of getting Shawn out of his clothes, and the mess that would be made if he didn't. So he propped his brother against the wall. "Just hold this up for a bit," he said.

"All right." Obligingly, Shawn braced his weight against the wall. "She thinks it's just sex, you know."

"Aye, well . . ." Working as fast as he could, Aidan crouched to take off Shawn's boots, which, he noted in disgust, had been tied into nasty little knots. "Women are the oddest of creatures."

"I've always liked them myself. There's so many varieties. But this is like having a lightning bolt smash right into my heart so it's all hot and bright and shaky. I'm not letting her go, and that's the end of it."

"That's the spirit." He got the boots off, and the jeans, and working briskly as a man with experience in such matters, efficiently stripped his brother down to the skin.

Knowing what was to follow, he shrugged out of his own shirt and tugged off his pants. "In you go."

"I can't go anywhere. I'm naked. I'll be arrested."

"I'll post your bond, not to worry." And not without sympathy, Aidan turned the shower on full cold and shoved his beloved brother under the heartless spray.

Oh, the scream all but peeled the skin off his face, and the curses that followed battered his ears. But Aidan held ground, dodged a fist when he had to, and clamping Shawn in a headlock, held him mercilessly under.

"You're drowning me, you bastard."

"Not yet." In a ruthless move, Aidan used his free hand to yank Shawn's head back by the hair so the icy spray showered his face. "Just shut your mouth and hold your breath, and you'll live through it."

"I'll kill you dead as Abraham when I'm out of here."

"You think I'm enjoying this, do you?" Laughter rose into his throat as he yanked Shawn's head back again. "You'd be right. Head clearing?"

Since Shawn's answer was a glug, Aidan gave it another minute, then switched off the spray. He was wise enough to move quickly out of range before tossing his brother one of Darcy's fancy towels. "Well, you're a sorry picture, but your eyes are clear. Are you going to be sick on me now?"

Though his limbs were weak as a baby's, Shawn wrapped the towel around his waist and tried for dignity. "Drowning me's one thing, insulting me's another. I ought to break your face for it."

Crisis passed, Aidan decided, then lifted a brow. "It appears someone tried to break yours. Did Brenna put that bruise on your chin?"

"No. Her father did."

"Mick O'Toole?" Aidan paused in the act of drying his own chest. "Mick O'Toole popped you one?"

"He did. But we've come to terms now." Shawn stepped out of the shower, annoyed that the blissful cushion of whiskey had been washed away, so now he could hurt all over — face, hand, leg. And heart.

"At a guess I'd say you got drunk together."

"That was part of the process." He flipped down the lid of the toilet, sat, and as he dressed again he filled Aidan in on the morning.

"You've had a busy day." Aidan laid a hand on his shoulder. "I can ask Kathy Duffy to do the whole of the shift."

"No, I can work. It'll keep my hands busy while I figure out what to do next." He stood up. "I mean to have her, Aidan, however it has to be done."

"You gave me advice once, on matters of the heart. Now I'll return the favor. Find the words, the right ones, and give them to her. I imagine there's different ones for different women, but when it's all cleared away, it means the same."

Before he came down again, Shawn tidied himself up as best he could and did the same for

310

Darcy's bathroom. Nothing was worth the spitting lecture she'd spew over him if he left it as it was. Since he felt the beginnings of a filthy head coming on, he rooted out the makings of the hangover remedy his family called Gallagher's Fix and downed a full glass of it.

He couldn't say he was feeling his best, but he thought he could get through the day now without making a bigger muck of things.

From the look of sympathy that Kathy Duffy sent him when he entered the kitchen again, he imagined he wasn't looking his best either.

"There now, lad." She clucked over him and had a strong cup of tea ready. "You just drink this and gather your wits. I've got things under control for now."

"I'm grateful to you. I know I left things turned 'round here."

"If a body can't indulge himself foolishly now and again, what's the point?" She bustled around as she talked, dealing with the fry pan and the pot she had simmering. "I've got the fish cakes doing and they're selling brisk. You had fresh cockles, so I did up the soup, and it's ready for serving now if any's a taste for it. Now most are wanting chips, but I've done up some pan boxty as well."

"It's a treasure you are, Mrs. Duffy."

She pinked and fluttered at that. "Oh, go on with you. It's nothing your dear mother wouldn't have done for one of mine if the need were there." She flipped fish cakes onto plates, spooned up chips that had drained, and added bits of parsley and pickled beets.

As if timed to a turn, Darcy came in to pick up the orders. "Well, the dead have arisen," she said with a quick study of her brother. "Though you look like you need to be buried."

"Oh, he's just a little shaky on his pins is all. Don't poke at him, Darcy, there's a good girl."

Shawn sent his sister a wide and sour grin behind Kathy's back as she loaded her tray. "We'll need two servings of your soup, Mrs. Duffy, and another of the fish cakes, with the boxty, and one further of fish and chips. And all would care for the green salad you were kind enough to make while my brother was indisposed."

"In two shakes, darling."

Darcy balanced her tray, and after shooting an evil look at Shawn, she headed out, singing "Whiskey for Breakfast."

"I'll deal with the frying, Mrs. Duffy, if you wouldn't mind seeing to the salads."

"Are you feeling up to it, lad?"

"I am, yes, thanks."

"It's best to keep busy, but mind your hand. Those are nasty scratches." She gave him a little pat as they passed each other. "And when Brenna comes in later to work, the two of you will make it up, mark my words."

If she'd smacked him over the head with the rolling pin, he'd have been less staggered. "Brenna?"

"I'm thinking the two of you had a bit of a spat,"

Kathy went on, cheerfully scooping up salad. "Lovebirds don't always sing pretty tunes."

Recovering, Shawn narrowed his eyes at the door. "Darcy." He said it darkly, bitterly, and with a hint of the violence he intended.

"Darcy?" With a rumbling laugh, Kathy lined up the bowls. "Now why would I need Darcy to be telling me what I can see with my own eyes? Wasn't I in the pub myself last night?"

"I barely spoke to Brenna last night in the pub." Sulking now, Shawn set the cakes to sizzling. "We were, the both of us, busy."

"I might expect that sort of answer from most men, but you're a poet, and you know very well just how much can be said with a look. The two of you clicked eyes together every blessed time you stepped out of the kitchen. Nothing I haven't been expecting for years."

"Oh, bloody hell." He muttered it, well under his breath, but the woman had ears like a rabbit.

"Now, what's the matter? It's a pretty business seeing the two of you starting to dance in the same direction."

And a mouth, Shawn thought, that flapped like a sheet in a gale. "Ah, the thing of it is, Mrs. Duffy — and I'm hoping you'll take this as delicate as it's meant — if, as things are, Brenna hears any talk of the two of us . . . dancing in the same direction, as you put it, she'll do a very fast jig the opposite way."

Judging the progress of the frying, she reached up for soup bowls. "And since when has Mary

Brenna O'Toole heard anything if it didn't please her to? The girl's ears are as stubborn as the rest of her — and good luck to you with her."

He shook the fry basket to drain more chips. "You've a point there, well taken."

"I've known the two of you since you were both bumps under your mothers' aprons." She ladled up soup and was generous with dumplings. "And ten years back — aye ten, as I recall it was the summer my Patrick broke his arm falling off the cabin roof, where he had no business being in the first place. Ten years ago this summer I said to Mr. Duffy as we sat out in the pub of an evening, and Brenna sat with her family at a near table, and you were playing one of your tunes on the fiddle while your father worked the bar . . ."

She trailed off as she set the bowls aside for Darcy. "I said to him, as I watched her watching you, and saw that now and again a glance of yours would land in her direction, there's something that will come around when the time's right."

"I never thought of her that way back then."

"Of course you did," Kathy said comfortably. "You just didn't know it."

When it was time for the evening shift, Darcy lay in wait for Brenna. And nearly missed her, as Brenna came in the front instead of the back.

"You missed a great crowd today." Darcy sauntered over. It took only a strategic shift of her body to corner Brenna by the coatrack. "Shawn was late for work," she continued in a whisper, "and was drunk besides. What's going on?"

"I can't talk about it now. I made a mess of things, I can say that much."

Darcy laid a hand on Brenna's shoulder until she finished her study. "You look terrible. Was it a big fight or a little one?"

"It wasn't a fight at all with Shawn." She glanced over at the kitchen door, wondering how they were going to deal with it all, and with each other, now. "Got drunk, did he? Well, now, I wish I'd thought of that. Let me go on to work, Darcy. It's going to be a long night, and the sooner it's started, the sooner it's done."

If anyone expected her to leave it at that, they didn't know Darcy Gallagher. At the first opportunity, she was in the kitchen. She took a good look at her brother as she relayed orders. Though he was a bit rough around the edges still, he appeared sober and steady.

"Brenna's come in." Darcy noted with interest that Shawn's steady motion with the rolling pin broke. "She looks unhappy. And so do you."

He went back to rolling out the pastry for meat pies. "We'll be all right."

"I'll help you."

He flicked his eyes up. "Why?"

"Because she's my oldest and dearest friend in all the world, and you, though an accident of fate, are my brother."

Humor flickered across his face. "We'll be all right, Darcy," he repeated. "It's for us to work it out."

"You're turning down the assistance of an expert in this particular field of battle."

He began to score the dough, measuring it into neat squares. "I'll hold you in reserve, if it's all the same to you."

"Well, it's your choice, after all." She started out, stopped, turned around. "Does she matter?"

Knowing how well his sister read faces, Shawn kept his head lowered. "Do you think I don't know what comes out of my mouth goes in your ear, then off your tongue and into her ear?"

"It won't. If you ask me."

He looked up then. Loyalty was her finest trait, as far as he was concerned. And he knew she'd sooner break her arm than her word. "Then I'm asking you. I feel it's my life up on a thin and slippery line. Step off one way, the ground's solid, off the other it's a bog. You sink in, and it's over."

"Then watch your step," Darcy advised, and went back into the pub.

The noise level was already rising. It would be a din, hushed down once the music started, and peaking again at every break the band took. Brenna worked the taps with both hands, even while she listened to Jack Brennan lumber his way through a joke he'd heard about a princess and a frog. Though her heart wasn't in it, she laughed at the end.

When the band began to set up, she ordered herself to pay no mind, no mind at all. But her gaze wandered over nonetheless and locked on the blond singer.

Just the type Shawn would drift back to, she thought. Shallow bastard. What would it take him? A month, a week, a bloody night before he rolled atop another woman?

"I'm almost afraid to ask," Jude said as she slid onto a stool. "But can I have a mineral water?"

"You can." Brenna got the glass, remembered ice as Jude had that Yank preference for it. "Why would you be afraid to ask?"

"Because you look as if you want to punch someone. I wouldn't want it to be me."

"It'd more likely be myself, or that blonde over there."

"Eileen? Why?"

"To start, she has tits." Brenna set the glass down, ordered herself to put the rest aside. "You look well tonight, Jude Frances. Well and happy."

"I'm both. I've gained two more pounds. I can't get my trousers hooked anymore."

Brenna took orders and coin, continued to work the taps. "So you'll make use of all those maternity clothes Darcy talked you into. Don't you want a table — a chair for your back?"

"No, I'm fine here for now. I'm just staying long enough for the first set, and a bowl of soup."

"You want a meal?" It came out as an accusation, making Jude stare.

"Well, I'd considered it."

"You'll want a table," Brenna said briskly. If Jude ordered from a table it would be Darcy's job to go into the kitchen.

"No, I don't. I've gotten some bits and pieces

317

about trouble between you and Shawn. You can't deal with it, Brenna, if you can't so much as open that door and shout out an order for soup."

"Maybe I don't want to deal with it." When Jude only folded her hands on the bar, Brenna hissed out a breath. "You know, I'm finding married women a pain in the ass." She finished building a Guinness, pulled a pint and a glass of lager, and exchanged them for the price. "You've got fairy tales on your brain," she continued. "That's not how it is here."

"I might agree with you but for one thing. Well two things. Carrick and Lady Gwen."

Brenna snorted and started another pair of pints. "They've nothing to do with me. I'll tell you how I'd end a fairy tale," she continued, thinking of Jack Brennan's joke. "In mine, the princess doesn't kiss the frog, but dines well on frog legs at end of day. I'll get your damn soup."

Spoiling for a fight, she strode to the door, shoved it open. Shawn was at the stove, a wooden spoon in one hand, a spatula in the other. The heat had his hair curling just a bit, and he needed a trim. He hadn't bothered to shave, which was an odd thing for Shawn. But under the day's growth on his jaw was unmistakable bruising.

Before she could speak, the warm, liquid voice of the blond singer drifted into the room. It didn't matter if it was unreasonable. It didn't matter if it was uncalled for.

It just pissed her off.

"I need an order of soup."

318

"It's hot and ready," he said easily, because he gauged her mood. "I've my hands a bit full here, if you wouldn't mind spooning it up yourself."

"Everyone's hands are full," she muttered, but she got down a bowl. "What happened to your face?"

He swiveled his jaw. "I wasn't watching my step."

"Aye. I heard you got yourself a snootful. Well, that's no answer."

Since she'd decided to snipe at him, Shawn reasoned, she wasn't going to wallow and brood. Much better all around. "It served at the time."

She filled the bowl, set it on a plate. "And now?"

He wanted to lean over, just lean to her while both their hands were occupied and close his mouth over hers. Instead, he lifted a shoulder. "And now I'll have to be more careful where I step." For the hell of it, he began to hum in harmony with Eileen's lovely voice.

"You think it's as easy as that, do you? Well, it's not. We'll talk about this after closing."

He let her have the last word since it was exactly what he'd intended to say to her. When she stalked out, her face fierce, he went back to work with a lighter heart.

A couple of tourists from Cleveland overindulged. Brenna helped Aidan steer them toward the B and B, on foot, as it was feared they'd break their necks if they attempted to ride their bikes even that far.

319

Gauging his timing, Shawn slipped out. "Ah, well, you got them off, then. I was thinking you might need an extra pair of hands."

"No, they should be able to stumble their way into bed." Aidan watched them lurch and weave down the street and shook his head at their off-key rendition of "Whiskey, You're the Devil." "A pair of Yanks straight out of school. Well, but what's a Grand Tour without one drunken night in an Irish pub, after all?" He caught Shawn's eye, figured the meaning. "It's been a long one, so we'll call it a night. Thanks for helping out, Brenna."

"It's not a problem. Good night, Aidan."

"It's been longer for you and me," Shawn said when he and Brenna were alone on the street.

"It has, but it's not done. I'd like a walk on the beach if it's the same to you."

"All right." He didn't take her hand, but walked beside her, his own hands in his pockets. "It's a fresh night. Full of moon."

"That's lucky. We won't freeze or fall on our faces."

He had to laugh. "You're such a romantic fool, Mary Brenna."

"A fool, from time to time. I was foolish with you, knowing my sister's feelings."

"With or without you, I couldn't give her what she thinks she wants from me. There's no getting past that. I'm sorry she's hurt, and sorrier still that it was you she struck out at. But in thinking it through, I don't know if there was a way it could've been avoided."

"I could have waited until her feelings for you faded off, as they will."

"So, I'm the forgettable sort."

She glanced up at him, then away. "That scores your pride, but it's the way it is. She's barely twenty and can't see through the stars in her eyes."

"But there're none in yours."

"I see clear enough. I started this with you, and I'd end it. I was prepared to end it. But that's not the way to solve the matter. Mary Kate won't forgive and forget just because I step away from you. If she's to grow up, she needs to learn how to face the hard things."

"So, you've decided for all of us, then."

Because he stopped, she turned to him. Moonlight streamed at his back, spilling over sand and sea like liquid pearls. And in its light she saw his eyes weren't calm and easy, but very near to furious.

"Someone has to."

"And it's always you? Maybe I've had enough of you. Maybe I prefer having my life on balance instead of being in the middle of two women who want to bite and scratch."

Nearly as shocked as she was offended, she snapped at him. "I don't bite and scratch, and I wasn't looking to fight Mary Kate or anyone over the likes of you. It just happened. And as far as you having enough of me," she added, "that's a different tune you're singing than the one I heard only this morning."

"I know a variety of tunes. And as you think so

little of me, I'd suspect you'd be relieved to part ways in this area. Both of us can find sex elsewhere when we're in the mood for it."

"It's not just sex."

Ah, he thought, finally. "Isn't it?" He stepped closer, backing her toward the sea. "Isn't that what you said you wanted from me?"

"Yes." What was going on in those eyes of his? she wondered. They were black as night, with thoughts and feelings she couldn't read. "But we have a caring for each other. I won't have you cheapen what's between us that way."

"But you'll say what I'll have and won't, what I'll do and don't?" He snatched her up seconds before she backed into the surf. "Why would you want a man touching you who could be so easily ordered about?"

"Shawn." He had her up, her feet dangling inches above the ground. Her heart began to boom. "Set me down."

"You want me to touch you. Even now, thinking you can point and I'll go here, or I'll go there, you want my hands on you."

"It's nothing to be proud of."

He jerked her up another inch. "Fuck pride."

And when his mouth crushed down on hers, it was rough and ruthless. She might have resisted, might have shoved and struggled. But she did none of those things.

She gave, because he so rarely demanded. She gave, because she needed to. As her body began a fevered quaking, she said his name.

"I could have you, right here and now." He dropped her abruptly on her feet. "Think about why that is. I have."

She couldn't think at all, not with her insides churning and the blood roaring in her head like the sea at her back.

"I'm going home."

"Go, then. I won't stop you." He tucked his hands back in his pockets so he wouldn't be tempted to do just that. "Mind this, Brenna. I won't come to you. Once you work out what's inside you yourself, you know where to find me."

She walked away. Shawn could say what he would about pride, but she needed herself. She didn't start running until her boots hit the street.

"That's the way you charm the ladies, is it?" Carrick stood in the shallow surf and lifted the silver pipe he held to his lips to play a quick tune. "What strange ways you mortals have."

"I know what I'm about here."

"I'm sure you think you do. You pea-brain. If you love the woman, why do you let her wiggle away like that?"

"Because I love her." The fury he'd barely held in check broke out now as he rounded on Carrick. "And you didn't do so very well in your own time with your own woman, did you?"

Carrick's eyes flashed, a wild blue that matched the lightning that split the star-strewed sky. "You're looking to take on the likes of me now, Gallagher the younger?" He stepped out of the surf on boots that were soft and dry. "Didn't your dear mother ever warn you about what comes of challenging the Good People?"

"You don't worry me, Carrick. You need me. It's come down to you, with all your power and all your tricks, needing a mortal man. So hold your threats and your light shows. They don't impress me."

Temper simmered, settled. "Hah. The woman thinks she knows what's in you, but she's yet to dig deep enough. Have a care you don't show her too much too quickly and scare her off."

"Go to the devil."

Carrick flashed his teeth. "He won't have me," said he, and faded away to the tune of his pipe.

Seventeen

Brenna went to early Mass. The little church with cool morning light coming through the glass smelled of candle wax and holy water. It always seemed to her that holy water carried a faint metallic scent. When Brenna was a child Mollie told her it was the blessings in it. She often remembered that, found comfort in that, whether she dipped her fingers in the church font or the water of Saint Declan's Well.

A baby was fussing in the back pew, little fretful squawls that his mother tried to hush with murmurs and pats. Brenna didn't mind it. It was rare to sit at Mass and not hear a baby whimpering or wailing, or children squirming, starched clothes scratching against worn wooden pews.

She liked the familiarity of it, as much as the ritual. It was a fine time and place for thinking, which to her mind was the same as praying half the time.

She had choices to make. And if she wanted to repair the damage that had been done, she had to make them quickly. When there was a crack in something it only widened if you didn't tend to it. Let it go long enough, a crack became a break, and you had a hell of a mess on your hands.

There was damage now to her relationship with Mary Kate, a split that could undermine the foundation of blood and heart. She'd had a part in causing it. Left as it was, that damage could run through and fracture the bond of her entire family. How it was repaired would determine whether that bond held firm or showed the scars.

The same was true of Shawn. There was a foundation there, built over a lifetime of affection and shared memories and friendship. She wouldn't stand aside and watch it crumble.

Choices, she thought, of where to begin the repairs and how to go about them. Each choice took steps, and only she could take them. Best if she began now.

She slipped out a few minutes before the service ended. That way she avoided anyone who wanted to chat or gossip or ask after her family. She drove home, a bit nervous in the stomach regions, but with her mind made up as to which step to take first.

"There you are." Mollie, dressed for church, met her at the door. "I heard you go out earlier."

"I've been to Mass."

"Oh, well, the lot of us are about to go ourselves."

"Mary Kate'll have to go later." Brenna moved in and started up the stairs. "She can use my lorry."

"Brenna, I want no fighting in this house on the Lord's day."

"There won't be," Brenna promised. She had a mind to fight elsewhere, should it be necessary.

She got to the top of the steps just as her father came out of his room. His face was red and glowing from his shave, his hair showing the forks of his comb like little furrows in a sandy field. Her heart all but broke with love for him.

"Dad."

It was awkward, and he imagined it would be so between them for a little while yet. But there were tears swimming into her eyes. That he couldn't bear. "Your mother's gathering us up for Mass."

"I've already been."

"Ah, well." He shifted his feet. "I'm after an early start in the morning. Those back steps of O'Leary's finally fell through, as we've been telling them they would. Of course, O'Leary fell through with them, which is no more than he deserves for letting them rot as he did. We'll start there first thing."

She understood that either of them could have dealt with the job alone. That he was having them work together healed the widest crack in her heart. "I'll be ready. Dad —"

"We'll be late for Mass if you don't shake out the lead," Mollie called up.

"Tomorrow's as good as today," was all Mick said, and touched his hand lightly to Brenna's arm as he passed her.

She took a deep breath. "Not for everything," she muttered, and pushed open the door to her sisters' room.

Alice Mae sat patiently on the side of the bed, her good shoes polished, her hair brushed to a rose gold gleam. Mary Kate primped in front of the mirror, adding a coat of mascara to her lashes. Her eyes were still a little swollen from weeping, but her mouth formed a thin sharp line when she saw Brenna.

"Alice, darling, Ma's calling. Go on now."

Mary Kate gave her hair one more toss. "I'm coming with you, Alice Mae."

"No, you're not," Brenna corrected and stepped in front of the doorway. "You'll have to make a later Mass."

"I don't have to do anything you say."

"You can come with me and have this out away from the house, as I've promised Ma there'd be no fighting in it. Or you can sulk day and night like a child. If you want to be a woman, Mary Kate, I'll be in my lorry waiting."

It took less than five minutes for Mary Kate to saunter out of the house and climb into the lorry. She'd added lipstick, Brenna noted as she zoomed out into the road. She couldn't understand why so many females saw paint as a kind of shield or weapon.

Then again, she knew her ancestors had painted themselves blue before screaming into battle.

As she figured it as neutral turf, or if anything leaned a bit toward Mary Kate's side, she drove to the cliff hotel and parked. She got out and began to walk, knowing her sister would follow.

"And where are you going?" Mary Kate demanded. "Somewhere you can toss me off a cliff?"

"Somewhere I think the both of us will respect enough not to start pulling hair or punching."

They followed the path, crossing the cliffs, where the air still had a bite. It seemed winter wasn't quite ready to surrender to spring. But there were wildflowers beginning to show their faces and tuneful birds that sang out as high and loud as the crying gulls.

She passed the ruin of the cathedral once built in the name of Saint Declan and moved beyond his well, beyond the three stone crosses, toward the ground that held the dead and their markers.

"This is holy ground," Brenna began. "And I'm standing on it when I tell you I wronged you. You're my sister, my blood, and I didn't consider your feelings, not as I should have. I'm sorry for it."

It threw Mary Kate off, and that alone was enough to stir her temper again. "Do you think that makes up for it?"

"I'm thinking it's all I can say."

"Are you giving him up?"

"I thought I would," Brenna said slowly. "That was part pride. 'I'll give him up for her,' I thought. 'Then she'll see how I'd sacrifice to keep her happy.' The other part was guilt that I'd done something to hurt you, and ending things with Shawn would be my penance for it."

"I'd think you'd have more guilt than pride in the way you've behaved."

Temper flashed once, a bright warning in her eyes. Then Brenna snuffed it. She knew her sister, and she knew just how clever Mary Kate could be in inciting anger to overpower her opponent's reason.

"I've no guilt over what's been between myself and Shawn, but only that what is between us has hurt and embarrassed you." The cool delivery only added impact to the words. "And for that I was prepared to turn from him, as a lover, and perhaps as a friend as well. Then, reconsidering, it seemed to me that doing that would be something akin to giving in to a child's tantrum, and that's hardly treating you or your feelings with respect."

"You're just twisting it all around so you can have what you want."

Suddenly the four years separating them seemed like forty. And made Brenna unbearably tired. There were tears in Mary Kate's voice, hot and spiteful ones that reminded Brenna of times they'd squabbled over a new toy or the last biscuit in the tin.

"Do I want Shawn? I do. I haven't figured it all out as yet, but the wanting's there, and I can't deny it. I'm facing you here, woman to woman, and telling you he wants me as well. I'm sorry, Mary Kate, for the unhappiness it causes you, but he isn't looking at you that way."

Mary Kate's chin came up, and Brenna thought her own would have done the same under the circumstances. "He might if you weren't warming his bed."

That caused a hitch in her stomach, but she nodded. "The fact is, I am in his bed. And I won't be rolling out of it to make room for you. Yesterday I might have, because I couldn't stand seeing you so hurt and knowing I was part of the cause. But I'm looking at you here, Mary Kate, in clear light with a clear head. And you're not hurting now. You're just mad."

"How do you know what I feel for him?"

"I don't. Tell me."

She threw up her head so her hair flew in the frisky wind. "I love him." It was a passionate and almost sweetly dramatic declaration. Brenna gave her full marks for it, knowing she herself could never have pulled it off so impressively.

"Why?"

"Because he's handsome and sensitive and kind."

"Aye, he's all of those things — as is the Clooney dog. What of his flaws?"

"He doesn't have any."

"Of course he does." The fact of them smoothed out Brenna's nerves and made her feel oddly sentimental. "He's stubborn and slow to move and absentminded. There are times you'll be talking to him and you might as well be talking to yourself, as his brain's gone off somewhere else. He lacks ambition and needs to be prodded along every other step or he'd stay happy in the same place forever."

"That's how you see him."

"I see him as he is, not as a pretty picture out of a book. Mary Kate." She stepped forward, knowing it was too soon to reach out. "Let's be honest here, we two. There's something in the way he looks, in

331

the air of him that makes a woman want. I understand how he makes you feel in that area. And I've wanted him myself since I was no older than Alice Mae."

Something flickered in Mary Kate's eyes. "I don't believe you. You don't wait for anything."

"I thought I'd get over it. Then I thought I'd make a fool of myself." Brenna pushed at her hair, wished she'd thought to tie it back before coming up the cliff. "In the end it was more than a wanting. It was a needing."

"You don't love him."

"I think I might." The minute the words were out, Brenna pressed a hand to her heart, as if someone had just delivered a blow to it. "I think I might," she said again, then just slid down to her knees. "Oh, sweet God Almighty, what am I to do?"

Mary Kate could only gape. Her sister had gone dead white and was rocking on her knees and clutching her chest as if she was having a seizure. "Stop that. You're playacting."

"I'm not. I can't. I can't seem to breathe right."

Suspicious, Mary Kate walked over and gave Brenna a hefty thump on the back. "There."

Her breath whooshed out, wheezed in. "Thanks." She sank weakly onto her heels. "I can't deal with this now, I can't. I shouldn't be expected to. It was bad enough the way things were, but this won't do. It won't do at all. This fixes nothing, but only shifts the weight. Damn it."

Since Brenna made no move to get up, Mary Kate sat down. "I think I could forgive you if you were in love with him. Are you just saying you are so I will?"

"No. And I didn't say I was, I said I might be." Desperate, Brenna grabbed her sister's hand. "You're to tell no one. I want your word you're to say nothing of this, or I'll strangle you in your sleep. Swear it to me."

"Oh, for heaven's sake, why should I go around telling anyone? So I can look like a bigger horse's ass?"

"It'll probably go away."

"Why should you want it to?"

"In love with Shawn Gallagher." Brenna rubbed her hands over her face, ran them back into her hair. "What a pretty mess that would be. We'd drive each other crazy inside a year — me always wanting to get things done, him dreaming the time away. The man can't remember to plug in a cord, much less fix one that's gone off."

"What difference does that make? You can fix it. And dreaming's what he does. How else could he make up all that music?"

"And what's the point of making it up if you do nothing with it?" Brenna waved it away. "Oh, it doesn't matter. It's not what either of us was after when we started. I'm just doing the bloody female thing, and it annoys me. Why do women have to turn attraction into love?"

"Maybe there was love hiding under the attraction all along."

Brenna lifted her head. "Why do you suddenly have to get wise?"

"Maybe because you're not treating me like a foolish girl anymore. And maybe because when I look at you right now, it occurs to me that it might not have been love I was feeling for him. It didn't make me go pale and tremble, that's for certain. And . . ." She sat back, a faint sneer on her face. "Maybe because it's satisfying under the circumstances to see you look weak and terrified. You damn near pulled my hair out by the roots yesterday."

"You got your licks in."

"Well, it was you taught me to fight." At the memory of it sentimental tears clouded Mary Kate's eyes. "I'm sorry I called you a whore. I did it the first time out of anger, and the others out of spite." She dabbed at her eyes. "And I'm sorry for the things I wrote about you in my diary — well, sorry for some of them."

"We won't let it matter." Their fingers linked. "I don't want him, or anyone, between us. I'm asking you not to make me push him away."

"So you can feel righteous and me guilty? No, I'll have none of that." A ghost of a smile flitted around her mouth. "I can get me own man when I want one. But . . ." She angled her head. "There's one thing I'd like to know."

"What would it be?"

"Does he kiss as well as it seems he would from looking at him?"

"When he puts his mind to it, he can melt every bone in your body."

Mary Kate sighed. "I had a feeling."

She walked to the cottage, but her mind wasn't much clearer when she arrived than it had been when she'd started out. There was rain coming, a soft one, Brenna thought, from the way the sun was shining under the clouds.

A good day to curl up by a fire, she thought. But of course there wasn't a puff of smoke rising from the chimney at Faerie Hill Cottage. Shawn forgot such things twice as often as he remembered them.

His car was gone, so she imagined he'd taken himself off to church. She'd wait. She passed through the garden gate, and glancing up, half expected to see the quiet green eyes of Lady Gwen watching. But nothing stirred, mortal or otherwise.

She stepped in, nearly tripped over his work boots that lay where he'd kicked them off the night before, with a good coating of dirt on the heels. She nudged them aside with the toe of her own, then crossed over into the little front parlor to build a fire.

His music sheets were scattered over the piano, and a cup that would have held his tea was sitting carelessly on a table. As was a squat green bottle that held a clutch of flowers from the front garden.

He would think of such things, she mused. He wouldn't remember to clean off his boots, and neither did she more often than not, but he'd take the time and have the thought to put flowers out.

Why didn't she think of things like that? She liked a house with flowers, and with candles sitting about. And the scents they created together that made the air delicate. She would think of cleaning the chimney out, and laying by turf or wood, but she would never think of the little touches that turned house to home.

Hanging curtains was one thing, she decided. Thinking of lace was another altogether.

After the fire was going, she rose to wander to the piano. Had he worked here last night? she wondered. He'd been angry with her. Did he work off a mad here as well as dream?

His heart's in his song. She frowned as she sifted through the pages scribbled with notes and words. If that were true, why did he leave his music all tossed about this way? Why didn't he *do* something with it?

How could she care so much for a man who lacked basic drive? Surely it wasn't enough for a man to have such a light inside him if he didn't use it for something.

"These pearls I now lay at your feet," she murmured, reading his work, "are only moon-shed tears. For every time my heart does beat, it weeps for you across the years. Night by night the spell holds fast, until the day love breaks the past."

So he sings of legends, Brenna thought — and waits for what?

She set the sheet aside again when she heard his car.

He'd seen the smoke and knew it would be Brenna. What he would do about it, he was less certain. He had to hope, as he did with his music, that the next passage would just come to him.

He stepped into the house and turned as she walked to the parlor doorway.

"There's a chill in the mornings yet. I lit your fire."

He nodded. "Do you want some tea?"

"No." She couldn't read his face, and it worried her. "You were angry with me last night. Are you still?"

"Not as much."

"Well . . ." The sense of awkwardness was something new, and not at all welcome. "I thought I should tell you I had some words with Mary Kate this morning. Private words."

"Then it's better between you."

"It is, yes."

"I'm glad of it. With a little time, I hope she'll be comfortable with me again as well."

"She'll be embarrassed for a while, but as for the rest . . . after I pointed out all of your flaws, she thinks perhaps she's not in love with you after all."

He lifted his brows. "That was clever of you."

"Shawn." She laid a hand on his arm when he started into the room, so they stood, framed in the doorway. "I'm sorry for how we left things last night."

"I'm sorry" were words that didn't slide easily off her tongue, he knew. So they meant more. "Then so am I."

"And I don't mind your flaws — or most of them — very much."

She smelled of Sunday, shampoo and soap, and her eyes were full of apologies. "Then it's better between us as well?"

"I want it to be."

He crossed over, sat in the single chair that wasn't full of sheet music. "Why don't you come sit with me awhile, Mary Brenna?"

Her eyes twinkled as relief sparkled through her. She thought she knew what he was about. She couldn't think of a finer way to make up. After walking to him, she sat on his lap, angling herself so their faces were close. "Friends again?"

"We ever were."

"I hardly slept for worrying we'd never be easy with each other again, though I know we promised we'd stay friends."

"And we will. Is friends all you're wanting to be just now?"

For an answer she closed the distance between them and laid her lips on his. Her little sigh slid into him, warm, familiar now. He drew her closer, lingering over the kiss, drawing it out soft and sweet before trailing his lips up to her brow.

Then he tucked her head on his shoulder, circled his arms comfortably around her. Puzzled, she sat still, waiting for his hands to move in the way, and to the places, she expected. But he only held her while the fire smoked and simmered, and the rain flowed in to splat and patter.

Gradually she relaxed against him, sinking into the comfort and coziness, lulled by the intimacy of silence.

She'd never had a lover like him, one who understood her, who was content to cuddle away a rainy morning. Was that why she'd fallen in love with him? Or had she always felt the same without knowing it? Whatever the answer, it had to be dealt with, explored and examined until the pieces fit.

"I'm wondering," she began, "if the next evening you have free you'd like to go with me up to Waterford City. I'll take you to dinner."

He smiled into her hair. She'd taken her time working up to courting him, but this was a fine start at it. "Would you be wearing that dress you put on for the Dubliner some time back?"

"I could."

"I like the way it fits you."

"If I'm wearing a dress, we'd best take your car. I'll give it a good going-over today. Your engine's missing, and your oil's filthy. From the quick look I had under the hood, I'd say the last time your battery connections were cleaned was when I did it myself."

"I prefer leaving such matters to the experts."

"You're just lazy about it."

"There's that as well. Was that one of the flaws that has Mary Kate reconsidering?"

"It was. You're a feckless sort, Shawn Gallagher."

"Well, now, 'feckless' is a harsh word."

"I'm sorry if it insults you." She shifted, and didn't look sorry at all. "But you must admit ambition isn't your middle name."

"I've ambition enough when it matters."

"Doesn't your music matter?"

He'd leaned forward to nip at her ear, but she'd thrown him off his rhythm. "What does my music have to do with it?"

Careful, Brenna, she thought. Take the pieces apart, but don't damage them. "You sit here and make it, then leave it all tossed about."

"I know where everything is."

"The point is, what are you doing with it?"

"Getting pleasure from it."

A block here, she noted, studying the way his face closed up. It would take deft hands to work around it — but she was determined to do it. It was one of the steps that needed to be taken.

"That's fine and good, but don't you want more? Don't you want other people to have the pleasure of it as well?"

"You don't even like my music."

"Now when have I said that?" At his bland stare she shrugged. "Well, if I did 'twas only to annoy you. I like it very well. And now and then when you've played one of your tunes in the pub or at a *ceili*, others have too."

"That's friends and family."

"Exactly. I'm a friend, aren't I?"

"You are."

"Then will you give me a tune?"

He shifted, wary. "What do you mean, 'give you a tune'?"

"Just that. Let me have a song, for my own. A barter, for fixing your car." On impulse she got up, gestured to the piano. "You've dozens, and they're

340

just lying about. I'd like to have one."

He didn't believe that for a minute, but he couldn't see the trap or the harm. "It's some mood you're in, O'Toole, but all right. I'll give you one."

He rose, but when he started to push through the piles, she slapped his hand away. "No, I get to pick it. It's only fair." She snatched up the one she'd been reading, the one, she realized, she'd been picking out on the keyboard when Lady Gwen had first shown herself. "I like this one."

"It's not finished yet." He couldn't put a finger on the point of his panic, he only knew he felt it. "It needs work."

"It's the one I want. You wouldn't be stepping back from a bargain, would you?"

"No, but —"

"Good." She folded the sheets in a way that made him wince, and tucked them in her back pocket. "It's mine now, and thank you." She rose up on her toes, kissed him lightly. "I'll drive you to the pub, drop you off for work. That way I can bring your car back to my house where my tools are. I'll have it running smooth for you."

"I've a bit of time yet."

"Well, I don't. I've considerable to do today. If I brought your car down to you before closing, would you give me a lift back?"

He tried to put the song out of his mind. She'd forget it soon enough, he decided. "Back to where?"

She smiled slowly. "Here would be just far enough."

She had one stop to make before she drove home to change and get out her tools. With Shawn safely at the pub, Brenna drove down to Jude's house and parked.

Jude was out in the front garden, getting a jump on spring. Her gloves were already dark with dirt, and there were a number of sketches on the walkway beside her. At Brenna's approach, she sat back on her heels and tipped up the straw hat she was using to protect her head from the drizzling rain.

"Something wrong with your lorry?"

"No, I'm doing some work on Shawn's car, as he'd rather be nibbled by ants than lift the bonnet. Your drawings are getting wet."

"I know. I have to stop. I just wanted to hurry spring along."

"Ah, you've sketched out your ideas for your gardens." Crouching, Brenna used her back to protect the papers. "Like a blueprint. That's a clever notion."

"It helps me see it. Let's go inside, out of the wet." She started to rise, then shifted and put a hand on the slope of her belly. "My center of gravity's changing."

"Another few months, you won't be able to get up off your knees without a rope and pulley. Here, I'll get these." Brenna picked up the sketches and Jude's garden basket.

"I saw Colleen Ryan going into the market the other day. She's due any minute. She waddles,"

Jude said as they stepped into the house. "It's very sweet, but I intend to glide, Madonna-like, through my term."

"You keep thinking that, darling."

Brenna carried the basket back to the little mudroom off the kitchen and spread the drawings out on the counter to dry.

The kettle went on. The biscuit tin came down.

"I told Aidan I'd come into the pub for lunch." With a sheepish grin, Jude bit into a sugar cookie. "But I'm always hungry these days. Nothing spoils my appetite."

"Expecting looks good on you, Jude. I remember the first time I saw you, a year ago, standing in the rain at the door to Faerie Hill Cottage, looking lost. You're found now."

"What a lovely way to put it. Yes, I'm found now. Things I wanted, and could hardly admit even to myself that I wanted, happened."

"You made them happen."

"Some of it." She nibbled on the cookie while Brenna paced the kitchen. "And some things are meant to be. You have to be willing enough, brave enough, to let them happen."

"When you discovered you loved Aidan, did you tell him? Straight out?"

"No, I was afraid to. I didn't trust myself enough."

Brenna's eyes sharpened. "Or him?"

"Or him," Jude admitted. "Before I came here, I never made things happen, and it wasn't courage that had me letting them happen around me or to me. It was fear and passivity. I had to learn the difference. To take charge of some things, to trust others to fall into place."

"But you had to take steps."

"Yes. Are you in love with Shawn?"

Frowning, Brenna sat. "It seems I am. I'm not ashamed to say it's a shock to the system."

"Love looks well on you, Brenna."

At the turn of her own words, Brenna let out a short laugh. "It doesn't feel well. But I suppose I'll get used to it. I'll get the tea," she said when the kettle sputtered.

"No, sit. Have you told him?"

"Not bloody likely." As a thought struck, Brenna looked over quickly as Jude dealt with the tea. "I know married couples tend to tell each other most everything, but —"

"You don't want me to mention this to Aidan."

"I don't."

"Then I won't."

"Thanks." Brenna let out a breath. "It's a matter now of taking those steps, and figuring out which come first. As well as I know him — Shawn, I'm meaning — he's not as predictable as I thought before we . . . changed things between us."

"The dynamics are different between lovers than they are between friends. Even lifelong friends."

"I've discovered that. Still, I know he often takes a good kick in the ass to get moving in some areas. I'm taking that first step with something that bothers me the most, and that I think, underneath, means the most to him." Shifting her seat, she tugged out the sheets of music.

"One of his songs?"

"I badgered him into giving it to me. There's talent here, isn't there, Jude?"

"I think so."

"Why doesn't he pursue it? You understand how the mind works."

"You're asking a former, and mediocre, psychology professor." Jude set the pot on the table, fetched cups. "But my educated guess would be that he's afraid."

"Of what?"

"Of failing in the thing that matters most. What if it isn't good enough? What if he isn't good enough? There are a lot of us who circle that abyss, Brenna." She poured out the tea. "You're not one of them. You just roll up your sleeves and build a bridge over it."

"Then I'm after building one over his. He gave me this song, and I can do what I like with it. I want to send it to someone who'd know about such things. Who'd know if it's worth buying."

"Without telling Shawn."

"I won't feel guilty about that," Brenna muttered. "If it doesn't work out, he'll never have to know, will he? And if it does, how can he be anything but pleased? I'm not sure how to go about it, or who to send it along to. I thought you might have some ideas on it."

"I'd be wasting my breath trying to talk you out of this?"

"You would."

Jude nodded. "Then I'll save it. I don't know anything about the music business. I could ask my agent, though I don't think she'd . . ." As an idea formed, she trailed off, worked on it. "What about Magee? He's built theaters. He has to know people in entertainment. Maybe he'd have some connections."

"That's a good notion."

"I can get you his address. You can write to him."

Brenna ran her fingers over the notes and the words on the sheet in front of her. "That takes too long. Do you have a phone number?"

Eighteen

The soft rain became a pounding, and the pounding a flood swept in by gale-force winds that beat against the coastline and rocked the boats at their moorings. For the best part of a week it was too rough to cast a net. From shore to horizon was nothing but angry, churning gray slashed by white-caps that looked keen-edged enough to slice through a hull.

Those who made their living from the sea waited it out with the grim patience honed in them over generations.

Wind screamed against windows and doors in a constant banshee call and snuck through any crack or crevice to chill the bones. Smoke belched back down chimneys in nasty, fitful streams. Plucking fingers of wind tore a few shingles from the roof of the market so that they careened away like drunken birds. One swooped down and sliced at the back of young Davey O'Leary's head as he rode his bike home with a quart of milk and a dozen eggs. The head required seven stitches. The eggs were a total loss.

Flowers that had wintered over happily enough and those that had begun to show their spring faces were chewed to pieces by the last teeth of winter. Dooryards went to mud.

Tourists steered clear, and reservations were canceled as the storm gleefully battered Ardmore. Power and phone lines gave out on the third day.

The village huddled down, as it had time and again, to weather the storm. Under more than one roof the mood was edgy. Young children, bored and restless, drove their mothers mad. Tears and warmed bottoms were daily occurrences.

Brenna and her father, shielded with slickers and Wellingtons, stood knee-deep in mud and worse as they searched out the break in the Duffys' septic system.

"Filthy work, this." Mick rested against his shovel.

"More than one lowlander's going to find himself wading in shit if this keeps up."

"If those bastards from Waterford had showed up, we'd have the tank pumped out, at least."

"If they ever get here with their big pumper, I say we toss them headfirst into the muck."

"That's my girl."

"Christ Jesus, what a smell. But I think here's the matter, Dad."

They hunkered down, rain beating over their heads, and studied the old cracked line with identical expressions of interest and thoughtfulness on their faces. "It's just as you figured, Dad. The pipe's old and gave out under the added pressure. It runs from tank to field and bursting's turned

Mrs. Duffy's nice yard into a dung heap."

"Well, once she's cleared out Kathy'll have herself a well-fertilized garden, won't she?" As the stench was enormous, Mick breathed through his teeth. "It was a good job of you to think of going and getting the PVC pipe ahead of time. We'll replace it and see what's what."

With a grunt, Brenna got to her feet. They squished over to the truck together. The work was nasty, but the teamwork routine. As they worked, she shot little glances at him.

He'd said nothing about Shawn, not a word. And though she understood her father would have some delicacy of feeling about the situation, she couldn't stand having it between them. Unsaid, it was a wedge, and she needed to knock it loose.

"Dad."

"Ha, nearly got her now. Bitch may be cracked, but she's tough on the joinings."

"Dad, you know I'm still seeing Shawn."

Mick rapped his knuckles hard against the pipe and his tool squirted out of his hand like wet soap. Keeping his eyes lowered, he plucked it out again, then wiped it on his equally filthy trousers. "I suppose I do."

"Are you ashamed of me?"

He worked another moment in silence. "Never have you done anything to shame me, Brenna. But the fact is, you're stepping onto boggier ground than we're swimming in. Working with you, respecting and admiring your skills is on the one hand. But on the other, you're my daughter. It's not an easy thing for a man to discuss such areas with his daughter."

"Sex?"

"Damn it, Brenna." Under the filth on his face, his cheeks went pink as peonies.

"It's there, isn't it?" When the ruined pipe was wrenched free, she shoved it aside.

"So is the shit I'm sitting in at the moment, but I'd just as soon not dwell on it. You've been reared as best as your mother and I could, and the steps you take as a grown-up woman are your own. You can't ask me for my blessing in such a thing, Brenna, but I'm not judging you, either."

"He's a good man, Dad."

"When did I say he wasn't?" Exasperated, embarrassed, and wanting an end to the topic at hand, Mick scooted, slithered so they could fit the new pipe.

"It's just . . . what Mary Kate said last week. She was mad as spit, and we've come to our terms on it. But I don't want you to think that it's cheap between us."

The girl, he thought, was as ever like a terrier with a bone. She wouldn't have done until it was chewed to her satisfaction. "What Mary Kate said to you was uncalled for between sisters, and it's pleased I am the two of you have made it up. As for the other . . . do you care for him?"

"I do, of course. Yes."

"And respect him?" The slight hesitation had Mick looking over the pipe, meeting Brenna's eyes. "Ah, well, now."

"I do respect him. He has a good brain when he bothers to use it, and he has a kind heart and a good humor. That doesn't make me blind to his faults. I know he's lazy about things, and careless with his own talents."

"On this I do have something to say, though you'll go your own way no matter." He straightened, rolled his shoulders. "You don't fix a man the way you do a fault in a pipe or a leak in a roof. You take him as he is, Mary Brenna, or you don't take him at all."

She frowned. "It's not like that, but more of a turning in the right direction."

"Right for who?" He gave her a pat on the arm. "Adjustments can't be all on one side, darling, else the balance goes off and what's being built just falls down."

For Shawn, Brenna's appearance at the back door in the middle of the lunch shift was a shock to all his senses. She was filthy from cap to boot and, even with the distance, let off an aroma that watered the eyes.

"Mother of God, what've you been doing?"

"Septic tank," she said cheerfully. "We scraped and hosed off the worst of it."

"You missed a few spots from where I'm standing."

"Well, we've got to do what we can to put Mrs. Duffy's yard back together, so we didn't bother with all of it. But the fact is, we're near to starving."

He held up a hand. "If you're thinking of coming

in here, O'Toole, pause and reflect."

"I'm not coming in. I told Dad I'd walk up and get us a couple of sandwiches to keep us going. And we could use a couple bottles of beer."

"Step back out and close the door."

"I will not." To annoy him, she leaned against the jamb. "I'm not hurting anything way over here. Whatever makings you have handy'll do. We aren't particular."

"That's obvious enough." He bumped back the orders he'd been filling and got out bread and meat.

It amused her to see him work with a great deal more speed than was his habit. "We'll be a couple hours yet. Then I've a few things to do."

"I hope bathing's one of them."

"It's on the list. From the looks of things in here, the weather's not slowing down your business."

"Half the village is in day or night. People look for company as much as anything else, and a change of view from their own four walls." He layered meat and cheese generously. "We've a *seisiun* going most the time and a few heated tempers over whatever sporting match is on the telly now that we've got the generator running."

"It's keeping us hopping as well. I don't think we've had an hour free, Dad and me, since the storm rolled in."

"I'm looking forward to it rolling out. Haven't seen sun nor star in a week now. Tim Riley says she's breaking, though."

It was easy talk, weather and work, the sort she

could have with anyone she knew. Wasn't it nice, she mused, that she liked having it with Shawn best of all? That was a kind of treasure, one she hadn't cherished enough in the past.

"Well, whether Tim's right or he's wrong, I was thinking I might wander up to Faerie Hill later on. Say a bit after midnight."

"The door's open, but I'd appreciate you cleaning off your Wellies first." He put the sandwiches in a sack, added a couple of bags of crisps and two bottles of Harp. When she started to dig out payment, he shook his head. "No, this is on the house. I don't think I want any coin you might have in those pockets."

"Thanks." She took the bag, rested it on her hip. "Aren't you going to kiss me?"

"No. But I'll make it up to you later."

"See that you do." With a grin that might have been flirtatious under different circumstances, she sauntered off and left him to close the door.

She was a woman of her word, and she opened the door of his cottage at the stroke of midnight. Too early, she knew, for him to be home from work. But she liked the quiet of the place, the mood of it when she was there alone.

She took off her boots at the door, as Shawn often did himself, and wandered around in her stocking feet lighting candles and oil lamps, as the power had yet to be restored. And as she did, she was half hoping Lady Gwen might show herself.

Wasn't it the perfect time for a ghost, after all? A

stormy night alive with rain and whistling wind, a little cottage alight with candles and the glow of a fire.

"I know you're here, and there's no one but me." She waited, but the air was still, the only sounds the ticking of the cottage as it settled and the incessant call of the wind. "I wanted you to know that I think I understand what you were telling me that first time. His heart's in his song, and I have listened. I hope what I did was the right thing."

Again she fell silent, and again only silence answered her.

"Well, a lot of help you are." Irked, she marched upstairs.

She didn't need any ghostly visitations or words from beyond to tell her what to do and how to do it. She knew what she was about. She had a man she intended to keep. Since her mind was set on it, it was just a matter of seeing to the details.

She lighted the fire here as well, and banked it for the night. After setting the flame to a pair of candles, she dropped onto the bed, propped the pillows at her back, and settled down to wait.

And the day's work caught up with her.

There was no wind, no rain. The sky was midnight silk studded with stars that flashed ruby, sapphire, citrine. The moon, full and white, sailed high, spilling its light over a sea as calm as a lake.

The wings of the white horse beat like a heart, steady and true. Astride him, the man in silver rode with his back straight and proud while his dark mane of hair streamed back like a cape.

"It wasn't wealth or stature or even immortality she wanted from me."

It seemed not odd at all to be riding with the prince of faeries and sweeping over Ireland. "What was it she wanted from you?"

"Promises, vows, words that come out of the heart. Why is it that saying 'I love you' is so hard for some?"

"Saying it lowers all shields."

He turned his head, his eyes bright and bitter. "Exactly so. It takes courage for that, does it not, Mary Brenna O'Toole?"

"Or foolhardiness."

"If love doesn't make a fool of us, what will?"

The horse swooped downward at a speed that had her heart bounding with excitement. She saw the light glow against the window glass, and the shape and shadows of the cottage on the faerie hill.

Hooves sent sparks shooting when they met ground.

"A simple place," Carrick murmured, "for so much drama. There, that pretty garden gate. It might be the wall of a fortress, for I can't pass through it as once I did."

"She walks the cliffs as well, your love."

"She does, I'm told, but we can't so much as see each other, though we might stand near as side by side."

There wasn't bitterness in his eyes now, but sorrow. And, Brenna thought, a painful kind of longing.

"At times I feel her there, or catch the scent of

her hair or her skin. But not once in a hundred years times three have I been able to see or to touch or so much as speak my heart to her."

"You cast a harsh spell on the both of you," Brenna commented.

"I did, yes, and I have paid for that rash moment of temper. You know of such things," he said.

"I do, indeed. And fortunate it is I haven't the power to conjure or cast."

"Mortals." Amusement softened his face. "You've no concept of what powers you hold, and so you use what you have most carelessly on yourselves and each other."

"That's pot calling kettle."

"As you see it," he agreed with a nod. "But there was no faerie magic in what began between me and Gwen. I neither tricked nor lured her to me, as some tell the tale. She came to me willing, until her father forbade her. Until he promised her to another for fear of me."

"I believe the truth of that." Because she did, she laid a comforting hand on his arm. "A maid had less say in such choices then."

Carrick tossed his leg over the horse, slid down. "Then make yours."

"I have." She mirrored his move, watched his mouth twitch. "But I'll follow through in my own way."

"Listen," was all he said.

The music drifted out on the air, wove around her like a silk net. "It's Shawn playing. The song he gave me. Oh!" She closed her eyes. "It fills the heart right up. There's nothing in your raft lovelier than that," she said, reaching down to open the gate.

But it held fast, no matter how she pushed or pulled. "I can't open it." Panicked, she whirled around, but horse and rider were gone. She turned back, gripping the gate with both hands, shoved.

"Shawn!"

"There, now." She was in his arms, and there was a chuckle in his voice. "You were dreaming. An excitable one."

"Dreaming." Her mind was full of mists and stars and music. "I couldn't open the gate. I couldn't get in."

"You are in."

"I am in. God, I'm fuzzy-brained yet. I must've dropped off like a rock." She pushed at her hair. "Give me a minute to wake up."

"I've some news that might clear the cobwebs."

"What is it?"

"Aidan's taken with your drawings of the theater."

As he'd suspected they would, the clouds in her eyes cleared immediately. "Really? Is he?"

"He is, yes. So pleased, in fact, he's already spoken of them to the Magee."

"What did he say?"

"Which of them?"

"Both, either." She gripped his arms and shook. "Don't play with me, Shawn, or I'll have to hurt you."

"Sure and that's a frightening thought, so I'll tell you. I can't relay exactly what Magee said, as it was Aidan who spoke with him, but it seems that the man's interested enough to want to take a look at what you've drawn up." Shawn toyed with her hair as he spoke, a new habit he was enjoying. "So they're going off to New York City, and we'll see what we see."

"It's a good design."

"It looked good to me."

"It would work and work well." Worrying over it, she gnawed at her lip. "Any dunderhead would see that it blends with what's here, adds to it rather than overpowering. He won't get better from any of his fancy architects."

"You have to work on your confidence, Brenna. So much modesty's unseemly."

She only snorted. "But how is Magee to know that if he can't actually *see?* The way the pub sits and how the land is and so on."

"He has photographs," Shawn reminded her. "Finkle took dozens while he was here."

"It's not the same. I should talk to Magee myself, is what I should do."

"You may be right, but wouldn't it be best to give it a bit of time, then see what he thinks before jumping in boots first and pushing at him?"

"Some take a good push." Her lips slanted into a sneer. "As yourself is a perfect example. When is Aidan sending them? Maybe I should take another look at them first."

"They're already on the way. He shipped them

off in yesterday's post, by special courier as Magee requested."

"Well, then. Well." They would stand or fall on their own, she thought, as Shawn's song would. She nearly blurted out that she'd already spoken to Magee herself, and that between them they were keeping the man busy looking over their efforts.

No, better to wait, then give Shawn the results instead of the worry of wondering.

"And what are you thinking of so hard and long?"

"The next steps, and what happens after they're taken. It seems when one thing changes, everything changes with it."

"I've thought the same myself." Look at us, he thought, and brushed her hair back from her face.

Her pulse stumbled. Another change, she realized, that his just touching her could cause that sudden and vivid awareness. "Does it worry you?"

"No. But if it concerns you at the moment, I'd rather just take you dreaming again." His lips cruised over hers as he laid her back. "If you hold on to me, we'll go together."

"I want to be with you. You're the only one." It was the closest she could come to lowering her shields.

He took her dreaming, gliding up, sinking down with the lights of the candles and turf fire shimmering everywhere. There was a tenderness in her she hadn't explored before. A welling need to give whatever was asked, and give gently.

They undressed each other. No tugs, no pulls

this time. Fingers slid over skin, and lips followed, lingered so that each caress, each taste was precious. Sigh answered murmur. A mingling of breath.

Desire, without the red flash of flames, was gilded at the edges. Even when he urged her up to that fine and trembling peak, the glow held steady.

They watched each other as he slipped inside her.

It was like coming home.

His lips curved as they lowered to hers, another link. Her hands lifted, framed his face, held him there, just there while the beauty of it had tears swimming to her eyes.

"Come with me." She murmured it against his mouth. "Let go and come with me."

Her breath caught as she began the tumble, then released in a sigh when he took her hand and fell with her.

His mouth was on hers again before the mists cleared. "Stay."

She shouldn't. Even as he shifted to draw her against his side she thought of all the reasons why it was best if she left now, crept quietly into her own bed.

"All right," she said and settling her head on his shoulder, slept.

Of course, by dawn he'd shoved her to the edge of the bed. That was a little something they'd have to work on, Brenna thought as she got up in the half-light. She'd be damned if she'd spend every night of her life fighting for space on the mattress.

Begin as you mean to go on, her mother often said. Well, she'd begin by shoving her elbow into his ribs several times a night until he learned to share.

But her eyes were warm, watching him as she dressed. And the kiss she gave him before she left was unashamedly loving. "We'll get a bigger bed," she whispered, then hurried out to get home before her mother came down to make breakfast.

An hour later, he woke alone and vaguely dissatisfied. Couldn't the woman have said good-bye at least? That was going to change. In fact, the whole business was going to change, and sooner than she might expect.

He wanted her in his life altogether, and not just for snatches of time in his bed. He rose, and gauging his time, figured he had plenty of it to have a look at the land he'd gotten word was for sale.

Nineteen

The price was as steep as the lay of the land, but Shawn liked the feel of it. As he stood in what was no more than a drizzle now, he could see the water from one direction, stone gray to mirror the sky, and calmer now.

The storm had died in the night, but the beach was littered with shells and kelp and debris that had been heaved out of the sea.

He imagined they would face the house that way, with at least one good-size window in the front room so they could watch the moods of the water.

In back there was the rise of distant mountains, shadowy bumps up into the cloudy sky. Then on either side was the fall of hills and fields, the deep, wet green shimmering through winding ribbons of mist.

He didn't have the talent to build a house in his mind, sketch one on paper, or take materials and tools and make it a reality. Not as Brenna did. But he could, particularly when the interest was personal, conjure up a glimmer of it.

He wanted a music room — well, not just for music, he thought, as he walked away from the area that he thought most likely for planting a house. It would have to be comfortable and welcoming so others would feel easy about coming in and staying awhile. But a room, and not a tiny, cramped one, where he could have his piano, and his fiddle. He'd want a kind of cabinet — perhaps Brenna could build it — for his music. And a stand, or whatever could be devised for a good tape recorder.

He'd always meant to record his music, and it was time to begin. If he ever meant to get to the next step, which he did in his own time and way, and polish a few of his pieces, the recorder was essential. Then he'd see about choosing one and going about the business of peddling the tunes.

Because the thought of it stretched his nerves, he shook his head. But not quite yet, of course. Not quite yet. He had a great deal to do first, and more than enough time.

He and Brenna had to come to terms first, and the house had to be built. Then they'd want to settle into it, and into each other for a while. He would get to the other business by and by.

The road leading to the plot he was considering was a worse mess than the track that led from Ardmore to Faerie Hill, then down to the O'Tooles' house. Still, it wouldn't worry him overmuch, and if it troubled Brenna it could be leveled some or widened or whatever. That was a business he'd leave to her.

It wasn't a big plot, but enough for a sturdy

house and garden. Room enough, he calculated, for a cabin as well, as she'd want one for her tools and perhaps a workshop. She would need that just as he would his room for music. They'd do very well with their separate interests, he thought, and was grateful neither of them was the type who needed to be in each other's pockets day and night.

They had mutual and opposing ground, and he thought it a nice mix.

There was a skinny stream in the far back, and a trio of tough-looking trees that put him in mind of the three crosses near Saint Declan's Well.

The man who wanted to part ways with the land had said that there was a turf bog behind them and that no one had bothered to cut it for years. He himself hadn't cut turf since he was a boy and went out with his grandfather on his mother's side. The Fitzgeralds had been more people of the land and the Gallaghers people of the town.

Shawn thought he might enjoy it, if his life and comfort didn't absolutely depend upon it.

He wandered back toward what was grandly called a road, where the hedgerows grew tall and had the first haze of spring on them. As he did three magpies darted by like bullets shot from the same gun in rapid succession.

Three for marriage, he thought, and decided it was more than sign enough for him.

When he drove away toward the village to work, he considered himself a landowner, as hands had been clasped and shaken on the deal.

Brenna worked at home the early part of the morning. The wind had torn a few shingles from the roof, and a couple of leaks had sprung with the rain that had been driven hard by the wind.

It was simple enough work, no more than a patch here and there, and it gave her a fine opportunity to sit in the wavering sunlight and look out at the water.

When she built a house, she thought, she'd choose higher ground so her view of the water would be from windows rather than a rooftop. It was good to look and see the boats out again and know that life was sliding back into its regular rhythm.

And maybe she'd have some sky windows as well, so she could look up and see the sun or the rain or the drift of stars. It was time for a home of her own, she knew, though she'd miss the sounds and scents of family.

But there was something inside her that told her the time was now for the next stage of what she was and where she was going. There'd been a different tone between her and Shawn the night before, and it had changed everything in her once and forever. Her mind and her heart were in one place now.

It was time to tell him, to ask him. To browbeat him if there was no choice. Whatever it took, the O'Tooles were going to be planning another wedding.

God help them all.

She scooted over to the ladder, climbed down.

Leaving her toolbox by the back door, she went in to tell her mother the job was done and she'd be on her way.

When the phone rang, she picked it up without thinking, then guiltily tucked the receiver under her chin and wiped the shingle grime off her hands onto her jeans. "Hello."

"Miss O'Toole?"

"This is one of them."

"Miss Brenna O'Toole."

"Aye, you've hit the target." Automatically Brenna pulled open the refrigerator door and perused the contents. "What can I do for you?"

"Would you hold the line, please, for Mr. Magee?"

"Oh." She shot up straight, bumping the door with her hip and slamming it on her own hand. She bit back a yelp. "Yes, I could do that. Goddamn it," she added in a mutter when she heard the line click, and sucked at her sore fingers.

"Miss O'Toole, Trevor Magee."

"Good day to you, Mr. Magee." She recognized his deep, smooth voice from the time she'd waded through what had seemed like an army of assistants to speak with him. "Are you calling from New York City?"

"No, actually I'm on my way to London."

"Oh." Her initial disappointment in not taking a call from New York vanished in a fresh thrill. "Are you calling from an airplane, then?"

"That's right."

She wanted to shout for her mother to come

366

quick, but thought it would sound just a little too countrified. "It's kind of you to take time out of your busy schedule."

"I always make time for what interests me."

He sounded like he meant it and that the reverse was entirely true as well. "Then perhaps you've had time to look at the package Aidan Gallagher sent you."

"A good look. You and your father are quite a team."

Because her hand was throbbing, she pulled some ice out of the freezer. "We are. And I have to add, Mr. Magee, I know Ardmore and what suits it."

"I can't argue with that, Miss O'Toole."

She thought she caught a hint of amusement in his tone and braced herself. "Perhaps you could tell me what your thoughts are on my design, then?"

"It interests me. I have to look at it more thoroughly, but it interests me. Gallagher didn't mention where you had studied design."

She narrowed her eyes, then decided if it was a trap it was best to fall into it now as opposed to later. "On the job, sir. My father has worked in the trade all his life, and I learned at his side. I would imagine you had some of the same sort of experience with your own father."

"You could say that."

"Then you know a lot can be learned by the doing of things. Between the two of us, my father and I, we handle most of the building and repairing in Old Parish. And if we don't, we know who does. As that, we'd be some considerable help to you with your project. You'll find no better than the O'Tooles in Old Parish — or all of Waterford, for that matter. You're planning to build in Ardmore, Mr. Magee, and it's good business, I'm sure you'll agree, to use local skill and labor when you're able. We'll be happy to send you references."

"And I'll be happy to see them. You build a strong case, Miss O'Toole."

"I can assure you I build better with wood and brick than with words."

"I'll see that for myself, as I'm hoping to carve out a day or two to visit the site personally before too much longer."

"If you let us know the particulars, my father and I will be happy to meet you at your convenience."

"I'll be in touch."

"Ah . . . I don't mean to worry you, Mr. Magee, but I'm wondering if you had a moment to look at the music I sent along to you."

"Yes, I did. I'm not sure I understand. Are you representing Shawn Gallagher?"

"No, I'm not, no. It's . . . a bit complicated."

"Then he doesn't have representation?"

"Ah, no. Not at the present time." How the devil did this sort of thing work? "You could say I'm acting on his behalf in this particular instance on a personal level."

"Hmm."

She winced, thinking there was entirely too much knowledge in that small and casual sound. "Would you mind telling me what you thought of it yourself?"

"Enough to buy it if Gallagher's selling, and to want a chance to negotiate for his other work. I assume he has other work."

"He does, yes. Scads of it." She forgot her throbbing hand, dropped her ice in the sink. While her feet danced, she fought to keep her voice cool and professional. "You're saying you'd buy the tune. But for what purpose would that be?"

"For the purpose of recording, eventually."

"But I was under the impression that you build things."

"One of the things I've built is a record company. Celtic Records." He paused, and sounded amused when he spoke again. "Do you want references, Miss O'Toole?"

"Well, now, could I be getting back to you on that? I'll need to discuss this with Shawn."

"Of course. My New York office knows how to reach me."

"Thank you for your time and consideration, Mr. Magee. I hope to meet you in person before much longer. I . . ." She simply ran out of words. "Thank you."

The minute she hung up the phone she let out a shout of triumph, then raced through the house to the front door. "Ma, I've got to go! I'll be back when I can."

"Go?" Mollie dashed out of the back bedroom

to the top of the stairs in time to see her daughter's lorry bullet into the road. "That girl. If it's not the first thing it's the second. Go where, I'd like to know, and is my roof finished or isn't it? I'll give her both sides of my tongue if I have to listen to water plopping into buckets one more night."

Before she could go back to work, she saw Shawn's car pull in. "All this coming and going around here," she muttered and started down the steps. "It's making my head spin."

She pushed open the door and waited while Shawn made his way to her. "Good morning to you, Shawn. I'm afraid you've just missed Brenna. She went tearing out of here not a minute ago like her trousers were afire."

"Ah, well." He cleared his throat. "I wasn't actually coming by to see Brenna."

"Weren't you now?" She gave him a considering look, but knew better than to wait for him to explain himself. That, she knew from experience, could take half the day, and she'd as soon be sitting down for part of it. "Well, then, I'm all that's left. Come inside, why don't you, and we'll have a cup."

"I'd be grateful." He ducked inside behind her and trailed her into the kitchen. "I don't want to take much of your time."

"Lad, you've been in and out of this house since you could toddle. No one's ever booted you out the door before, and I'm not after starting now." She waved a hand toward the table and went about the business of making tea. "Brenna's a heart and mind of her own. As I'm sure you know."

"That I do. I thought I should come 'round to see if . . . to make certain you . . ."

She had to take pity on him. "Are you afraid I don't love you anymore, my handsome lad?" The worry in his eyes faded away as she reached over and scrubbed a hand over his hair, as she'd done as long as he could remember. "There's no danger of that changing. Now if you'd taken up with my Katie, I'd have boxed your ears to the back of your head."

"I never meant to give Mary Kate any . . ."

" 'Encouragement' might be the word you're after. Your tongue's tied today, boy, and that's not the usual case, for you've a slick one. Here now, I've a cinnamon bun left from breakfast. I'll warm it for you and you'll tell me what's the matter."

"You make me miss my mother, Mrs. O'Toole."

"I'll stand in her stead, as she would in mine." She bustled around the kitchen, knowing it would put him at ease. "Is Brenna giving you headaches, then?"

"I'm used to that — I don't mind it so much. I think I give them back to her in fair measure. I, ah, I'm thinking Mr. O'Toole told you of our discussion a couple weeks back."

She sent him a look designed to wither a man. "If you're meaning on the day he came home drunk, that he didn't. I gathered well enough he'd got the whiskey from you, as he hasn't a world of choices where he could walk off, drink his belly full, and walk back again in so short a time."

"He didn't speak to you of it."

"Closed up like a clam."

"Well, you see, he was angry, and rightfully so, until I told him how things were."

"And how are things, Shawn?" Mollie set down the pot, waited.

"I'm in love with Brenna, Mrs. O'Toole, and I want to marry her."

She stood still a moment, then laid her cheek on top of his head. "Of course you are, and of course you do. Don't mind me. I've got to sniffle a bit."

"I'll be good to her."

"Oh, there's no doubt in my mind of that." Dabbing at her eyes, she turned to get out the warmed bun. "You'll be good for her, too, and she for you."

"The other part of it is, I've been working her around, so to speak, so she'd come to the idea herself. You know how she is when she's got her teeth into a notion."

"Clamps down until she gets what she's after or it isn't worth having anymore. I always said you were a bright lad, Shawn."

"Thousands wouldn't," he said easily. "I thought I could wait, you see. I'm not one who needs to hurry as a rule. But it seems I can't wait for this. I bought land today."

She wasn't half as surprised as he thought she was, and nearly twice as pleased. "Goodness, boy, you can move fast enough when you've a mind to."

"She'll have her house as she wants it. I'm not fussy about such matters."

Mollie opened her mouth, closed it again. Men,

she knew very well, always said such things and believed them as well. Then they drove a woman to distraction picking at the details. But that was for Shawn and Brenna to find out for themselves. "She's always had a mind to build her own," she said at length.

"I know it, and why shouldn't she? She's a talent for such things, and a liking for the work. Myself, I've no driving urge to pick up a hammer or saw. But I make a good living, and I'll have a better one yet when the theater goes in. There won't be a worry about putting a roof overhead, or keeping one there."

"Shawn, are you asking for my permission to ask Brenna to marry you?"

"For your blessing. It matters to me as much as it will to her."

"I'll give you my blessing." She took his hands in hers. "And for all I love her, my sympathy as well. She'll run you ragged."

"I need a favor." Brenna burst into the pub through the back just as Aidan was taking the chairs down. Timing was everything here, she thought as she fought to catch her breath. Shawn would be coming in any minute.

"Well, now, you look full of surprise and secrets." He tucked a chair under a table. "What's the favor?"

"First off, I can't tell you the secret." Automatically she began to tip down chairs herself. "I have to ask you to do the favor blind."

He got a good look at her then — the flushed face, the wildly glowing eyes, the foolish smile. He recalled a very similar look on his wife's face at a certain moment. "Oh, Lord, Brenna, never say you're breeding."

"Breeding?" The chair nearly slipped out of her hands. "No, no!" And though she laughed it off, she found it interesting to discover she wouldn't have minded it. "It's nothing like that. Aidan, is there any way you could arrange for Shawn to have the evening off?"

"The whole of it?"

She heard the pain in his tone, sympathized. "I know it's a lot to be asking, and at the last instant as well. But it's important. I'll work this weekend for no pay to make up for it. I'll go down and talk to Mrs. Duffy myself to see that she'll fill in."

"Why the devil doesn't Shawn ask for time himself instead of sending you in to look at me with those big eyes?"

"He doesn't know." She moved closer, running a hand down his arm. "Another part of the favor is that you don't tell him I asked. Could you just send him home somehow at the beginning of shift?"

"He'll certainly wonder why, won't he?"

"I haven't had time to think it all out." She whirled away, paced, but couldn't clear her head. "Oh, you'll think of something, Aidan. Please."

"It's a matter of the heart, I suppose. And you're using mine against my good business sense." He let out a windy sigh. "I'll work it out for you."

"Oh, you're the best and the finest." She leaped

into his arms to plant a hard, noisy kiss on his mouth.

"Look at this, will you? If she's not after one brother she's after another." With a lazy yawn, Darcy sauntered in. "That's a married man, I'll have you know, you sneaky slut."

"I've got one for you as well." Before Darcy could evade, Brenna rushed over and gave her the same treatment.

"Sweet Mary, now she's after the girls, too." But Darcy's sleepy chuckle faded away. She gripped Brenna's arms. "Brenna, are you pregnant?"

"Oh, for heaven's sake. No. Can't a body be happy without a baby in the belly? I've got to go, he'll be coming in. You don't tell him I was here. Please. I'm grabbing a bottle of the French bubbly you keep in the back. Put it on my account, would you?"

She dashed out the way she'd dashed in and left Darcy rubbing her mouth. "And what was all that about?"

"I haven't a clue. But she's something up her sleeve, and Shawn's not to know."

"Secrets. I could get it out of her in five minutes."

"No doubt you could," Aidan agreed. "But let's let her have her surprise."

"I've already had mine." Darcy went behind the bar for her change apron. "She's in love with him."

"Does that trouble you?"

"No, but for the fact that the Gallaghers are tumbling like ripe fruit from a tree."

Aidan moved behind the bar with her to check the till. "Afraid it's catching, darling?"

"I would be, was I not immune to such weaknesses." She heard the back door open again. "And speaking of clueless, there's himself now." Filled with affection and sentiment, Darcy headed for the kitchen to torment her brother.

"What do you mean I can go?" Up to his elbows in potatoes, Shawn turned his head to stare at Aidan. "Go where?"

"On your way. Kathy Duffy'll be right along."

"Well . . . why?"

"To cover for you." Aidan had thought of a way, and saw no reason not to have a little fun at his brother's expense while he was about it. "You have the evening off as you asked. Though it's damned inconvenient."

Shawn shoved peelings into the garbage. "I never asked for the evening off."

"Well, it must've been your evil twin, then, or I've just had a brainstorm." Fixing a scowl on his face, Aidan pulled open the refrigerator and plucked out a bottle of water. "I told you two days past when you asked that I'd work it out."

"But I . . . you've been dreaming. I've ten pounds of potatoes here to deal with. Why would I be making stovies if I was planning on having the evening free?"

"That's a question I can't answer, but I've Kathy Duffy coming in, and there's no need for both of you tonight."

"I've no plans but to do my job here. You've mixed something up."

Enjoying the timing, Aidan turned to Darcy as she came in. "Darcy, did Shawn ask for this evening free or did he not?"

"He did, a couple of days back. Selfish bastard." Not one to let an opportunity pass, she flashed a challenging look at Aidan. "And since you're so bloody accommodating with our brother, I'm wanting Saturday afternoon off for myself."

"Saturday afternoon." Aidan nearly choked on his water. "You can't have a weekend day off as we're heading into spring."

"Oh, so it's all right for him." She pointed a finger toward a baffled Shawn. "But it's a different matter entirely for me."

"I don't need the evening off."

"You've got it," Aidan snapped, and ground his teeth as Darcy folded her arms. "A weekday evening's a different matter from a weekend afternoon."

"All right, fine, then. I'll take the evening off Monday next. Unless me being female means I don't get the same considerations as this one." Satisfied that she'd boxed Aidan in, she flounced out.

"I don't remember asking for tonight off," Shawn said vaguely.

"Aye, and you don't remember to tie your bootlaces half the time." Seriously annoyed, Aidan jerked a thumb at the door. "Out with you, you troublemaker."

Shoving up his sleeves and squaring his shoulders, Aidan went out to deal with his treacherous sister.

She had everything under control, and quite the job of work it had been. It had to be special, and as close to perfect as she could manage. Shawn Gallagher would see he wasn't the only one who could fuss and fiddle and set a nice scene.

She'd been to the market and got all the makings. While Shawn had been busy cooking at the pub, she'd been doing the same at the cottage. Maybe she didn't have his flair with such things, but she wasn't altogether helpless.

She'd chilled the wine and had even ferreted out a tin pail she'd scrubbed to use as an ice bucket. The champagne glasses she'd borrowed from Jude. Flutes, she'd called them, Brenna thought. And elegant they were.

She'd set a nice table, if she said so herself. A pair of pretty plates and cloth napkins, the flowers she scavenged from her mother's garden and the one at the cottage.

Candles, she thought as she lighted them. Surely everything was in place for an atmosphere of romance and celebration.

Oh, she couldn't wait to see his face when she told him about his music. It had been a test of will and restraint not to shout out the news to everyone she'd passed that day. But it was for Shawn first.

After they'd celebrated the thrill of it, and his future, lifted a glass or two, she'd tell him the rest. She couldn't — wouldn't — fumble with the words. Hadn't she practiced them in her head all of the day?

"I love you," she said now, out loud to the empty room. "I think I always have, I know now I always will. Will you marry me?"

There. She rubbed the heel of her hand against her heart, as it was galloping like a wild horse. It wasn't so hard, really. Maybe her tongue felt a little thick and clumsy, but she'd said it straight out without stuttering.

And if he balked or refused, she'd just have to kill him.

As her ears were pricked for it, she heard the sound of his car as he turned into the street. All right, Brenna. She closed her eyes, steadied herself. Here we go.

Damned if he'd asked for an evening off. Still stewing about it, Shawn shoved open his garden gate. He should know, shouldn't he? And if he had, wouldn't he have made plans for it? He knew what was going on in his own life, for Christ's sake.

Not that he couldn't adjust. He'd ring Brenna and see if she was agreeable to having an evening together. He'd throw a meal together, or it was early enough that they could go out to the hotel restaurant.

Aidan and Darcy had to be having him on, though for the life of him he couldn't think of the purpose.

The minute he stepped into the house he caught the scent of cooking, then the flicker of light back in the kitchen. What now, was all he could think. Had Lady Gwen taken to making meals while he was away from home?

When he walked in, he was as surprised to see Brenna as he would have been to see the ghost.

She was wearing a dress, which was odd enough. But she was standing, smiling, with candlelight all around her, the good, rich scent of stew simmering, and a bottle of champagne in a rain bucket standing on the counter behind her.

"What's all this?"

"It's dinner. Beef and Guinness stew. The one thing I can make that no one has trouble choking down."

"You cooked?" He rubbed his forehead as if he had a headache brewing.

"I've been known to on the rare occasion."

"Yes, but, did we . . . Well, we must've," he decided, scanning all the pretty preparations. "This is beyond a bit of absentmindedness. I think something must be wrong with me."

"You look fine to me." Since he wasn't going to make a move, she did, walking to him to kiss him. "More than fine." This time her hands slid over his face, and the kiss went dreamy. "It's glad I am to see you, Shawn."

He started to question it all again, then as Brenna's mouth moved warm over his, thought it was foolish to bother. "It's a pleasure coming home to you."

Get used to it, she thought and smiled as she stepped back. "I've been waiting. All but jumping out of my skin," she admitted. "I've things to tell you."

"What are they?"

Words leaped to her tongue but she bit them back. "Let's have this open first."

"I'll do it." He nudged her away from the champagne, then lifted his brows at the label. "The pricey stuff. Are we celebrating?"

"We are." She caught the look in his eye, and the way his fingers suddenly stilled on the foil. "If you ask me if I'm breeding I'll brain you. I am not."

Her eyes were laughing as she spoke. He kept his on them as he twisted the wire. "You're in a rare mood."

"I am. There are some things that don't happen every day of the week, and a rare mood's what you get from them when they do." She felt as bubbly as the wine he poured. Taking her glass, she lifted it. "This is to you, Shawn."

"And what did I do?"

"We should sit down. No, I can't. We'll have to stand. Shawn, you've sold your first piece of music."

Twenty

The puzzled smile slid away from his face. "I've done what?"

"You've sold your song, and there'll be others as well. But the first's the biggest thrill, isn't it?"

Very deliberately, he set his glass down again. "I haven't put any music up for sale, Brenna."

"I did. Well, in a way I did. The song you gave me, I sent it off to the Magee in New York City. He called me today, just this morning, and said how he wants to buy it. And that he wants to see your other work." She spun in a circle, too excited to see how cool his eyes were as they watched her. "I didn't think I'd get through the day without telling you."

"What right did you have to do that?"

Still beaming, she sipped champagne. "To do what?"

"To send my music off that way, to take it on yourself to show a stranger what was mine?"

"Shawn." She put a hand on his arm to give him a little shake. "He's buying it."

"I gave it to you because you asked me — because I thought you wanted it for yourself, and that you valued it for that. Is this what you planned all

382

along, to send it off somewhere, have another put a price on it?"

Something was wrong, badly and dangerously wrong. The only way she knew how to deal with it was temper. "What if it was? It got results, didn't it? What good is it to make songs without doing something with them? Now you can."

He met heat with ice. "And it's for you to decide, is it, what I can and should do, and how and when I should do it?"

"You weren't doing anything about it."

"How do you know what I'm doing or not, planning on doing or not?"

"Haven't I heard you say a thousand times you weren't ready to show it for sale?"

The minute the words were out of her mouth, she recognized her mistake. Even as she searched for a way around it, he was plowing on. "That's right, you have. But that didn't suit you, didn't sit well with the way you want things done. What good is it, you're thinking, if you can't make a living from it. If you don't have coin to show for it at end of day."

"It's not the coin —"

"My music is the most personal thing in my life," he interrupted. "Whether I ever make a pound from it doesn't change what it is to me. You don't understand that, Brenna, or respect that. Or me."

"That's not true." She was beginning something other than anger. It was a cl~
gut, in the throat, that had noth¹

temper. "I only wanted you to have something out of it."

"I had something out of it."

She'd never seen anger so cold, so controlled. There was no mistaking it in that rigid face, those hard eyes. It made her feel like a bug not worthy of being squashed. "For Christ's sake, Shawn, you should be dancing instead of hammering at me. The man wants to buy your song. He thinks it should be recorded."

"What he thinks matters more than what I do?"

"Oh, you're twisting this all around. You have an opportunity, and you're too stubborn to take it."

"Is that how it is between us? You make the decisions, you do the thinking, and I'm just to follow, to fall in line and be grateful you're looking out for me as I'm too half-witted to look after myself?"

"Why are you turning this one thing into everything?" Her hand shook as she dragged it through her hair. "Didn't you arrange for the man to look at my design?" It struck her suddenly that she'd forgotten about that, about everything Magee had said to her about her own work. She'd forgotten all that in the thrill of his offering for Shawn's.

"I did," Shawn countered. "And you can't see any difference in that, Brenna, than this? I talked to you of showing your design, I didn't go behind your back with it, or pull tricks."

"It wasn't a trick, wasn't meant as one." But she was beginning to see the wrong turn, and the sinking sensation in her stomach layered sickness over understanding. "You never said you didn't want to do something with your music. It was always you weren't ready."

"Because I wasn't ready."

"Well, if we're stuck on that one point, I say you were." Fear made her lash out. "And so does a man who appears to be something of the expert on such things. Damn you, you gave the song to me, and I did what I chose with it. I thought you'd be pleased, but it's not a mistake I'll make again."

He stared her down, viciously pleased when she began to tremble. "And neither will I." Without another word, he turned and walked out of the house.

"You son of a bitch." She kicked the door behind him. "You shortsighted, ungrateful, *simple* bastard. This is the thanks I get for trying to do something for you. If you think I'm running after you, you'll have a long wait."

She snatched up her glass, downed the contents. Bubbles exploded in her throat, set her eyes to watering.

To think of all the time and trouble she'd gone to, only to have him act as if she were some sort of shrew or bully. Well, she wasn't crying over it, or him for that matter.

She braced her hands on the counter, leaning forward and breathing slow to try to relieve the horrible pressure in her chest.

Oh, God, what had she done? She just couldn't get her mind around where she'd gone so completely wrong. The method, yes, there she had surely mis-stepped. But the results . . . How could something she'd thought would be a joy to him whip out of her hands to lash at them both?

She turned, wanting to sit down until she felt steadier, and saw Lady Gwen. "A lot of help you've been. His song, you told me. His heart's in his song and I was to listen. Isn't that just what I did?"

"Not closely enough," was the answer. Then Brenna was alone.

He knew how to walk off a mad. He'd done so before. He trooped over the fields, letting the moonlight guide him. Thinking wasn't the order of business, movement was.

He climbed the cliffs, let the wind and the water clear his head. But the anger wouldn't pass. He'd given his heart to a woman who thought very little of him as a man.

Sent off his music, had she? And to a stranger, a man neither of them had met face-to-face or measured. And not a word to him about it, just following her own whim and expecting him to shuffle right along in her wake.

Well, he wasn't having it.

Didn't she think he could see her line of thinking? Just how simpleminded did she think he was? Oh, Shawn's an affable sort, and clever enough in his way, but he'll not get off his arse unless someone plants a boot on it.

So this was her boot this time around. If the man's going to sit about and play with music half the time, we'd best see if we can do something practical with it.

It was his music, not hers, and she'd never troubled herself to so much as pretend to understand or appreciate it.

And what did this man Magee know about it anyway?

Celtic Records, Shawn's mind murmured. Come now, you've looked into such matters enough to know just what Magee and his like know about it. Why pretend otherwise?

"Neither here nor there," Shawn muttered and heaved a rock over the cliff. Hadn't he already turned it over in his head that once he'd met Magee for himself, gotten a feeling on the man, he'd consider the possibility of showing him a piece of music?

A piece *he* chose. A piece *he* decided was right. Because by Christ it was *his* work and no one else's.

And when was the last time he'd decided a piece was finished and ready and right?

Approximately never, he was forced to admit and heaved another rock for the hell of it.

Magee wanted to buy it.

"Well, fuck me." Struggling to separate his anger from the rest, Shawn sat on the ledge.

How could he explain to anyone what he felt when he pulled notes and words out of himself? That there was a fine and quiet joy in that alone. And that the rest, the *doing* something with it, as Brenna put it, made him feel like he was standing way out on the edge of a cliff. He hadn't been ready to take the leap.

Now he'd been pushed, and he resented it. No matter that the result was something he wanted, the pushing was uncalled for. And that's what she'd never understand.

So where were they, then, if they had no better understanding of each other than this?

"Pride's an important thing to a man," Carrick commented from his perch on the rocks.

Shawn barely spared him a glance. "I'm having a personal crisis here, if you don't mind."

"She's slashed a gash in yours, and I can't blame you for taking the stand you have. A woman ought to know her place, and if she doesn't, she needs to be shown it clear."

"It's not a matter of place, you arrogant jackass."

"Don't take it out on me, boy-o," Carrick said cheerfully. "I'm with you on this one. She overstepped, no question of it. Why, what was the woman thinking, taking something of yours and going off with it that way? No matter that you'd given it to her, a kind of gift, one might say. That's nothing but a technicality."

"Well, it is."

"And so I'm saying. Then as if that wasn't nerve enough, what does she do? Fixes it up so you've the evening free —"

"She fixed it up?" For lack of something more satisfying, Shawn heaved another rock. "I knew I wasn't crazy. Damn it all."

"Playing with your mind, that's what she's about." Carrick waved a hand, then tossed the little star that clung to his fingertips out over the water, where it trailed silver light. "Cooking you a meal, making everything, herself included, pretty for you. A more devious female I've never known. You're well shed of her. Maybe you should take another look at her sister, after all. She's young, but she'd be malleable, don't you think?"

"Ah, shut up." Shawn got to his feet and strode off, scowling at the merry sound of Carrick's laughter.

"You're sunk, young Gallagher." Carrick sent another star over the water. "You've not quite resigned yourself to having your head under, but there you are. Mortals, why is it that half the time they'd rather suffer than dance?"

This time when he flicked his wrist he held a crystal, smooth and clear as a pool of water. Passing his hand over it, he watched the image swimming inside. Fair of face, she was, with eyes soft and green as freshly dewed grass and hair pale as winter sunlight.

"I miss you, Gwen." Holding the glass to his heart, he called for the white horse to ride the sky, as he did night by night. Alone.

The house was empty when he got back, and that's what he'd expected. It was, he told himself, what he wanted. The solitude. She'd put the food away, and that surprised him. Knowing her temper, he'd expected to find she'd hurled pot and pan or whatever else around the room.

But the kitchen was tidy as a church, with only the faint scent of candle wax clinging to the air.

Since it made him feel churlish to find it so, he got himself a beer and took it into the parlor.

He hadn't intended to play, but to sit by the cold fire and brood. But by God if he was going to have an evening off shoved down his throat, he'd spend it doing something that pleased him.

He sat, laid his fingers on the keys, and played for his own pleasure.

It was the song he'd given her that Brenna heard when she walked back toward the garden gate. Her first reaction was relief that she'd found him. The second was misery, as the song was salt in a fresh wound.

But it was a misery that had to be faced. She put her hand on the gate. And it held fast against her. She shoved it, yanked at the latch, then stepped back in shocked panic when it refused to open.

"Oh." A sob rose in her throat. "Oh, Shawn. Have you closed me out then?"

The music stopped. In the silence she fought back the tears. She wouldn't face him with them. But when the door opened, she hugged her arms hard, digging her fingers in to keep those tears at bay.

He thought he'd heard her call, a teary whisper in his mind. He'd known she was out there, whether it was sense or magic, didn't matter. She was there, standing under the spill of moonlight. Her eyes were wet, her chin was up.

"Are you coming in, then?"

"I can't . . ." The weeping tried to get the better

of her, and she ruthlessly battled it back. "I can't open the gate."

Baffled, he started down the path, but she leaped forward, gripped the top of the gate in her hands. "No, I'll stay on this side. It's probably best. I went looking for you, then I figured, well, you'd come back here sooner or later. I, ah, I had to think it through awhile, and maybe I don't do that often enough. I . . ."

Was he ever going to speak? she thought desperately. Or would he just stand there looking at her with eyes shielded so she couldn't see into him?

"I'm sorry, I'm so truly sorry, Shawn, for doing something that upset you. I didn't do it with that in mind, you have to know. But some of what you said before is true. And I'm sorry for that as well. Oh, I don't know how to do this." Frustration rang in her voice as she turned her back on him.

"What is it you're doing, Brenna?"

She stared straight ahead, into the dark. "I'm asking you not to cast me off for making a mistake, even a big one like this. To give me another chance. And if there can't be anything else between us now, that you won't stop being my friend."

He would have opened the gate to her then, but thought better of it. "I gave you my word on the friendship, as you gave me yours. I'll not break it."

She pressed a hand to her lips, held it there until she thought she could speak again. "You mean so much to me. I have to clear this between us." Steadying herself, she turned around. "Some of what you said was true, but some was wrong.

Some of the most important parts were wrong."

"And you'll tell me which was which?"

She flinched at the icy sarcasm, but couldn't find enough of her temper to scrape together for a retort. "You know how to aim and shoot as well as any," she said quietly. "And it's all the more effective as you do it so rarely."

"All right, I'm sorry for that." He had to be, as he'd never seen her look quite so wounded. "I'm angry still."

"I'm pushy." She drew a breath in, let it out, but the ache was still there. "And single-minded, and I can be careless with people even when they matter to me. Maybe more when they matter. I did think, well, the man's doing nothing with this music of his, so I'll have to do it for him. That was wrong of me — wrong to put the way I'd do things or think about them onto what was yours. I should have told you, as you told me."

"On that we agree."

"But it wasn't wholly selfish. I wanted to give you something, something important, something that would make you happy and matter to you. It wasn't about the money, I swear it. It was for the glory."

"I'm not looking for glory."

"I wanted it for you."

"What does it matter to you, Brenna? You don't even care for my music."

"That's not true." Temper spiked a bit now, at the sheer unfairness of it. "What am I, deaf and stupid now as well as a bully? I love your music. It's beautiful. It never mattered to you what I thought, anyway. Christ knows, poking at you about it over the years never riled you enough to prove me wrong. You've been wasting a gift, a kind of miracle, and it makes me furious with you."

Glaring at him, she swiped tears from her cheeks. "I can't help that I feel that way, and it doesn't mean I think less of you, you blockhead. It's because I think so much of you. And then you go and write a song that reaches right into my heart, that touches me the way nothing ever has before. Even before it was finished, weeks and weeks ago, when I saw what there was of it there on the piano, just tossed there like you couldn't recognize a diamond if it jabbed your eye out, I loved it. I had to do something with it, and I don't care if it was wrong. I was so proud of what you can do I couldn't see past it. Damn you to hell and back again."

She'd rocked him onto his heels, staggered him. He whistled out a breath. "That's quite the apology, that is."

"Oh, fuck you. I take back every bit of any apology I was foolish enough to make."

There, he thought, was his woman. This time he laid his hands on the gate and gave her a look of wicked satisfaction. "It's too late, I already have it, and I'm keeping it. And here's something back at you. It always mattered what you thought of my music, and of me. It mattered more what you thought than anyone else in the world. What do you say to that?"

"You're just trying to get 'round me now because I'm angry again."

"I've always been able to get 'round you, darling, angry or not." He nudged, and the gate opened smooth and silent. "Come in through the gate."

She sniffled, wished for a tissue. "I don't want to."

"You'll come in regardless," he said, snatching her hand and yanking her through. "Now I've some things to say."

"I'm not interested." She shoved at the gate again, cursed violently when it didn't budge.

"You'll listen." He turned her, trapped her, caught her hands before she could think of making fists out of them. "I don't like what you did, or how you went about it. But your reasons for it soften that considerably."

"I don't care."

"Stop being a twit." When her mouth fell open, he lifted her a couple of inches off the ground. "I'll get tough with you if I must. You know you like it when I do."

"Why, you . . ."

When she fumbled for words, he nodded. "Ah, speechless, are you? It's a refreshing change. I don't need someone directing my life, but I don't mind someone being part of the direction. I won't be pushed or tricked or manipulated, and if you try, you'll be sorry."

"You'll make me sorry?" she all but sputtered. "I'm already sorry I did the first thing to try —"

"Brenna." He gave her a casual little shake that

had her mouth dropping open again. "There are times you're better off to just shut your mouth and listen. This is one of them. Now, as I was saying," he went on while she blinked at him. "Being tricked is one thing, but surprised is another matter. And I'm thinking that, under it all, you wanted to surprise me with something, like a gift, and I threw it back at you. For that, Brenna, I'm sorry."

The fear and sorrow were sliding away, but it was hard to resist grabbing onto the tail of them. "I don't think a great deal of your apology, either."

"Take it or leave it."

"You're awfully damn pushy yourself all of a sudden."

"I've my limits, and you should know them well enough by this time. So . . . how much is Magee willing to pay me for the tune?"

"I didn't ask," she said stiffly.

"Ah, so you can keep your fingers out of some pies. It's good to know."

"You're a hateful man. I told you it wasn't about the money." She pushed at him, and rather than humiliate herself with the bloody gate again, stomped down the path. "I don't know how I could have been blind to that part of your nature all these years. How I could have thought myself in love with you, I'll never know. The very idea of spending my life with the likes of you gives me a cold chill."

He couldn't stop the grin. It was so lovely to have all the parts of his life nicely in order again.

"We'll get to that in just a minute. It matters that it wasn't about money, Brenna, matters that you weren't thinking, 'Well, if I'm going to be with this man he'd damn well better prove he's man enough to make a living off his talents. And since he won't, I will.' "

"I don't give a tinker's damn how you make your living."

"That's what I'm seeing now. It was more of, 'I want to be with this man, and feeling as I do about him, I want to help him with that which matters to him.' It's a lovely thought, but that doesn't change the fact you should've left it to me."

"You can be sure I'll be leaving such matters, and everything else, to you in the future."

"If that vow lasts a week, I'll expect to see pigs flying over Ardmore Bay. And in case you're wondering in that calculating brain of yours, I'll be contacting Magee myself, and I'll send him music if what he says convinces me — which is what I intended to do once he came here and I got his measure."

She stopped at that, eyed him suspiciously. "You were going to show him your work?"

"I was, most likely. I'll admit that dozens of times in the past I've come close to sending it off and then pulled back. When something comes out of you, it's precious. There was a fear of others finding it wanting. It was safer not to risk it. I was afraid of losing something that mattered to me. Does that make me less in your eyes, Brenna?"

"It doesn't, no. Of course it doesn't. But if you

don't ask," she said, remembering her father's words, "the answer's always no."

"I'm not arguing your point, just your methods. Now tell me this, if Magee had said to you, 'Why, what are you sending me this silly amateur music for? Whoever wrote it has no talent whatsoever,' would you have thought less of me?"

"Of course not, you pinhead. I'd've known that Magee had no taste other than what he may have in his own mouth."

"Ah, well, now, that's tidied up a considerable mess. Can we go back to the part where you're in love with me?"

"No, because I'm not anymore. I've come to my senses."

"That's a damn shame, that is. You'll have to wait here a minute. There's something I need from inside."

"I'll not stand out here. I'm going home."

"I'll only come after you, Brenna," he called over his shoulder as he walked to the door. "And what I have in mind is best done here, and in private."

She considered climbing over the gate just to spite him, but the whole emotional mess had made her tired. It might as well get finished now as later.

So she waited, arms crossed. When he came out, he carried nothing, which only made her scowl.

"The moon's full," he commented as he went to her. "Maybe there's others have more to do with the timing of all this than we know. But it was meant to be in moonlight, and it was meant to be here."

He slipped a hand into his pocket, kept it there. "I had a plan at one time, how I'd let you chase me down, wear at my resistance and convince me there was nothing for me to do but give up and marry you."

Her eyes went blurry with shock. "I beg your pardon?"

"Do you really think you were tugging me around like a puppy on a leash? Is that the kind of man you want when the day is done, O'Toole? The kind you want walking beside you through life, fathering your children?"

"Is this a game you've been playing?"

"Partly, and as much as you were. Game's over now, and I find I want this done more in what might be the traditional manner. Brenna." He took her hand, not at all displeased that it was trembling. "I love you. I don't know when it started, years ago or weeks. But I know my heart's lost to you, and I wouldn't have it another way. You're what I want, all there is of you. Make a life with me. Marry me."

She couldn't take her eyes from his face. The whole world was in his face. "My head hurts," she managed.

"God bless you." With a half laugh, he took her hand, kissed it. "How could I not love such a woman?" He kept her hand firm in his as he took the ring from his pocket.

The pearl gleamed like the moon, white and pure, in a simple band of gold. "A moon tear," he told her, "given to me to give to you. I know

398

you don't wear rings as a rule."

"I — they — with the work they get caught and banged around."

"So I got a chain for it as well. You can wear it around your neck."

He would have thought of such a thing, she realized. Such a small and lovely detail. "I'm not working at the moment."

He slid it onto her finger, and her hand steadied under his.

"I suppose it suits me, as you do. As the whole of you suits me. But you won't make me cry."

"Yes, I will." He touched his lips to her forehead, her temple. "I bought you land today."

"What?" Tears might have dazzled her vision, but she managed to step back. "What? Land? You bought land? Without a word to me, without me laying eyes on it?"

"If you don't like it, you can bury me in it."

"I might. You bought land," she said again, but her voice had gone dreamy.

"So you can build us a house, and the two of us can fill it into a home."

"Damn it. There you are, you've made me cry." She threw her arms around his neck. "Just hold on a minute, I'm a mess." With her face buried against his shoulder, she breathed him in. "I thought it was just a longing for you, and that would be enough for both of us. I do long for you, but it's not enough and it's not all. Oh, this is where I want to be. And I did chase you down, nothing will convince me otherwise."

She drew back enough to touch her lips to his. "I had it all worked out what I would say to you tonight, and now I can't remember just how it was to go. Only that I love you, Shawn. I love you as you are. There's nothing I'd change."

"That's more than good enough. Will you come inside now? I'll warm your supper."

"It's the least you could do after you let it go cold." She linked her fingers with his. "You won't insist on a big, fancy wedding, will you?"

"I don't see how when I've a mind to have us wed as quick as can be managed."

"Ah." She leaned against him. "I do love you, Shawn Gallagher. There's one more thing," she said as they walked toward the cottage. "Won't you need a name for your song, the one Magee wants?"

"It's 'Brenna's Song,' " he told her. "It always was."